D0546003

THE JOURNEYS OF SOCRATES

For information about Dan Millman's work:

www.danmillman.com

The

JOURNEYS

of

SOCRATES

DAN MILLMAN

HarperCollins*Publishers*

HarperCollins*Publishers*
77–85 Fulham Palace Road,
Hammersmith, London W6 8JB

The HarperCollins website address is: www.harpercollins.co.uk

First published in the US by HarperCollins*Publishers* 2005
This edition published by HarperCollins*Publishers* 2005

1 3 5 7 9 10 8 6 4 2

© Dan Millman 2005

Dan Millman asserts the moral right to
be identified as the author of this work

A catalogue record for this book
is available from the British Library

ISBN 0 00 719816 7

Printed and bound in Australia by
Griffin Press

All rights reserved. No part of this publication may be
reproduced, stored in a retrieval system, or transmitted,
in any form or by any means, electronic, mechanical,
photocopying, recording or otherwise, without the prior
written permission of the publishers.

I dedicate this book to the man I called Socrates, and
to you, my readers,
who asked me to tell his story.

Had I realized the trials my old mentor had faced and
the agonies suffered, I would have listened better,
and cherished even more the time we spent together.
I hope that I've done him both honor and justice
in sharing this journey into the life of a loving sage,
into the soul of a peaceful warrior.

DAN MILLMAN

Every journey has a
secret destination of which
the traveler is unaware.

MARTIN BUBER

PROLOGUE

I'VE KILLED DMITRI ZAKOLYEV.

This thought, this stark reality, played over and over in Sergei's mind as he lay belly down, straddling the moss-covered log, paddling as silently as he could through the frigid waters of Lake Krugloye, twenty-five kilometers north of Moscow. He was fleeing the Nevskiy Military School and his past—but he could not escape the fact of Zakolyev's death.

Following a course roughly parallel to the shoreline, Sergei peered through the darkness to the wooded hills appearing and disappearing in the mist. The lake's black surface, lit by faint slivers of moonlight, shimmered with each stroke. The sloshing water and bitter cold distracted Sergei for a few more moments before he thought again of Zakolyev's body, lying in the mud.

Sergei could no longer feel his hands or legs—he had to make land before the waterlogged timber sank beneath him. Just a little farther, he thought, another kilometer before I head for shore.

This means of escape was slow and dangerous, but the lake had one distinct advantage: Water left no tracks.

Finally he angled in toward the shore, slipped from the log, and waded through the waist-high water, sucking mud, and sharp reeds at the water's edge, up the sandy shore, and into the dark forest.

Sergei was fifteen years old, and a fugitive. He shivered not only from the cold, but from a sense of destiny, as if all the events of his life had brought him to that moment. As he threaded his way through thickets of pine and birch, he thought about what his grandfather had told him, and how it all began . . .

T HAT AUTUMN OF 1872, chill winds blew west across the moss-covered Siberian tundra, sweeping over the Ural Range and north across the taiga, vast forests of birch and pine, lichens and shrubs, bordering the city of St. Petersburg, the crown jewel of Mother Russia.

Just outside the Winter Palace, wool-capped bodyguards of Aleksandr II marched along the Neva River, one of ninety waterways that flowed beneath eight hundred bridges, then past rows of small apartment buildings and church spires topped with crosses of the Orthodox Church. Not far from the river were city parks with statues of Peter the Great and Catherine and Pushkin—tsar, tsarina, and literary master—all standing sentry, bordered by street lamps just lit in the fading light of day.

Biting breezes snatched the last yellow leaves from thinning branches, tossed the woolen skirts of schoolgirls, and tousled the hair of two young boys wrestling in the front yard of a two-story home near Nevskiy Prospekt. In the bedroom window on the second floor, a gust of wind ruffled the curtains where Natalia Ivanova stood framed in the window. She pulled her shawl over her shoulders, closed the window a little, and gazed down into the small yard where her little son, Sasha, was playing with his friend Anatoly.

Anatoly ran toward Sasha, trying to tackle him. At the last instant, Sasha stepped aside and threw Anatoly over his hip, just the way his father had taught him. Proud of himself, Sasha crowed like a rooster. Such a strong boy, Natalia thought—like his father. She envied her son's energy, especially now, when she had so little of it herself—tired most of the time since her belly had swollen with their second child. Natalia's fatigue was no surprise. Yana Vaslakova, her neighbor, friend, and midwife, had warned her: "A woman of your fragile nature should not bear another child." Yet she bore this new life and prayed daily for the strength to carry this child to full term even as the fainting spells had begun and a great fatigue had penetrated her bones.

Natalia hugged herself and shivered, wondering how little boys could play outside on a chill evening like this. She called out the window, "Sasha! Anatoly! Soon it will rain. You boys come in!" Her weary voice hardly carried over the wind. Besides, six-year-old ears heard only what they wished.

With a sigh, Natalia returned to the small couch where she'd been speaking with Yana and sat with a sigh, brushing her long black hair. Sergei would be home soon. She wanted to look as pretty as she could.

Vaslakova said, "You rest, Natalia. I'll let myself out and shoo the boys inside." As her friend went downstairs, Natalia heard the patter of rain on the sill, then something else, directly overhead—the scuttle of young feet and mischievous squeals. They've climbed the trellis again, she thought. In the mixture of anger and anxiety felt by all mothers of small boys who fancy themselves invulnerable, Natalia cried up to the rooftop, "You boys climb down from the roof this instant! And be careful!"

Laughter and more scuffling as the boys wrestled on the rooftop.

"Come down now or I shall tell your father!"

"All right, Mamochka," Sasha called sweetly to curry her favor. "Just don't tell Father!" More giggles.

As Natalia turned back to lay her brush down, everything changed in one sudden, sickening lurch. Young laughter turned to descending screams. Then silence.

Natalia ran to the window. To her horror, two bodies lay below.

The next moment, it seemed, Natalia found herself outside, kneeling in the mud. As she cradled her lifeless boy in her arms, the tears and rain running down her face, she rocked to and fro in the timeless rhythm of a mother's agony.

Then a knotlike pain in her womb ripped her back from the abyss, and Natalia became vaguely aware of Vaslakova and a man standing beside her. As Vaslakova helped Natalia to her feet, the man tried to lift the burden from her arms. Natalia fought him off but froze when a boy's shrill cry rang out—she looked quickly down to her Sasha, but it was the other boy, Anatoly, whose leg was broken.

Vaslakova helped Natalia inside before the pain took her again. She doubled over and collapsed in the doorway. Where is Sasha? she wondered. He should come in. It is cold, so cold.

When she awoke, Natalia found herself in bed, attended to by the midwife. All at once she knew: The baby is coming . . . too soon . . . two months early. Or have the months passed without my notice? she thought. Where am I? Where is Sergei? He will know if this is a dream. Sergei will smile and stroke my hair and tell me that Sasha is fine . . . that everything is all right.

Ah! The pain! Is something wrong? Where is my Sasha? Where is Sergei?

Sergei Ivanov arrived home to find neighbors in his front yard, standing in the rain. He saw their faces and rushed inside. Vaslakova told him the news: Sasha was dead—a fall from the rooftop. Natalia had gone into labor . . . the bleeding wouldn't stop . . . nothing to be done. Both of them gone.

But their baby lived. A son born so early he probably wouldn't survive. Vaslakova had seen many births, many deaths. Death is easy, she thought, but hard on those left behind. A priest would soon arrive to perform last rites for Natalia and Sasha, and likely the infant as well.

Vaslakova placed Sergei's tiny son in his arms and told the distraught father that the child was too weak to suckle, but a little goat's milk, squeezed from a cloth, might sustain the boy if he lived through the night.

Sergei looked down at the wizened little face of the infant boy, swaddled tightly in a blanket Natalia had made. He barely heard Mrs. Vaslakova say, "Natalia's last words before she faded away . . . she said she loved you with all her heart . . . and asked that you give her son into the care of her parents . . ."

Even while dying, Natalia had thought about what was best for her child . . . and her husband. She knew that Sergei, a member of the *streltsy*, elite bodyguards to the tsar, could not care for their tiny son. Could she also have foreseen that every time he looked at the boy, he would think of this dark day?

The priest arrived and baptized the infant in case he should die, for the sake of his soul. When he asked the infant's name, the distracted father replied, "Sergei," thinking that the priest had asked for his own name. So it was done: The child took the name of the father.

Midwife Vaslakova offered to care for the child through the night.

Sergei nodded slowly. "If he lives until morning . . . please deliver him to his grandparents." He told her the address and their names—Heschel and Esther Rabinowitz. Jews. This did not sit well with him, but they would love the child and raise him safely. So he did as Natalia had asked. Sergei could never refuse her anything—in life or in death. That day in autumn marked the beginning of Sergei Ivanov's descent into death, even as his tiny son was clinging to life.

Eight years later, on a dark October night, Heschel Rabinowitz sat alone in the third railway car on a train bound for Moscow. He gazed out the window in thoughtful repose, half dozing in the manner of old men, hardly aware of the passing forests or settlement huts just visible in the first light of dawn. Heschel dozed and dreamed and stared. Memories moved through his mind like vistas flashing past the train's muddy window: his daughter Natalia in a red dress, her face bright . . . a photograph of Sasha, the grandson he had never met . . . and the beautiful, aged face of his beloved Esther. Gone now, all of them.

Heschel squeezed his eyes tightly as if to shut out the past. Then his eyes relaxed and he smiled as another vision appeared—the face of a three-year-old boy with eyes too large for his skinny body, reaching up to his grandfather . . .

The conductor's voice, announcing the train's arrival, jarred Heschel from his reverie. With a yawn, he stood painfully, stretching his joints. He pulled his old coat tightly around him, scratched his snow white beard, and adjusted the wire-rimmed spectacles on his large nose. Departing strangers jostled the old Jew, but he took little notice. Holding his satchel protectively in front of his chest as one might carry an infant, he descended to the platform and shuffled through a cloud of steam in the cold morning air. He looked skyward. Soon the first snow would fall.

Heschel straightened his cap and focused his wandering mind toward the north. He would have to find passage in the cart or wagon of a willing farmer, half a day's ride into the hills.

It would not be an easy journey. Heschel's back, eroded by countless hours at his workbench, was curved like the violins he fashioned from aged maple, spruce, and ebony. Heschel also made precision clocks. He had learned both trades as a boy—one from his father and the other from his grandfather. Unable to favor one craft over the other, he would first construct a violin, then a clock, alternating for variety. Even at his age, despite the aches in the joints of his fingers, he worked diligently, shaping each violin as if it were his first and each clock as if it were his last.

Soon after Heschel had learned these two crafts, his father had left him the workshop and journeyed to the East to trade in gems. Later his father's wealth and generosity enabled Heschel, a Jew, to continue living within the city of St. Petersburg, where he and his wife, Esther, had shared an apartment.

Heschel reflected on these memories as he carried his satchel out of the train station with a slow, halting gait, toward the main road out of the city.

A few hours later he sat against a sack of potatoes as a farmer's cart bumped up the narrow, muddy roads rutted with wagon tracks, pockmarked by the hooves of horses and oxen, then on foot to the school on the shore of Lake Krugloye in the hills north of Moscow.

As he hiked down into the valley, Heschel thought of the many letters he had written over the past five years and the same number of refusals he'd received. Several weeks before, he had sent a final letter to Chief Instructor Vladimir Ivanov: "I have not seen Sergei since he was taken to the school. My wife has died. I have no one left. This may be my last chance to see my grandson."

When Ivanov's letter had arrived, allowing the visit, Heschel had left immediately.

Now, chilled by the snow-laden wind on his neck, he lifted the collar of his wool coat. Two days, he thought—such a short time to pour my life into an eight-year-old boy. Then the words of Rabbi Hillel came into his mind: "Children are not vessels to be filled but candles to be lit."

"I don't have much fire left," Heschel murmured aloud as he wove his way through birch and pine, down the cold and rocky grade dusted with snowflakes. His painful joints reminded him of his corporeal existence—and this one final errand. The sound of wind faded as Heschel's mind slipped back into the crevices of memory, taking him back five years to the day a young soldier came to their door with a letter from Sergei's father, instructing that his son should be taken to the Nevskiy Military School . . .

An hour later Heschel approached the main gate of the school and surveyed the enclosure, bordered like a castle with walls about four meters high. Just ahead he could see a spartan complex of blockhouses. No hedges or adornment softened the stone battlements, where, he surmised, efficiency and function molded the young soldiers' lives.

A cadet showed Heschel across the large courtyard into the main building and down a long hallway to a door and sign that read, V. I. Ivanov, Chief Instructor.

He removed his cap, brushed back his thinning hair, and entered.

Part One

———

THE BITTER
AND
THE SWEET

I have a sad story to tell, and a happy one.
In the end, you may find that they are one and the same,
for the bitter and the sweet each has its season,
alternating like day and night, even now,
as I pass through the twilight hours . . .

FROM SOCRATES' JOURNAL

. 1 .

SERGEI WAS WORRIED, that October day, when he was summoned to his uncle's office. Being summoned—a rare event for any young cadet—usually meant bad news or punishment. So, in no hurry to stand before the chief instructor's stern face and downturned brows, Sergei wandered across the school compound at a distinctly unmilitary pace.

He was supposed to think of Vladimir Ivanov not as his uncle but as Chief Instructor. He also was not supposed to ask personal questions, though he had many—about his parents and about his past. The chief instructor had said little about either one, except on that day four years ago when he'd announced that Sergei's father had died.

Each spot Sergei passed in the inner courtyard held memories of earlier years: the first time he'd ridden a horse, bouncing wildly, clinging to the reins in a death grip . . . one of many fistfights he'd gotten into due to a quick temper, then lost due to his frail disposition.

He passed the infirmary and the small apartment of Galina, the elderly school nurse, who had watched over him when he'd first arrived. She had wiped his nose when he was sick and brought him to meals until he found his own way around. Too young to live in a barrack, he had slept on a cot just off the infirmary wing until he was five. It was a lonely time, with no place of his own and nowhere he fit in. The cadets treated him like a mascot or pet dog—petted one day, beaten the next.

Most of the other boys had mothers or fathers at home; Sergei had only his uncle, so he worked hard to please the chief instructor. His efforts, however, only earned the wrath of the older cadets, who called him "Uncle's Vlad's boy." They would trip, push, or punch him at every opportunity—a moment's inattention might mean bruises or worse. Older cadets routinely bullied the younger ones, and physical beatings were commonplace. The instructors knew about it but looked the other way unless someone was seriously injured. They tolerated the fights because it spurred the younger boys to toughen up and stay alert. It was, after all, a military school.

The first time Sergei was accosted by an older cadet, over in the corner of the compound, he started swinging wildly, sensing that if he backed down there would be no end to it. The older boy gave him a good beating, but Sergei managed to get in one or two good punches, and the boy never bothered him after that. Another time he had come upon two cadets beating a new boy. Sergei had attacked them with more rage than skill. They had backed off, treating the whole thing like a joke. But it was no joke to the new boy, whose name was Andrei and who had been Sergei's only real friend ever since.

Just after his fifth birthday, Sergei was moved into a barrack with the seven- to ten-year-olds. Older boys lived upstairs, and anyone over sixteen lived in another building. The older boys ruled the barracks. Every cadet dreaded a move to the next floor, where he again would be the youngest and therefore the prey. Meanwhile, Sergei and Andrei watched each other's backs.

Of the years prior to his arrival, Sergei had only hazy impressions— as if he had been cocooned in another world, not yet awakened into this one. But sometimes, when he searched his memory, he glimpsed fleeting images of a large woman with arms as soft as bread dough and a man with a halo of white hair. Sergei wondered who they were; he wondered about a great many things.

He had gazed at maps of Mother Russia and other countries on the classroom walls, and his finger had circled the globe on his teacher's desk, tracing lines across sky blue seas and lands colored orange, yellow, purple, and green. But he no more expected to visit such places than he thought to visit the moon or stars.

His world—until that day in October of 1880—was defined largely by the stone walls, blockhouses, barracks, classrooms, and training grounds of the Nevskiy Military School. Sergei had not chosen this place, but he accepted it, as children must, and passed his early years in orderly routines of class work and physical training: military history, strategy and geography, riding, running, swimming, and calisthenics.

Whenever the cadets weren't in their classrooms or on work assignments, they practiced fighting skills. In the summer Sergei had to swim under the cold waters of Lake Krugloye while breathing through a hollow reed, and practice elementary skills with the saber, and shoot arrows with bows he could barely bend. When he was older he would shoot pistols and carbines.

It was not a bad life or a good life, but the only one he knew.

A s SERGEI DREW CLOSER to the main building, he tucked his dark blue shirt into his matching pants and gazed down at his boots to see if they were clean. For a moment he wondered whether he should have fetched his more formal coat or gloves but then decided against it. Most of the taller boys looked trim in their uniforms, but on Sergei everything looked baggy. When he finally grew out of one size uniform, they gave him another hand-me-down.

Still daydreaming, he shuffled down the long stone hallway toward his uncle's office, and thought about the last summons, four years ago. He could still recall his uncle's lean face and severe countenance as the chief instructor told him to sit. Sergei had climbed into a chair with his legs dangling—he could barely see over the top of the desk—and his uncle had spoken the few words now imprinted in Sergei's memory: "Your father, Sergei Borisovich Ivanov, has died. He was once an elite bodyguard to Tsar Aleksandr. He was good man and a Cossack. You must study and train hard to become like him."

Sergei did not know what to feel or how to respond, so he only nodded.

"Do you have any questions?" the chief instructor had asked.

"How . . . how did he die?"

Silence. Then a sigh. "Your father drank himself to death. A great waste." Then Sergei was dismissed. He was sad that his father had died, but proud that he had a Cossack's blood coursing through him. And for the first time, Sergei thought that he might someday grow strong like the father he had never met.

W HEN SERGEI finally reached the door of his uncle's office and was about to knock, he heard his uncle's muffled voice inside. "I will allow this visit, but several others disagree . . . They have no love for Jews, the killers of Christ."

"And I have no use for soldiers, the killers of Jews," said an older voice Sergei didn't recognize.

"Not all soldiers hate Jews," his uncle replied.

"And you?" said the other voice.

"I hate only weakness."

"As I hate ignorance."

"I am not so ignorant as to be tricked by your Jewish intellect," said the chief instructor.

"And I am not so weak to be intimidated by your Cossack bravado," said the older voice.

In the silence that followed, Sergei found the courage to tap three times on the heavy oak door.

It opened to reveal his uncle and an old man. Sergei's uncle spoke curtly: "Cadet Ivanov. This is your grandfather."

The elderly white-haired man rose from his chair. He seemed happy to see Sergei. Then he spoke softly, almost in a whisper—it sounded like a name: *Sokrat* . . . Socrates.

. 2 .

Hᴇsᴄʜᴇʟ ʀᴇᴀᴄʜᴇᴅ ᴏᴜᴛ to embrace his grandson; then, realizing that the boy did not recognize him, he lowered his arms and more formally reached out to shake the boy's hand. "Hello . . . Sergei. It's good to see you. I would have come long ago, but . . . well, I am here now."

Chief Instructor Ivanov broke in: "Get your things ready, Cadet Ivanov—I will allow you two nights' leave." And to Heschel he added, "See that the boy returns by midday Sunday. I expect him to be ready to train. He has much to learn."

"That he does," said Heschel, taking Sergei's hand. "So do we all."

When the chief instructor dismissed them both with a wave of his hand, Sergei hurried to the barrack to gather a few belongings. Then he and his grandfather took their leave, passing through the dark hallways, out the iron gate, across the fields, and up a snow-dusted path toward the forested hills.

Heschel, somewhere in his eighties—he had stopped counting when Esther died—walked with faltering steps. Sergei, intoxicated by a sense of liberation, skipped ahead, then stopped to knock the snow from a tree branch or sniff the air while waiting for his old grandfather to catch up. The boy had no words to explain or express his elation or this new sense of himself. It was as if he were no longer just another cadet now, but a real boy with a grandfather. He belonged to a family.

They angled through the trees until they came to a stone outcropping and a large boulder. Heschel took out a map and showed it to the boy. "You see the lake and the school? Here is the boulder, shown on the map, and there is our destination," he said, tapping an *x* he had drawn in dark ink. Sergei had learned only the rudiments of map reading, but he knew enough to understand and to remember.

After folding the map and slipping it into his old wool coat, Heschel peered up the snowy path. Then he checked his pocket watch and frowned. "We must reach our destination before dark," he said. And they started up the steep grade.

Sergei was accustomed to following instructions and not asking questions. But as they climbed his mind overflowed with curiosity. "Are we going to your house?" Sergei asked.

"My house is too far away," Heschel answered. "We'll spend the next two days and nights with Benyomin and Sara Abramovich. I have known Benyomin for many years."

"Do they have any children?"

Heschel smiled, having anticipated the question. "Yes—two of them. Avrom is twelve years old, and little Leya is five."

"Their names sound . . . strange."

"They are Jewish names, and tonight we celebrate Shabbat—"

"What's a Shabbat?" asked the boy.

"Shabbat is a sacred day set aside for rest and remembrance."

"Like Sunday Sabbath?"

"Yes. But Shabbat begins Friday night when the first three stars appear. So we will have to make good time."

As they trekked upward, the old man concentrated on each careful footstep while the nimble eight-year-old hopped up from rock to rock like a mountain goat. Sergei heard his grandfather's breathless voice behind him. "The stones are slippery—be careful, Socrates."

There was that name again. "Why do you call me Socrates?"

"It was our special name for you, ever since you were a baby."

"Why?"

A faraway look came to Heschel's eyes as his mind drifted to the past. "When your mother, Natalia, was just a girl, I would read to her from the Jewish Talmud and the Torah, and from other books of wisdom, including the commentaries of the great philosophers. Her favorite was a Greek named Socrates. He lived a long time ago . . . and he was among the wisest and best of men." Heschel looked away, into the hills or the sky, and said, "We called you our little Socrates because . . . it made us feel close to your mother—to our daughter."

"Did my mother like Socrates for his wisdom?"

"Yes, but even more for his virtue and strength of character."

"What did he do?"

"Socrates taught the young men of Athens about higher values, virtue, and peace. He claimed to be the most ignorant of men, but he asked clever questions that revealed both falsehoods and truth. He was a thinker, but also a man of action. As a youth, Socrates wrestled, and he was a brave soldier until he finally put war behind him. I suppose you could say that he was a . . . peaceful warrior."

Satisfied for the moment, Sergei turned to gaze back down at the snowy landscape. The afternoon sun sparkled off the white hillside, illuminating the trees and moss and lichen. Invigorated by the crisp, cool air and by this adventure, Sergei bounded ahead again, then forced himself to stop so his grandfather could catch up. As he waited, Sergei thought about the word *Jew*. He had heard it uttered at the school, most recently in his uncle's office.

"Grandfather," Sergei called down the trail, "are you a Jew?"

"Yes," panted Heschel, approaching slowly. "So are you . . . your mother was Jewish, and your father . . . well, he was not . . . but you have Jewish blood."

Sergei looked down at his hands, reddened by the cold air. So he had Cossack blood and Jewish blood. "Grandfather—"

"You may call me Grandpa if you like," he said, sitting down on a snow-covered rock to rest a moment.

"Grandpa . . . would you tell me something about my mother . . . and my father?"

Hearing this, Heschel stopped, brushed the snow from another large stone, and beckoned Sergei to sit beside him. After a time, Heschel told the story of Sergei's birth—all that he had learned from Vaslakova, the midwife, who was with Natalia on that fateful day. Then he added, "You were a single ray of light on a dark day, Socrates. And you had a mother and father who loved you . . ."

Sergei glanced back to see his grandfather wiping tears from his cheeks. "Grandpa?"

"Just give me a moment, my little Socrates—I'll be all right. I was just thinking about your mother—about Natalia . . ."

"What was she like?" Sergei asked.

Heschel's gaze grew vacant; then he continued in a wistful voice, "Every daughter is lovely in her father's eyes, but few were as wise or gentle as your mother. She would have been a prize for any Jewish man worthy of her—that is, if he didn't mind a little debate." He smiled, but it quickly faded. "I don't know exactly how she met your father—perhaps in the market—then she brought him home to meet us and we learned that he was not Jewish. Even worse, he was a Cossack and bodyguard to Tsar Aleksandr, no friend to our people."

"But he loved my mother, and he was good to her. You said—"

"Yes, yes—but you see . . . your mother could not marry your father unless she renounced her Jewish faith and converted to the . . . Christian Church." Heschel stopped to let Sergei absorb the enormity of this terrible thing.

"Did she stop speaking to you?"

"No." Heschel's face contorted again, and he could not speak.

"Grandpa . . . are you all right?"

Heschel held up his hand. "It was I who stopped speaking to her. I treated my daughter as if she were dead." He started to cry again, this time openly, as his words poured out. "I don't expect you to understand how I could do such a thing, little Socrates—I don't understand myself. But cruel words poured from my mouth. I turned my back on her as I believed she had turned her back on her people. I could find no other way. Your grandmother Esther had no choice but to do the same, although it broke her heart."

Heschel forced himself to go on. "Esther wanted desperately to speak with her daughter—to embrace her one more time. Did she think

I wanted anything less . . . ?" Heschel said this to himself, his mind again drifting to the past.

When he spoke again, he sounded weary. "When Natalia wrote to tell us about our first grandchild, your brother Sasha, Esther and I had a terrible argument. She begged me to let her go to her daughter, to see her grandson. But I would not let her . . . I would not even allow my beloved Esther to answer Natalia's letters.

"We never did get to see little Sasha," he said. "We learned about his childhood only from Natalia's letters of love. I could not bear to read them myself . . . but your Grandma Esther would tell me of their contents. We never spoke with your mother or saw her again. Not while she lived."

Heschel blew his nose and wiped his cold wet cheeks on the sleeve of his coat.

A light snow had begun to fall again as they stood and continued upward. Heschel grasped Sergei's hand and said softly, "There is one more thing you should know, Socrates: The midwife who brought you told us . . . Your mother was able to hold you for a little while before she died."

Sergei thought about this, then added: "Why did she die, Grandpa?"

"Why does anyone die? It is not for us to know." Heshchel stopped again for a moment, reached down slowly, and plucked a blood-red flower from the snow. "Your mother was fragile, yet strong, like this winter blossom. It is pure and innocent, yet I've just plucked it from the snow. God picked Natalia. It was her time. I only wish . . ."

Once again Sergei's grandfather withdrew from this world, and his face took on a more peaceful visage. "Yes, Esther," he said to a ghost Sergei could not see. "I know . . . it will be all right."

Heschel put his hand on the boy's shoulders as they walked on in silence, side by side, and Sergei thought more about what his grandfather had told him—how his mother had held him before she died. For a little while, he didn't feel so cold anymore.

Now he knew the story of his birth, and of the deaths surrounding it. He sensed too, as much as any eight-year-old can, that his grandfather would carry his own sorrows, like a weight in his knapsack, to his own death, when all burdens would be lifted. But for now the boy saw that his grandfather's brow had relaxed, and he was glad for it.

Then Heschel emerged from his memories and spoke again: "So that is how things are, little Socrates—I lost my daughter and my wife; you lost your mother and father. Each of us is alone now, but we have each other. This is the truth, and it may hurt. But the truth sets us free . . .

A COLD SUN, barely visible through the blanket of clouds, disappeared behind the trees. Somewhere in the darkening woods ahead, as a wolf's howl marked the coming dusk, a clearing came into view, then a cabin. A soft light poured from its windows, offering the promise of comfort and warmth. The falling snowflakes, gray in the twilight, sparkled white as they drifted down in a final moment of glory before settling to the earth.

The cabin appeared well built with a plank-and-shingle roof and smoke rising from a stone chimney. Heschel stepped up onto the porch, removed his cap, and shook the snow from his boots. Sergei did the same as Heschel knocked firmly on the large oak door.

After a warm welcome and much-needed washing, Sergei and Heschel sat at the table with the first real family in Sergei's memory. The mother, Sara, a small-boned woman with brown hair almost covered by a white babushka tied beneath her chin, brought food to the table. Visitors were rare here, and friendly faces all the more so. Sergei stole glances at the children. Avrom, a tall, slender boy of twelve, appeared formal but friendly; Leya, a pretty little five-year-old with a mop of copper-colored hair, glanced shyly back at him.

Sergei's eyes drank in all he could of their orderly home. He felt shabby in his plain clothing next to Avrom in his coat and smooth trousers and Leya in her dark dress and white babushka like her mother's.

The father, Benyomin Abramovich, explained to Sergei, "During our Sabbath we set aside all of our weekday concerns and devote ourselves to literature, poetry, and music. This day reminds us that we are not slaves to work. On Shabbat we are free of the world."

Sara lit two candles and said a blessing. After Benyomin recited a prayer over wine, he invited Heschel to say a prayer over two loaves of a bread braided like a rope, which they called *challah*. Sergei gazed at the array of food set out before them as Sara pointed out each dish: a thick barley soup, chopped eggs, a spicy beet salad, crackers, chopped vegetables from the garden, potato knishes, rice with apples, and a honey cake with stuffed apples for dessert.

As everyone ate their fill, Sara apologized with a shrug of her shoulders. "In this weather I would have included chicken broth, but the chicken declined . . ."

So this is what a mother is like, Sergei thought, gazing at her. He envied these children for getting to see her every day, and wondered whether his own mother had looked like Sara Abramovich.

It was the best meal in his memory. There was laughter, and easy conversation. The evening glowed with a special light, provided by a fire on the hearth and candles everywhere, and he was embraced as a member of their family. It was a night he would never forget.

THE NEXT DAY passed quickly. Avrom taught Sergei to play checkers. As they played, Sergei noticed a scar on Avrom's forehead over his right eye. Avrom saw him staring and said, "I was climbing a tree and fell—I think a branch did this," he said, pointing to the red line. "Mother said I almost put my eye out. Now she won't let me climb so high anymore."

That afternoon, when the sky cleared, the family went for a walk in the woods, where Benyomin pointed out the trees whose wood he harvested for Heschel's violins and clocks.

When they returned, Heschel took a spontaneous nap that began midsentence. Later, he woke up grumpy, not quite sure where he was. Sara brought him a cup of steaming tea, then left him to come around on his own.

That evening, when the first three stars appeared, the Sabbath ended with more blessings recited over wine and candles. As Benyomin lit a new fire on the hearth, Heschel reached into his sack and took out gifts—spices and candles for the adults and sweets for the children. Then Benyomin handed Heschel a violin that Heschel himself had crafted, and the old man began to play.

Sergei stared openmouthed. It was as if his grandfather had come alive in a new way. No longer a mere mortal, he was now a Maker of Music. The instrument sang of private sorrows in one moment and lifted their spirits in the next. Leya danced and twirled as Avrom and Sergei clapped for her.

When his grandfather finished, the cottage was full of light. Sergei lay down in front of the hearth and slept in the fold of a family, and he dreamed of music.

On SUNDAY, soon after dawn, they said their farewells. Sergei took in every impression he could, so he might draw upon these memories back at the school. He memorized Sara's face and voice . . . Benyomin's laughter . . . Avrom, his face buried in a book . . . Leya sitting by the fire . . .

He wondered if he might someday be like Benyomin Abramovich, with a wife like Sara and with children of his own.

Before they parted, Sara Abramovich knelt and embraced Sergei; little Leya gave him a hug too. Avrom and Benyomin shook his hand. "You are welcome here anytime," said the father.

"I hope to see you again," said the son.

Grandpa Heschel pulled on his winter coat and lifted his sack over his shoulder. Sergei looked up at Heschel and realized that this kind old man, after eating all his meals alone in an empty apartment, had also found comfort in this home. With a last wave, they turned and headed down the path into the forest.

The body can forget physical sensations. After feeling cold for hours or days, one can sit for a few minutes by a fire, and it's as if the cold never existed. How different are the emotions, which leave traces in memory that come alive with each recollection. In the difficult days and years of his life that followed, Sergei's memories of that family—of a fire on the hearth, the smell of fresh-baked bread in the stone oven, and Avrom and Leya, not cadets but regular children his age—would help sustain him.

Sergei had attended many masses in the school chapel when Father Georgiy spoke of a heavenly realm. But Sergei had never understood heaven—not until those two days with a family in that cabin in the woods.

Except for the crack and shush of a snow-laden branch breaking, and the rhythmic crunch of their feet in the snow, Sergei and Heschel descended in silence. Words would only intrude in the thoughts and feelings they each savored. Besides, they had to concentrate on each step; the path was more hazardous on the downward journey. When Sergei slipped once, and reached out to grasp his grandfather's hand, Heschel said, "You're a good boy, Socrates."

"And you're a good grandpa," Sergei responded.

TOO SOON, IT SEEMED, the school came into sight. Sergei looked up at his grandfather's face, now drawn and weary. A long journey awaited the old man, back to an empty apartment, inhabited only by memories. Sergei felt a sudden impulse to go with Grandpa Heschel to St. Petersburg, but he couldn't find the courage to speak. It had been his father's will that he be raised at the military school. Besides, Sergei would not be permitted to leave.

They reached the edge of the school grounds, then drew near to the main gate.

They stood for a long time as the autumn sun passed overhead. Finally, Heschel spoke: "My little Socrates, no matter what the coming years may bring, even in the most difficult times, remember that you are not alone. The spirits of your parents—and your grandma Esther, and your grandpa Heschel—will always be by your side . . ."

Staring down at his feet, Sergei felt his shoulders sink with the full weight of their parting. He knew that he might not see his grandfather again.

Heschel bent down and straightened his grandson's shirt and coat, then pulled him close. Sergei feared his grandfather was about to leave him then, but instead Heschel smiled and said, "I have something for you—a gift from your mother and father." He reached inside his coat and held out a silver chain, from which dangled an oval locket. The boy blinked as its silvered surface caught a ray of light.

"The midwife gave it to me on the same day she gave you into our care," Heschel told him. "This locket belonged to your mother. It was a gift to her from your father. The midwife told me that your mother wanted you to have it when you were old enough. You are old enough now."

Heschel placed the locket and chain in Sergei's open palm. It had touched his mother's skin . . . and now it was his to keep.

"Open it."

Sergei looked at his grandfather, uncomprehending.

"Here, I'll show you—" Heschel opened the clasp, and inside Sergei saw a small photograph—the face of a woman with dark curly hair and skin like milk, and a man with high cheekbones, an intense gaze, and a dark beard.

"My . . . parents?"

His grandfather nodded. "I think it was her most precious possession, and now it is yours. I know you will keep it safe."

"I will, Grandpa," Sergei murmured, still in awe, unable to take his eyes from his parents' faces.

"Quickly now, Socrates, listen carefully! There is something else—I couldn't bring it with me—another gift, hidden in a meadow near St. Petersburg." He reached again into his coat and pulled out a folded piece of paper and spread it out on his chest so that the boy could see it: a map that marked a spot by a tree in a meadow, bordered on three sides by forest, near the banks of a river. The map also had other markings.

"You remember the story I told you on the way to the cabin—the one about my favorite spot in the forest, the meadow on the banks of the Neva River where I learned to swim? Here it is, just north of St. Petersburg," he said, tracing a line with his finger. "And here's the city . . . and boat docks . . . and the Winter Palace. If you follow the river ten kilometers north of the palace, out of the city and into the forest, you will come to a clearing . . ."

He turned over the paper to reveal a more detailed drawing of the shoreline, a tree, and a small *x*. "This is where the box is buried, on the side of a tree opposite the river . . . the only large cedar tree standing alone near the center of the meadow. The tree was planted by my own grandfather when he was a boy. And there, in the box I buried between the two roots, you will find it."

Grandpa folded the map and placed it in his hands. "Maps can be lost, or stolen, Socrates. "I want you to study it carefully, in private. Commit every line and every marking to memory. Then destroy the map. Will you do that?"

"I will, Grandpa."

They walked to the gate. "Remember this gift. It has . . . great value, and will be waiting for you. When you find it, remember how much we love you—how much we all loved you . . ."

Sergei nodded, unable to speak. Heschel looked up into the sky and took a slow, deep breath—the kind he took when he had completed a new violin or clock and was pleased by what he saw. "That is good," he said. "That is good." He then lowered his gaze. "I want you to know, Socrates . . . to share this Shabbat with you—it has been one of the great joys of my life."

With that, Heschel Rabinowitz turned and set out toward the hills, murmuring to himself, "Yes, Esther . . . yes, it will be all right now . . ." Sergei watched him grow smaller, until he faded from sight, out of Sergei's life and into his memory.

. 4 .

W<small>ITH THE MAP TUCKED SAFELY AWAY</small>, Sergei entered the gate.

Late for chapel, he ran through empty halls to his barrack and dropped his knapsack into his footlocker. As he turned to leave, Sergei noticed a traveling bag on the bunk next to him, vacated several weeks before. This bag might indicate a new arrival.

He quickly slipped the locket and map into a hole in his mattress—the safest hiding place he could find. Then he hurried down the hall toward the chapel. His half run slowed to a walk as he thought of his grandfather, stooped over now, hiking slowly up toward the main road.

Sergei made the sign of the cross and asked God to keep his grandfather safe and give him strength for his journey. It was the first time he remembered praying with all his heart, the way Father Georgiy had instructed. He'd never had a reason to do so before.

He hoped his prayer might be answered, even if Grandpa Heschel was a Jew.

As he opened the chapel door, a fleeting thought came to him: Who am I? A Jew? A Christian? A Cossack?

Sergei walked quickly down the aisle. Several boys stole glances at him, smiling either in friendly greeting or gloating that he would be punished for his lateness. He looked up at Father Georgiy, standing in his black robe before the raised altar and icons of Christ, Mary with child, and St. Michael, St. Gabriel, and St. George, the guardian of their school and patron saint of Russia. The sun cast rainbows of light through the stained-glass window.

A hymn had begun; Sergei found his place and joined in, but his mind drifted. Both Father Georgiy and his grandfather Heschel had spoken of a God he couldn't see. To Sergei, God was a cabin in the forest, and heaven was a mother's embrace . . .

"Grandpa," he had asked on their return to the school, "what do the Jews say is the path to heaven?"

Heschel had smiled upon hearing this and said, "I do not speak for all Jews, nor am I wise enough to know this, Socrates. But I believe that one day you will blaze your own path . . . and find your own way."

As THE SERVICE ENDED, Sergei snapped out of his reverie and joined the orderly lines out of the chapel. That's when he first encountered the new cadet—tall and unsmiling, three or four years his senior. They happened to walk side by side up the narrow aisle as they filed out of mass. There was room for only one person at a time to pass through the door, and Sergei was about to step aside and let the new boy go first when the taller cadet shouldered him aside so roughly that Sergei nearly fell into the pews.

This first act of dominance would define their relationship.

It turned out that the bag on the bunk between Sergei's and Andrei's did belong to the newcomer. His name was Dmitri Zakolyev. From that day on, Sergei would think of him only as Zakolyev, a name he came to fear and despise.

Rumor had it that a man had brought Zakolyev to the entrance, handed an envelope to the cadet at the gate, and said, "Here is payment," and without another word or even a backward glance, the man had turned and left.

Being twelve years old, Zakolyev should have been assigned to a sleeping room on the next floor among the eleven- to fourteen-year-olds. But they had a temporary shortage of beds upstairs—something about airing the mattresses because of lice. So for his first week the new cadet had to sleep in the "little boys' barrack," as he called it. He took his embarrassment out on everyone around him—especially on Sergei and Andrei, since their bunks were the closest.

In the following weeks Zakolyev elbowed his way to a certain status in the student hierarchy and earned a grudging respect from his peers—the kind one might give to a passing snake or bear.

Everything about Zakolyev seemed larger than life. He had huge hands, with knuckles scarred and calloused from punching trees or stones, and big ears, mostly covered by straw-colored hair that he left as long as he could get away with. Zakolyev hated the mandatory haircuts; he hated anything mandatory. His other features were fair enough, but they didn't quite fit together. And he had a pasty complexion, as if the skin on his face never got enough blood.

What stood out most were Zakolyev's eyes—flint gray and cold, deep-set above a prominent nose—eyes that made you shiver. His eyes never changed when this strange boy smiled, a frightening, mirthless grin that appeared when others might frown or cry, revealing Zakolyev's crooked teeth. Anyone who stared at those teeth might lose some of his own. Nor did anyone stare at his birthmark—a red-white blotch on his neck, just beneath his left ear—another reason he hated the haircuts.

In a school where power meant respect, Zakolyev quickly established dominance over the younger cadets as well as most of his peers. He possessed a self-assurance that drew the admiration of some cadets who competed for Zakolyev's approval, which he doled out in small portions so that it seemed rare and valuable. Disgusted by this fawning display of servility, Sergei did his best to stay out of Zakolyev's way—a fact that did not escape the bully's notice.

Zakolyev came to be feared not only for his brutality but also for his unpredictable nature. Quiet one moment, cruel the next, he might lash out for the least cause or for no reason at all. Once he befriended a smaller boy, defending him against several bullies; the next day he gave the boy a worse beating than the hapless cadet would have suffered at the hands of his previous assailants.

Zakolyev seemed to view everyone at the school—cadets and instructors alike—as either potential followers or obstacles, and each was treated accordingly. An acute observer of human nature, he was wary of all those in authority who were older, stronger, or more powerful. Those people he would deceive or manipulate; the rest he could coerce.

Sergei was never certain how he got on Zakolyev's bad side. Maybe it was because he saw through Zakolyev's ruses and refused to be intimidated. Still, he avoided confrontation, knowing the extent of the bully's wrath if provoked. There were other bullies in the school—probably a third of the upperclassmen—but none as dangerous as Zakolyev.

Andrei became Zakolyev's whipping dog—"runt of the litter." Andrei studied the bully's expressions the way a dog watches its master to learn whether it will be fed or beaten. Sergei also received his share of bruising and humiliation. He did his best to fend off the bully's angry blows, but never struck back because it would have driven Zakolyev into a frenzy.

Sergei observed how Zakolyev made his own rules but followed none, unless he was under the direct gaze of an instructor. Then he would make a pretense of obedience but do as he pleased once the instructor was out of sight. In one eerie incident, Zakolyev was mercilessly kicking a fallen cadet when two instructors rounded the corner. Instantly, Zakolyev knelt down like a ministering angel, and all the instructors saw was him calmly and gently touching the contorted, moaning face of the cadet. "I think he's had some kind of seizure," Zakolyev said in a concerned voice. The injured boy dared not contradict him. Not then, and not later. After that story got around, Zakolyev more or less took charge.

He could even manipulate some of the senior cadets. Sergei saw how it worked: At first he might ask only small favors, until they got used to saying yes, but gradually his requests increased until they became demands. Occasionally, when a senior cadet had had enough and refused to be intimidated, there would be a fight. Zakolyev won for two reasons: First, he showed no sense of fair play; second, he didn't seem to care what happened to him. That made him a formidable foe— one who fought with the instincts of a cornered wolf.

Among the cadets, especially the younger ones, an atmosphere of fear now pervaded the hallways and training grounds. Zakolyev required immediate obedience to any "request," and his punishments for insults real or imagined were absolute and inescapable. He never forgot or forgave, and eventually all transgressors suffered. It became easier to submit than to resist.

ON THE LAST NIGHT before Zakolyev was moved upstairs, Andrei stepped around a corner and collided with the older cadet, causing Zakolyev to stumble. Furious, he put all his weight into a punch to Andrei's belly. Andrei fell to the floor groaning, gasping for air as Zakolyev stepped over him, walked to his bunk as if nothing had happened, and lay back with his hands behind his head.

Sergei rushed to Andrei's side, his fists clenching with rage as he helped Andrei back to his bunk. Sergei looked up at Zakolyev, who stared down with that icy smile. Sergei stared right back—a small gesture of defiance.

Later that night, as Sergei drifted to sleep, he thought wistfully of that cabin in the forest—of Sara Abramovich and Benyomin and Avrom and Leya, wishing he were with them. He dreamed that he had awakened by their hearth on a Sabbath morning, with Avrom and Leya nearby, and that he was part of their family and the school had been only a dream after all.

Morning came as a great disappointment.

IN THE DAYS AND WEEKS following Zakolyev's move upstairs, that late winter of 1881, school returned to its usual rhythms of class work and combat training, meals, chapel, and sleep. But early one morning a senior cadet woke Sergei and his bunkmates at dawn and led the twelve sleepy boys—wearing only shorts and hugging towels and bundles of clothing to their chests—down the long passageway beneath the school.

It was cold and dank in the dim light. Dripping water echoed along the walls as twelve pairs of bare feet slapped the wet stone floor. Shivering, the young cadets came to a massive iron door. It creaked as the senior pushed it open. Sergei stepped outside and found himself on the shore of the lake, now glowing in the first light of day. Chunks of thin ice and slush, remnants of winter, still floated in the shallows. The eastern hills stood in dark silhouette, and all was quiet. Not for long, however.

"Take off your shorts!" ordered the leader as he removed his own clothing and waded out into the frigid water, up to his shoulders, up to his neck; then he submerged for a few seconds. He surfaced, his cheeks red, and returned to the shore, with tiny bumps showing on his now rosy skin. The senior cadet took his towel and rubbed himself briskly, then issued the command: "All of you into the water!" But Sergei noticed that the senior was fighting back a grin in anticipation of their agonies.

Like the other boys, Sergei edged into the water, gasping and screeching, followed by spasms of shivered laughter. The cold cut into his skin as he ducked under the water, then clambered quickly out and rubbed himself dry. The boys pointed to one another's blotchy red faces and chests and arms. Sergei remembered the flush of warmth, and the giddy exhilaration—but not an experience he wanted to repeat anytime soon.

As he and the other boys slipped into their clothing, the senior announced, "You will do this immersion every morning from now on! You will never like it, and you will never get used to it—but it will make your body and spirit strong. Such disciplines will shape you into soldiers who can defend the Tsar and Mother Russia from foreign invaders. And the best of you will be chosen for the elite bodyguard."

The elite bodyguard . . . will I follow in my father's footsteps? Sergei wondered.

. 5 .

A FEW WEEKS LATER Sergei's group was about to start riding practice when Lieutenant Danilov called out, "Sergei Ivanov, come with me!" Sergei guessed that they were going to the chief instructor's office. At the first summons, years before, he'd learned of his father's death; the second time he'd found his grandfather waiting for him. So he didn't know whether to feel excitement or dread.

He found out soon enough. "I just received word that your grandfather has died," the chief instructor, who waited a few moments for Sergei to absorb this information, then added, "He must have made arrangements—so you would know when the time came. You may go to the chapel if you wish to pray for his soul. That is all," he said.

Sergei did not go to the chapel. He returned to his empty barrack, and after checking to make sure he was alone, retrieved his mother's locket and gazed at the photograph. Now his Grandpa Heschel had joined his parents, and was with Grandma Esther. This locket would remind him of them all.

He placed the silver chain around his neck, deciding to wear it whenever he could safely do so.

Then Sergei took out the map and committed every line to memory, until he could close his eyes and trace it in the air with his finger. When he was sure, he tore it into small pieces, scattering them in several different receptacles.

ONE MONDAY AFTERNOON in March of 1881, the school was shaken by news that dwarfed Sergei's personal concerns and reminded him that he was part of a larger world—a world of conflict and turmoil. On this windy day, he and about fifteen other cadets were outside in the compound, training with wooden sabers, when a bearded Cossack rode in through the main gate. They all stopped to watch this proud rider pass.

When all the cadets were convened in the chapel, the Cossack was introduced. His name was Alexei Orlov. He had once served with Sergei's Uncle Ivanov in a Cossack regiment. Then the chief instructor announced that the Little Father, Tsar Aleksandr II, had been assassinated.

That evening they returned to the chapel for a special mass so the instructors and cadets could pray for the tsar's soul. Like the other boys, Sergei dressed in his best uniform—dark blue with shiny buttons down the jacket and the academy logo, a two-headed eagle with a rose and saber in its claws.

Alexei Orlov stood straight and tall, his handsome face turned somber with grief. He said, "Cossacks are a free people, loyal to the Tsar and to the Mother Church." He offered a respectful nod to Father Georgiy before he continued: "I was among those serving as the tsar's royal guard. Despite our best efforts to protect the Little Father, he was killed by an assassin's bomb. The Tsar Liberator, who had emancipated millions of serfs, reformed the legal systems, and allowed greater freedom than ever before, was nevertheless hated by revolutionaries dissatisfied with their lot. Aware of the threat to his life, the Little Father had varied his travel routes under our direction. I was not yet on duty at that time, but one of my men told me what transpired."

Orlov continued. "As the tsar's carriage reached the upper section of one of the city's canals, a young man suddenly loomed up and threw what looked like a snowball between the horses. The bomb exploded but wounded the tsar only slightly. His Imperial Highness insisted on getting out to express his concern for a Cossack and a delivery boy who had been severely wounded.

"As Tsar Aleksandr turned toward the carriage, another man made a sudden movement toward him. There was an explosion. Within the hour, both the assassin and the Little Father died of their wounds. The man who threw the first bomb informed on his comrades. We know that at least one of the conspirators was a young woman named Gelfman—a revolutionary and a Jew."

When Sergei left the chapel, he found himself walking alongside his uncle. The chief instructor looked down and said under his breath, "If your father were alive, it would not have happened ... not on his watch."

Soon Sergei heard news of the coronation of Tsar Aleksandr III— and fragments of conversations about a wave of violent pogroms sweeping through Russia and Ukraine as word spread that a "cadre of Jews" had murdered the Little Father. That rumor turned out to be false: The sixteen-year-old, pregnant Gelfman woman, who later died in prison, was the only Jew, a naive but idealistic girlfriend of another revolutionary. Still, the pogroms continued.

Mutterings about revolutionaries and Jews continued at the school, especially among those closest to Zakolyev. This talk made Sergei conscious of his own Jewish blood. He grew more concerned, as the weeks passed, for the Abramovich family. In this dangerous time, their isolation in the sanctuary of the wooded hills might work in their favor—but it could just as easily work against them. What might happen if a roving band of brigands, or even Cossacks, came upon a family of Jews in the forest?

Sergei decided he had to warn them.

T HAT NIGHT he slipped past several cadets on guard duty and passed down the long tunnel under the school to the back door by the lake. He had traversed that hallway so many times he could do it blindfolded. His eyes might just as well have been covered, since no lamps were lit there at night.

Sergei pushed open the heavy iron door with a creaking sound that made him grit his teeth. He wedged a small branch between the jamb and door to keep it open, then moved quickly around the school's perimeter. Skirting the field, he found the stone outcropping that marked the beginning of the path. Now he had to rely solely on memory and instinct. Fortunately, the night was clear, and a waxing moon provided enough light for him to make his way.

Despite the darkness, he had to hike at a much faster pace than he had the last time. Having slipped out without being caught, he now had to contend with other dangers: hungry wolves—or getting lost. If he lost his way, he could find the school in the morning, but by then his absence would have been discovered. Such absence without leave was a serious infraction; he would be punished severely.

Two years earlier, several older cadets were caught after they sneaked out during the night. They had to walk between two long rows of cadets, who whipped them with heavy reeds. At the end of the line they were whipped by the instructors. Then, the bruised and bleeding cadets were put in isolation cells without food or water for three days.

After that, no one had repeated the offense—until now.

During his march up the moonlit trail, Sergei made his plan: Once he found the cabin, he would inform Benyomin about the assassination, the pogroms, and his grandfather's death. He'd accept a single cup of tea, which Sara would insist on giving him, along with another embrace—then he would take his leave and return to the school before dawn.

Sergei was breathing hard but keeping his pace as he hiked up the steep trail. His light frame and improved endurance served him well. As he was awash in the adventurous optimism of youth, a bold idea occurred to him for the first time: He could be leaving the school for good. What, after all, was keeping him there? He would miss Andrei of course—and perhaps even his Uncle Vladimir. He might feel a certain nostalgia for the school grounds. But he would not miss the day-to-day life—and he would gladly put Dmitri Zakolyev behind him forever.

Sergei was wearing the locket; he had no other possessions worth keeping. If only he could find the courage to ask! Could he claim

Avrom and Leya as his brother and sister, and Sara and Benyomin as his parents? Would it be possible? Yes, he decided. He would be helpful, and no burden at all. He would make them proud. Excited by this possibility, Sergei pushed onward. The moon was nearly overhead. It couldn't be much farther—

In the next moment, thick clouds covered the moon, shrouding the forest in darkness. Sergei could scarcely see his hands in front of his face. He looked up to see stars spread across the sky to his left and right. Only the moon was obscured. He shuffled forward, his arms reaching out in front of his face, feeling his way, sensing that he was nearly there—

Abruptly, he froze with a chilling realization: It wasn't clouds obscuring the moon. It was smoke. But not the smoke from the hearth—it was something else.

Sergei found himself careening headlong toward the cabin, racing around the boulders, lurching into the small meadow, to stop dead still, his mouth agape. Where the cabin had once stood he now saw only charred ruins. Flickering illumination from still-burning timbers lit the nightmarish scene.

Stumbling through the ruins like a drunken man, he found no living thing. Sergei prayed that the Abramovich family might emerge from the forest to greet him. Together they might rebuild—

No, he told himself—the truth: Their lives, and his hopes and dreams, were burned to cinders. Coughing and wiping his smoke-blackened face, he searched the piles of smoldering rubble and found the damning evidence he most feared: the blackened bones of a forearm and hand reaching up through the timbers.

Squinting from the heat and fetid air, Sergei threw off the smoking logs to reveal a man's skeleton with glistening flesh still clinging to the bones. The stench and sight of it made Sergei retch onto the earth and ashes. The body was almost certainly that of Benyomin Abramovich. Forcing himself to dig farther, Sergei found what remained of a little girl's shoe and wooden doll. He had to face what he wanted to deny: The rest of the family lay buried somewhere beneath the smoking nightmare that was once a home.

With his eyes burning from the acrid air, Sergei stumbled and ran back down through the wooded hills. At some point he threw himself, fully clothed, into an icy stream to clean the smell of death from his hair and clothing. But he couldn't clear his mind, where questions raged: Why didn't I come sooner? I might have saved them! Only one day earlier . . .

His head throbbed, and his breath came in gasps.

An hour before dawn, with nowhere else to go, Sergei finally reached the school and entered the iron door, still ajar. Moving carelessly, he shuffled into his barrack and fell exhausted into a troubled sleep and a barren dreamscape that stank of death.

When his eyes opened to the wan light of the day, Sergei thought, for a moment, that it was all only a nightmare, until he saw the soot still staining his hands.

He could tell no one, not even Andrei, what he had seen.

Part Two

———

SURVIVAL
OF THE
FITTEST

What is to give light must endure burning.

VIKTOR FRANKL

. 6 .

SERGEI'S TENTH, eleventh, and twelfth years marched by like good soldiers in well-ordered days, each one like the ones before. He fell into a trancelike routine at school, going through the motions doing as instructed, growing in strength, in height, in skill. He faced each task as it came but without any real sense of meaning or purpose. He still thought about his grandfather on occasion, and about the Abramovich family. But each time they came to mind, the specter of smoldering ruins rose up before him.

Little had changed among the cadets. The strata of power and influence remained the same. Zakolyev, now sixteen years old and living in the senior barracks, had almost killed an older cadet in a fight. Sergei heard two of the senior cadets muttering that Zakolyev had acted "like a crazy man" and beaten their friend with a chair. The cadet's injuries were reported as an accident.

A few days after the beating, six of the injured cadet's friends overpowered Zakolyev and gave him a beating of his own. Zakolyev had learned an important lesson: He might overcome one man but not many. After that, Zakolyev seemed quieter, less domineering. But over the following months, every one of those six boys suffered a painful "accident." One boy tripped on a loose stone; another was struck by a falling object; a third rounded a corner and collided with an unspecified object; a fourth fell down the stairs. None of them would talk about their accidents; they feared for their lives.

On a hot summer's day in 1885, a few months before Sergei's thirteenth birthday, the Cossack Alexei Orlov returned. Chief Instructor Ivanov announced, with some satisfaction, that after negotiation with higher authorities, he had succeeded in getting Instructor Orlov assigned to the school.

"As you will soon learn," his uncle continued, "Alexei Igorovich Orlov is as skilled as any man alive at tracking, outdoor survival, riding, and combat. I have seen him stand atop a galloping steed and leap over a tree branch, landing lightly again on the horse's back. Even our Instructor Brodinov might find Alexei Orlov a challenging foe in hand-to-hand combat." Sergei glanced at Instructor Brodinov, who scratched his balding head and nodded.

This high praise from his uncle turned out to be fully justified. In the coming weeks Alexei the Cossack, as the cadets referred to him, had occasion to demonstrate his skills. Sergei found himself observing their new instructor the way he had once watched his uncle. He admired the confident yet relaxed way the Cossack walked, and his friendly manner—as if he didn't need to bluster or posture or threaten because he knew he was deadly.

Sergei felt as if he were awakening from a long sleep. Suddenly he wanted to learn from Alexei Orlov; he wanted to *become* him. Now it seemed manly and romantic to be a warrior—like his father.

Sergei had heard older cadets talking about women—making jokes about what men and women did together to make babies. This subject, which he had previously ignored, now fascinated him. And it was generally agreed that to win a woman a man needed to be able to defend her from other, lesser specimens; he must fight off brigands and protect the weak. In short, he must be like Alexei, the sturdy Cossack with wavy brown hair and a neatly trimmed beard, whose face lit up when he smiled.

Orlov's one physical flaw—a saber scar on his neck—only added to his dashing persona. He told the boys that the scar served as a reminder about the value of practice, which he had pursued intensely since that mishap. He was never cut again.

Unlike the other instructors, Alexei the Cossack treated Sergei and the others with courtesy and respect. He expected even the slowest students to surpass him someday, allowing the young men to believe that anything was possible. "When we're in the woods," he told the cadets, "you may call me by my first name—as if we are colleagues and friends. But you must work hard to earn this friendship."

Sergei would have done anything for him.

Alexei, he learned, had grown up in a village of Don Cossacks. When Alexei's father was killed in battle, he had redoubled his training. Driven by a deeper awareness of the reality of death, and by a desire to make his father proud, he was finally taken into the tsar's elite guard.

"You will become Russia's finest soldiers," he told these young men, "and you will leave your mark upon the world." The cadets believed every word he spoke.

"True warriors," the Cossack added, "bring death only when necessary and protect life, including their own, whenever possible. What good to conquer an enemy in battle, only to be vanquished by hunger or cold? Napoleon and his men were defeated not only by Russian soldiers but also by the Russian winter. So my aim is to show you not merely how to kill, but how to live—how to survive on the bare essentials of life, relying on no one but yourself. There is a difference, however, between knowing how to do something and actually doing it. You will discover that soon enough."

Since his hike in the forest with his grandfather years before, Sergei's love of the wilderness now reawakened in the form of a wanderlust. He found himself gazing at the mountains in the distance. He continued applying himself in the classroom and in wrestling, riding, swimming, saber, and shooting—but survival training became his passion.

The cadets made camouflaged shelters out of pine branches and learned the skills of hunting and trapping and fishing. Alexei showed

them how to find edible plants—nature's medicines he called them—
and how to avoid poisonous plants and other hazards of the wild, such
as bears, snakes, and insects. They learned how to adapt to different terrain and any kind of weather. "Outdoorsmen do not seek hardship or
adversity," Alexei explained. "Nor do we delight in sleeping on the cold
earth or suffering unnecessary discomfort. We use our wits and skills to
soften nature's sharp edges."

One morning before training, Alexei paced back and forth in front
of the attentive cadets, gesturing with his arms as he spoke: "We
Cossacks are a peaceful and devout people, but fearsome when provoked. When the gospel is read, we draw our sabers halfway out as a
gesture of our readiness to defend church and country.

"Legends abound of the Cossacks' nearly magical skills in horsemanship and combat. Our people can make sounds to imitate the gait and voice
of different animals; we can howl like a wolf, cry like an owl or a hawk to
signal our compatriots. But it is not magic; it comes from training."

The younger boys begged him to demonstrate, which he did so
well that he could hardly continue after that because the young cadets
were all howling and making animal sounds too. "Stop!" cried Alexei
in mock consternation. "You sound like a barnyard of animals in mat-
ing season." This predictably sent the boys into peals of hysterical
laughter, which no other instructor would have allowed—and that was
why they loved him. Even the younger boys quieted down at the
prospect of learning more.

"The Cossacks bow to no one but the tsar. We fight his enemies, but
beyond this we make our own laws. For example, we will not allow soldiers to arrest runaway serfs whom we have accepted into our commu-
nities, yet we kill any marauding bands, and form a Great Wall like that
of China—a living wall that can move faster than any enemy, protecting
Mother Russia on the frontiers and borders of this vast land.

"Won't soldiers make you give back the serfs?" asked one of the
younger boys.

"Soldiers do not 'make' Cossacks do anything," Alexei answered.

"We have developed effective fighting methods on any terrain and in all kinds of weather—on frozen rivers, in snowy forests, and on tropical plains—against many different invaders, fighting styles, and weapons. I will teach the best of you some of these skills."

Sergei smiled, seeing some of the younger boys sit up straighter, trying to look taller and stand out as more disciplined than their peers. Alexei then led them all into the woods once again. When a few of the younger boys treated this time as play, throwing berries at each other instead of paying attention, Alexei appeared to ignore their antics, until he stopped abruptly and said quietly, "Those who listen, live."

The cadets froze as he added, "If any of you gets lost or injured—or if you die during survival training, which can happen—it will be your failure. But it will also be my failure . . . so you must take care."

There were no slackers after that.

Through Alexei the Cossack, Sergei came to take pride in his father's lineage. Alexei's strengths even earned the grudging admiration of Dmitri Zakolyev. For all Zakolyev's flaws, he trained harder than most for reasons of his own. When the Cossack gave Zakolyev an occasional nod of approval, a jealous Sergei strove even harder to earn Alexei's respect.

As the weeks and months passed, Sergei began to win more wrestling matches than he lost, even with some of the older boys. He also learned to shoot a rifle and pistol while riding across the nearby fields, imagining himself a great Cossack. During this period Sergei outgrew his clothing almost as fast as he was issued larger sizes. His uniforms no longer looked baggy; he felt new strength coursing through his arms and legs and chest.

On a cold morning during Sergei's fourteenth year, he overheard Lieutenant Danilov talking with one of the senior cadets. At the word *Jew*, he listened more closely, and caught a few more words: ". . . Constantine Pobedonostov, the tsar's procurator declared

. . . one-third of the Jews forced to convert, one-third expelled . . . the rest killed . . . pogrom . . . Cossacks." Times were growing darker for the Jewish people—as his grandfather had predicted.

Friday afternoon, after a survival training session, Sergei managed to catch Instructor Orlov in a rare moment alone and asked if he could walk with him back to the main gate. Alexei's smile and nod gave Sergei the courage to ask, "Are Cossacks killing Jews?"

When Alexei kept walking in silence, Sergei feared that his instructor might ask, "Why are you so concerned about Jews?" Instead, he said, "Your uncle told me a little of your history, Sergei. I understand your concern. But . . . to answer your question about whether some Cossacks have killed Jews . . . I would have to say yes.

"Cossacks feel a deep connection to the Tsar and the Mother Church. The ways of Jews seem strange to us. But we are a free and tolerant people. Those who plague, pillage, plunder, and hunt Jews like animals are not Cossacks but nationalists who resent any outsiders. True Cossacks have honor, Sergei. We engage in battle with the enemies of Russia; we do not slaughter a devout people even if they are different."

He paused before adding, "Yet among even the Cossacks there are lesser men who have raped women after battle and who have behaved badly. There is no doubt that violence against Jews has increased, at the hands of angry peasants, the Okhrana—the secret police—and even soldiers on orders of the tsar. And a small number of Cossacks may have also raided Jewish settlements. It is a shame."

Not long after his conversation with Alexei, between classes, Sergei was washing his face in the latrine area when Zakolyev entered, brushed past him, and said, "Well, if it isn't Sergei the Good."

Sergei was caught off guard. Is that what Zakolyev thought of him? How should he react? If he ignored the comment—pretend it hadn't happened—he would suffer for it. So he shrugged and muttered, "Not always so good." Then he exited the latrine as soon as he could.

Sergei had no wish to fight Zakolyev, four years his senior and equally dedicated to his training. But he thought: Alexei the Cossack would not let a bully dominate him, so neither will I.

After that he began to observe Zakolyev during hand-to-hand combat matches, seeking to discover the older cadet's weak points.

It never occurred to Sergei that Zakolyev was also watching him.

A few days later Instructor Orlov called the cadets together and told them, "Tomorrow morning at sunrise you will all set out on a seven-day survival test. You will work in pairs, each composed of a senior and junior cadet." He then instructed the older cadets to choose a younger partner.

Zakolyev chose Sergei. The phrase "survival test" took on a new meaning.

THE NEXT DAY at dawn Instructor Orlov explained, "Now that you understand the strategies of survival, you and your partner will hike to an isolated part of the forest, away from the others, to the spot marked on your map. Each team of two will work together to survive. Now remove your clothes."

The cadets were not sure they had heard correctly; it was late April of 1887, and although the snow had begun to melt, patches still lay on the ground and a chill remained, especially at dawn. "You may keep your shorts," Alexei said, "but you must walk barefoot to learn the importance of footwear. Each of you may take one of these," he said, issuing a knife and sheath to each cadet and a small military shovel to each pair. "I expect you to return here by midday seven days from now—well rested, well fed, in good health, and wearing footwear and clothing you made yourself. Any questions?"

As Sergei undressed, he stole a glance at Andrei, who gave him a worried look about spending seven days with Zakolyev.

Sergei had to run to catch up with the older cadet, who had already taken the shovel and map and set out toward the forested hills.

Four hours later, after following a small stream up into the thickly wooded hillside, they arrived at the location marked on the map. Or Sergei guessed it was the right location, since Zakolyev had made no move to show him the map. It looked like a good spot—a small clearing about fifty meters from the stream. The stream meant fish, and equally important, it meant animal trails leading to the water. An overhanging rock wall formed a shallow cave that would serve as a partial shelter; the rest they could build.

Sergei examined his feet, reddened with cold—numb, already blistered—and was about to find material to make various traps when Zakolyev issued his first order: "Make us a fire!" So he found dry moss and small twigs for a starter fire. He then tried striking his knife against several different stones to create sparks but made little progress, so he shaped a fire stick and began rubbing for friction and heat and blowing gently. It took longer than he had thought, but soon he had heat, then smoke, then glowing embers. Despite the blisters on his hands matching those on his feet, Sergei felt a primal excitement when the twigs burst into flame. He had made fire in training sessions, but this was for real. This meant survival.

Meanwhile, Sergei noted, Zakolyev had gathered branches, stones, and the tuberous fibers they could weave into string for their snares. So, after placing some larger branches on the fire and then larger logs he had cut from a fallen tree with the shovel, Sergei approached Zakolyev to help construct their traps.

"Go get your own materials!" said Zakolyev. "This is for *my* traps."

So that's how it was. Sergei knew better than to refer to the crackling flames as "*my* fire."

He moved quickly into the forest to find the materials he would need for his traps. After some difficulty, and with an eye to the sun's lengthening afternoon shadows, he managed to build and set seven traps at likely spots upriver and upwind of their site along animal trails. He made two fish traps and set snares and deadfalls—and where a supple sapling grew, he made two spring traps near the stream. He was careful to camouflage them well.

By the time he returned to camp, dusk had brought cold gusts of wind from the north. Shivering, he slapped himself and danced around to keep warm. He found Zakolyev completing a primitive shelter from birch branches and leaves, propped against the hillside next to the fire. It had room for only one.

The fire, now little more than embers, needed more logs. Sergei gathered a few and set one on the fire Zakolyev had claimed. Then he gathered more twigs and logs and built a fire of his own.

By the light of his fire, Sergei managed to throw together a makeshift overhang of interwoven pine branches near another granite overhang. He finished just as a light drizzle began. The cloud cover served as an insulating blanket, keeping the night from turning frigid.

Shivering, wet, and naked except for his shorts, Sergei sandwiched himself between layers of pine boughs he had gathered, shifting until he found a warmer position. Zakolyev's huddled form, faintly visible in the glow of his fire, revealed that he had made similar preparations.

Sergei lay awake for a few moments, too cold to sleep, and listened to the rain. Despite the cold and hunger that churned in his belly, a wave of satisfaction washed over him. He had set snares, made fire, found shelter. For the present, he was alive and well. In the morning he would check his traps, and they would see what the day would bring. These thoughts gave way to a deep fatigue that pulled Sergei over the edge of sleep.

W HEN S ERGEI next opened his eyes, his breath misted in the chill morning air. He scrambled out of his bed of pine branches, hoping for a patch of sunlight, but found none this early. Leaving Zakolyev asleep, he walked gingerly on sore feet to the stream, where he drank, then splashed the icy water over his face and chest and shoulders. Brushing the water from his body, he slapped himself all over, and ran in place until his body warmed. He then returned to camp, grabbed his knife, and headed upstream.

Although he had marked trees at eye level near his traps, Sergei couldn't find the first snare. Alexei had reminded them, "The wilderness teaches hard lessons and has little tolerance for mistakes." Why didn't I pay better attention? Sergei thought, chastising himself for his carelessness. Backtracking, he finally found the second trap he had set. It was empty.

But nearby, in a spring trap he had placed along the trail, he found an exhausted weasel, dangling in midair, struggling weakly. He approached the animal cautiously. As he reached up to grasp the weasel, it made a low growl and sliced his hand with a sudden swipe of its claw. Then it tried to bite him.

With a primitive rush of energy, Sergei grabbed the back of its head and slashed the weasel's throat so forcefully he nearly took off its head—and narrowly missed cutting his own wrist in the process. The creature kicked a few times, blood pulsing from its neck. Then it was still, and dead.

Panting and trembling, his heart pounding, Sergei found the presence of mind to open the snare rather than cut it; he would need it again. He hoped the killing would be easier in the future. But then he thought, Should killing get easier? Do I have the right to take a creature's life? No, he decided, only the power. He did what had to be done under the circumstances. He felt no animosity toward this animal, which had only tried to defend itself. And Sergei had killed only to survive. He thanked the weasel for its life, which would sustain his own. He would not waste it.

In killing that weasel, he had put a part of his childhood behind him. He realized that his life too could be snuffed out in a moment. It had nothing to do with fairness, only chance. By paying attention—through knowledge and skill—he might better his odds. This was his first real lesson in the wilderness. As he padded quietly toward the next trap, Sergei wondered what kind of snares might be waiting for him on his own path into the future.

The third trap was empty and undisturbed; so were the fourth and fifth. The next had snared a squirrel, which he killed as quickly and mercifully as he could with one blow of a large stone. The remaining traps were empty, except for the last, in which he found a large rabbit. This meant food for several more days, and new shoes as well.

The cut on his hand from the weasel's claw was beginning to throb. So he swung his arm rapidly around to make the cut bleed and cleanse the wound. Then he washed and scrubbed and scoured the shallow gash with sand from the stream. Finally, he peed on it, remembering Alexei's dictum that fresh urine could help guard against infection.

After Sergei tied the creatures together with several vines, he reset the last snare and turned back toward the camp. He didn't expect any more catches until the next morning, but he would check again in the late afternoon. Just in case.

The hunt had awakened his instincts and sharpened every sense. He listened to rainwater dripping from budded branches overhead and birdsong in the distance. His eyes drank in every hue and texture of the forest as he headed back to camp. He found a morose Zakolyev skinning his catch—a single squirrel, one small meal and one shoe.

Sergei knew it would not go well for him when Zakolyev saw his three animals, but he could hardly hide them. So he casually walked up and dumped the other squirrel next to Zakolyev's, followed by the weasel and rabbit, saying diplomatically, "These are from our other traps."

Zakolyev stared at them. All he said was, "Sergei the Good does it again," before turning back to his skinning. Sergei butchered the carcasses as well as he could. It was messy work, made worse by his inexperience. In training, he had only helped butcher one rabbit and a deer.

By early afternoon they had hung strips of meat from vines tied between nearby trees. They stretched the skins on frames made from flexible saplings. The weasel skin wasn't large enough to cover Sergei's shoulders, but it was a start. When he handed Zakolyev the squirrel skin and said, "For your other shoe," the senior took it without comment.

They cooked strips of rabbit flesh, their first meal in nearly two days. With a full stomach, Sergei brought back more saplings and pine boughs to reinforce his makeshift shelter.

That night, as Sergei and Zakolyev squatted by their respective fires, neither having spoken more than a few words, Sergei watched the stars appear, sparkling like ice crystals scattered across a velvet sky. White smoke and glowing embers rose up, then disappeared into the night.

After a glance toward Zakolyev, staring into the flames of his fire, deep in thought, Sergei slipped into the cover of pine branches. As he drifted into sleep, he wondered: Why had Zakolyev chosen him?

THE NEXT MORNING Sergei found a squirrel crushed by one of his deadfalls; another trap had snared a raccoon near the stream—the same trap that had caught the weasel. Rather than trying to grab the hissing, growling animal, he fashioned a club from a heavy log and knocked the creature unconscious before taking its life.

Sergei also found two fish in the fish trap before returning to camp.

Zakolyev's traps had caught only one squirrel and a sickly looking skunk—good for its hide but not for meat. When he saw Sergei's bounty, Zakolyev just stared at him, saying nothing.

Awkwardly, Sergei set down the two fish, the squirrel, and the raccoon on a flat rock. "I got lucky," he said. "We can eat well."

After the meal, his stomach satisfied, Sergei went out exploring— anything to distance himself from his sullen companion. He spent about two hours making a wide circle around the camp, checking the streams for fish and familiarizing himself with the surroundings. He was returning to camp when he heard the distant tapping sound of a deer's hooves. He froze, waited, and listened. Silence . . . a few more hoof sounds . . . then silence. Sergei was downwind of the sounds, which would make it less likely for the animal to detect his scent. Sergei crouched low and moved in slowly and quietly.

A few minutes later he spotted a huge buck, barely visible, about twenty meters away, nibbling on fresh shoots of grass. Every few moments its large ears would turn, and it would look up. Sergei stayed absolutely still. The deer moved a few more meters in his direction. That's when Sergei realized that he was standing on a deer path, between the deer and the stream.

A crazy idea occurred to him: He'd hunt the buck. There was no time to go back and get Zakolyev. It had to be now, or he'd lose the chance. This one creature would provide them with enough food and clothing to meet all their needs. So, driven by a primitive urge, Sergei slowly shimmied up a tree right next to the deer trail.

Once he reached a thick branch directly over the trail, Sergei found a stable position and waited. He could no longer see the deer, but he would wait as long as it took, on the chance it would pass under him.

About fifteen minutes later, there it was—walking and grazing below him. Now or never, he thought. Hardly breathing, his knife in hand, Sergei dropped from the branch and landed on the buck with a thud, one arm wrapped tightly around its neck. As the creature kicked wildly, Sergei reached around and cut its throat—once, then another cut. The panicked buck, bleeding profusely, kicked with renewed frenzy. Sergei realized that if he fell off, the buck would likely gore him with those antlers before it bled out. So, before he was thrown, in a hunter's act of mercy, he aimed just above the front foreleg and stabbed deeply into the buck's side, through its ribs and into its heart.

The creature fell over and lay still.

As he panted hard, his own heart pounding, Sergei's elation was mixed with sorrow for the death of this great stag.

On the way back to camp, he remembered something Alexei had told them: "When in the wilderness, you must become wild."

Entering the clearing, blood-soaked and breathless, Sergei told what he had done. A skeptical Zakolyev went back with him to find the proud creature lying dead.

Sergei watched Zakolyev as his face changed from surprise to a controlled rage. The senior pulled out his knife and began to gut the deer. "Come on!" he ordered Sergei. "Don't just stand there—make yourself useful!"

They left most of the internal organs for the scavengers, then made litters and dragged the carcass back to camp. It took them the rest of the day to butcher the animal, stretch the hide, and prepare the strips of meat. It was such a large buck that they now had enough food to last the rest of their stay in the forest. More important, with the other animals, mostly trapped by Sergei, they had enough for fur-lined shoes from the rabbit and deerskin shirts and leggings. Sergei also had a raccoon cap.

That night, before dusk, Sergei washed the blood off his bare chest and legs. Then he padded through the forest and dismantled his traps. There was no sense killing more animals.

It took a good part of their final two days for each of them to fashion a pair of stiff buckskin pants and shirt. They had to let the hide soak for hours in the stream before scraping off the hair and flesh and washing the hide several times more to remove any grease. They couldn't tan them properly, lacking salt or lime. But they rubbed the hides with the brains of the deer, then with ashes from the fire, as they had been taught.

Finally, after cutting leather thongs—narrow strips to tie together the leather shirt and pants—they were clothed like real woodsmen. That final day passed quickly. Zakolyev only spoke to Sergei when necessary, every remark curt or insulting. Finally the older cadet stomped out of camp and left Sergei in peace.

Then, an hour before dusk, Sergei thought he heard the distant cry of an animal. He went back to tending the fire. Then he heard it again. It was Zakolyev, calling his name. Going quickly to investigate, he heard the cry more clearly: "Ivanov!"

Sergei found Zakolyev at the bottom a steep and slippery embankment over the stream. It was so slick with moss that Sergei almost lost his footing as well. In the fading light he could just see Zakolyev struggling to free his ankle, wedged between two rocks.

Furious—as if Sergei himself were somehow responsible—Zakolyev snarled, "Don't just stand there, idiot. Get a branch! Hurry!"

Sergei had his knife, but it hadn't occurred to him to bring the military shovel, which also served as a hatchet. "I'll be right back!" he yelled, and ran as fast as he could in the deepening dusk to retrieve the tool. On his way back from camp he spied a straight and sturdy branch that might be used as a lever. He hacked at the limb until it came free.

By the time Sergei got back to him, Zakolyev was so furious he could hardly speak. This was the ultimate shame, and Sergei knew it. Not only had he out-trapped Zakolyev, and caught and killed the great buck, but now Sergei the Good was rescuing him—maybe saving his life.

Sergei knew that if he was able to free Zakolyev, there was no way to predict what might happen next, but it wasn't likely to be a humble thanks or a handshake. He felt an impulse to leave Zakolyev there. But it passed.

Once Sergei got the heavy branch under one of the stones, it didn't take long to move it enough for Zakolyev to pull his ankle free. The ankle was sore but not broken. Sergei knew better than to offer any further help. He silently handed him the sturdy branch for a walking stick and left him alone.

A dread came over Sergei as he walked back to camp. He knew that in saving Dmitri Zakolyev, he had made an enemy for life.

WHEN ZAKOLYEV finally returned to camp, Sergei busied himself by adding branches to his lean-to, fearing that a single word, or even a look, might set off Zakolyev. Sergei needed more branches overhead because the heavy clouds threatened rain, and he hoped to sleep well this final night in the forest.

As it turned out, he hardly slept at all.

Sometime in the night, after drifting off, Sergei was startled awake by flashes of lightning in the distance—then the explosive crackle of thunder. His eyes snapped open—a strange sense of foreboding passed through him. Something was wrong. Just then the lightning flashed again, and he saw—or thought he saw—legs and a torso just outside the shelter. He turned his head imperceptibly, nearly frozen with fear. The lightning flashed again to reveal a momentary glimpse of Zakolyev, squatting nearby, staring down. There was a knife in Zakolyev's hand. Sergei felt he was about to die.

The light vanished in an instant. Unable to breathe or make even a sound, Sergei stared into the darkness. Another flash of light revealed that the figure was gone.

Could he have dreamed it? Imagined it? He couldn't be sure. Sergei lay back, gulping shallow breaths as the downpour continued and the thunderclaps receded in the distance. He lay awake for hours, alert to any sound that stood out against the patter of rain . . .

The next time his eyes jerked open it was dawn. He had survived the night. He sat up quickly to see Zakolyev, still asleep under his lean-to.

As Sergei broke apart his shelter and scattered his fire, Zakolyev rose, took his knife and the shovel, and without a word walked out of the camp.

Later, making his own way back through the rocky, forested terrain, Sergei thought about what he had experienced over the past seven days. He now knew that he could survive in the wild, like Alexei and others before him.

He made it back to the meeting place by midday, as Alexei Orlov had instructed. Soon most of the original thirty-two cadets had returned. Some distance away, Sergei spied Zakolyev standing in the middle of a group of half-naked younger boys. Zakolyev saw him too—he pointed toward Sergei and said something to the boys. They laughed.

Ignoring them, Sergei looked around for Andrei, wondering how he had fared, but his friend had not yet returned. When Sergei turned back to Zakolyev and his admirers, some of the young boys snickered. One of the bolder cadets, probably trying to please his idol, said in a sarcastic tone, "Found your way back, did you?"

Sergei stared at the young cadet; he could only imagine what Zakolyev must have told them all.

As the group of boys walked away, one of them called back, "It was lucky Dmitri gave you part of the hide, or you'd be as naked as some of the others!" Then he scurried off to follow his leader.

Finally Sergei spotted a tired but happy-looking Andrei approaching with his older companion. They had pieced together rough-looking long shirts but no pants, and pieces of leather were strapped to the soles of their feet with thick cords. Sergei surveyed all these half-naked cadets wearing motley skins made of rabbit, raccoon, shrew, skunk, fox, and squirrel, and he smiled with new confidence.

It had been one of the most intense experiences of Sergei's youth. He hoped it was the last time he would ever have to spend time alone with Dmitri Zakolyev.

. 8 .

AFTER SURVIVAL WEEK, Sergei returned to the daily routines at the school aware of changes not only in his inner world, but in his body as well. He looked at himself in the mirror and now saw a muscular young man, with hair growing under his arms and elsewhere. He began to think about women more often—about their bodies and their mysteries, all in a confused state of longing.

He also noticed flaws and hypocrisies in the adults around him: Brodinov preached about the importance of training hard and staying fit while he grew heavier with each passing month, and Kalishnikov would lean over his desk in the classroom and pontificate about telling the truth while he told lies about the Jews.

Sergei's life now seemed even more complicated and confused than ever before. He thought again about what it might be like to leave this place, to find a home and people more like him.

Sergei felt the urge to be free in a world where few freedoms existed—except in the wild. And even nature had its own strict rules and consequences. Questions and dilemmas raged inside him. He had never thought much about the future; now it preoccupied him.

When the chief instructor allowed it, Sergei made more frequent visits to his uncle's library. Vladimir Ivanov owned an impressive selection of books, and Sergei read works ranging from religious philosophy and military science to ancient Greek philosophers such as Plato, who described the lives and teachings of Socrates and the other sages and statesmen.

Sergei soon made a startling discovery: Certain phrases seemed to unlock within him a vast storehouse of insights about subjects he had never before contemplated—questions he had never asked: What is the purpose of living? What constitutes the good life? Are people innately virtuous or selfish? Sometimes he had to shut a book, close his eyes, and hold his head in his hands as his heart raced with excitement—not merely because of the words he read, but because of the doors they opened. It was like discovering foreign lands in his mind.

Then came Sergei's fifteenth birthday, summer's end in 1887. He thought of his mother on that day, as he thought of her on every birthday and other times as well. He slipped the chain of the locket around his neck and under his shirt. He wore it almost daily, taking this risk for the simple pleasure it provided him in a place where few pleasures existed, simple or otherwise. After dark—or before training or the cold-water immersions—he would hide it again within his mattress.

IN DECEMBER of that year, Chief Instructor Ivanov made a rare appearance during morning exercises in the school compound. In recent months Sergei had seen little of his uncle, a distant and private man who remained behind the scenes. So the chief instructor's presence spoke of the importance of this announcement. Without preface or explanation, he said, "Step forward if you hear your name called." He began reading from a list. Sergei heard the names of several senior cadets; then his own name was called, and those of a few of the more hardworking boys his age, including Andrei. Sergei stepped forward with the others. Why are we being singled out? he wondered. Finally his uncle called out the last name on his list —"Cadet Dmitri Zakolyev."

His uncle then announced, "You twelve have been selected for special training and duty as elite soldiers and possible future bodyguards to the tsar. You are to be congratulated." These were the closest thing to encouraging words any of them had heard from the chief instructor.

Out of the corner of his eyes, Sergei could see proud smiles forming on some of his companions' faces. He was glad to see Andrei smile as well. But Sergei had nothing to grin about; it only meant that his life had changed once again at the whim of others. And, worst of all, he would see more of Zakolyev.

After Chief Instructor Ivanov dismissed all but the chosen twelve, he began to pace slowly and speak in measured tones, as if he were imparting secrets for their ears only. "Thus far," he said, "you have learned what all young soldiers must learn—the fundamentals of wrestling and boxing, horsemanship, water skills, basic weapons, military strategy, and survival in the wild. The other boys will continue to refine these skills. But elite bodyguards need elite training."

He paced in silence before continuing. "Long before the birth of Christ our savior, Greek merchants traded with tribes on the shores of the Black Sea. As centuries passed, Sarmations were overrun by Germanic Goths, who fell to Asiatic Huns, later defeated by Turkic Avars. Then, twelve hundred years ago, heirs of the Vikings gave way to eastern Slavic peoples who settled in a land now called Ukraine, home of the Kievan Rus. These various peoples, who spoke a hundred and forty different languages and dialects, who had risen up through a history of sacrament and sacrifice, of struggle and blood and toil, formed the largest country in the world, known by its peoples as *Rodina* . . . Mother Russia."

Sergei remembered this speech vividly—not only because his uncle spoke so rarely, but also because he saw the chief instructor pause and wipe away tears that came to his eyes at the mention of *Rodina*, this land he so loved. He quickly recovered, however, and said, "Throughout her history, Russia's people—not only Cossacks and soldiers, but farmers, merchants, and others called to duty—have been forced to repel invaders from the north, south, east, and west. We have fought on sandy plains, frozen rivers, muddy bogs, and thick forests. Our varied enemies forced us to develop a versatile system of combat. As elite soldiers, you will be shown an approach to fighting more natural and more lethal than anything you have studied."

The chief instructor then called out, "Alexei Orlov!" The Cossack stepped forward. Chief Instructor Ivanov turned back to the twelve boys. "We need a volunteer," he said. Anatoly Kamarov, one of the senior cadets and the wrestling champion, stepped forward. Gesturing in a good-natured way, his uncle said, "Please attack Instructor Orlov." Cadet Kamarov crouched and circled Alexei, who only smiled and stood relaxed, not even bothering to face the cadet squarely. When the cadet thought he saw an opening, he lunged in and threw a front kick.

Alexei hardly moved, but the cadet was suddenly off balance and falling awkwardly to the ground with a thump. It was as if the cadets were watching a magician rather than a fighter. This performance was repeated several times before his uncle thanked Kamarov for his courage and Alexei for his demonstration. "The tsar has many loyal soldiers," he continued, "but those who protect him and serve on special missions must be able to overcome even the best soldiers. So at this point your training will intensify to the breaking point, and sometimes beyond. Anyone who wishes to step down may do so with honor. To remain in the regular barracks, step forward. You will have our permission to contribute to the regular ranks of brave men."

The chief instructor waited. No one stepped forward. "There is no shame in the regular ranks," he repeated. "It takes wisdom to know your limits and courage to speak out." Sergei stood frozen like the others.

"So be it," said his uncle. "Effective immediately, the regular cadets will continue to train with Instructor Brodinov. The elite group will train under the supervision of Alexei Orlov."

THE NEXT DAY their elite training began. As soon as the cadets had assembled in two straight rows, Alexei told them the Cossack code: "The life of your friend is more important than your own. It is your duty to risk your life to save a comrade, and to defend the Tsar and the Church."

He paused as they absorbed this—Sergei felt lifted to a place above his usual world—and then the atmosphere changed abruptly with Instructor Orlov's next words: "Each of you must now pass an initiation.

It may seem cruel, but it serves many useful purposes. You are about to suffer pain and injury. Each of you must choose whether to receive a deep knife cut or have your arm struck by a hammer with a force that may break it.

"You will be the first, Cadet Ivanov," he announced. "The others will follow." Sergei stepped forward, but hesitated before speaking. Confronted with two painful options, which was the best choice; which was the worst?

"Well," said the Cossack. His voice was quiet, and patient—but persistent. "Which shall it be?"

Sergei thought a moment longer. Then he said, "I choose the blade."

Immediately, but without pleasure or rancor, Alexei sliced open his arm. For an instant Sergei felt no pain—only the shock of watching the skin of his arm part to reveal the thin white layer of fat. Then the wound filled with blood, as the deep, throbbing pain began, and the blood ran down his arm and dripped to the earth.

"You two," said Alexei, pointing to two of the older cadets. "I want one to stitch up Cadet Ivanov's wound and the other to apply a field bandage. Do a clean job—you will soon have your turn." He gestured toward a table with various bandages and splints and supplies. Galina, the old nurse, stood by to supervise. She told Sergei to drink two small glasses of vodka to help dull the pain. He did so—and wanted a third but could not bring himself to ask.

After the nurse sprinkled a powder into the gaping wound, she held his arm and watched an older cadet clumsily stitch his skin with a curved needle. Sergei turned away, clenched his teeth, and tried not to gasp or cry out each time the needle pierced his skin.

The throbbing pain had increased and the needle punctures made him wince, but he held on as Cadet Yegevny pulled the thin twine taut, drawing the edges of the wound tightly together. After what seemed an interminable few minutes, Sergei's wound was covered with a bandage, and the pain faded to a deep ache.

"You're a brave boy," she said. He hardly heard her, distracted as he was by the continuing tests a few meters away. At least the worst was over for him.

Now every cadet stared in morbid fascination as the next boy, after seeing Sergei bleed, chose the hammer. He yelped then whimpered but did not faint when Alexei hit him with the hammer. They all heard a *crack* but couldn't tell whether the bone had broken. The cadet came over, breathing rapidly, in great pain. Two other cadets applied a splint while the rest of the cadets observed.

They continued in this manner, with some choosing the knife and others the hammer. Andrei hated blood and chose the hammer. He cried out but gathered himself together once it was over. Zakolyev chose the knife and didn't even flinch. In fact, he smiled throughout.

One of the cadets had declined to take the test. Alexei told him, with formal courtesy, to return to Brodinov's group. Soon a line of eleven pain-racked cadets remained, standing at the medical station. Most drank the vodka and, like Sergei, wanted more.

At the end Alexei called them all together and said with great formality and respect, as if each had leaped across a chasm that separated them from the other cadets: "Sometimes words alone cannot teach. Each of you has received an injury, as you might in combat. The wounds will heal. Meanwhile, learn from your body. Will yourself to heal quickly. Continue to function despite your injuries, as you would have to do in battle.

"This was not a lighthearted exercise," he continued, "and I do not enjoy inflicting damage. But it was necessary. Now you've experienced a small degree of the pain that you, as soldiers, will inflict on the enemy when necessary. This is the ugly reality of battle. Never forget that it is better to wound ten men than kill one. The wounded require more care and slow the enemy, and I tell you this for higher reasons as well.

"Wounds may heal, and a soldier can return to his family, but death is permanent, and an adversary's soul rests heavily upon your conscience. So kill an enemy only when there is no other way. Now return to your rooms until your next class and think about what I've told you."

The cadets were issued pants with a red stripe down the sides, just like the officers. As the eleven walked back toward their respective barracks, Sergei noticed a certain camaraderie among them, forged by the common bond of having endured this painful lesson together. Only Zakolyev walked alone—ahead of the others.

One of the older cadets had taken a bottle of vodka from one of the instructors—a daring act. Now, as a show of trust and bravado, he shared it with the others. They passed around the bottle, and Sergei got drunk, and funny, and sick. Later he found himself craving more, but there was no more to be had. Then Sergei remembered that his father had drunk himself to death, and he wondered if there was something in his blood too.

His wound healed within a few weeks, but he would have a scar to remind him of the day he became one of the elite.

Soon after, their special unit had to go without food for seven days, with no water either for the last two days. The purpose of this, according to Instructor Orlov, was multifaceted. "First," he said, "you will overcome the instinctive fear of not eating, so that if you are cut off during a battle, it will be of little consequence to you whether or not you have food. Second, occasional fasting purifies the body and strengthens the constitution."

"Third," whispered one of the cadets, "not feeding us saves the school money." Several of the other cadets stifled laughs. But no one was laughing by the end of the first day. They all felt ravenous, and not in the best of spirits the second day either, when another cadet dropped out, so ten remained. They were assigned extra work and training during this period—their lack of food was no excuse to rest or slack off.

During those seven days Sergei and the others experienced periods of lassitude alternating with a sense of lightness and higher energy.

The last two days without water were the hardest. They ended the fast with purifying rituals involving a kind of second baptism. "You become elite soldiers through elite training," Alexei reminded them. "One day some of you may make the shift from soldiers to warriors, like the three hundred Spartan *Skiritai* of ancient times who held the pass at Thermopylae for three days against three hundred thousand invading Persian soldiers."

"What happened to them?" asked one of the other boys.

"They all died," said the Cossack.

Sᴇʀɢᴇɪ ꜰᴇʟᴛ ᴇᴠᴇʀʏᴛʜɪɴɢ quickening—his thoughts, desires, his mind and body. He moved into the men's quarters, where Zakolyev, now nineteen, was a senior cadet. Meanwhile, Sergei's training with Alexei continued in firearms, camouflage, field medicine, winter survival, and hand-to-hand combat.

A few weeks later the elite instructor announced, "Today we will practice choke holds and escapes. When your partner tries to strangle you, do what you can to escape without inflicting serious damage to your fellow cadet. Explore possibilities. Find out what works, and what doesn't. When you are choking your practice partner, he will not be able to speak, so he will slap his hand on his leg to signal you to release the choke immediately. Otherwise, he will pass out . . . but if you hold it too long, you might just kill him. So do *not* hold a choke after your partner has slapped!"

Near the end of the day, Zakolyev chose Sergei as his partner. The moment Zakolyev's arms wrapped around his neck, Sergei couldn't breathe, couldn't speak. As the choke tightened, Sergei's head felt like it was exploding. Spots floated before his eyes. He slapped his thigh once, then again, as he was sucked down into a maelstrom of panic, an encroaching darkness.

Finally Zakolyev released the hold. Sergei collapsed to a sitting position, semiconscious. He looked up to see Zakolyev staring at him. "What's that around your neck?" asked the senior cadet.

"N-nothing," Sergei answered, furious at himself for having forgotten to remove the locket beforehand. A moment's carelessness, and there would be hell to pay.

"Let me see it," Zakolyev said casually.

Zakolyev had a way of asking for things that made it seem unreasonable, even silly, to deny him. Sergei almost found his hand reaching for the clasp before he came to his senses. "No," he said. "It's personal." Zakolyev shrugged and walked away to work with another cadet.

With a few final comments, Alexei ended the class and departed. All of the cadets, except for a few still practicing, filed out of the practice room. Anxious to find a few moments alone, Sergei was turning to follow his departing classmates when he heard Zakolyev's chilling voice close behind him. "Now you can show me your little treasure."

Sergei knew instantly that Zakolyev didn't merely want to just see it; he wanted to possess it. "Like I said—it's private. I want to keep it that way."

As Sergei turned to leave, Zakolyev's right arm again wrapped around his neck; the other locked behind his head. Sergei willed himself to fight the panic, to breathe, but there was no breath, only an agony of pressure bursting in his head. Through the gathering darkness he caught a final glimpse of a few of the straggling cadets, who glanced in their direction then turned and walked away, thinking that they were still practicing. But this was no practice—Zakolyev could kill him.

As the light faded from his mind, Sergei experienced a flickering premonition, an image of his lifeless body sprawled on the floor. Then blackness.

W HEN HE CAME TO, Zakolyev was gone. So was the locket.

From that moment on, Sergei became obsessed with reclaiming the locket. Zakolyev would not, could not, be allowed to steal Sergei's only tangible connection to his parents.

The two were not scheduled to train together for a few days. So Sergei searched in the senior barracks, on the grounds, and behind the classrooms where Zakolyev would smoke and drink—but could not find him.

Sergei's concentration suffered; he could think of nothing else but taking back what was his.

Three days later he caught up with the senior and confronted him. "Give it back!" Sergei shouted, the anger burning in his belly.

A few other early arrivals circled around, drawn in by the unfolding drama.

"Give back what?" Zakolyev said calmly, apparently amused.

"You know what."

Zakolyev smiled that hateful smile. "Oh, you mean that little girl's trinket you had around your neck?"

"Give it to me . . . now!" he said, his voice a growl.

"I told you . . . I don't have it."

"You're a liar!"

Zakolyev studied him as he might observe a bug, intrigued that Sergei the Good, nearly four years his junior, was crazy enough to make such demands. Still, the boy would have to be punished—

Sergei's kick caught Zakolyev unaware, snapping his knee to the side. Zakolyev let his knee give way and twisted his body to trap Sergei's leg, forcing him to the ground. Now the muscular senior sat on Sergei's chest and methodically started pounding on his face.

Sergei's hands came up protectively as the blows rained down, and he managed to strike back once. Using his fingers as a spear, Sergei thrust them into Zakolyev's eye, infuriating him.

Just then Brodinov showed up and broke them apart. But not before Zakolyev had broken Sergei's nose, loosened some teeth, and cracked his cheekbone, sending him to the infirmary.

The next day Sergei peered through eyes swollen almost shut to see Andrei kneeling by his bedside. In an excited whisper, Andrei reported, "Zakolyev has a black eye and a limp. It was a brave but foolish thing to do, Sergei. I heard Zakolyev tell some older cadets that if you ever troubled him again, you might have a serious accident.

"And that's not all: There's a rumor that one of the other cadets saw Zakolyev choke you after class and take the locket. Somehow the instructors heard about it," Andrei added, smiling. "Brodinov demanded that Zakolyev return the locket, but Zakolyev insisted he didn't have it. They know he's probably lying, but no one can prove anything, and no cadet would step forward to accuse him. Zakolyev has to sit in detention all his spare time as long as you're in the infirmary. Now he's been punished like any other cadet; it's out in the open. Some say that he's going to be expelled."

Then Andrei's elation vanished. "I think you've made a bad enemy, Sergei. But I'll watch your back."

"And I'll watch yours," Sergei managed to reply. He felt no elation at Zakolyev's punishment or satisfaction in Zakolyev's shame. It would only make things worse; he would never return the locket now.

SERGEI SLEPT and daydreamed through the rest of the day. But that night he awakened from a deep sleep to find Alexei the Cossack standing nearby in the shadows. He was dressed not in the school uniform, but rather in his Cossack garb—the way he had first appeared years before, when he rode into the compound to bring news of the death of Tsar Aleksandr II. For a moment Sergei thought he was seeing an apparition.

Then Alexei spoke, and Sergei knew he was awake. "Practice holding your breath, so you will not be concerned about lack of air. It's not the lack of air that causes blackout; it's the pressure of depleted blood. So if you are ever choked again," he whispered, "relax completely—it will give you twenty or thirty seconds."

Alexei looked up and away for a moment, as if searching for the right words. "Life can be hard, Sergei, so you must be harder. But remember too that softness can overcome rigidity. A river can cut through stone. It only takes time. All you need is a little more time . . ."

Alexei added, "You did a brave thing, confronting Dmitri

Zakolyev. Your father was also a brave man . . . a good man, as you will become . . . Yet I don't think you are destined to become a soldier."

Hearing his last words, Sergei felt a pang of deep disappointment, but then Alexei smiled at him as one might smile at a friend. And before Sergei could say anything, or thank the Cossack for his guidance, Alexei Orlov stepped back into the shadows and was gone.

THE NEXT MORNING Andrei returned to Sergei's bedside with the news: "Alexei the Cossack is gone! He had to report back immediately to the palace, and he left before dawn. Instructor Brodinov will continue our training. Chief Instructor Ivanov conveyed to us Instructor Orlov's farewell and regards. Then he said—let me see if I can remember—he said, 'This is a soldier's life. People appear and disappear. Comrades may fall in battle right next to us, but we must continue without missing a step.' After that he dismissed us until the afternoon—that's how I could come to see you." Andrei paused. "You know, I think the chief instructor will miss Instructor Orlov."

Not as much as I will, thought Sergei.

. 10 .

On a bitter cold day in January, 1888, Sergei was released from the infirmary. Still intent on recovering his locket, he considered his options. He realized the futility of another confrontation; if he again challenged Zakolyev, he would likely get beaten again. Or he might get lucky and hurt the older cadet. Either way, Zakolyev would not tell him where he had hidden the locket.

The wisest thing he could do was to watch and wait. As Alexei had said, some things take time and patience. But he would not forget. Sergei knew he had made a formidable enemy. But then, so had Zakolyev.

Another change had occurred since that night Alexei had visited. A part of Sergei's dedication had departed with the Cossack. He now felt a growing sense of detachment, as if he were an observer rather than a participant in the life around him.

In the coming months he spent more time alone, in the quiet of his uncle's library. He would turn the globe on his desk, letting his fingers drift to the north, south, east, and west.

Soon after the spring thaw Sergei was sitting in the library reading the dialogues of Socrates when the strangest thing happened: Out of nowhere, a vivid image appeared in his mind—a rough-hewn face with a nose that looked as if it had been broken, chin and cheeks covered with a beard, and coarse, curly hair. Yet the face had an air of strength and integrity, with eyes that reminded Sergei of thunder and lightning.

Then Sergei heard the words, "I am a citizen not of Athens or of Greece but of the world . . ." In a flash Sergei realized that this vision was none other than Socrates himself. The apparition spoke only six words before it vanished: "A new world . . . to the west . . ."

Then all was quiet. Sergei was back in his uncle's library at the Nevskiy Military School. He had no idea what had happened or why. He did not believe that the spirit of the Greek philosopher had actually visited or spoken to him. After all, the words were not in Greek but in his own language. Yet the words came from somewhere . . . What new world? Where to the west? Sergei recalled something that Andrei had told him years before, after they had met: "I wasn't born in Russia, but in a land to the west, across the sea . . . in a place called America."

Perhaps my own mind created his face and drew forth these words. But why? Sergei thought. He looked once more in the book, hoping for another vision. Finally, he replaced the book on the shelf and was turning to go when something caught his eye—a letter lying askew on his uncle's desk. Curious, Sergei stole a glance:

NOTICE:

To Vladimir Borisovich Ivanov,
Chief Instructor, Nevskiy Military School:
In one week's time, a garrison of soldiers will pass your school on the way south to the Pale of Settlement for Jewish duty. All seniors and elite cadets will join this garrison for three months. This field experience will prepare your cadets for duties to come. Remind them they act in the name of the Tsar, the Holy Church, and Mother Russia.

Vasiliy Aleksandrovich Artemov
Field Commander

Jewish duty. The words chilled Sergei. As one of the elite group, he would be expected to harass innocent people—people like his grandfather, like the Abramovich family. Once again, the charred remains of their cabin appeared, and the air stank of death . . .

He would not do it. Not for his uncle; not for the tsar himself.

Sergei had come to a crossroads and his choice was clear. The time had come for him to disappear in the night. He would go to St. Petersburg to find the gift that his grandfather had left for him. This buried treasure might enable Sergei to purchase a ticket on a great steamship. Then he would go to America, where they did not send soldiers to kill people because they were Jews.

As this decision penetrated him, he reflected on what would surely follow: They would conduct a search, so he would have to travel fast and far. And he could never return. Sergei felt a pang of guilt as he reflected upon his father's decision to send him here and his uncle's willingness to take him in and provide a home and a way of life. He would be turning his back on them. But it was a life he could no longer abide. He was not only his father's son; he was also his mother's. And it was her blood calling to him now.

Sergei felt as if he were about to leap from that tree onto that wild buck once again. He couldn't know what the future might hold, but it would at least be a future he would choose for himself.

Having made this decision he knew that he must depart soon—that very night. But not without leaving a letter for his uncle. He owed him that. Sergei snatched up a blank piece of paper from his uncle's desk and a fountain pen and wrote:

Dear Chief Instructor Ivanov,

I offer my apologies for leaving in this manner. I go to find another life. I have taken a map, a compass, and some supplies I will need for my journeys.

Under your care, I have become stronger, and I have learned much. Someday I hope to make you proud. I believe that you have a good and kind heart. I wish that I could have known you better.

I will remember you always and hold a place for you in my prayers.

Sergei signed the letter, folded it, and put it in his pocket. Before he left the office, he searched hurriedly and found what he was looking for: a map that might prove useful, and from a file drawer he quickly grabbed the few documents in his folder.

THAT NIGHT Sergei slipped into bed with his clothes still on. His knapsack was packed with whatever essentials he could gather, including the documents, which he had wrapped in oilcloth for protection. He had packed dried food pilfered from the kitchen, along with a survival knife and the small and versatile military shovel, as well as fishing line, map, and compass.

During the evening meal Sergei looked around the hall and said a silent farewell to Andrei and his fellow cadets. Before bed he walked to the barrack window and gazed out across the central compound, where he saw his boyhood self, clinging fiercely to the mane of that horse on his first ride.

After curfew he feigned sleep until he heard the familiar sounds of slumber; then he slipped the letter to his uncle under his pillow. Someone would find it soon enough, and his uncle would send the best cadet trackers, maybe even one of the instructors. But they would not find him; they had trained him far too well.

Once again he reviewed his escape plans. First he had to slip past the sentries—he knew their routines well enough. And during their last cold-water immersion, he had seen a log floating in the shallows . . .

SERGEI AWOKE with a start. What time is it? he thought. Have I overslept? He slipped out of bed and peered through the narrow window to see the moon still rising, nearly overhead. The time had come. He lifted his pack and padded soundlessly out of the room, barefoot, carrying his boots, moving like a shadow along the wall to avoid any creaking sounds on the stairwell, then down a long corridor, where he saw a crack of light under the door of his uncle's office. He passed through the old oak doorway and down the stone steps. After lacing his boots he hurried down the tunnel's full length—a hundred meters, slanting downward under the main building and grounds as it followed the curve of the gentle slope.

His heart pounding with excitement, Sergei finally stepped out into the moonlight on the shores of the lake. He slowly shut the great iron door. The lapping sounds at the water's edge seemed unnaturally loud with all else quiet, except for a distant loon singing across the water. As he stood there, a young man alone in the night, the bird's melancholy song pulled at his chest.

Taking a deep breath, Sergei walked toward the place where he had spied the floating log. It was gone. His boots made slushy sounds as he moved downwind, searching for the log through reeds and waist-high grasses.

Under cover of a gathering mist, Sergei knelt down among the reeds. Finally he spotted the old timber, but it now appeared too water-logged to float . . .

Just then Sergei heard nearby footsteps. Still squatting, he froze and peered through the high grass. What he saw made the bile rise in his throat. It was Zakolyev, the bully, the tyrant, the thief. Had he followed Sergei? Or was this just some bizarre coincidence?

ZAKOLYEV, ALSO CARRYING A PACK, stared straight ahead, peering through the mist as if searching for something . . . or someone. Sergei had only a moment to decide whether to remain hidden and let him pass or stand and confront him. The first choice seemed far wiser; he could avoid a confrontation and remain undetected. But then he would never learn Zakolyev's purpose. As Sergei weighed caution against curiosity, Zakolyev drew close, and Sergei spied the faint glint of moonlight upon a chain around Zakolyev's neck. His decision made, he stood and hissed, "Dmitri Zakolyev!" just loud enough for the older youth to hear.

Zakolyev jerked his head around but didn't seem surprised. "So," he said. "Out enjoying the evening air?"

Sergei stared into that ghostly face as he closed the space between them. "Give me the locket, then go where you wish—to hell for all I care." He had spoken louder than he had intended, but his voice would not likely carry far through the mist.

Zakolyev shook his head, as if disappointed. "Good Sergei . . . wasn't one beating enough for you?"

They both knew that a fight might attract the sentries' attention—so they had reached a stalemate. Several thoughts flashed through Sergei's mind: What would the others think about two cadets disappearing on the same night? Would his uncle assume they had gone together? Not likely. They might conjecture any number of things . . .

Then he remembered the letter to his uncle. Yes—at least the Chief Instructor would know—

As if reading Sergei's thoughts, Zakolyev pulled a sheet of folded paper from his shirt. "Such a nice farewell letter to your uncle Ivanov," he said smugly, flashing that hateful smile again. The blood pulsed in Sergei's temples as Zakolyev slowly tore the letter to bits and threw it into the water lapping at their boots.

Feeding on Sergei's expression, Zakolyev said, "You should know I have spies everywhere, Ivanov. How could you be so stupid?"

The locket, Sergei told himself. Concentrate on that—the rest can't be helped. "Give me the locket, and I won't yell out an alarm," he said.

"Go ahead," Zakolyev replied. "Scream like a stuck pig for all I care."

"Are you so sure I won't?"

"Like I said—go ahead."

Sergei's mind searched for a solution. "Then keep the locket. I only want the photograph of my parents, Dmitri. Give me back this one thing, and we will not part enemies."

In the silence that followed, Sergei knew his answer. He lashed out with a front kick to Zakolyev's midsection. The kick caught the older boy square in the solar plexus; Sergei heard the air whooshing out of him as he doubled over. Sergei followed up with a knee toward his head, but Zakolyev managed to redirect the kick and Sergei found himself spinning off balance. Then Zakolyev had his arms around Sergei's neck, and his every instinct told him that Zakolyev intended to kill him this time.

A moment of panic washed over him, followed by a cold clarity. His first impulse was to lock Zakolyev's arm with his chin, bend quickly forward at the waist, and throw his adversary—but the placement of Zakolyev's weight told Sergei that his opponent was prepared for that. So he did the unexpected and turned his head toward the crook of Zakolyev's elbow. It was a mistake, and Zakolyev knew it and took full advantage. But he didn't know that having his air cut off did not concern Sergei, who could now hold his breath for more than two minutes. As long as Sergei relaxed, he might buy some time . . .

He felt the familiar pressure building and saw the first of the black spots. He feigned a frantic struggle for a few moments, waiting as long as he could, then he went completely limp, as if unconscious. Now Zakolyev either had to release him or hold his dead weight up off the ground. Playing dead bought Sergei a few more precious seconds. More black spots appeared. If Zakolyev did not release him soon—

All at once Zakolyev let go, and Sergei felt his back thud to the muddy ground. Lying still, his eyes closed, he sensed his opponent standing directly over him, one boot on either side of his head. He stayed dead for one second . . . two . . . three. With explosive speed, Sergei simultaneously grabbed the backs of his opponent's ankles. At the same time, Sergei lifted both his knees to his chest and thrust one leg up and back, directly into Zakolyev's groin. It was a solid shot. Zakolyev made a noise between a grunt and a deep groan and went down, unable to move.

As Zakolyev vomited onto the muddy ground, Sergei rolled to his feet. Grasping a short, clublike log heavy with moisture, he swung with a burst of strength and smashed Zakolyev along the side of his skull, knocking him unconscious. He lifted the log again, high over his head, ready to crush the bastard's skull, when something stopped him.

At war with his own impulses, Sergei willed himself to drop the log. And in a fit of unspent rage, he grabbed Zakolyev's knapsack and flung it as far as he could into the lake. The muffled splash made no more sound than a duck landing on the quiet waters.

Zakolyev may awaken soon, Sergei thought. So he knelt down and quickly removed the locket from his neck. Sergei fastened the clasp behind his own neck and picked up his knapsack to hurry off. He glanced back one last time at Zakolyev—he lay askew and absolutely still. Sergei couldn't see any rise or fall of his chest. That's when the question arose: Could I have have killed him?

Sergei had hit him hard—maybe too hard. Even in the pale, fog-shrouded moonlight, he could make out the dark wetness on Zakolyev's scalp, and his eyes, half open and staring, sightless. Sergei put his hand to the older cadet's throat. No pulse.

With a shudder, he backed away from the body. Away, away, away, said his mind. He slipped back down among the reeds, and with a strength born of desperation, he managed to pull the large timber out into the water. It still floated. With his pack fastened tightly to his back, Sergei lay on his belly, with his legs straddling the log, and pushed off. The numbing chill on his arms and legs cleansed his mind of thought for the moment. Balancing precariously, he heard only a gentle slosh of water as he began to paddle away from the shore. A moment's distraction would roll him, rucksack and all, into the lake.

He paddled out into a thick cover of fog. No sentry could spot him now; neither would he be able to see the shore. If he paddled too far out, he could lose himself forever in the expanse of icy water. Even this brief exposure left him shivering uncontrollably from the cold, and from the shock of what he had done.

I've killed Zakolyev. I'm no longer a runaway but a fugitive, he thought. Never mind that it was an accident. It will not look that way.

Everyone knew I held a grudge against Zakolyev over my locket.

He thought of going back, of explaining—explaining what? That he had been running away and so had Zakolyev? The letter was gone. There was no evidence, no excuse that would satisfy his uncle. What was done was done. Zakolyev was dead, and Sergei would have to live with it for the rest of his life.

11

A NEAR SPILL into the icy water pulled Sergei back to his senses. The past is behind me, he thought. Focus on this moment. He paddled away from the Nevskiy Military School, pulling through the water with all his strength to fight off the chill now creeping into his bones. His chest heaved with the effort, as the full import of his circumstances bore down on him.

Another few minutes, then to the shore . . .

Sergei's destination was the mouth of a stream that emptied into Lake Krugloye about six hundred meters east of the school. Estimating that he had traveled nearly that distance, he paddled into the shallows, abandoned the log, and walked through waist-deep water, mud, and reeds up onto the shore. Shivering, his teeth chattering, glad to be back on solid ground, he took careful, measured strides over the rocky soil.

After he had hiked briskly for another hundred meters east along the shore, Sergei's blood began to warm. But he worried that he had passed the stream. He stopped and listened intently—there it was, a rushing sound ahead. Dropping on all fours, he crawled through the thick foliage until he found it.

Sergei sloshed up the shallow streambed, then headed south another hundred meters. After reaching a rocky area where his tracks disappeared, he walked backward in the same tracks he had left and returned to the stream, leaving this false trail behind him, just in case.

He continued upstream before finally turning east. His pursuers could only guess at his direction.

If he were only a runaway, they would soon give up the search. But now everything had changed: Zakolyev's death meant he could no longer go north to St. Petersburg; they would notify authorities there. His search for his grandfather's treasure would have to wait; so would the voyage to America. One year, or two, or longer . . .

Now he must flee to the mountains far to the south, and put his pursuers, and the ghost of Dmitri Zakolyev, behind him.

Sergei circled back within a thousand meters of the school before he turned east again, then south through the forest and into the wooded hills. He heard a distant wolf howl as he pushed on into the night, breaking into a run whenever moonlight and terrain allowed.

He had once heard of men from Mongolia or Tibet who could run hundreds of kilometers, over rough terrain in the dark of night, while gazing straight up into the sky. But Sergei's eyes were fixed not upon the heavens but peered ahead as he ran through the misty darkness.

He hoped that the dawn would shed new light on his path through the forest, through his life. How did all this happen? he asked himself. Seven hours before, all was well; life was routine. I was an elite cadet, respected well enough by my instructors and fellow cadets. And now . . . Have I made the right decision or the worst mistake of my life? No, he decided. I did what I had to do.

The alternative—Jewish duty—was unthinkable. Only he had not intended to leave a corpse behind.

The manhunt would begin in a matter of hours. He would travel fast to the faraway mountains of Georgia, twelve hundred kilometers to the south.

There he would find safety and sanctuary.

THUS SERGEI'S JOURNEY BEGAN in the spring of 1888. It took him east and south, along the River Kiyazma.

In those first days of flight he glanced back repeatedly, haunted by the sense he was being pursued. Each night he fought with shadows in his dreams; each morning he immersed himself in the river, washing away the last traces of the night. He made camp in the late afternoons, finding or building shelter, then hunting, fishing, or foraging as need arose.

Several weeks later, when Sergei reached the great Volga, he found an abandoned skiff in some bushes on the shore. Its flat bottom had several small leaks, which he filled with tree sap. Soon he was rowing his way downriver.

As time passed, Sergei measured his days by the rhythms of the circling oars. His life merged with the river and with a sense of the eternal. On warmer days he dove into the clear, deep water to bathe, with one end of a length of twine tied to his ankle and the other end to the skiff. After the river had washed the sweat from his body and soothed the heat from his blistered palms, Sergei climbed back in and lay in the sun as the rowboat drifted down the widening waterway past ever-changing landscapes.

The days lengthened, and his shoulders turned copper. Some days he ate little or nothing; on others he feasted. From bamboo cane growing along the river he made a primitive spear, then a bow, fashioned from the flexible limbs of a yew tree, and arrows made of thick reeds flocked with quail feathers, their tips weighted with stones sharp enough to pierce tough hides. He bow-hunted hares too far off to spear.

In this manner, through the summer and early autumn, Sergei journeyed a thousand kilometers downriver until he reached the Caspian Sea, continuing south along the coastline. About a hundred kilometers south of Makhachkala, he reluctantly abandoned his little skiff and set out on foot, east toward the Caucasus Mountains of Georgia.

As he hiked south and west toward the mountains, Sergei occasionally glimpsed a *stanitsa*, a fort where Cossacks were stationed. Sergei doubted that news of Zakolyev's death had traveled this far, but he could not forget that he was a fugitive; he resolved to avoid contact with military men. He would bide his time in the high country for one or two full cycles of the seasons, maybe longer, until he could safely return to St. Petersburg, where he might find the gift of great value his grandfather had buried.

Sergei broke his resolve only once, in the first chill days of autumn. Out of a loneliness that came with the season, he risked passing through a farming village of free Cossacks. As he gazed wistfully at smoke rising from warm hearths, his eyes drifted down to a young woman returning to her cabin. She glanced toward him and nodded and smiled, stirring a longing to become part of a community, to find a home. Sergei had never been with a woman, and he yearned for this too, wondering whether he might one day have a family of his own.

H<small>IS ASCENT</small> into the mountains took several weeks. It would be a cold winter in the high country, yet the mountains promised the solitude he needed.

He searched for a more permanent camp and protection from the elements. By late autumn he found what he was looking for: a cave not far from a waterfall, with salmon and trout, and a beaver dam not far away. He built a sturdy lean-to against the face of the cave, which had an opening above his fire pit. He packed the lean-to with a thick clay to keep out the coming winds and snow. And before the streams froze and game grew scarce, he hunted and dried as much food as possible. That, with some ice fishing, would have to last him until the spring thaw.

On the clear days Sergei explored the local surroundings, hunting or trapping what he could, but mostly he hibernated like the bear, and he slept, and he dreamed. Huddled in his burrow when the winds howled outside, he stitched together a fur coat and gloves lined with tufts of fur to keep his hands from freezing. He lined his worn boots as well.

Most mornings Sergei would rub snow on his naked body, then

exercise to maintain his vigor. Then he would slip back into his furs and burrow back into his cave. It was a long winter of solitude.

The spring of 1889 was worth the wait. Sergei caught sight of a bear and her cubs in a meadow far below. Later, near dusk, he spotted a shy leopard passing like a shadow along a snow-covered ridge. He rarely spoke aloud, and then only to reassure himself that he still had a voice. But sometimes he practiced birdcalls, and he howled with the wolves at night.

In this manner, the seasons passed into a second year of his mountain hermitage. Autumn came again, and one morning it struck Sergei how everything had changed—how he no longer belonged to a school, a society, a religion, a group, or even a culture. He was a woodsman. He hardly recognized himself when he stopped to drink in a highland pond and glimpsed a rippled reflection of his bearded, sun-burnished face. Even his eyes had changed and were somehow deeper. He was eighteen years old, but the face he saw was that of a mature man—a mountain wanderer.

Once a visitor to the wilderness, he had become a part of it.

In THE SPRING OF 1891, nearly three years after he first took flight, Sergei was squinting directly into the rising sun as he threaded his way through a narrow canyon. Its vertical walls stood four meters apart, forming a narrow alleyway. He stepped carefully over stones left slippery from a recent rain. His senses were sharpened by necessity, but apparently they were not sharp enough: As he stepped around a huge boulder in his path, Sergei nearly found himself facing the largest bear he had ever seen.

Its back was turned to him, but only for a moment. As the bear turned, Sergei backed away as quickly as he could while the creature snuffed the air and decided what to do. Fresh from her winter lair, well rested and full of terrible hunger, the bear saw him not as a man, but as a meal.

Sergei did not, in fact, know whether he was about to be killed by a she-bear or a he-bear. But as the creature rose up and towered above him, this distinction seemed unimportant. Several things happened at once: The bear dropped to all fours and thundered toward Sergei, who pulled off his rucksack, threw it down, and scrambled up the nearest rock face. He had never known that he could climb so fast—that *anyone* could climb so fast.

Throwing that rucksack gave him precious seconds, and his rapid climb had saved his life—at least for the moment. Just out of the bear's reach, he hugged the sheer wall.

The bear reached up and swiped razor claws within centimeters of his quaking boots. Sergei's legs shook so badly he could barely retain his footing.

The frustrated bear paced and growled, then tore open his pack. Sniffing for food and finding none, it lumbered off, disappearing down one end of the narrow passage. Sergei climbed down a few steps, listened as the seconds passed, then leaped. He landed hard and rolled to his feet. With a quick glance behind, he grabbed up his torn pack, knife, shovel, and other essentials, and sprinted away.

He knew that if the bear returned, it would have no problem running him down; that thought provided a burst of speed that took him down the rugged course of that mountain.

By late afternoon Sergei stopped to rest. He sat beneath a rocky overhang, sorting through the remains of his torn rucksack and ripped blanket. He built two fires, one on either side, to keep warm. Only later, when he reflected on his near-death encounter did Sergei fully grasp how close he had come to violent death. That incident affirmed, in a way no words could have done, the value of his life and the opportunity it represented.

That night he fell into a troubled and restless sleep, in which his mind replayed his narrow escape from the bear, then two bears, and three, which shifted into human predators roaming the steppe, and villages burning . . . then the charred Abramovich cabin, the cries of innocent people as mounted men rode them down with whips and sabers . . .

As the faint light of dawn illuminated the snowcapped peak of Mount Elbrus, Sergei went to the stream to clear his mind.

Soon after, he began his long trek north, out of the mountains and up through Ukraine. It was time to return to St. Petersburg—time to seek the buried treasure that might take him to a new land across the sea.

Part Three

GAIN

AND

LOSS

From the beginning,
love has been my undoing . . .
and my redemption.

FROM SOCRATES' JOURNAL

12

As SERGEI IVANOV was setting out on his long trek north, a different sort of man, riding a stolen horse and carrying a Cossack saber, pursued another course. With a certainty possessed only by sages or zealots, Gregor Stakkos aimed to become a leader of men. "Leaders make their own laws," he said aloud, rehearsing speeches waiting to be spoken, riding through southern Russia in the region of the Don Cossacks.

His plan was simple: He would join, and eventually lead, a Cossack band. As a boy, he had heard of the Zaporozhian Cossacks—and the Kuban, Terek, and Don Cossacks as well—and of their clever tactics and fighting skills. He also knew that they often welcomed strangers who showed bravery in battle. He would find his place among these warriors; then he would rise above them.

They would call him *Ataman*—leader—as Cossacks called those in power. Beyond this single-minded ambition, he had no other aim but one: to rid the land of Jews. He despised them for reasons not entirely clear, even to himself.

Gregor Stakkos was not troubled by uncertainty. He feared nothing, except the screams that plagued him nearly every night. He hated falling asleep. In the waking world Gregor had no equal; against the netherworld he had no defense. Unable to turn away, he could not shut out the staccato shrieks and jagged, bloody images that appeared in the night. His limbs were strong, but he had no power to banish that grisly scene from his ninth year of life, when he had lost both parents in a single night—murdered by a monster.

Gregor's father was a former officer in the tsar's army. Then, after an accident left him lame, he had smelled of vodka ever since. The colonel, as Gregor called him, had lived with his wife and young Gregor in the back of a small outpost store near the city of Kishinev.

On a cold night in December, as on many other nights, Colonel Stakkos sat fuming in a drunken sulk. He sought a reason for his anger but found none, until Gregor ran inside to escape the great gusts of snow and went straight to the hearth, to sit quietly and whittle, trying to shape another hollow reed into a flute. It was all he did at night— whittle quietly and stay out of his father's way.

The colonel, startled by the slamming door, found an object for his smoldering rage. Which meant that Gregor would either have to flee outside into the cold until the colonel passed out, or he would have to take another beating.

Such beatings were neither rare nor brief. And every time the colonel's heavy belt raised welts on Gregor's back, the boy's mother would look away in dismay, busying herself with the cleaning, never raising a hand or saying a word in her son's defense.

The senior Stakkos stood and tottered toward Gregor, blocking the exit. "Little bast'rd," he muttered. "Come take y'r med'cine, you son of a dog . . ."

"But I'm *your* son, Father," said the boy.

"Thass wha' you think," the colonel slurred. "'Bout time you knew. Took y'in when y'r father gave y' away . . . some Jew kid . . . the mother'd run off'r died, dunno which . . ." The colonel fumbled with his belt buckle and pulled the heavy leather strap free. "Now come 'n' get yer beatin'! Didn't want no damn kid . . . wife said you'd help with the chores . . . dirty Jew . . . should've known . . . good f'r nothin' . . . useless . . . you owe us your—"

The colonel never finished his sentence. Because on hearing these words and learning that he was a Jew, Gregor swiveled around and with surprising ease caught the belt and jerked it from his old father's hand.

"Get away from me!" Gregor screamed, striking out with all his might; then Gregor saw the whittling knife in his hand, glistening red, and his father, stumbling back, eyes wide. The colonel fell, grabbing blindly at the table, knocking over the chair, striking his head with a sickening thud on the cast-iron stove. He lay still, staring into nothing.

Gregor turned to face his mother, who was gaping wide-eyed. "Oh, my God, my God!" she cried.

I finally got her attention, Gregor thought, his hand shiny and red, as she began to scream again—but this time she cried out, "Monster! Monster! You've killed him!"

That's when the monster came, and Gregor saw a blade sink deeply into the woman's belly, and she screamed, and the sound cut through him, and he saw a knife flash again, and the monster stabbed her until he was spent and the cries faded to a whimpering and she lay quiet.

Gregor dreamed of a fire, the flames leaping high into the air and the smoke mingling with the falling snow. Neighbors came and found the ruins and the boy who had dreamed it all, sitting in the snow, and they took him in.

. 13 .

By MIDSUMMER, Sergei had skirted the eastern edges of the Pale of Settlement, that region of Russia from the Baltic to the Black Sea, where most Jews were required to live. In a few more weeks he would pass west of Moscow on his way north. Now nearly nineteen, with long hair and beard, he was no longer recognizable as the young, clean-cut youth who had fled the Nevskiy School, so he risked the open road, at times even riding in the wagon of a farmer or merchant.

As he trekked through the summer heat, Sergei reviewed all that his grandfather had told him. He hoped that his memories of Grandpa Heschel's map might somehow guide him along the way. He had committed the map to memory ten years before. He knew that something valuable was buried north of St. Petersburg . . . in a meadow . . . on the shore of the Neva River . . . ten kilometers north of the Winter Palace.

In late September of 1891, on a muggy summer's afternoon, St. Petersburg finally came into view. Sergei entered the city, walking along cobblestone streets. Some passersby, more accustomed to seeing aristocratic city folk than a wandering woodsman dressed in buckskin and worn boots, gave him wide berth. Their stares made Sergei self-conscious for the first time in a long while; he decided to get cleaned up to blend better into his new surroundings.

Seeing city people in their carriages, and the lamplighters at their work outside shops and businesses reminded Sergei how long he had lived without any need to pay for food, clothing, or lodging. He hadn't a single kopek in his pocket, but if he found the gift, he might then have the resources to afford a room, a hot bath, and a barber. That, and more.

He made his way to the Neva River, not far from the Winter Palace, and headed north with a growing excitement. He now saw the map clearly in his mind's eye: the river and, near its bank, bordered by forest on three sides, an *x* marking the spot beneath a large cedar tree. That tree, he remembered, was planted by his grandfather's grandfather when Heschel was a boy. Sergei walked in the deepening darkness and finally lay down in a forested area just north of the city, on a bed of leaves on this humid night.

Early the next morning Sergei found his way to the large meadow ten kilometers north of the palace and began.

He searched for but found no lone cedar tree marking the spot—no tree of any kind.

Just then, a sudden breeze at his back—or maybe an instinct developed in the wild—caused him to turn. He spied four riders in the distance, two hundred meters away and closing fast. It might be nothing, but when riders are racing toward a lone man, it is rarely a good sign. Sergei had nowhere to run in this open field, so he took a deep breath and did his best to relax. He couldn't help wonder: Are they still hunting for me? What has happened to my instincts? Have I grown complacent?

From this distance they looked like Cossacks, with black fur hats and capes flapping in the wind. As they loomed closer, he could see their red vests, loose black pants, and black boots. Then he saw the sabers hanging at their sides and rifles strapped across their shoulders.

For a moment he thought they might ride him down, but at the last moment they reined in their horses, spread out, and surrounded him, as if they were hunting and he were the prey. The hairs stood up on the back of Sergei's neck. He forced himself to take slow, deep breaths, willing himself to stay calm despite his pounding heart. His combat skills were strong, but against four trained men with sabers . . .

"Greetings," he said, forcing a confident demeanor.

"Your name?" demanded their leader.

"Sergei . . . Voronin," he answered, reluctant to use his last name. Two of the men turned to look at each other, suspicious, but it ended there.

"Do you live nearby?" the leader asked him.

"No—as you see," Sergei answered, "I'm just a traveler, come to visit St. Petersburg." Then, speaking more boldly, he said, "Do you question every visitor to the city?"

The leader answered curtly, "We're looking for unauthorized Jews who might be wandering about." He gave Sergei a hard look, searching for any signs of fear. "You haven't seen any, have you?"

"No, I have not," he said with all the bravado he could manage, wondering if they knew about Zakolyev's death . . .

Sergei waited in silence. Then they all turned at the sound of wagons approaching on a nearby road. After a few moments, the leader apparently decided that Sergei might be more trouble than he was worth. "Let's go!" he shouted, and they were off. Cossacks or not, they rode well—and could fight too, Sergei ventured. The way they were armed, if they had tried to apprehend him, things would not have gone well.

T HAT INCIDENT left Sergei troubled—something about how those two riders had looked at each other . . .

Still, the incident had resolved itself well enough—and now he had more pressing business. Finding no cedar tree in the meadow, he hiked farther along the banks of the Neva, then backtracked in case he had passed the site. But Sergei found no other meadows that better fit his grandfather's description. He was certain he had reconstructed the map in his mind. This had to be the meadow—but without the tree, how could he ever find the treasure?

The September afternoon turned hot. Hoping to clear his mind, Sergei set aside his knapsack, removed his clothing, and immersed himself in the cold, clear waters. After a few minutes he waded up onto shore and squatted in the shallows, feeling the cold gravel between his toes as tiny waves lapped at his feet. He imagined his grandfather as a boy, floundering in these same waters, learning to swim . . .

Sergei washed his clothing, hung it to dry, and rested in the sun. All the while, he pondered the possibilities: It's exactly as my grandfather described, he thought—except for the missing tree. He could still recall his grandfather's voice: "A small x by a lone cedar tree . . . a box is buried, on the side of the tree opposite the lake, between two large roots . . ."

After putting on his still-damp clothes, Sergei crisscrossed the meadow, searching for any signs of the tree.

He walked to the edge of the meadow, turned to face the center, and knelt down. Only then did he see a slight mounding in the soil near the center of the meadow. He returned to that spot and found the trace of a tree root—a good-sized root, now dead and rotted, just below the uneven surface. Sergei's pulse quickened.

He fetched his shovel from his knapsack and dug, searching for any remaining roots. Soon he had cleared a three-meter circle and found a pattern of disintegrating roots that seemed to radiate outward, indicating where the tree must have stood.

The map had shown the x between two roots and away from the lake. He looked toward the lake and stood on the opposite side of mound where the tree had grown. Then he marked off a square and began digging—shallow at first, then deeper, until the shovel hit something solid. He fell to his knees and cleared away the soil with his hands.

With growing excitement, Sergei found a box and pulled it free of the soil's tight embrace. "I found it, Grandpa!" he cried aloud, as if Heschel stood nearby. The box was bigger than he had imagined, and heavier as well. Kneeling on the rich earth, Sergei pried it open to find a large canvas bag inside. Would this treasure pay for his voyage across the sea— maybe allow him to purchase land or even a house?

He opened the drawstring and reached inside, trying to guess by feel alone. It felt like wood. Another box? He pulled the object out to reveal . . . a clock.

Sergei stared numbly, unable to sort out the mixed emotions. It made sense—Grandpa Heschel did make clocks as well as violins. And it was a fine clock, to be sure. But the truth was, he had hoped for something more valuable.

Then he noticed something else: a small bag, tied to the back of the clock. He touched it and heard a clinking sound—it sounded like pieces of metal or—

He opened the small sack to find five gold coins and a folded piece of paper. Eagerly he opened the paper and read: "To my dearest grandson, Socrates. Always remember that the real treasure is within." It was signed, "Your loving grandfather, Heschel."

Sergei's eyes stung and spilled over as he read his grandfather's words again. Tears born of fatigue from the long journey—or perhaps it was the longing to see his grandfather once more. He imagined how Heschel must have smiled as he placed the five shining coins into the pouch—a small fortune for a young man who had never before had a coin in his pocket.

Sergei had little sense of the cost of anything, including passage to America, but these coins might be worth a hundred rubles or more. Still, he would have to earn more before his departure. Sergei Ivanov would not arrive in America a pauper. No, he would have money for a new beginning. And he would have his grandfather's clock.

He slipped Heschel's note and the coins into his coat. Gently setting the clock down beside him, Sergei reburied the box and covered it, and out of long-bred habit, he erased all signs of his presence. Then he admired the clock once again, with its fine glass cover over the face and the carefully carved and polished wood. He turned it around to view the short pendulum and weights. That's when he noticed something etched into the wood on the back. Blowing off a fine coating of dust, he could make out letters and numbers—a street address, quite likely his grandfather's old shop . . . or even his apartment!

Sergei felt a sudden impulse to visit his childhood home. But then he thought, My appearance may frighten whoever lives there. I'll need a bath . . . a haircut . . . and new clothing for my voyage . . .

The sun was already dropping to the west; his search had taken the better part of the day. Placing the clock back into its sack, he decided to stay one last night in the woods.

. 14 .

THE DAY was already warm on that September morning when Sergei exchanged one of his coins for rubles and purchased shoes, dark pants, a shirt, and a coat. He carried this bundle of new clothing to the barber, then the bathhouse. Afterward, he paused to glance at his clean-shaven, well-groomed self in the mirror, surprised by his youthful appearance.

Later that morning he would inquire about the cost of passage to America. Then he would secure a room. But first he had to find his grandfather's apartment.

Carrying his knapsack and few belongings, including his grandfather's clock, Sergei looked again at the piece of paper on which he'd written the address. When he looked up, he saw a vision that made him forget where he was going: She stood less than ten meters away, across the street, apparently bargaining with a street vendor. Her gestures were so animated, her expressions so full and graceful, that she seemed to appear in color while the rest of the world faded into gray.

Sergei couldn't quite make out her words—only the sound of her voice, which wafted across the cobbled street like the aromas of fresh bread and flowers. She seemed to be getting the best of this vendor, who alternately frowned and smiled. Then, she threw her head back and laughed, and Sergei thought that no music could ever be as sweet as that sound.

He could just make out hair of auburn, the rich color of autumn leaves, beneath her headscarf, framing the glowing face of this slim young woman about his age, with a full mouth and large eyes.

But it wasn't only her appearance that had drawn Sergei to her. He had, after all, seen other pretty women during his journeys. This was different, a visceral feeling, a tug at his heart, and something else . . . a sense of recognition, as if he had seen her, known her before, in this life or another—or in a dream . . .

Yes, that was it—a powerful feeling came to him that he had seen this woman, this place, in a dream! A sense of destiny gripped Sergei; he had to meet her.

As it was, he couldn't seem to pull his gaze from her. When she completed her business and moved off through the street market, he followed. Entranced by her retreating form, Sergei was nearly struck by a carriage. "Young fool!" yelled the irate carriage driver as Sergei dodged out of the way without taking his eyes from her.

He saw her stop to touch the shoulder of a ragged old man and drop a coin into his hand. After a few more words, she moved on, crossing the street—

Looking both ways, she turned to catch Sergei staring at her—he realized that his mouth was hanging open.

Had he detected a bemused smile on her face before she looked away? Yes! And she glanced back again! Maybe he could find the courage after all to—

The shrill cry of a child behind him snapped Sergei's head around to see a mother trying to comfort a little boy who had fallen and bumped his head. The mother held his head and murmured to the boy, who was already calming down . . .

Sergei quickly turned back to the young woman. She was gone.

He raced forward, searching right and left, scanning the tangled lines of vendors calling out their best prices. So, Sergei, who could easily track a hare or deer through the brush, had just lost this most beautiful quarry of all.

He felt wretched, consoled only by the hope that she might return the next day.

After lingering there for half an hour longer on the chance she might reappear, Sergei reluctantly gave up as he recalled the purpose that had brought him into the city of St. Petersburg.

Thirty minutes later he ascended the stairs of a vaguely familiar address, knocked, and just had time to straighten his coat and brush back his neatly trimmed hair before the door opened and he saw the dead come back to life.

He stood frozen, his mouth agape. More than ten years had passed, but her face had hardly changed. She gazed back at him with a puzzled look, a vague sense of recognition . . . It was the face of Sara Abramovich.

"It's me," he said—"Sergei Ivanov—Heschel's grand—"

"Sergei?" she said. "I can't believe it's you!" Sara clasped his hands and drew him inside. He followed her obediently, in a kind of trance. In his mind she was still incinerated with her husband and children ten years before.

"Mrs. Abramovich . . . how did you—?"

"I still can't believe it!" she repeated. "As soon as we arrived here, I sent word to the school, but they wrote that you had gone—"

"The children are . . . all right?"

She smiled. "Quite all right—but as you will see, they are no longer children. Sit for a moment, Sergei. I'll make us tea and tell you everything." She led him into a sitting room brightly lit by the morning sun, then she went into the kitchen, leaving him on a chair by the windows, overlooking the cobblestone street below.

He touched the chair; it was somehow familiar. The polished wood floor as well. He had played on that floor. He heard her call out from the kitchen in her high, soft voice, "Oh, Sergei, your grandfather would be so happy to know you are here!"

"And where are Avrom and Leya?" he asked loudly enough for Sara to hear as water boiled over the *primoos*, the kerosene burner.

"They no longer go by their old names . . . nor do I," she said, emerging from the kitchen with tea and small cakes. "Now eat! I made these myself, last night. You must tell me how you found—"

"Mrs. Abramovich—Sara—*please*," he said, interrupting her. "How—how are you . . . here?"

"How handsome you've grown," she said, ignoring his question. Then she turned to the old windup clock on the wall. "Oh, will you look—the clock has stopped again. I never know the right time anymore! In any event, I expect the children home soon. Oh! I haven't told you—Avrom is now named Andreas, and Leya is now Anya, and I . . . I am Valeria Panova. Our new names were arranged by your grandfather, just in case anything should ever . . ." Her words faded into silence, and her eyes took on a faraway look.

"Sara—Valeria . . . what happened?" Sergei asked again. "How did you and the children escape?"

Valeria turned to Sergei and looked into his eyes. "Escaped?" she asked. "How could your know—" She gripped his hand more tightly, for courage. "And why do you ask about the children, but not about Benyomin?" Hearing the tremor in her voice, Sergei answered with care: "In March of 1881," he began, "almost a year after my grandfather and I visited you—after the tsar's assassination—there was talk around the school about Jews. I was worried about your family. So I sneaked out of the school at night and found the path into the mountains."

"In the night? But . . . you were so young!"

"I had to warn you . . . so I found my way to the cabin . . . I must have arrived right after it happened . . . If only I had arrived sooner. I wished it so many times . . . nothing was left . . . only a pile of smoking rubble. But I . . . found a body that I believe—that I'm certain—was your husband.

Valeria's face slowly collapsed, and she cried.

AFTER A TIME Valeria gathered herself and told him her part of the story. She spoke slowly, as if not sure where to begin. "You know that Benyomin loved to work with wood. He admired beavers for their ability to build lodges with secret tunnels. So when Benyomin built our cabin, he dug his own tunnel from the root cellar extending forty meters to a concealed trapdoor in the forest. I remember chiding him about this odd project . . . It took him longer to dig that tunnel than to build the rest of our cabin. But his foresight saved our lives."

Valeria sighed and looked out the window for a few moments before adding, "It might have saved Benyomin's life as well, had he not run back. I thought about it later. Many times. I should have known that he would meet them at the door, to keep them from finding the tunnel. Oh, Sergei, they came so quickly—then the cabin was on fire . . .

"They must have expected all of us to run outside . . ." Her words trailed off for a time before she said in a rush, to get it all out, "After he hurried us all into the cellar and closed the door, Benyomin quickly handed me and Avrom—Andreas—a knapsack, with food and the papers your grandfather had arranged, with new names, just in case . . .

"We walked quickly, crouching, into the tunnel. It was pitch-dark, but he was right behind me . . . then he was no longer there. I only heard his voice, muffled by the earth, far behind. 'Run!' he said. 'When it's safe, go to St. Petersburg!' Those were the last words my husband ever . . ."

Valeria's eyes filled with tears and she sighed deeply before continuing: "We waited in the tunnel for an hour or more. Once, I felt the pounding of horses' hooves above us, and a dusting of earth fell through the stifling air. Then there was only silence. We waited like moles in the earth. We smelled the smoke. I knew that Benyomin would not return to us." A pained look crossed her face, and she spoke more quickly. "I wanted to run back, to beg him to come with us . . . only the children held me back. Only the children . . ." She paused again, then added, "Just before dawn we slipped out and made our way through the forest. We slept under cover in the day and traveled by night until we reached St. Petersburg."

Sergei imagined Sara and Avrom and Leya, without any training or skills, making their way those many kilometers on foot, as Valeria continued, "My husband saved our lives by his cleverness and courage, and your grandfather gave us a new life. We were a shambles when we arrived. We didn't know where else to go but this apartment—"

"But by that time my grandfather had died—"

"Yes, but he had made arrangements. We had become like a part of his family by the time Heschel brought his little grandson to visit." She touched Sergei's hair, and for a moment Sergei felt like that boy again.

"Most Jews," Valeria continued, "are required to live in the Pale of Settlement, far to the south, where conditions are hard, and where the pogroms continue. My husband refused to be told where to live and decided to build our cottage in the forest. Heschel was able to make a different choice. His regular income allowed him to live in St. Petersburg . . . in his own apartment, which he left to us."

"But why did you have to change your names?"

Realizing that Sergei knew little of Jewish traditions, Valeria explained, "In the Talmud it is written: 'Four things can change the fate of man: charity, humble prayer, change of name, and change of action.' After we were attacked in the mountains, we left our old names, our old identities, behind us. Now we blend in. We attend services of the Russian Orthodox Church. Heschel even arranged for baptismal papers, to complete our masquerade.

"Andreas and Anya both cling to their Jewish faith, but only in private. They understand the risk that Heschel took, and the expense . . . and it was their father's wish to keep us safe. In our hearts we are still Sara, wife of Benyomin . . . and Avrom and Leya. But you must call us by our new names, Sergei . . . for all our protection."

Sergei nodded, resolving to remember, though it would seem strange at first.

Valeria's thoughts returned to her children. "Heschel's apprentice, Mikhail, has trained Andreas; he is now a violin maker. He is more serious than his father, but so like him in other ways. And Anya has also grown into a woman of good character and—"

Just then the door opened. Sergei rose and turned to see a woman framed in the entry, her cheeks flushed, her arms filled with packages.

Sergei's legs nearly gave way, and his mouth dropped open once again. He could not believe his eyes, for he was staring at the same young woman from the marketplace. She was Anya, and she was smiling at him, puzzled and radiant.

H ER EYES were as green as emeralds, illumined by an inner light. Her curly hair, highlighted gold by the sunlight, crowned a kind and open face. In that moment, as Anya's lips parted in another smile—as she set her parcels on the hallway table, and her hand reached up to brush back a stray curl—Sergei fell in love for the second time that day.

It was as if he had lived in one world and was suddenly catapulted into another one more refined and elevated.

The rest of the evening passed in a dream.

When Valeria reminded Anya that Sergei had visited when she was a little girl, a look of recognition came into her eyes, and something else as well, mysterious and intangible, that gave him hope.

Anya and her mother went into the kitchen, and the light seemed to fade in her absence. Sergei felt a pang of disappointment when Valeria returned alone, even when she said, "I hope you'll stay with us for a few days, Sergei. Your grandfather would want this, and so do I. You'll find the spare room quite comfortable—"

"Is it all right with . . . Anya if I stay?"

Valeria put her hands on her hips. "The last time I checked, Anya was not in charge of this household, but I'm sure she has no objections. None at all."

When Anya returned, she looked even more lovely, in a deep blue dress that highlighted her figure. Sergei knew it was rude to stare, but he couldn't help it. At least he had enough presence of mind to close his mouth. Then their eyes met, and for a few moments the world vanished.

The spell was broken by Valeria's voice: "Sergei, would you put a few more logs on the fire while Anya and I prepare the evening meal? Andreas should be home any minute, and you two can get reacquainted."

They had retreated to the kitchen, and Sergei was feeding the fire, when the door opened and Andreas entered. Still slim and lanky he had not changed greatly from his boyhood self. Valeria emerged from the kitchen and made the introductions. Andreas greeted Sergei in a formal but not unfriendly way, as he had done years before.

Then came dinner and small talk, but Sergei could hardly concentrate; he kept glancing at Anya, hungry for another look into her eyes. When he told of his plans to emigrate to America, Sergei thought he detected a trace of disappointment on her face. Did she feel something for him, or was she just being polite?

Then Sergei remembered the clock. Excusing himself, he retrieved his knapsack, returned to the dining room, and took out the timepiece, briefly explaining how his grandfather had given him a map years before, and how he had only just found it, buried in a meadow outside St. Petersburg. "It was my grandfather's last gift to me," Sergei said, handing it to Valeria. "As you can see, it had this address . . . on the back. I believe it belongs here, on your mantel . . ."

Valeria smiled. She passed it to Andreas, who set the hands and arranged the weights and pendulum so that it began its rhythmic swing. Even after all these years beneath the earth, it worked perfectly, ticking like the beat of Sergei's heart as his gaze returned to Anya . . .

"A beautiful timepiece," said Valeria. "We can leave it on the mantel for now. When you take it with you to America, it will remind you of the time we had together."

In the guest bed that night, Sergei finally drifted to sleep, acutely aware that Anya slept only just down the hallway. He hoped that she might also be thinking of him . . .

And she was.

In THE FIRST FEW DAYS of his visit, Sergei helped fix things around the apartment, making himself useful. Still, it felt strange to see Andreas off to work each day while Sergei tinkered around the house. He also offered to help pay for groceries—an offer that Valeria graciously refused.

Sergei knew that the sooner he found employment, the sooner he would have enough saved beyond his four remaining gold coins to finally voyage west, across the sea. His deepest wish was that he might buy two tickets—not in steerage but in the more expensive second class.

He went out each day after that. Ten days later he found a job at a foundry, in the industrial section at the outskirts of the city. He would assist the blacksmiths who shaped and repaired horseshoes and carriage wheels as well as decorative metal fences and gates for homes of the wealthy. It was hard work, but after his active life in the wild, Sergei welcomed the fatigue of honest labor.

When he returned home each evening covered with sweat and grime, Valeria heated water and insisted that he take a hot bath before supper. He did so but continued his long-standing practice of pouring a bucket of cold water over himself afterward.

Sergei needed these cold-water dousings more than ever, given his ardor for Anya. He thought about her many times each day, certain that he could not leave without her.

One night at dinner, in the most important and difficult minutes of his life, he announced that it was his deepest wish that Anya would consider him as a suitor for her hand in marriage. He had planned, out of respect, to direct his words to Valeria, with Anya a spectator to his declarations. But when the moment came, Sergei spoke to Anya directly, with her mother and brother as witnesses. "As surely as I have ever known anything, I want to dedicate my life to your happiness, if only you will consent to our engagement."

Sergei did not know where such eloquence came from, or such courage. In the next moments he might be both rejected and made a fool. He watched Anya for any sign.

Valeria broke the silence: "Anya, I expect you have some things to do in the kitchen—no, I think in your room. It seems that Sergei and Andreas and I have things to discuss."

Anya responded softly, but with firm resolve: "Mother, I'm quite sure I have nothing more pressing in the kitchen or my room than what happens here. I shall stay."

Then she turned to Sergei, and he looked at her face, and he knew her answer even before she spoke.

Andreas, however, was less than entranced. "Sergei," he began, "you say you want to share your life with Anya. What life would that be? What are your prospects for providing for her safety and security?"

It was the best and the worst question Andreas could have asked. For the first time in Sergei's life he wished he were a wealthy man. Meanwhile, the question remained, hanging in the air. What indeed could Sergei offer besides devotion?

He answered as well as he could manage. "I understand your concern, Andreas. I have only a modest salary, right now, but I have discipline. I've survived alone in the wild. My hands are skillful, my mind quick to learn, and I don't mind hard work."

Andreas responded as the man of the house and Anya's brother. "That is all well and good, but you've known my sister only a few weeks. You should take more time to get to know each other."

Sergei spoke to Andreas but again looked directly at Anya. "There is nothing in this world I look forward to more." Then, turning to Valeria, he said, "I love your daughter with everything I am or ever will be. I will do anything for her. And I will protect her with my life if need be. This I promise."

Sergei concluded, "I will go to school, work long hours, and improve myself in any way possible to bring Anya a good life."

"Still, Sergei—"

"Andreas, enough!" interrupted Valeria. "Let the poor boy eat."

"Sergei is not a boy, Mother," said Anya.

And Sergei knew that all would be well.

He could not know that a few days later all his hopes might be destroyed.

. 15 .

IT BEGAN with lighthearted conversation over dinner, when Valeria asked Sergei about his plans for the future.

"Well," he said, "I'll do whatever I can to better myself. There are many opportunities in America . . ."

All movement stopped around the table.

Andreas spoke first: "Did you say *America?* But I had assumed—"

"We *all* assumed," said Valeria, her voice flat.

Sergei stared at Andreas, then at Valeria. In a flash he understood. He had a job; he was getting settled. They all believed that his plans had changed—that he would continue to live there, with Anya, until they had found a suitable place nearby.

Sergei, for his part, had informed them more than once of his intention to emigrate and had presumed that they understood: He and Anya would make a new life together across the sea.

Valeria, broke the silence, saying, "You cannot take my daughter across the sea. I would never see her again."

"Mother," said Sergei. "Please. I know how much you love Anya, and would want better circumstances—"

"What 'better circumstances' do you refer to in this America-across-the-sea?" she demanded.

Sergei took a moment to gather himself. "You know the times have never been easy for Jews—with the Cossacks roaming, and the pogroms—"

"You don't have to tell us about Cossacks or pogroms!" Andreas interrupted, his voice strident. "We have ample evidence of animosity toward the Jews. We are reminded by our father's empty seat at the table. Why else do we play this sham of fitting in? Why do you see before you 'Valeria,' and 'Anya,' and 'Andreas'? Do not tell us of difficult times!"

"I apologize for my thoughtless words, Andreas. But don't you see—these difficulties are all the more reason for you and Valeria to come with us to America. Take back your names and your heritage! Build a new life! In America you can celebrate Shabbat openly, and families can worship however they choose."

Sergei turned to Valeria. "Mother, I don't wish to take Anya away from you. I only want to take her to a better life. Come with us!"

Valeria stood. "I . . . am going to my room now, to think. Anya, the dishes—will you . . ." She turned and hurried out, but not before they all saw the pain on her face.

Anya started to follow but stopped, knowing that her mother would call if she needed her. So Anya remained at the table with Sergei and her brother as they sat in silence. Sergei wanted to speak—to bridge this chasm that had opened, to heal this fresh wound—but he had said all that he could.

He wondered: Is it selfish of me to pull Anya from the only family and home she has known, to take her so far away? He turned to Anya as she stared down at her hands, and he raised her chin. When her eyes met his, she said in a whisper, "Sergei . . . whatever happens and wherever you go, I will stand by your side."

Sergei knew then that they would be married—that he would be her husband, and they could go to America. But how could she leave without her mother's blessings?

Sergei sighed, and thought how love and family could pose more challenges than a winter in the mountains. In the wilderness, the rules were simple—but there were no maps to the human heart.

"Mother won't go," Andreas said. "You know that, Anya. She is deathly afraid of the sea. She will never cross an ocean."

After that, they waited in silence.

Finally Valeria returned, and her voice halted any further discussion: "I will not go to America," she said. "I was born and will die on Russian soil. It is where my husband . . ." Her voice trailed off, and then she looked at Anya, squeezed her hand, and said, "Although I give my blessings for this marriage, I will never give my blessings for Anya to go across the sea . . . but I do give my permission. She must go where her husband goes.

"But I beg one thing of you both, if you bear any love for me: Do not leave right away. Give me a little time with my married daughter, so I can get to know my new son-in-law better."

Sergei, much relieved, could not refuse Valeria her one request. He agreed to stay for a few months longer. Only then did a smile come to Valeria's face. It was a brave smile, willed there by a mother's desire for her daughter's happiness.

"So be it," said Andreas, and he embraced Sergei as a brother.

A few days later, as Valeria busied herself with arrangements, she told Sergei, "You and Anya will have to be married by Father Alexey in the church, or it will not be legal. They will require your baptismal certificate, Sergei. I presume you were baptized at that military school, and that they have such records. So you should contact them soon . . ."

The *school* . . . Sergei's mind flooded with dark memories he had tried so hard to put behind him.

Since he had taken all his records, including the required certificate, this practical matter posed no problem. But Valeria's request was a painful reminder that Sergei could never contact the school. He had killed a fellow cadet and fled; he was still a fugitive.

Valeria knew none of this—and he would not tell her, or Andreas, or even Anya. Especially not Anya.

THEY WERE MARRIED on a Friday morning, November 6, 1891, in a small chapel—six weeks after Sergei's arrival in St. Petersburg. It snowed on that fall day, and the world was cold and beautiful and good. Sergei's boyhood dream about becoming a part of this family had come true.

Later that afternoon, at home, in a private ceremony before her mother and brother and a few close Jewish friends, they once again declared their love and vows in the Jewish tradition. It could not be a formal ceremony with a rabbi because Valeria could not risk bringing the required *minyan*, the minimum of ten witnesses, according to Talmudic law.

As a wedding gift, Andreas and Valeria gave Sergei and Anya a baker's cart that Andreas had painted like new—pulled by a reliable old horse—a splendid gift for rides in the country.

When the guests left, Valeria sent the newlyweds outside. "For your first walk together as husband and wife," she said.

"Is this walk a tradition I hadn't heard about?" Sergei asked.

"Yes. A new tradition we are just starting. Now go out and get some fresh air," Valeria ordered, falling into her role of mother-in-law as easily as snow fell from the clouds.

So Sergei and Anya bundled up and strolled through the frosted air. Falling snowflakes glistened in the golden light of a nearby gas lamp. The night air—the glowing lamps, the scent of snow mixed with smoke from many hearths—took on a new clarity, as if Sergei were seeing St. Petersburg for the first time through Anya's eyes, and she through his.

"Mother was right, you know, " Anya said. "She pushed us out to get some fresh air—and do you notice how especially *fresh* the air is tonight?" They both laughed. Then she removed a mitten and asked him to do the same. "I want to feel your hand, Sergei. I don't want gloves between us. I don't want anything between us . . ."

He looked at her. "Let's go back home," he said. "I think it's time for bed."

Anya smiled, and the flush that rose to her cheeks was not just from the cold.

They discovered that while they were out, Valeria and Andreas had moved their belongings into Valeria's larger bedroom and Valeria's things into Anya's old room.

"It is only right," Valeria pronounced, as she wished them good-night.

Earlier that day, Andreas had reminded Sergei that according to Jewish law, on Friday nights husbands are directed to give pleasure to their wives.

Sergei fully intended to follow the law to the letter. And maybe surpass it.

ON THEIR WEDDING NIGHT, Sergei showed his bride the locket, and told her about its history. Then he cut five strands of her auburn curls, wound them into a small coil, and slipped this lock of hair behind the photograph of his parents. "This locket was once my only treasure," he told her. "Now you are my treasure, so I pass it on to you." After that he held Anya in his arms under the warm covers of their marriage bed and said, "We were married the moment our eyes first met."

"When you were eight and I was five?" she teased.

"Even then—even before this life."

Then, after her initial anxiety melted away, she gave herself to him completely. Overwhelmed by desire, Sergei and Anya learned the ways of love as they lay together each night that followed, as they rose and fell in each other's arms.

One night in bed, Anya giggled softly at his touch, tenderly touched the white scar on Sergei's arm, and murmured, "This is the happiest I have seen my mother in years."

"She's happy because we traded bedrooms?"

"No, silly—men can be so dense! She's happy thinking about her first grandchild."

"Ah . . . then we will have to do everything we can to increase her joy," he said, kissing the hollow of her throat.

Anya pressed herself against him, her voice breathy in his ear. "Yes . . . we must begin working on the project right now." And they renewed their vows with each kiss and every caress.

After their first Friday night, each day that followed, Anya's enthusiasm for their embraces grew, and they shared a private joke as lovers do: Sergei might be fixing a lamp or reading in the sitting room or shaving, and Anya would slip up behind him and whisper in his ear, "What day is it today, my husband?"

Every day his answer would be the same: "Why, I believe that today is Friday."

And she would answer, "My favorite day . . . and my favorite night."

In the days and nights that followed, whether in the bedroom or kitchen or strolling through the streets and along the canals of St. Petersburg, Sergei told Anya of his young life. She also shared her past joys and sorrows. They shared everything with each other. Almost everything.

IN THE FOLLOWING WEEKS a vague foreboding, no more substantial than smoke or shadows, intruded upon Sergei's happiness. It was the sense one gets before an approaching storm. The source of his unease centered on his promise to remain for a time in St. Petersburg. If it had been up to him alone, Sergei would have booked passage on the next train to Hamburg and from there the first ship to America. He had resolved to honor Valeria's plea, but he could not delay much longer.

In mid-January he had a private conversation with Valeria, reminding her of his intention to leave for America as soon as feasible. "I will soon have enough money saved, Mother—one month, or two at the most. So prepare yourself for our departure."

"Of course, I understand," she said. "But everything is going so well, Sergei, and we are all so happy. You don't need to rush across the sea."

Every conversation on this topic ended this way, and Valeria kept finding things that needed repairing and asked if he might help a little with the expenses, so his savings grew ever more slowly. Still, Sergei could not refuse these requests; after all, he was living under her roof, and it was only right that he help with expenses.

Valeria's difficulty in accepting the idea of their departure created tension between them as the weeks passed.

Sergei's anxiety only grew as news of pogroms in the south and rumors of other isolated incidents reached his ears. But despite the urgency gnawing at his insides, day-to-day life in St. Petersburg was peaceful and good. Sergei convinced himself that his fears were exaggerated.

16

GREGOR STAKKOS set out each day with clear purpose, untroubled by the petty concerns or morality of lesser men. Lean and sinewy, but disinclined to meaningless labor, he stole food and funds and a better horse, leaving the injured or dead behind. Certain that he was a giver of life or death, with powers and rights above those of ordinary men, he already thought of himself as Ataman—Cossack leader. Soon enough, others would do likewise.

Men such as Gregor Stakkos have become leaders of nations—but to lead, they need followers with the loyalty and skills to become the leader's eyes and ears and limbs. He would soon gather such men. It was all planned. In the meantime, Stakkos observed and asked questions But he left no friends or goodwill behind.

One day Stakkos arrived at a Cossack settlement near the Don River, an outpost maintaining the southern border from marauders. After a few days' stay, he was confronted by a young man who claimed that Stakkos had stolen a knife. For this slander, Stakkos beat the boy badly, nearly putting out an eye. The knife was never found.

A few days later a young girl accused Stakkos of taking her by force. Because she was the daughter of the village Ataman, Stakkos had to leave quickly and seek a more suitable settlement.

I will have to show more restraint in the future, he thought as he sharpened his newly acquired knife.

As Stakkos rode away, he was followed by a tall, one-armed horseman about his age, a man the villagers called Korolev. Stakkos had already noticed and asked about this Korolev. He'd learned that everyone knew of him, but few knew anything about him. Korolev stood a full head taller than Stakkos himself, with chiseled features, deep green eyes, and long black hair tied in the back. A powerfully built and handsome brute, save for a large scar on one cheek, eyes too small and close together, and the missing left arm.

"He keeps to himself," an elderly Cossack villager had said. "Arrived half a year past but never fit in." Now this giant of a man was following Stakkos.

Stakkos stopped and confronted him. "What do you want?"

"I have seen you handle yourself. I want to find out if you are a worthy companion."

"I am no one's companion, but I can be a generous leader to those who ride with me."

"Then you will have to best me in battle," Korolev said as he dismounted. His voice had an odd sibilant quality, like the hiss of a snake.

Gregor Stakkos nodded, careful to hide his rising excitement behind a cold smile. "Let us find out." Although his adversary looked formidable, Stakkos's hidden power was his willingness to accept pain or death rather than defeat. This bravado impressed Korolev, who usually intimidated most men into cowering dogs before the fight even began.

They circled one another and then fought, each testing the other's ferocity and commitment. Korolev fought well—amazingly so for a man with one arm. In fact, he would have won, as he always did, except that he made one significant error. He had underestimated Stakkos, who took full advantage of the mistake and threw Korolev down, at the same time drawing his knife. With his knee on Korolev's massive chest and his knife on the giant's cheek, Stakkos said, "I see that you have some artwork to complement your pretty face. Would you like a matching scar on the other side? Or perhaps I should take off your other arm to improve your balance?"

"As you wish," answered the one-armed man, "but I will ride with you, in any case, and follow you while it pleases me."

"Well said. Then I will leave you as you are." Stakkos reached down to help Korolev to his feet, but Korolev sprang up on his own and mounted his horse. As they rode they spoke, not as trusted friends—they would never be that—but as allies.

When Stakkos asked direct questions, Korolev answered them without embellishment: The scar was self-inflicted as a boy to make his face "less pretty." The loss of his arm had come three years earlier, when he had attacked an ax-wielding man with nothing more than a knife. Before Korolev killed the man, the bastard had cut into Korolev's left arm so deeply that it would be useless and might become infected. So after he tore open his opponent's throat, he took the man's ax and finished the job, then jammed his stump into a nearby brazier to seal it. He lay sick for a time after that but survived.

Stakkos also learned that, like him, Korolev had left home early. Beyond that, he would say no more except, "There was trouble at home. They were afraid of me after that."

"They threw you out?"

Korolev shook his head. "One morning I woke and they were gone . . ." He stopped and turned his blue-eyed gaze on Stakkos. "What I have told you is for your ears alone. We must have this understanding: If you repeat it, I'll kill you—or die in the attempt. But more likely, I will succeed."

Nodding, Stakkos placed Korolev under the same conditions, adding, "I'm good to those who are loyal and not so gentle with those who betray me."

They looked into one another's eyes, and for the first time in his memory, Korolev felt something akin to fear. He shook it off and added one more condition: "I have a strong appetite for women. So when we take prisoners—"

"We will take no prisoners—"

"Before they die, I will have the women first. Do you agree?"

Gregor Stakkos agreed readily. Korolev could have his women. Stakkos would have his power.

In this way they formed a bond of sorts. Over time these two men would form the core of a new breed of Cossacks, with Stakkos as Ataman. And like-minded men would be drawn to this Ataman and his right-hand man as flies find their way to fresh dung.

17

IN MID-FEBRUARY, on a rainy morning just before they got out of
bed, Anya whispered, "I have something special to tell you, Sergei."

"Everything you tell me is special, my sweet."

She nudged him in the ribs. "This is more special. Are you listening? Really listening?"

He turned toward her, vaguely aware that after work he needed to
fix the basin in the kitchen. "When do I not—?"

She touched her finger to his lips. "A new life has begun inside me.
I can feel the baby . . ."

Sergei was not sure he had heard correctly. It was as if Anya had just
announced that she could float from the ground and fly. "A baby?" he
said. "Our baby?"

Anya laughed. "I don't recall making a baby with anyone else, but let
me think . . ."

"When did you know?"

"I suspected something in January but wanted to be certain. It must
have happened soon after we married. Maybe even on the first night,"
she said.

In a state of wonder, he reached out to touch her belly. "Can I feel
it moving?"

Anya rolled her eyes. "Sergei Sergeievich, you wise and silly man, he
is probably still no bigger than your fist. It will be months before you
can feel him kick like his father."

"His . . . ?"

Anya hesitated. "Yes, I think the baby is a boy, but—"

"Then a boy he shall be!" he pronounced, thrilled by the prospect of making his own family. "We shall have a house full of children, and . . ." Then he thought of Valeria. "Does Mother know?"

"Of course not! Do you think I would tell anyone before I told you?"

"We must tell her and Andreas! Our son shall be born in America!"

Anya leaned against him. "Yes, in America . . ."

"I'll teach him all I know—how to survive in the wilderness—"

Anya laughed. "Aren't we getting ahead of ourselves? We mustn't plan his future just yet. After all, he could be a she."

His eyes widened at the possibility. "A daughter? As graceful as her mother? Then she shall be a ballerina!"

Anya paused then, glowing with happiness. "Is life not a wonder, Sergei? Four months ago you didn't know I was alive. And now you're planning our daughter's life as a prima ballerina in the Mariinsky Theater—"

"Anya," he interrupted "Not in the Mariinsky Theater—our child will grow up in America . . ."

"Of course, Sergei—it was only a slip. Do they have ballet in America?"

"I expect so—and hot water in the kitchen, and indoor commodes . . ."

"No more trips to the *kolonka* at the corner to draw water? Or running downstairs to the toilet? Or heating bathwater on the *primoos?*" Anya asked. "That alone is enough to draw me across the sea! Oh, Sergei, if this is a dream, I never want to wake up."

He embraced Anya so gently that she laughed. "I won't break, you know," she said, giving him a quick squeeze before slipping out of bed.

Before Sergei left the apartment that day, they agreed not to tell Valeria until dinner, when they would all be together.

That night, Anya and Valeria brought in the food. Sergei sat grinning until Andreas finally said, "Well? What is it?"

From the expression on Anya's face, Valeria suspected the truth but waited, breathless, for confirmation.

Upon hearing the news, Valeria turned and rushed into the kitchen.

Sergei looked bewildered. Anya quickly followed her mother. A few minutes later Anya emerged, smiling as she wiped a tear from her eye, and explained, "It's okay. Mother just didn't want us to see her cry again. She is making a honey cake to celebrate."

With the coming of spring, Anya and Sergei took walks in the fresh evening air as her constitution allowed. In the early months she had some bad days, but now, in her fifth month, she felt in the best of health. On Sundays they took long walks and spoke of their future together.

On the last Sunday in May, in the sixth month of Anya's term, Sergei took her on her first ride to the meadow where he had found his grandfather's clock.

As they walked the perimeter of the meadow, in the shade of the trees, Sergei glanced often at his wife, checking to make sure she was all right. He needn't have worried—Anya thrived in the outdoors, pointing out birds, delighted by her brief sighting of a doe and her fawn.

Ankle-high grasses waved in a soft summer breeze, with red, yellow, and purple flowers scattered everywhere. "It's beautiful," she said. "Let's spread our picnic blanket over there." They ate their fill and spent a rare day alone. If Sergei had suddenly died and found himself in heaven, it could not have been so different from that day with Anya in the meadow.

The afternoon was marred only slightly by a cloud of dust to the east, reminding Sergei of the riders who had confronted him nearly a year before. He could just make out a small band of passing horsemen. A few minutes later he looked again and they were gone. But he was left with that restless feeling again, glad that they would soon leave for America.

That very night at dinner Sergei announced that he had saved enough for their tickets and initial expenses, and in a few weeks they would depart. He said nothing about his sense of urgency—no point in burdening others with his concerns.

When Anya took the dishes into the kitchen, Valeria came over and sat next to Sergei. Taking his hands, she said softly, "Sergei, have I not loved you and been good to you?"

"Yes, Mother, of course."

Having gained this concession, she continued, "You know that I may never see my daughter again, the world being what it is. May I at least see my grandchild?"

Sergei had seen this coming. Next, he thought, she will be asking us to stay until the child's confirmation or bar mitzvah. He would not be swayed so easily. "Andreas will marry," he responded. "Then you'll have many—"

"Who can predict?" she said, outflanking him. "Andreas has not yet thought of marriage, much less children. Sergei . . . I'm not asking you to stay forever—I would if I thought there were a chance—but can you at least find it in your heart to grant this one delay? Let me assist my only daughter as she gives birth to her first child!"

Sergei turned from Valeria's anguished, imploring face to see Anya in the doorway, listening and waiting in silence for his response.

Despite his misgivings, Sergei heard himself say, "All right, Mother. You will see the birth of your first grandchild—but as soon as we are able to travel, we will go without delay."

An ecstatic Valeria embraced him. "You are such a good man, Sergei—"

"And a good husband," said Anya.

18

WHEN GREGOR STAKKOS and the one-armed giant Korolev arrived at a village of Cossacks in the region near the Caucasus Mountains of Georgia, both spoke and acted with discretion. As mounted warriors, they were provisionally welcomed into the everyday activities of the settlement. They worked for food and lodging and bided their time, waiting for an opportunity to prove themselves.

They did not have to wait long. A few weeks after their arrival, Cossack warriors returned to the settlement after a scouting mission and told of *Abreks*—Chechen bandits—who had crossed the river to raid the Russian side. This time they had killed two Russians. On alert, expecting more raids, the Cossacks doubled their sentries, with each watching out for the other so no sentry could be taken without alerting the others.

Stakkos saw his chance to earn a hero's welcome. He had already drawn the admiration of several younger men with stories of his conquests. Some of the stories were true, and the rest were drawn from his imagination. The fact that the one-armed warrior rode with him only added to his reputation.

Stakkos told his young admirers, "I do not think we should wait for these Abreks to cross the Terek. Korolev and I will raid their camp this very night. We will find the Chechen encampment and kill them all. We will bring back weapons, horses, and boots. And some souvenirs—maybe an ear or two," he added, holding up a leather pouch. Two of the youths, impatient for glory and adventure, volunteered immediately; three more, not wanting to appear cowardly, followed.

So it was that Gregor Stakkos and his small band silently approached the enemy camp in the predawn darkness. He warned his men to save the single shot from each pistol until absolutely necessary—to favor the knife and saber for their silent efficiency.

These Abreks were hardened fighting men. But they had never expected such a daring preemptive raid. The seven young warriors would have slaughtered the bandits in their sleep had not one of the enemy gotten up to relieve himself and seen a movement in the bushes. He just had time to shout a warning before his cry was cut short.

Suddenly alert, the Abreks leaped up to grab for their knives, pistols, and rifles. Seeing his surprise unravel, Stakkos led a determined charge, nearly decapitating one warrior with his saber as he drew a pistol with the other hand and fired. The young men, inspired by their leader's bravado and Korolev's apparent invincibility, fought like demons.

Eight men and two women had lived in the enemy camp. Stakkos killed the first woman as she leveled a carbine at one of his men. Korolev captured the second woman alive and when he was finished with her, she was more than willing to die. In this manner, the Ataman and his first lieutenant, Korolev, initiated the first of many new traditions for these youths whom he now called "his men." And so they were.

Their band of seven returned to camp leading enemy horses, their tunics covered with blood—mostly that of their enemies. Only two boys had received minor wounds, which they wore proudly, like medals.

Gregor Stakkos had proven his abilities at strategy and leadership as well as his bravery in battle. They were welcomed as heroes, until the younger men bragged about their treatment of the woman. When the elders heard this talk, and saw the bag of "souvenirs," they spat on the ground, leaving a bitter taste to this day of bravery and infamy. So, after earning the adulation of the youth and the enmity of the elders, Stakkos left with five young Cossacks—the beginning of his band.

In the coming months, under the Ataman's authority, the band began scouting for small Jewish *shtetls*, cabins, or farms. At random, every month or two, they would ride in like a storm, leaving fire and death in their wake. Other times they rode on normal patrols, as did other Cossacks bands, hunting other enemies of Russia.

This pattern of roaming patrols, changing camps, and the random slaughter of Jews continued until a scouting party returned to camp. Soon after, the Ataman announced to his men, "Break camp. We ride north!" They moved like a force of nature, wreaking havoc along the way, each time disappearing without a trace.

19

JUNE SLIPPED into July and the full heat of a St. Petersburg sum-mer. Sergei decided that his uneasy feelings were normal for a husband and father-to-be. He had never before known such happiness, and he wanted nothing to change. I must have faith that all will be well, he told himself, recalling what his grandfather had told him: "Life is God's book, not ours, to write."

He pondered these words as he read *Bibliograficheskie zapiski*, which reported both facts and rumors about raids in the Jewish settlements to the south. He had that sinking feeling again in the pit of his stomach— but in a few short months his family would be on their way to America. And someday Valeria and Andreas might follow.

As each day brought them closer to their departure, family gather-ings took on an air of the sacred. Valeria became possessive of Anya and wanted to sit and speak with her daughter alone. Sergei was glad to accommodate a mother's wishes. He and Anya would have a lifetime together, but Valeria's time with her daughter was drawing to a close.

When Valeria came in and sat near him, he put down the news pub-lication.

"I hope you enjoyed your dinner, Sergei."

"I did, thank you."

"Anya has gone to your room to read. I thought we might talk."

"Of course."

With some difficulty, she said, "Motherhood is sweet, Sergei, but sometimes bitter. Because, those we most love, we miss all the more when they are gone. Now, when I speak with Anya, my words fall far short of what I want to tell her. I want her to know how much I love her . . . how much she means to me . . . but she cannot know, she will not under-stand—until her own child grows up. Then she will know . . . and she will miss me too, Sergei. She will miss me terribly."

Valeria began to cry softly. Sergei did not know what to do, so he just sat with her. He did not speak, for what words could console a mother when the hour came to part? After a time she released his hand, which she had been squeezing tightly, thanked him for listening, and started toward her room.

The next words he heard were not meant for him but only whis-pered thoughts: "A grandmother should be near her grandchild . . ." Then, with a sigh, Valeria disappeared through the doorway.

Her turmoil was clear: She wanted to come with them—but she could not, would not, allow herself to do so. Her roots lay in Russia, but her heart would soon cry out across the sea.

Even though her grandchild wasn't expected for many weeks more, Valeria grew more anxious by the day—not so much about the birth itself, but because it signaled her daughter's impending departure. So she and Sergei maintained a sort of détente. She cared for him, but he was also the man who would take away her daughter and grandchild to a faraway land.

As they waited those final weeks, Sergei gave his notice at work and planned their passage, obtained luggage, and helped Anya pack their few belongings. Meanwhile, Valeria kept busy, cleaning and preparing for the arrival of her grandchild. Arrival, then departure.

And his grandfather's clock sat on the mantelpiece, ticking away the hours.

On the third Sunday in July, Anya asked Sergei to take her to their "happy spot" in the meadow for a picnic, where she might cool her tired feet in the shallows of the Neva.

Sergei thought she should remain close to home, just in case. "Aren't you far along for a bumpy ride?" he asked.

"I feel farther along than any woman who has ever lived," she said. "Still, I'd welcome a carriage ride in the fresh air and a day alone with my husband."

An hour later, Sergei helped Anya up to her seat. A worried-looking Valeria handed Sergei the picnic basket. "We'll be home long before dark," he assured her. With a flick of the reins, they were off.

As they rode along the canal passing beneath Nevskiy Prospekt and turned north, Sergei said, "Anya, my sweet, do you believe in fate?"

"I believe in you."

"I know you do," he said, leaning over to kiss her hair. "But do you believe in destiny?"

Anya laughed. "How could I not believe when such strange and wondrous events brought you to me?" She rubbed her abdomen. "And now we have another miracle." Drawing one of his hands from the reins, she held his palm to her round belly. "Do you feel him?"

Sergei sensed nothing at first—then one thump, and another. "He is already practicing his kicks and punches," said Sergei, glad for this day, glad for this life.

Making their way out of the city limits and up a country road, they passed a farm. Anya smiled and waved to the farmer, who nodded back in greeting.

Soon after, they arrived at the meadow. Sergei had planned on setting their blanket in the center of the clearing, atop the rise where he had found his grandfather's final gift. But the oppressive heat sent them closer to the edge of the forest, where they set out the food, rested in the shade, and gazed out across the meadow.

20

DURING THE REIGN of Tsar Aleksandr III and the period of counterreform, violence increased against the Jews and gypsies. The *Chernosotentzi*, extreme nationalists, were one source of the scourge. Another source was Gregor Stakkos and his men.

Unlike the nationalists, Stakkos had no ideology; his hatred of Jews was personal, his motives unexamined. Unlike most Cossacks, who might kill enemies of the tsar but would not steal like common thieves, Stakkos had a passion for acquiring anything of interest or value before they burned all evidence of their crimes.

He left no witnesses to provide clues to their whereabouts, and was obsessive about security. He and his men would never ride directly toward camp; they would circle back over rocky terrain and streambeds, so they seemed to disappear like ghosts. Their raids produced rumors both terrifying and confusing.

Over the past few years, the Ataman had attracted restless youths and hardened veterans as they passed through towns and villages. Several women had joined too, for reasons of their own. A few were married or attached to new recruits. Some were willing to service the other men, so rules were made and order maintained.

During this time, Stakkos began a new custom: Every year or two, he would spare a Jewish infant and give the child over to the women to raise as a good Christian. This way, even as he murdered and burned, he adopted the mantle of "savior of children." Eventually, this nomadic tribe came to resemble the makings of a Cossack village.

Each small atrocity opened the way for a greater one, until no act was unacceptable. By their standards cruelty was necessary, even virtuous. Armed not only with swords and firearms, but with the certainty of any zealot, they indulged every kind of impulse.

In their temporary camps they appeared to be like ordinary villagers, with huts and hearths and women and children. But they were men without humanity. Intoxicated by a growing sense of invincibility, setting themselves above both law and decency, they thundered across Russia and wrought the horrors of hellfire on their victims.

Thus it was that Gregor Stakkos and his men rode into a peaceful meadow on a Sunday afternoon in July.

. 21 .

Sergei and Anya had just finished their picnic meal, and she rested her head against his shoulder on this languid afternoon, listening to birdcalls in the summer wind, blowing through the trees and across the Neva River.

As he was about to lie down in Anya's arms, Sergei saw a dust cloud rising in the distance. He sat up to see riders coming their way—most likely soldiers out on patrol.

Maybe if he had taken immediate action at first sighting—maybe if he had trusted that sinking feeling in the pit of his stomach—they might have gotten away. Leaving their belongings in disarray, he might have gotten Anya up onto the cart and whipped the old horse into a gallop. But such actions might have sent Anya into a needless and confusing panic. After all, it was just some men riding in their direction.

Riding fast. And now it was too late to flee. As the men drew near, Sergei thought he recognized one of the men, then another, who had surrounded him on the previous September. His dread grew when he saw among the fourteen riders a giant, one-armed man who looked like a Mongol warrior.

Then their leader pulled his horse up a few meters away. He was older now, and had a scar angled across his forehead, but there was no mistaking him. Towering above, astride his warhorse, and gazing down with a cold smile that Sergei would never forget, was Dmitri Zakolyev.

Sergei stood immobile, reeling from revelations and contradictory emotions: relief then regret that he had not killed Zakolyev, followed by a sense of impending doom.

He quickly turned to Anya, who was still sitting, not yet frightened, only puzzled, looking up at Sergei for a sign of reassurance. "I know him," he said. "We're old schoolmates." His mouth was suddenly dry, and his voice rang hollow. He looked back at Zakolyev.

"It's good to find you, Sergei—I believe you've already met a few of my men," he said, gesturing toward the four riders who had surrounded him months before. "When my scout told me of a man he had encountered who fit your description—a Sergei . . . Voronin, I believe he said—I was quite cross that he had not brought you back to the camp for a reunion. I was going to properly chastise him, but he assured me that he could find you again. And so he has. An opportune time for us to catch up, don't you agree?"

Not waiting for Sergei's response, Zakolyev continued, "I inquired about you for a considerable time, but no one had heard of Sergei the Good. And after the way we parted on such unfortunate terms, I truly wanted a chance to make things right. And now here we are, together again, and you with a pretty wife, no less. And with child . . ."

Zakolyev's voice was so gentle, his manner so courteous, that for a fleeting moment Sergei believed that his fellow cadet might have changed. Then some of the men smirked and laughed. The muscles on Sergei's arms twitched as he snapped back to cold reality.

"Well, Sergei," Zakolyev continued, "where are your manners? Will you not introduce us?"

Sergei's mind raced, taking stock of the situation: If Zakolyev was dangerous, his men were even more so—they were followers, anxious to please their leader, to rise in rank and status. No doubt they were well-trained fighters. He might be a match for a few, make a heroic effort—

But if he fought, Zakolyev would kill them both; perhaps if he pleaded and humbled himself, they might only spit on him, beat him . . . but what of Anya?

He would not allow his mind to go further.

Sergei searched desperately for the right words or action that might at least save the life of his wife and child. All this passed through his mind in the time it took for Anya to climb to her feet—Sergei reached quickly down to help her. She came to his side and took his hand. It was cold and trembling. Her hand drove him into a primal rage. Contain it, he told himself. Use it. But not yet . . . not yet.

"I asked whether you were going to introduce me to your woman," Zakolyev repeated, an edge in his voice.

"Dmitri," Sergei heard himself say, calling on better times. "Do you remember when I was under your guidance during our survival training? How we helped each other—?"

"I remember everything," said Zakolyev, cutting him off.

Sergei knew, upon seeing him alive, that Zakolyev must have been waiting for this day—that he must have rehearsed and anticipated everything that Sergei might say or do, every desperate attempt to escape. But Zakolyev had not foreseen the sweet surprise of Anya.

"I appeal to you as a Cossack and a man of honor," Sergei finally said. "Let my wife go home. I give you my word—"

A bored-looking Zakolyev raised his hand to silence Sergei. Then he asked, politely, as if he were merely curious—as if reminiscing about old times—"Do you still have that old locket?"

"I . . . I gave it away," he answered. "As a gift."

Anya's hand automatically reached up to her neck.

"Indeed you did," said Zakolyev. Then he barked, "Korolev!" and gestured with his head in Anya's direction. The huge one-armed man with the black braid dismounted and walked slowly toward Anya. The stench of him hit Sergei's nostrils—not just the scent of sweat, but the rank odor of a man possessed.

"Back off!" said Sergei, stepping between his wife and the muscular giant. "Call off your attack dog, Zakolyev!"

Korolev paused. The chieftain nodded toward his men, and six of them dismounted immediately and surrounded Sergei, with Anya outside the circle.

"What is this?" said Sergei.

"I need a man to search you," said Zakolyev.

"And the others?"

"In case you try something stupid."

Sergei decided to cooperate. So far, no one had been injured or even threatened. There was still a chance. But he stood balanced on a powder keg.

Then, as the keg exploded and all six men restrained Sergei, the giant grabbed Anya's wrist and dragged her away from Sergei.

In the next five seconds, with a burst of energy, Sergei disabled two of the men, one with a blow to the windpipe and the other with a kick to his knee. Both fell back, one gagging, the other unable to stand. But the other four managed to grasp his arms, his legs, his neck—a crushing weight of bodies as they took him down, smashing his face to the ground, immobilized.

Instantly, Sergei relaxed as if he had given up. He would wait for a few moment more, until they least expected it . . . but there were too many. He managed to lift his head and spit out dirt and blood, and watch in helpless fury as the scene unfolded.

ZAKOLYEV NODDED once again. Korolev released his one-arm grip on Anya's wrist, and rapidly, like a snake striking, ripped the locket from her neck and, in the same motion, backhanded it up to Zakolyev. Anya gasped and held her neck as a red line appeared on the soft throat that Sergei had kissed only minutes before. She was frightened now—terrified for her husband, for herself, but most of all for her child.

She would not take her eyes from Sergei. If she could imagine that no one else was there but the two of them, maybe she could make them all go away. Her eyes searched her husband's for a glint of hope, but found none.

Zakolyev spoke. "Thank you for keeping my locket safe all these years, Sergei. And on such a lovely neck." He sniffed the locket. "Ahhh, it has her scent. I rather enjoy the aroma . . ."

Some of the men laughed, and a blood red sea flooded Sergei's vision. "You have the locket," he growled from his belly-down position. "It's yours . . . and I'm at your disposal."

"Yes, you are," Zakolyev with his lifeless smile.

"Then let my wife go—she's not part of our business. Let's face each other if that's what you want . . . but for God's sake, Dmitri, we were fellow cadets—"

"I find you tiring," Zakolyev replied, as if bored. "I have always found you tiring, Good Sergei."

He turned to Anya. "Is our Sergei also good to you in bed?" he asked. "Does he say 'please' and 'thank you' before and after?"

Zakolyev's men barked like dogs thrown a scrap from their master. He was a cat playing with its prey.

Korolev tightened his grip on Anya's wrist, and she winced, beyond Sergei's powers to help. He could feel her dread; he knew her mind and heart. She had narrowly escaped from Cossacks as a child, and it tore at Sergei's guts to watch her brave face, even as her eyes spoke a single prayer: "Protect the life inside me."

But Sergei lay impotent, a pawn in Zakolyev's game.

As one man searched his pockets, the others let down their guard. Only for a moment, but it was enough. Sergei whipped his elbow up and broke the searcher's jaw. He managed to turn and kick another man in the groin when the others fell on him with again with crushing force so that he could hardly breathe. They forced him belly down again, pinning him.

Zakolyev spoke: "So you see, Sergei, how I have become a leader of men?"

Sergei spat out dust and blood. "I see what you've become."

"And you have remained what you always were—a weakling anxious to please the parents you never met." Zakolyev opened the locket. "Ah, yes, here I see your sainted mommy and daddy. I always liked this family photograph. I found it touching," he said to no one in particular as he stared at the tiny faces. His gaze shifted back to Sergei. "Then you stole it from me."

Sergei tasted bile rising in his throat. In that moment he knew that their luck had run out, that their prayers would not be answered, that his last act on Earth would be one of desperation.

Zakolyev turned to Anya and looked her up and down. Sergei tried again to throw the men off. "This bauble means nothing to me now," he said. "Maybe I'll even give it back to the pretty wife in exchange for a little kiss."

Anya's eyes, frantic now, like the eyes of a young doe, looked again to Sergei. Even now she had faith that he had a plan or power to save them. Even then, with her husband pinned by all those men, a thread of hope still remained—until Zakolyev said, "On second thought, with all the trouble I've gone to over my locket, I believe it's worth more than a kiss."

Wallowing in his power, knowing that Anya was Sergei's weakness, Zakolyev spoke to her, while looking straight at Sergei, "Little wife, it's such a warm day, why don't you remove a little clothing so the men can enjoy a look—" He nodded again to Korolev, who released his viselike grip on Anya's wrist and ripped open her blouse. She stood, terrified, trying to cover herself and to protect the child in her womb.

Sergei exploded with a superhuman ferocity, breaking free of the five who now held him down. "Run Anya! Run!" he cried out as he broke the ribs of another man. Then all the remaining henchmen save Zakolyev and the giant fell on him like an avalanche, burying him again under their weight, breaking his nose and cheek as they smashed his face down into the rocky soil.

Sergei felt no pain—only an overwhelming need to protect his Anya and his absolute inability to do so. He drew upon every skill, every ounce of strength or cunning he had, to no avail.

Two words spat from Zakolyev's mouth: "Hold him!"

A hand grabbed Sergei's hair and pulled his head up to watch Korolev release Anya's wrist and roughly squeeze her full breast. Anya spat in his face, in a maternal fury now, fighting, kicking, clawing at Korolev's eyes—

Enraged, his face bleeding, Korolev reached around Anya's head, grabbed her jaw, and twisted.

With a sickening sound, Anya's neck snapped. She died three meters from Sergei's reach.

Everything happened in slow motion after that. Sergei no longer felt as if he were in his body but rather floating above as Korolev threw Anya like a rag doll to the earth and she lay still, staring sightless into the pale blue sky. His benumbed mind refused to believe what his eyes beheld. It couldn't be true; it was only a nightmare; he was asleep.

But the nightmare wasn't over. Zakolyev dismounted, his brow furrowed, and walked toward Korolev. Drawing his sword, he approached the man who had just murdered Sergei's wife.

"Korolev," he said, his voice sharp, "you really must learn to control that temper of yours. You've spoiled a moment I had hoped to prolong."

The giant wisely remained silent, backed away, and remounted his horse, waiting for the Ataman's next words: "Well, not all is lost."

As Sergei stared, horrified, Zakolyev knelt by Anya's body and, almost tenderly, drew his saber across her swollen belly, opening her lower abdomen. Then he reached inside her and pulled out an infant, hanging the tiny newborn upside down, its cord still connected to its mother.

Zakolyev shook his head grimly as he saw, along with Sergei and the others, that his saber had cut too deeply—the infant was dead.

Disgusted by this ruined triumph, Zakolyev turned to face Sergei. "It was a boy," he said, dropping the dead child next to Anya's body.

Sergei screamed, trying to drown out the pain he couldn't bear. Out of the corner of his swollen eye, Sergei glimpsed a pistol swinging toward his head. Then he saw no more.

AFTER TAKING A SOUVENIR, as was his custom, Zakolyev remounted. Korolev dismounted again, drew his knife from the sheath at his side, and approached the unconscious Sergei Ivanov.

"Leave him," said Zakolyev. "I want him to live. I want him to remember."

"You have made an enemy for life—now my enemy as well," Korolev responded. "A man with nothing left to lose may be dangerous; it would be wise to kill him before he returns the favor."

"He's a weakling and a fool, and no threat to anyone," Zakolyev responded sharply, aware that his men bore witness to this conversation. "You have done enough damage for one day. Leave him!" It was not a request—and the Ataman did not like to repeat himself. Ever.

Korolev hesitated, but not for long. With a shrug, he returned to his horse and asked, "Ataman, why did he call you Dmitri Zakolyev?"

"It was a name I took in my youth," he answered. Then louder, he called out to all his men, including those limping or being carried back to their horses, "From this day on, Gregor Stakkos is dead! I never want to hear that name again. To commemorate this day, my name is now Dmitri Zakolyev—but you will call me only Ataman! To signal your assent, raise your sabers!" They drew their sabers and pointed them skyward. After a moment's pause, Korolev did the same.

Zakolyev and his men wheeled their stallions and rode out of the clearing. With a last look back at Sergei Ivanov, who lay facedown and still, Korolev turned and followed the others.

. 22 .

SERGEI IVANOV came back to life with a gasp—to another life, a hellish reality filled with the shrill cries of carrion birds. Leaping to his feet, flailing and screaming like a madman, he vented his rage on the winged harpies tearing apart the remains of his wife and child. His bloody head throbbing, he forced himself to look down, but his mind could make no sense of the shards of skin hanging from the bones of a tiny hand, stretched out toward the breast of a waxen figure whose abdomen lay open to the sun.

Wrapping his family's remains in the blanket, he tried to dig a grave, scraping at the earth with his hands until his fingernails were torn and bloody, but the hard soil of summer would not yield. He could not save them, and he could not bury them. So he pounded his fist against a flat stone, watching from faraway as his knuckles cracked open.

He would gladly have lain down with them upon the quiet earth but for his last duties—to find and kill Zakolyev and the man Korolev and then, if he still lived, to tell Anya's mother and brother what had happened.

A hollow man, he had no fear left in him; they could not kill a man from the netherworld. Seeing nothing beyond a dark tunnel, he stumbled and groped his way toward the river, where he vomited. When the ripples cleared he saw the face of a stranger who meant nothing to him—a weakling, a coward, a fool.

Anya, the love of his life, had thawed the ice of his past until it flowed into the warmer seasons of love. Now he was chilled to the bone, shivering as he staggered aimlessly through a world of shadow.

Another sharp pain pierced his skull, and a sickly light flashed behind his eyes. Sergei fell to his knees and prayed for an end to memory, for an end to suffering, but neither prayer was granted. He knew that his wife and child were dead. The purity and goodness in this world had died with them. There was no God left for him, no justice, no light remaining.

Then his head exploded again, the earth tilted, and he fell.

He awoke in darkness, and the pulsing pain returned. Finding himself on a soft bed, he threw off the covers and started to rise, but his legs gave way and he knocked over a table as he fell. An older woman appeared and helped him back into bed.

"You rest," she said. "Later we'll talk if you want."

"My wife, my child . . . in a blanket—"

"Hush now. My husband buried them proper where they lay. Now sleep."

When he awoke again, it was still dark. He heard snoring not far off as he rose on shaky feet, then sat back heavily. A demon whispered in his ear: "But for you, she would be alive." He could not deny this truth, nor bear the pain, nor end it. That would be too easy. His penance meant living with that truth every moment. He would die many deaths before he could join them. First he had men to hunt and a mother to face.

Sergei stood again, trembling, and found his clothes, now cleaned and folded next to the bed. He turned his head and winced. Reaching up, he felt a bandage; his hands had been washed and covered with a poultice. Dressing quietly, carrying his shoes in a shaking hand, he wove his way toward the door. In the bare outlines of predawn, Sergei found a pen and paper on an entry table and scribbled a few words: "Thank you. I will not forget your kindness."

Back in the meadow, in the early light Sergei knelt at the mound that marked his family's grave. He spoke words of love and sorrow—but when he tried to apologize, his words died in his throat. Despising himself, Sergei swore on his family's grave that he would avenge their deaths.

The tracks were not difficult to follow, at first. He traveled as quickly as he could manage on foot, limping through the day and part of the first night. His smashed nose, loose teeth, and swollen face left him in constant pain. That was good—it would keep him awake. But he had to maintain his strength, so he found a stick and sharpened it on a stone to spear a fish from a stream. He caught one and ate it raw as he stumbled onward, eyes on the ground, following the hoof marks. The next day he found bird's eggs, and he picked fruit. No fires, little rest, no appetite. He forced himself to eat, to keep moving.

Time passed in a daze of light and darkness, a sunlit then moonlit dreamscape of shifting shadows. As he pushed on, reading the signs, following a map of trampled earth, Sergei thought about his father, and he finally understood how a man could drink himself to death.

Like his father, Sergei had also lost a wife and son in a single day. Only Sergei's family was taken not by God, but by the will of twisted men. In taking their lives, Zakolyev and his men had ended Sergei's lineage, for he would not marry again—he knew this as surely as he knew these men would die by his hand. No mere punishment would suffice; no redemption was possible. He didn't want their contrition; he wanted their heads. From that day on, he would live for their deaths.

ON THE MORNING of the third day it rained—a sudden downpour—and the tracks disappeared. He found a few broken branches, then nothing. He had lost them. With this realization, he slumped to the ground, too weak to go forward or back.

Then he thought of Valeria. She would be crazed with worry. He had to complete the dreaded task.

On his return to St. Petersburg, Sergei's preoccupation was so deep that he did not notice the passing scene except to take bearings. When he stopped to drink from a pond, he saw reflected back to him a swollen, grime-stained face. He also saw something else: His hair had turned completely white.

Hours later, the spires of the city appeared, marking his return to the world of men.

GAZING UP at the apartment window, Sergei recalled the moment he had first asked for Anya's hand. A moaning sound escaped his lips. He walked slowly up the stairs and knocked upon the door. He heard the rush of footsteps and Valeria's voice, frantic yet filled with the relief. "My God, where have you . . ." When she saw Sergei standing alone, her words fell away.

Valeria's face was ashen, her graying hair disheveled. Dark circles had appeared under reddened eyes. Sergei was less recognizable than she. With his broken cheekbone, swollen nose and lips, hollow eyes, and stark white hair, he looked like a grotesque mask of his old self.

But Valeria knew who it was, and with a horrified glance she looked past him, searching down the stairs. "Where is Anya?"

Sergei stood mutely, unable to speak.

"Where is Anya?" she repeated, her voice a hoarse whisper. Then she looked into Sergei's eyes, and her heart knew the truth before her mind would grasp it: Anya had not come back. She would never be coming back.

Sergei caught her as she fell and set her gently onto the couch.

When her eyes opened, Valeria sat up abruptly. "Tell me what happened," she said in a monotone.

Sergei said only, "A band of evil men came to the meadow. I was overpowered and knocked unconscious. Anya was killed. I followed them to avenge her death, but I lost their trail . . ."

Valeria refused to accept this—far better to believe he was cruel or deranged to tell her such terrible lies. So Sergei sat with her in silence until the truth penetrated her heart. It was like watching her age and die.

She finally spoke in a voice so weary it was barely audible. "Six days . . . and six nights of not knowing. At first I feared that you had both run away . . . later I prayed that you had . . . I tried to convince myself it was so, but I knew that Anya would never . . ."

Then Sergei read her unspoken thoughts: Valeria had begged them to remain in St. Petersburg so she could see her grandchild. For this selfish act of love, she would blame herself for the rest of her life.

Sergei imagined Anya's brother, hard at work even now, losing himself in his craft while praying for his sister's safe return.

Valeria took a deep, gasping breath and with great effort asked, "Did you at least bury my daughter?"

He nodded slowly. "She's . . . in the meadow . . ."

He reached out to take her hand, but she pulled away, then spoke the words he most dreaded—the question he had asked himself a hundred times: *"How is it that Anya is dead and you are alive?"* Sergei had no answer, so she asked another: "Here, in this room, did you not promise to protect her—to give your life for hers? Did you not make this promise?" They both knew the answer.

His eyes looked into hers, searching. "Mother, I—"

Valeria stood stiffly and said, "You let them kill her. You are a coward, and no son of mine. Now leave this house."

He stood slowly, then entered their bedroom to fetch his few belongings. Sergei gazed for the last time at her pillow and touched the nightdress folded neatly for her return. He held it to his face and inhaled her scent. Images appeared—moments they had shared. The pain was so intense his legs gave way.

Sergei pulled himself to his feet, gathered his rucksack, knife, shovel, and a few items of clothing, and left as he had come, a lone wanderer without a family.

W HEN HE HAD GONE, Valeria leaned against the door. Her dry eyes stared at nothing. She hardly breathed until she realized that

Andreas would soon be home, and she would have to tell him. Then a gasp escaped her, a spasm of breath. "Oh! Oh!" she sobbed and couldn't stop.

Later, like a sleepwalker, she rose and walked across the living room, hugging herself, suddenly cold. The apartment, like her body, felt barren. She turned toward the hearth as another shrill cry of grief burst forth, a final acknowledgment that she would never see her daughter again.

Valeria pounded her fists upon the mantelpiece—once, and again—and her blows dislodged the clock resting there. She watched it tip and fall, somersaulting . . . this clock made by Heschel Rabinowitz, from wood prepared by her Benyomin's hand, tumbling down . . .

Its corner struck the floor, and with an off-key *clunk* it broke apart, scattering pieces that sparkled like jewels across the floor. But Valeria saw only ashes and dust before she collapsed on the living room floor.

H IS   FINAL   TASKS behind him, Sergei returned to the meadow where his wife and child now lay buried and prepared himself to die. He had thought it through: He would not let his life's blood stain the earth where Anya lay—he would only lie near her grave and let hunger and thirst do their work.

One day passed. Then two . . . then three . . . then he stopped counting. Hunger had long passed. His parched lips served as small penance, his death a mere pittance on a debt he would never clear.

He did not plan to rise again.

A stream of thoughts, sounds, and emotions rose into his awareness as he lay in dreamlike reverie, random images of bygone days mixed with what might have been: his father, drinking alone in a darkened room . . . his grandfather disappearing in the distance . . . Anya, nursing their child . . . children playing in a park in America . . .

Then mysterious impressions arose from the dark, mythic realms of his mind. He saw Charon, ferryman of the dead, a sulky old man waiting for him on the shore of Acheron, the river of woe, waiting to carry him across the river Styx to the underworld. But Sergei had no coin to give the ferryman and was doomed to wander through the mists, along the rivers of the dead.

Sergei saw the river before him as he stood naked on the shore of no return, gazing down into the black water, seeing only moon and stars reflected upon the rippling surface. Then it came to him that he was not imagining this—that his body had somehow risen from the dead, and he now stood on a small outcropping on the shore of the Neva. He leaned out, tipped forward, and fell down toward the moon and the stars . . .

The shock of hitting the surface roused Sergei's heart, and it beat strongly. He gasped, then drank deeply, and the waters had a strange sort of curative power. In a moment of grace, the demon of self-hatred was cast out from him, and he turned away from the path of death.

Sergei struggled out of the river like the first creature to emerge eons past from the sea. Dripping wet, reborn on this warm summer night, he heard the voice of Alexei the Cossack in his mind: "A man is measured twice—first by his life, and then by his death." Sergei's life had come to nothing, but his death could still count for something. He decided then that he would not throw away his life. Anya had fought bravely; he could do no less.

"Why are you alive?" Valeria had asked. He'd had no answer then, but now he knew that he had survived for a purpose. As he stood naked under the starry sky, his purpose crystallized, and it had carried him back from the underworld to the realm of the living.

The face of his grandfather appeared, then his mother and father, bringing a moment of sanity, the memory of love. But the moment passed; memories alone would not sustain him. Only one man had that power—and his name was Dmitri Zakolyev.

Sergei thought back on his deluded attempt to hunt down those men. How could he have imagined himself succeeding? Was he hoping for divine intervention, for a burst of superhuman strength? His training as a youth had prepared him to fight one, maybe even two or three untrained men, not an entire band of seasoned fighters. Dying was easy. It was time to live, to pursue this final purpose: He would train as no man had done before; he would suffer any hardship and develop such strength and skill that the next time he faced them he would be ready.

Even a dark purpose can keep a man alive.

On this night, as a warrior spirit possessed him, Sergei Sergeievich Ivanov became his father's son. With newfound clarity, patience, and resolve, he trusted that the necessary power would come in time. He would seek out those who might help prepare him. And when he was ready, he would find Zakolyev and Korolev—and he would send them to hell.

Part Four

———

THE
WARRIOR'S
WAY

*I had not always believed
that strength could come from brokenness,
or that the thread of a divine purpose
could be seen in tragedy.
But I do now.*

MAX CLELAND

. 23 .

IN THE SUMMER of 1892, nearing his twentieth birthday, Sergei Ivanov set out on his quest to become an invincible warrior.

As he walked south, Sergei could still picture Alexei the Cossack pacing before his enthralled audience of cadets, reminding them, "A wise soldier does not attempt to cut down a tree with a dull ax nor should he rush into battle unprepared. To defeat an enemy, you must know the enemy. To know the enemy, you must first know yourself. Face your own demons before you confront others on the battlefield."

Of late Sergei had made intimate acquaintance with his demons: He still had trouble focusing on a task for more than a few moments before the recent horrors rose up to haunt him. His tortured mind and emaciated body needed to heal before he could even begin to train seriously.

So he returned to the wilderness once again, where he found a quiet stream and made camp. There he set traps, and he fished and he hunted. He drank the pure water of rushing steams and returned to his cold-water dousings each morning. In the evenings he sat in quiet contemplation, gazing into the flames of his campfire.

At first his ribs stuck out, but as the weeks passed, the late summer brought ripe fruits to supplement his simple, nourishing diet. He began to stretch in a relaxed yet rigorous way, and he added strength-building exercises for his abdomen, back, arms, and legs. At first he recalled what he had learned as a youth, but as time passed he relied more on his instincts and created new ways to challenge his muscles. Life develops what it demands, he reminded himself, recalling the words of his Cossack instructor.

The hills and woods offered many opportunities to increase his vigor. He walked, then ran, uphill and upstream in waist-high water. He progressed to long, slow runs of ten kilometers and more over hills and rough terrain, with intermittent bursts of speed as spirit moved him.

Each day he imagined that he was facing the giant Korolev, then Zakolyev, then two, then three, then four. He fought phantoms, boxed shadows, ducked and evaded and rolled, refining movements he had learned in the past. He fought until he was drenched in sweat—ten minutes, twenty minutes, thirty minutes, or more—imagining enemies leaping out from behind the trees and boulders, from every possible line of attack, with every weapon. He formulated how he would respond—and he defeated them all.

It was easy enough to do in his imagination. But when the time came, he would have to end each confrontation in seconds, not minutes. To destroy these renegade Cossacks, he would seek out the best Cossack fighters and train with them.

By mid-October, Sergei was ready to travel farther south.

He JOURNEYED ON FOOT—walking, running, and fighting shadows, developing his stamina, looking for any opportunity to better himself as he traveled south along the River Don.

As the December winds blew and the snowfall deepened, it came to Sergei that he needed a horse. If he were to find the training he sought from Cossacks, he needed to arrive on a mount. Besides, a horse would allow him to cover more ground in less time, and time was precious.

The three remaining gold coins, and nearly two hundred rubles he had earned, remained in the pouch in his knapsack with his other possessions. The coins would enable Sergei to purchase a suitable horse; the rest would serve for future needs that might arise. When a man has learned to live without money, he thought, a few rubles can go a long way. This is good, because I have a long way to go. Sergei also thought about how he should have left some money for Valeria—but she would not have accepted it, and at the time he had not been able to think clearly.

He inquired at each farm he passed whether they had a horse for sale. Some days later, in exchange for the three remaining gold coins and fifty of Sergei's remaining rubles, a farmer was willing to part with a strong-looking stallion, and a blanket, saddle, bridle, and bit.

"He's a bit skittish—doesn't take to the plow or wagon," the farmer added as they closed the deal.

As it turned out, the horse didn't much take to a rider either. But Sergei had learned enough about horses in his youth to reach an understanding with the animal. After some bucking and bargaining, the stallion calmed down. Sergei named him Dikar, which means wild and crazy.

As the weeks passed, a bond formed between the man and horse. Sergei reminded himself that he rode an intelligent creature, not a mere possession like his knapsack or the saber or clothing he had purchased in a nearby town. So it was agreed: The horse would carry Sergei, and Sergei would care for its needs.

T HE WINTER went easier atop his mount, with Sergei wearing the Cossack waistcoat and the *burka,* a long felt cape, to keep out the winds that sometimes threatened to tear him from his mount. But Dikar was stolid enough, and if the horse could weather the storms, so could his rider.

Several months after heading south, just before the spring thaw, Sergei came to a settlement near the shores of the Don. This small community had the appearance of a simple village, but only the most ignorant of bandits would venture among these men and women, among the most formidable fighters the world had seen.

Chimney smoke mixed with falling snow as Sergei entered the settlement, passing between the first cabins of birch logs scattered under a sparse covering of birch and pine trees. The clearing was about two hundred meters from the river, on ground high enough to escape flooding should the Don overflow its banks. The forest stood near enough to form a windbreak in rough weather but not so close as to provide cover for unfriendly observers. A few boys scurried about; an elderly man, wrapped in a woolen coat, sat in a chair and smoked a pipe.

At the sound of hoofbeats behind him, Sergei turned to see a rider pull up alongside until their horses walked shoulder to shoulder. With a glance, he took in the man's traditional Cossack dress—the soft leather *cheviaki*, or boots, and a *cherkesska*, the belted, long-sleeved black coat, and a row of cartridge pouches on his chest. His burka, which served as a blanket, tent, or head cover from winter winds or burning summer sun, was folded neatly over the man's saddle. He also carried a saber at his side and carbine slung over his shoulder.

A few sturdy-looking women came out to greet the other riders who followed close behind. Several younger women carried infants on their backs, leaving their hands free to fight if need be, according to custom.

The Cossack riding alongside Sergei—about ten years his senior, with a powerful frame and shaggy mane of light hair—nodded in welcome. Taking his measure, Sergei sensed that this man could be a good friend or dangerous adversary. The Cossack asked in a clipped local accent, "Do you pass through, stranger, or look for shelter?"

"I come to learn."

"To learn what?" the man asked.

"To fight," Sergei responded.

The Cossack laughed and turned to smile back at a few other riders near enough to hear. "Well, you've come to the right place," he said.

"And found the right man," said one of his companions.

He introduced himself as Leonid Anatolevich Chykalenko. As the men were in need of some light amusement, that very afternoon a match was arranged in the barn—a relatively private affair, with friendly bets among the spectators. Sergei lost the first match and won the second, surprising Leonid and the spectators and earning their respect. The third was called a draw. Sergei found Leonid swift and skilled and clever in his tactics. But his own intense physical preparation and training had paid off. This match—the first with a real adversary since his overwhelming defeat against Zakolyev's men—boosted his confidence. He had expected to fare worse.

Sergei offered his compliments, telling the Cossack quite honestly that he was one of the most formidable men he had fought and that he had learned much of value during their match.

They parted with friendly farewells and a personal reminder that there were good people in the world—and for a fleeting moment, he felt a pull to stay for a time, here in this quiet village, and live as one of them. But the moment quickly passed, for his path led elsewhere and allowed no such delays.

Sergei met with a similar experience in the next Cossack settlement, and the one after. Each victory revealed the strength, speed, and skill he had acquired over those months, fighting with shadows. But Sergei finally realized that to defeat Zakolyev and his Cossacks, he would have to find something more. Friendly matches with a single opponent was one thing; battles to the death with multiple opponents were quite another. Sergei needed another mentor like Alexei, who rose not only above other men but above other Cossacks as well.

He recalled a conversation with Leonid Chykalenko and a few other men after their evening meal. As they gazed into the crackling fire on the hearth, Leonid had said, "I've heard rumors about a swordsman who lives alone in the forest, southeast of the Don—somewhere near a small settlement—a few huts, nothing more—hidden in the hills around Kotelnikovo. I was told that this man traveled widely as a youth . . . trained with the samurai of Japan . . . and gained audience with their last great ataman, the Shogun, where he disarmed one of their samurai before the warrior could even draw his blade."

"His name?" Sergei asked.

"No one knows for certain. But I've heard he calls himself Razin."

. 24 .

On a windy March day in 1893, Korolev returned from hunting with a deer carcass slung over his back. As he entered the temporary camp, he saw one of the new men, Stachev, a heavy drinker, stumble unevenly toward his hut, then fall facedown.

Oddly, the way Stachev fell reminded Korolev of that day when the Ataman had found the man he had sought—Ivanov and his woman—and had thrown him facedown, then let him live. A foolish thing to do, but no matter now—they had traveled far south again to the warmer plains between Kharkov and the river Dniepr. Besides, Ivanov was no more than a pissant to Korolev, certainly not worth remembering.

Yet the one-armed giant did remember, because of the change in Stakkos since that day. Not only had the Ataman taken a new name—Dmitri Zakolyev—but having settled that score, his mood had improved. Except for an incident that had occurred a few days later, Korolev recalled . . .

After every raid, as a cautionary measure, Zakolyev sent Tomorov the scout back along their trail to check for any signs of pursuit. And after the incident with Ivanov, Tomorov had returned to report: "I saw only a family traveling by wagon . . . and a lone man, stumbling along on foot."

When Tomorov saw Zakolyev's expression, the scout quickly added, "He couldn't have been the same man, Ataman—his hair was white and he looked old and sickly . . ."

Zakolyev sent Tomorov to find the man, kill him, and bring back the body.

When Tomorov returned empty-handed, Zakolyev announced that the band would move immediately.

A month later they found a camp far to the south and west, not far from Romania's Carpathian Mountains. From there, they patrolled the border like regular Cossacks. They also resumed their methodical raids, once every few months. Everything had returned to normal—including Zakolyev's nightmares.

Korolev knew of the Ataman's troubled sleep; he made it his business to know everything. The few men who courted his favor, and the women who were terrified of him, were quick to report anything of interest they had learned. But they could not inform him of the contents of Zakolyev's mind. Korolev would have cut off his braid to know what disturbed the Ataman's sleep. Yes, that would be worth something. He studied the Ataman as one might study an animal in its natural habitat. But Zakolyev remained an enigma, and Korolev did not like puzzles. He either solved them or smashed them to bits.

At first it seemed that Zakolyev had no weaknesses. He lived like a Spartan, no longer interested in the women. He drank rarely. In fact, the Ataman seemed a model of virtue, except for his penchant for killing the Jews. And that was just his nature, Korolev surmised: Scorpions sting; Zakolyev kills Jews.

Korolev found only one flaw in Zakolyev's armor, and that was the Ataman's strange attachment to children. Zakolyev actually *liked* the little beasts, especially the young suckling whelps who didn't know any better, who would smile and coo at the devil himself. Only when the children grew past infancy, and the Ataman saw the fear in their eyes, did he lose interest in them except as servants or new blood to carry on his dynasty.

Among those born or adopted into the tribe, the Ataman seemed especially taken with two of the new children—a boy, Konstantin, and a girl he had named Paulina. Just after her arrival—when her cry was heard in the night—Zakolyev had claimed the child as his own. He proclaimed that the woman Elena was the child's mother but that Shura would care for his daughter, since the older woman was better suited to maternal duties.

Once, after the infant girl had grasped the Ataman's finger, he remarked with paternal pride, "A strong baby, is she not?" Shura agreed, as she always did. Whatever the Ataman said became truth.

In her forties, Shura was the oldest woman and first female to join the band. Disfigured by scars on her cheek, neck, and one breast as a result of childhood burns, she was befriended by Great Yergovich, the only other elder in the tribe. He did not approve of the younger men inflicting their lusts on the poor woman, but things were as they were. Fortunately for her, she was one of the few women that Korolev ignored.

Shura had a foul mouth and would complain loudly to anyone who would listen. Mostly she talked to herself. Careful not to complain in front of the Ataman, she grumbled about little things like the weather or the knots in the girls' hair as she pulled out their tangles. The girls would run the other way when they saw Shura with her wooden comb.

Widowed years before when her man was killed in a drunken brawl, Shura had followed her son, Tomorov, when he had taken up with Zakolyev. The Ataman permitted her no motherly indulgence. "If the children in your care become a problem," he told her, "they will be left behind." She understood what this meant. She also understood that when the girls were old enough to attract any of the men, they would be used as the men pleased.

All but the child Paulina.

The Ataman's other favored child, Konstantin, knew his place and played the admiring pup. It was a natural role for this curious boy with large dark eyes and a tousle of hair to match. Sometimes Zakolyev smiled when he looked upon the boy; at other times the Ataman seemed melancholy—about what, Korolev could not guess.

For his part, Korolev could barely tolerate the Ataman's displays of sentiment—patting his favorites on the head and insisting that they call him "Father Dmitri." It was disgusting. Still, Korolev was glad he had found this one flaw, because once you know what a man cares about, you know where to stick the knife.

Korolev also disliked Zakolyev's passion for stealing the belongings of the dead Jews. Killing was one thing, but acting like a common thief was another. And the way the Ataman pored over these mementos back in camp made no sense. Taking money, gold, and jewelry one might understand—but coveting soiled goods, journals, and photographs of those they had killed? Trinkets and memorabilia? Korolev was not a superstitious fool, but any man could see that one should not bring such things back to camp.

Although the Ataman had grown more eccentric as time passed, he maintained his authority—and the raids remained the same: The scouts continued to ride at least two days' distance—north, south, east, or west, never the same direction twice. They would note the locations of isolated huts, cabins, or small farms, observing from a distance until they could determine who lived there and whether they were Jews. Sometimes one scout would leave his horse with the others and walk to the door asking directions. If they saw women, all the better.

Eventually two other women, Oxana and Tatyana, had joined the band—bored girls plucked not unwillingly from their native villages. Now four of the nine children in the tribe had been born to Elena, Oxana, or Tatyana, but no one kept track anymore.

Despite their normal appearances, the men and women of Zakolyev's camp were outsiders and outlaws. Friendly enough to their own kind, they had abandoned any veneer of civilization when seeking prey. Murdering on orders of the Ataman—some with reluctance, others with pleasure—they had given their souls to Dmitri Zakolyev and become extensions of his mind, servants of his will.

Sᴇʀɢᴇɪ ʀᴏᴅᴇ ꜱᴏᴜᴛʜ along the river, then east, where he found several more Cossack camps. He considered seeking more contests but thought better of it. To defeat Cossacks he had to reach beyond them. That meant finding the swordsman Razin. Leonid Chykalenko's mention of this man seemed more than chance. Now committed to this goal, his search became a single-minded passion.

Looking for a few small huts hidden in the shade of a forest was no simple task, however. Sergei asked many locals, but their directions were vague and conflicting. After three months he began to doubt the man's existence. He had, after all, heard legends about many great warriors, but most were folktales. Still, his search continued.

A few weeks later Sergei's pulse quickened when he came upon a likely group of huts in the forest. Finding an old woman peering out of a makeshift door, he asked if she had heard of a skilled swordsman living nearby. She stared at him for a time, as if trying to discern his intentions—then she pointed toward a thatched roof in the distance, barely visible among the trees. Her door closed before he could thank her.

Sergei rode to the hut, dismounted, and knocked lightly on the door. No answer. He tapped again. Suddenly he felt the sting of a saber point between his shoulder blades.

Sergei considered spinning and taking the saber as he had been trained but thought better of it. If this swordsman had wanted to kill him, he already would have done so. A husky voice behind him said, "Your business?"

"I wish to learn from the sword master Razin," he said. The point of the saber pierced deeper into his skin.

"Who sent you?"

"A . . . a Cossack . . . he had heard of your skills . . ."

"I don't teach. Go away!" Lowering his blade, the man stepped past Sergei and closed the door to his hut.

Sergei knocked again.

"Go away!" he repeated in a guttural voice—a menacing growl that made Sergei shiver. Yet he persisted.

"If I could explain—I believe that I am meant to learn from you—"

The door cracked open. "Do not disturb me again!" said the gruff voice. Sergei caught only another glimpse of sharp cheekbones, fierce eyes, sun-darkened skin, and shaved head—before the door slammed again.

Sergei had found his sword master—the one teacher who might make the difference between success and failure. He had searched too many months to turn around now. He remembered something Alexei had said—or was it his uncle Vladimir? "The warrior must commit fully to any action."

Infused with a sense of destiny, Sergei decided to sit in place until Razin accepted him as a student, or until he died.

Dikar had not volunteered for hardship duty, so Sergei led the stallion twenty meters off into the forest near a stream and hobbled him under the cover of pine trees. It was cold, but not frigid; short of a late blizzard, Dikar's winter coat would keep him warm enough. He had eaten a generous helping of hay at a farm the day before and could graze at the river's edge.

Sergei returned and sat cross-legged, his back against a tree, in front of this reclusive master's hut. An hour passed . . . two hours . . . four hours. His body grew cold and stiff, then numb. He could no longer feel his hands or arms or legs. A fit of shivering came and went, and then he grew drowsy. Sometime in the night he fell over and painfully forced himself back to a sitting position. The motion brought back a little circulation, biting painfully at every nerve.

He grew hungry, but the hunger passed. The new day, clear and cold, brought a stream of memories—some welcome, others not: Anya and Sergei walking, laughing, through the sun-lit streets of St. Petersburg . . . then the horror came, and he saw Zakolyev's dead smile, and Korolev, tearing her clothes—

Sergei sat up straight, his resolve turned to iron.

As the sun crept overhead, providing scant warmth, it occurred to him that Razin didn't even know he was here. The reclusive master might have gone away. Even as these concerns arose, he heard the door open, then barely audible footsteps recede into the forest and, later, return. No, Razin could not fail to notice Sergei's vigil but was apparently ignoring him.

By nightfall of the second day, Sergei wasn't sure he could move if he'd wanted to. His tongue snaked out from between cracked lips in search of water, even if from the random snowflake. By dawn, time ceased to have meaning. Light and darkness. Another night, then a third day. During moments of clarity, between random dream images, Sergei wondered whether he had lost his mind. Where did determination end and obsession begin?

The day passed by. Darkness came again. He drifted in and out of awareness. Then he saw a trace of light, but remembered nothing more.

A VOICE CALLED HIM BACK into the world. "All right," it said, from a faraway place. Suddenly louder: "I don't want your corpse stinking up my place. Get up!"

Sergei tried to move but couldn't. He felt strong arms lift him, but he couldn't stand. So Razin left him sitting and returned with a pail of water. He poured most of it over Sergei's head—like heaven raining down—and it woke his arms and legs. Sergei couldn't tell if the water was hot or cold. Then Razin gave him a sip of water. "Not too much!" he said curtly.

After a time Sergei could move a little more. He rubbed his feet with increasing vigor. Finally, he rolled over and struggled to stand, dizzy and weak. Razin brought him into the hut and gave him a dried apricot. "Chew it slowly!" he said, handing Sergei warm tea and a cube of sugar through which to sip the liquid in the Russian manner.

"Sit there!" he said, directing Sergei to the large fireplace. Over the fire hung a large iron cooking pot. Inside was a steaming soup of grains and winter vegetables, with a little meat. "Stir the soup well, then fill both our bowls!" he instructed, and left Sergei alone for a time.

He did as Razin had asked.

When Razin returned, he told Sergei that he was to eat by the fire; Razin would eat at his small table. Then he gave Sergei more water to drink.

When Sergei had finished, Razin told him to wash both their bowls, adding, "I may consent to teach you. We will see . . ."

Razin pointed to the cooking pot over the hearth. "Most important—for my soup every night." He showed Sergei his stores of barley, oats, and kasha—buckwheat groats—and a small garden of winter vegetables he was to tend. He pointed to the pit toilet outside. "Keep it clean!" So Sergei was to cook Razin's food, sweep the floors, wash his clothes, and clean his latrine.

Gesturing back toward the old woman's hut and the small barn nearby, Razin said, "Keep your horse there. Go now and take care of it. Then return and begin your chores."

Sergei rose and left the hut. He attended to Dikar, feeding him a portion of oats and barley, then took him to the small barn, where he removed the saddle and blanket. Then he returned to the hut.

OVER THE NEXT FEW DAYS Sergei did his best to please this sinewy old warrior, without success. Razin always seemed irritated, barking one order after another. Without comment or complaint, Sergei made soup, stirring the vegetables and groats with a large wooden spoon, covering it to simmer with the heavy iron lid. Razin only grunted when he tasted it. After he ate, he indicated with another grunt that Sergei could also take some.

Between chores, Sergei went foraging in the forest, gathering eggs and catching a few rabbits. He also managed to walk Dikar, explore his immediate surroundings, and do some limbering exercises.

As the week turned to two, then three, Sergei went beyond what Razin demanded and made simple improvements and repairs—fixing the door and a loose window that rattled in the wind. But after all of Sergei's sweeping, cleaning, washing, folding, and cooking, Razin said nothing about teaching him.

Four more weeks had passed; it was the middle of May. He could wait no longer. That evening, as he served the food, Sergei said, "Master Razin, I hope—"

"Not Master Razin," the sword master interrupted. "Just Razin."

He nodded, then continued: "I've done my best with my duties . . . I hope you have found them satisfactory."

Razin answered with a grunt.

"I need to know whether I have earned the right to train with you." Razin glared at Sergei in a way that made the hairs stand up on his neck. He started to turn away, but the question remained unanswered, so Sergei added, "I am on a mission; I can't delay much longer. It's a matter of life and death."

Razin turned back to face Sergei. "It is always a matter of life and death with you young people."

Sergei decided to reveal his purpose; there seemed to be no other way to gain Razin's cooperation. "Some men posing as Cossacks murdered my family. They will kill many more innocent people. I have to stop them. You had promised to teach—"

"I promised nothing!" Razin said, then stormed out of the room.

Sergei was at a loss. Was this old man a charlatan? Was Sergei being used, taken as a fool? Had he spent all this time for nothing?

That very evening, as Sergei sat near the fire stirring the stew, he was suddenly struck in the head with such force that the blow nearly knocked him unconscious. Stunned, thinking a log had fallen from the ceiling, he rolled over.

Razin was standing over him, holding a wooden staff.

The man's face was blank—no scowl of anger, nothing. He turned calmly, walked over to his chair, leaned the staff against the wall, and sat. Then he took out a book and began to read. Sergei's hand went to his bleeding scalp, where he felt a large lump rising.

So Razin was crazy. And mean-spirited. Sergei was about to head for the door, but something held him in place. It was already night, after all; he would think more clearly in the morning.

As soon as he drifted off, *whack*—he awoke in a panic, sitting up, waving his arms at nothing. He glimpsed Razin's back as the old man returned to his cot.

Rubbing the welt on his shin, Sergei finally fell back to an uneasy sleep, but just before dawn he was awakened in a similar fashion, to a new bruise. Yawning, he went outside for his morning immersion in the stream. The icy water numbed his aching body.

That day, and every day for the next week, each time Sergei was distracted or preoccupied, Razin would strike, quick and silent as the wind. Sergei would have defended himself, but Razin continually caught him unaware. Pain became such a constant that Sergei forgot what it felt like to be free of it.

Each time he was nearly ready to end the abuse, Sergei reminded himself that he was not a prisoner—that any moment he could walk out, mount Dikar, and ride away. That thought kept him in place. One more day, one more hour, one more minute. This might be an initiation for all potential students—a test of sincerity. If he passed this, Sergei felt certain that Razin would teach him something of value.

Day and night the blows rained down—ten, twenty, thirty—until he lost count. Meanwhile, he continued with his duties and slept with eyes half open.

Two nights later, Sergei jerked awake without knowing why. He did not sense Razin near, so he was about to go back to sleep. But just then the idea came to him that he would turn the tables . . .

It took him nearly twenty minutes to move the five or six meters from his sleeping pad to Razin's cot, feeling his way through pitch darkness until he reached the cot. Anticipating the surprise he was about to deliver, Sergei lifted the straw pillow he had carried and swung it down—

It struck an empty cot. *Where was Razin?*

The hairs stood up once again on the back of his neck as Sergei realized that Razin might even now be stalking him in the darkness—not with a stick, but with a sword. He whirled around—

No one was there. Disappointed, he walked back to his mattress, where he found Razin, asleep in his bed.

Sergei didn't sleep the rest of the night. And in daylight he felt a constant state of nervous alertness and anxiety, expecting a blow any moment, feeling his way around corners, ready to raise a protective hand.

Then it happened, when he least expected it: One evening, just as he was lifting the lid off the pot to stir the stew, his arm abruptly moved the lid above his head, just as Razin's blow came whipping down. The stick clanged against the iron lid. Surprised, Sergei spun around to find the sword master gazing at him.

A broad smile spread across Razin's face.

Emboldened, Sergei said, "Does this mean my training can begin?"

"No," Razin answered. "Your training is finished."

Not until that moment did Sergei grasp the scope of Razin's gift. All those attacks . . . all that time . . . the sword master had been teaching him to move instinctively. That was the method behind his apparent madness.

His initiation complete, Sergei Ivanov was ready to go.

THE NEXT MORNING, Sergei had saddled Dikar and was about to mount when he sensed someone behind him and spun around to see Razin standing nearby.

Razin grunted in approval. "Good. You haven't wasted my time."

"So you think I'm ready to face these men?"

"Of course not! But you may be ready to learn . . ."

Razin was a man of few words, so Sergei thought he had finished.

But as he mounted Dikar, Razin added, "There is a master—far better than I. "

"With the sword?"

"With everything. Anything. Nothing. I saw him fight a hundred opponents . . . he was never defeated. He could throw a man without touching him."

Razin paused again. "He once lived on the island of Valaam . . . in Lake Ladoga. He may be there still . . ."

Razin stopped himself, deciding he had said enough. With a nod, he turned and disappeared into the woods.

. 26 .

As Dikar carried him west toward the River Don, Sergei thought about the two long journeys he had made to the south of Russia—after fleeing from the school and now, to hunt down Zakolyev and the others. They were likely raiding in this southern region, in the Jewish Pale of Settlement to the west. Sergei thought again about Razin's final words. But he had no intention of riding a thousand kilometers north once again to seek a mysterious warrior from years past on an island in Lake Ladoga—another master who would not likely teach him anyway.

But the mention of Lake Ladoga—less than a hundred kilometers from the meadow where his wife and child lay in the cold ground—brought a sharp stab of anguish. No, he would not delay his hunt any longer. He turned his horse west.

That May of 1893, Sergei crossed the Don and headed south toward Ukraine, the Dniepr River basin, and the Jewish territories.

Two days later, the enormity of his task sank in: Sergei traced his finger across a few centimeters of his map. How easily his fingernail traversed hills and seas, flying over prairie, forest, and farmland. But when he gazed out at the terrain before him—rivers to ford, rocky grades, and vast stretches of land—he realized what little chance he had to find his quarry. With nothing to go on but rumors, it was like trying to catch a fly that someone had seen buzzing through a room three days before.

AFTER MONTHS riding zigzag patterns—passing Kharkov, Poltava, Kiev, and across the region—Sergei had made almost no progress. One Jewish shopkeeper had heard talk of Cossack brigands to the west; other locals were certain such men were last seen in the east . . . or north . . . or south. One farmer reported hearing from a friend who had heard from another friend about phantoms who rode in the night to kill and burn, then dissolved into mist before the morning light.

Another year passed, an eternity of days in which hope dwindled with the passing hours and died with each sunset, then was born anew but diminished with the dawn. By August of 1894, under a baking sun, as he wiped his brow and sweat stung his eyes, Sergei thought fondly of winter snows. Dikar was thirsty and ornery, pulling at the reins and dropping his head at any sign of water. Summer passed much like the previous spring.

That autumn Sergei turned twenty-two on the open plains, riding from one settlement to the next. He found the ruins of several farms but nothing more. No tracks or traces remained by the time he arrived. Maybe that farmer was right; he might as well have been following ghosts.

In the summer Sergei had slept under the starry sky; now that the autumn winds had come, he and Dikar took shelter when they could in the barn of a farmer.

That December, after marking his map with the burned-out farms he'd found, and putting dots where people had heard rumors of attacks, Sergei hoped a meaningful pattern might emerge, but he found no order at all. Discouraged, he rode on. There was nothing else to do.

As flakes of scattered snow drifted down near Vinnitsa, on the shores of the Southern Bug River southwest of Kiev, a farmer gave Sergei the news that Tsar Aleksandr III had died and the reign of Nicholas II had begun. Meanwhile, the hunt continued.

By the end of a long winter, growing doubts pulled Sergei into a deepening depression. He had trained. He had fought skillful Cossacks. Razin had honed his instincts. But Sergei was nowhere closer to finding Zakolyev than the day he had lost their tracks three years before. Had he wasted those years? Would he spend three more years, or six or ten like them?

Even Dikar walked listlessly, like a riderless horse. The pale sun had no power to thaw the rivers or his bones. But Sergei rode on despite fading hopes, under gray skies, through falling snow. In moments, Sergei believed he had already died and now rode through a purgatory of lost souls. That night, thinking of Anya, he put his head in his hands and wept.

But spring did come, and another summer, and the seasons brought warmth if not hope. Then, on an afternoon in October, when the sky was threatening a cold rain and the wind began to gust, Sergei set up camp in the woods outside of a small town. He hobbled Dikar to graze, then set out to stretch his legs by walking into the village where he might find a clue, or scrap of information, or maybe a friendly face.

Just outside the town walls, he encountered four men, roughly dressed—sauntering as if they had been drinking. Sergei kept his gaze forward, but one of the men blocked his way and accosted him. "Why do you come to our village, stranger? Do you need food or vodka or women?"

"You will find the vodka better than the women!" said one of the others, elbowing the first, apparently their leader. All four of them laughed.

Sergei smiled. But when he tried to walk around them, their mood changed abruptly. A second man stepped into his path. Then the leader explained, "You must pay the toll to enter the town on this road."

To avoid trouble, Sergei shrugged and turned to leave, only to find the others blocking his path. "This way is even more expensive," said one of them, the largest.

"I don't wish to trouble you," Sergei said. "I'm only looking for a band of—"

Their leader interrupted him, mistaking Sergei's courtesy for weakness or fear. "Maybe you didn't hear. You must pay us. Now."

Clearly, these ruffians were set on robbing Sergei and giving him a beating in the bargain. He observed them calmly as they took his measure, a lone, white-haired man.

"I don't want any trouble," said Sergei. "Just let me pass and I'll wish you a good day."

"Not without your toll," said the self-appointed leader, pulling a knife from his belt. He moved closer; the others followed. Just as the thug with the knife stepped forward, Sergei kicked the inside of his knee, throwing him off balance; he then grabbed the man's hair and twisted the knife from his hand. Having disarmed him, Sergei threw him to the ground. The others, surprised, were caught off balance, giving Sergei time to deal with the two closest men. He stunned one with a trinity of blows and held the other off with a kick. Then the fourth ruffian got in a lucky shot from behind—he clipped Sergei on the side of his head—and for a moment everything went dark. On the ground, Sergei felt a kick to his side, then another.

Lying there, covering his head, Sergei saw flashing images from a time past, when he suffered other such blows, outnumbered by Zakolyev's men. Suddenly enraged, which may have saved his life, Sergei rolled abruptly away from the men and came up facing them. He took down the first man who came in, then disabled the next man with a stomping heel kick to the thigh. The third man threw a sloppy, glancing kick. Sergei grabbed his leg and twisted—he heard a snap and a cry of pain. Then his arm went up instinctively and deflected a punch he didn't even know was coming. Kicking his heel back and up, he connected with the groin of another man behind him. At that point the last man still standing lost heart—and they all withdrew, limping off, sulking.

Panting, Sergei took stock: His head hurt, and his ears were ringing—he would be sore the next day—but he had no disabling injuries. Shaking it off, he continued into town to make the usual inquiries.

Learning no more than he already knew, he returned to the forest to spend another quiet night with Dikar for company, as he had done many nights before.

That evening, from under his lean-to, Sergei gazed into the flames of his crackling fire. He thought of the four swaggering drunks who had nearly beaten him. "Never underestimate an adversary," he muttered to himself, recalling Alexei's advice of years before. Then another proverb came to mind: I hear and I forget; I see and I remember; I do and I understand.

Sergei now understood that drunk or not, those men likely had been soldiers in their youth and were hardened by past battles. He had underestimated them—a nearly fatal mistake and a lesson he would not forget.

His own combat experience was limited to boyhood wrestling matches, a few fights, and his struggle with Zakolyev outside the school long ago, then his utter devastation by Zakolyev's men . . .

As Sergei's eyes grew heavy, scenes flashed before him of his training these past months: fighting shadows, and Leonid, and Razin. That's when the sword master's words came back to him—about the master of combat on an island in Lake Ladoga . . .

He fell into a restless slumber and dreamed he was fighting phantoms . . . five Zakolyevs, ten Korolevs, then more and more and more . . .

Then they vanished and he found himself lying on his straw bed in Razin's hut, unable to move, staring up at the swordsman standing over him, about to strike—not with a stick but with a saber. Sergei could only stare, wide-eyed, as Razin cut downward—

Jarred awake by a crack that sounded like a gunshot, still half dreaming, Sergei threw his body to the side to avoid Razin's anticipated blow just as a large tree branch crashed down, with a crackle and a thud, smashing the lean-to where he had been sleeping seconds before. The ground shook with the impact. Sergei leaped to his feet, confused, half expecting to see Razin there, until dreams and reality sorted themselves out.

He took a deep breath, a new resolve taking shape in his mind. Then he turned toward Dikar, to find that dreams and reality had merged horribly once again. Dikar's body lying crushed and broken beneath the trunk of the fallen tree. He rushed to the stallion but found no signs of life.

Using his shovel, Sergei dug for half the day in a deep sorrow. When the large area was hollowed out, he rolled his brave and loyal horse into the shallow grave. Finally, he covered him and spoke a few words. "You carried me far, valiant friend, and never complained."

A sense of loss overwhelmed him. He had lost too much in his life— parents, grandfather, wife, and child—and now this innocent animal, a good and loyal a companion. The sharp pangs of loss reminded Sergei once again of the reason for his journey. Not that he needed any more reminders. After stripping off his sweat-stained clothing, he immersed himself in the icy stream, dressed quickly, and ate the last of his stored food. Then he set out on foot, leaving behind the saddle to mark his horse's grave. He followed the river Don, north once again.

Razin was right, thought Sergei; I'm not ready to confront Zakolyev or the others. Not until I've found the master on Valaam. If he exists at all.

As he hiked over rolling hills and across broad plains, another understanding grew in Sergei's mind: To bring down Zakolyev and his minions, he could not just train with another master. He would have to become one.

I T TOOK SIX MORE MONTHS to reach St. Petersburg on foot. Sergei drew upon all his survival skills and will, each step of the thousand-kilometer trek. Leaning into frigid winter winds, he was bone tired as he drew near the city. He arrived as unkempt as before, with his beard and long white hair.

Seeing Valeria and Andreas was out of the question; he would not open old wounds. Far better to leave them to whatever peace they had made with their loss. Neither would he rent a room for the night. He would need his few remaining rubles for passage by boat across Lake Ladoga to the island of Valaam.

Near dusk, on the banks of the Neva, he reached the meadow and his family's grave. The site was now overgrown, but the small marker remained. Before he slept, Sergei sat by the weathered mound of earth and spoke to Anya. He renewed their marriage vows in spirit and promised again that her death would serve some higher purpose. He also renewed his pledge to save innocent lives by ridding the world of Dmitri Zakolyev and his henchmen. Then he bid Anya good-night as he had while she lived: "You are my heart," he told her, reaching down and touching the earth where she rested.

His dreams that night were peaceful and sad, filled with love and longing. He felt Anya with him, and her hand stroked his hair, and her kisses cooled his brow as the night winds blew.

So it was that in the spring of 1896 Sergei walked to the docks and boarded the next boat bound for the monastery island.

Part Five

———

THE
MONASTERY
ISLAND

Softness triumphs over hardness, gentleness over strength.
The flexible is superior over the immovable.
This is the principle of controlling things
by going along with them,
of mastery through adaptation.

LAO-TZU

. 27 .

DURING THE TWELVE HOURS it took for the two-masted ship to sail across windblown waters, Sergei spoke with several pilgrims on their way to the monastery. He learned that Valaam was the largest of many islands in Lake Ladoga but measured only seven kilometers side to side, with a few smaller islands just offshore. Dense forest and steep cliffs guarded the island's coast, but as the schooner rounded an out-cropping, a small bay came into view, followed by the topmost tower of the main monastery—a huge, gleaming white fortress, eight centuries old, with spires of brilliant blue topped with gold. It was as if he were sailing into a bay of dreams.

Another pilgrim spoke of tranquil inner lakes hidden in the primeval forest, bluffs, and glades. In addition to the main monastery, the center of community life, he said, smaller, secluded hermitages called *sketes* were scattered about the island. These were inhabited by monks seeking deeper seclusion. Even more isolated were the tiny her-mitage huts and caves, and even some holes in the ground where her-mit monks worked and prayed in complete solitude. The pilgrim added, "It is said that no one lives there but the monk and God, until only God remains."

One returning brother told him that the monastery had been destroyed numerous times in the past, since the pacifist monks refused to fight, even when Swedes annexed the island before Peter the Great finally reclaimed it. Strange, thought Sergei, looking for a warrior in a community of nonviolent monks. He expected that this kind of man might stand out in such a place. In any case, if this master lived on the island, Sergei would find him.

If he wanted to be found.

S ERGEI MADE A TEMPORARY CAMP that spring in an isolated section of the forest covered with lichen, ferns, and growing blossoms. In the days that followed, he crisscrossed the island, walking past the small farm that supplied the island with milk and vegetables, past isolated sketes and tiny hermitage huts scattered about the woods.

As the weeks passed, Sergei carefully watched the black-garbed monks. He also tried to catch a glimpse of the hermits, in case one of them was the man he sought.

Since Razin had seen this warrior many years before, he would be middle-aged now, in his forties or fifties, possibly older. Whether monk or recluse, if this master still lived among them, he might reveal himself to Sergei simply by the way he moved.

As the weeks passed, Sergei started recognizing familiar faces among the various brothers, and several of the elder fathers, as they went about their duties. One such man stood out in his memory: Sergei was in the main monastery building when he noticed one of the black-robed elders, a man with a snowy beard and long white hair, ministering to a bedridden monk in the infirmary, giving the monk his last rites. A few minutes later, on his way back down the hallway, Sergei saw the same old monk, his eyes closed in concentration as he laid his hands upon the chest and forehead of another patient. At one point—seconds or minutes might have passed—he looked up and gazed directly at Sergei, who stood transfixed . . .

The spell was broken as a younger monk brushed by to enter the room. He glanced back to see Sergei's expression and smiled. "The father's name is Serafim. He is a *starets*."

Sergei later learned that the term *starets* referred to elder fathers of extraordinary character and wisdom. He made a note to speak with this Father Serafim, who might be old enough to recall the warrior he sought.

Meanwhile, he continued to question other monks. He could not openly state that he was seeking a master of combat on an island of pacifists, so he phrased his question this way: "I once heard about a man who lived here. He was a skilled soldier before he found peace. Have you heard of any such man?" His inquiries attracted puzzled looks. No one seemed to know anything, and he found no signs of any such warrior.

As summer slipped into autumn, and frigid breezes began gusting off the lake, new doubts arose as to whether this master existed at all—at least on Valaam.

Even as Sergei watched the brothers, they had been observing him, the young pilgrim with white hair, who wandered the island asking questions. Soon after, a monk who introduced himself as Brother Yvgeny brought the following message: "The elders know of your presence here but not your spiritual purpose. Since you seem to follow some inner calling, you may stay for a time if you are willing to serve. Are you so willing?"

"Yes, I am," Sergei answered.

Satisfied, Brother Yvgeny continued, "Since you cannot live outdoors through the winter, you are to live and work at the skete St. Avraam Rostov. This hermitage is located five kilometers to the south. It is separated from the main island by a narrow channel—"

"I'm familiar with the location," said Sergei.

"Good," the monk replied. Then he added one last thing: "You will be allowed to stay there for seven days only. When the elder returns, you may ask his permission to remain and serve the brothers in hermitage. Otherwise, you will need to leave the island soon. In another few weeks, high winds and blocks of ice make the lake impassable until the spring."

Sergei had only one question: "The father whose permission I need . . . what is his name?"

"Father Serafim," replied the monk, and with a nod, he departed.

Sergei gathered his belongings, removed all traces of his camp, and found his way to the rocky shore, where he descended stone steps and was taken by cutter across the channel. He arrived in the late afternoon, when all the monks had retired to their cells for several hours of prayer. During this time Sergei walked quietly through the skete—the small kitchen, dark hallways, and common room now empty. A good place and time, he thought, to practice.

On the fifth morning after his arrival at St. Avraam Rostov skete, as Sergei swept and cleaned, he asked one of the brothers when he could speak with Father Serafim.

"He should return in a few more days," the monk replied before departing for other duties. Sergei continued with his afternoon tasks until the brothers retired and it was time for training.

In the waning light, as Sergei headed toward the common room, he passed Father Serafim's empty cell. Curious, he stopped and peered through the open doorway into the darkened room. He found no furniture except for a small table and a chair. And in the corner, where a bed would normally be, stood an open coffin.

With a shiver, he continued down the hallway.

Except for distant thunder, marking an approaching storm, the silence was so profound at Rostov skete that Sergei's breathing seemed unnaturally loud, and the dim lighting lent a dreamlike quality to the winter evening.

As Sergei moved through a warm-up routine, practicing kicks and strikes in the air, a lone figure appeared in the dimly lit doorway holding a candle. This sudden apparition startled him, until Sergei recognized the face of Father Serafim. Sergei started to speak but found that he had no voice.

The old monk's stillness, and the way he stood watching, reminded Sergei of a snow leopard before it springs on its prey. Then a flash of lightning filled the room with stark, garish light, turning the monk's face into a death's head—a skull with a scraggly mane of white hair, whose empty sockets stared at nothing.

In the grip of a primal fear, Sergei stared at this apparition in the darkness—until Father Serafim raised the candle higher and Sergei saw only an elderly monk, his serene face illuminated by the flickering flame.

The next instant the doorway was empty. It wasn't that the father had turned and walked away or even backed into the shadows. He was standing there, then he wasn't. Sergei heard no footsteps receding down the hallway.

I must have closed my eyes, or looked away for a moment, he told himself. Only he couldn't remember doing so.

Two hours later, in the candlelit room, Sergei served a meal to the six brothers in residence. He expected to see Father Serafim, but his place remained empty.

As soon as the meal ended, Sergei said to Brother Yvgeny, in whispered tones, "I saw Father Serafim this afternoon. Why was he not—"

"You say you saw him?" said the brother.

"Yes, he was in the doorway."

Shaking his head, Brother Yvgeny said, "You must have seen someone else. Father Serafim is not due back until tomorrow."

W HEN THE ELDER RETURNED on the following day, as expected, he summoned Sergei to his tiny cell and beckoned him to sit on the only chair. A soft glow seemed to surround the old monk. His mane of long white hair and full beard made him appear somehow larger, more imposing. Sergei, overcome with a sense of awe and reverence, had never before met a man of such spiritual presence.

"I am Father Serafim," the elder said softly, then smiled. "But then, I believe we've already met . . . at the infirmary, wasn't it?"

Sergei cleared his throat and, with difficulty, found his voice. "Yes—yes it was. I'm pleased to meet you again, Father. And I'd like to ask your permission to stay in this hermitage through the winter."

The father closed his eyes, took a slow, deep breath, and remained that way for nearly a minute. He finally opened his eyes and said, "It is unusual for a layman to stay in a skete, but . . . I've looked into it. You may remain through the winter—possibly longer . . ."

Seeing Sergei's eyes steal a glance toward the coffin, the father smiled and said, "The box serves as my bed, but also a reminder to make use of the time God has given me. And one morning, when I do not rise, it will save the others some trouble."

It just didn't seem like the right time for Sergei to ask Father Serafim if he had met any great fighters.

. 28 .

Thus began Sergei Ivanov's official residence at the Avraam
Rostov skete, living with celibate, ascetic monks in hermitage, eating
their plant-based diet, observing silence during meals, and searching
for the man who wasn't there. There never seemed to be an opportunity to speak again with Father Serafim. He was often away doing his
healing work at the monastery, tending to the needs of the brothers in
residence, or praying in solitude. With silence at meals, and Sergei's
duties before and after, he rarely crossed paths with the father at an
opportune time.

Meanwhile, on occasional errands to the main cloister, Sergei continued his search for the elusive—or nonexistent—warrior.

About six weeks after their first brief meeting, he encountered Father
Serafim gazing out the window at a snow-covered landscape. Sergei
approached quietly, so as not to disturb him, and for a moment shared
the winter scene, seeing it through the old monk's eyes . . . the emerald
green pines . . . shrubs with tiny red bulbs dusted by snow . . .

By the time Sergei came to his senses, the monk was walking away.
"Father! Father Serafim!" he called, startled by the volume of his own
voice.

The elder monk turned. "Yes, Sergei?"

"I've been meaning to ask you—but now I'm not sure how. You've
been here a long time, I take it?"

He nodded.

"Well, during that time, some years ago . . . did you happen to know, or see . . . someone—a monk or pilgrim—who was a skilled fighter? Some kind of master?"

Sergei suddenly felt dull and silly as this old starets looked at him, a blank expression on his face.

"A fighter, you say? A soldier?" said the father. "I . . . have nothing to do with such people." Excusing himself, he departed.

Sergei could think of no one else to ask and nothing more to do. Nonetheless, all that winter he worked diligently, serving wherever he could, and he joined the brothers in their customary two meals a day—porridge, bread, mash and vegetables, sometimes with fish, and herbs. They drank *kvass*, a beverage made from bread, and tea on holy days. It was a simple, ascetic life of work and contemplation and training.

During one of these times of reflection, Sergei realized with a shock of regret that he had never taken time to write to his uncle Vladimir— an oversight all the more serious as he recalled how Zakolyev had destroyed his farewell letter. To this day, his uncle might still believe that Sergei was dead.

So he composed his thoughts and set quill to paper:

Dear Chief Instructor Ivanov,

I write this long-overdue letter to express my apologies for leaving the school without your consent—and my regret for not having written to you sooner. I did what I had to do, and I offer no excuses. I thank you for the kindness and care you showed me during my early years. It is not forgotten. You are not forgotten.

I have enclosed a map I took from your library. I return it now, somewhat the worse for wear. It has served me well, and I thank you for this "loan." As to the knife, shovel, compass, and other supplies, I will one day return them or pay for them.

I am now twenty-three years old. During the course of my long journeys through Russia, the skills I learned at the Nevskiy Military School enabled me to survive arduous conditions in the wild. Despite the

manner of my departure, I want you to know that both your care and
your training may yet serve some higher good.

I respected you and your position as chief instructor, but I have
always thought of you first as my uncle and family. You were the closest
man I had to a father. You will forever remain in my memory and in
my prayers.

Your nephew,
Sergei Sergeievich

As he sealed the letter with candle wax, he saw his uncle's stern face
in his mind. Sergei no longer felt the awe of his youth but rather a deep
affection for this good man, Vladimir Borisovich Ivanov.

That letter completed a small part of his past; a far greater portion
remained unfinished.

THROUGH THE SHORT BITTER DAYS, Sergei followed the
same routine: work, reflect, train, eat, and sleep. It was like being back
at the Nevskiy Military School—as if he had gone nowhere, done nothing. Each day his frustration grew.

More than three months had passed since Sergei had begun his residence. He thought back to his time at the school, among soldiers, when
he had wished for a sense of peace. Now, in this place of peace, he
sought a warrior.

Meanwhile, he continued training on his own, going through the
motions without any sense of progress or change. Winter outside, winter inside. Sergei faced the truth that he might soon be leaving, having
wasted another year of his life.

Then, all at once, Sergei's fortunes changed.

Who can say how such things happen? Perhaps it was a matter of
timing or luck—or a master's change of heart. But on the last day of
March 1897, as Sergei was completing the movements of his routine,
ending in a stance with his arms in a guarded, ready position, he noticed
Father Serafim watching him.

The old monk's arms were crossed over his broad chest. He was shaking his head as if to say that all of Sergei's skills added up to nothing. "Whatever are you doing?" asked the puzzled father.

"I'm training . . . preparing myself," Sergei answered.

"In a real battle," said Father Serafim, "there are no warm-ups, no rehearsed techniques, no rules." He shook his head again. "I don't believe that such movements will prepare you to face the men you hunt."

For a few moments, Sergei's mind whirled with competing questions: How did the father know about the men? Could this man be—?

"Yes," said Father Serafim, answering his unspoken questions. "I am the one you seek, and I know why you're here. But you do not."

"What?"

"You still believe that you were sent by Razin, but you were sent by God. And when you leave, you will not be the same man who arrived."

He spoke with an authority that seemed to stretch back into eternity. And those words marked the beginning of a different way of training and living than any Sergei had ever encountered.

W ITHOUT ANY FURTHER WORDS, Serafim took up the role of teacher as if it were both natural and inevitable. He began appearing in the common room each afternoon to observe practice. One day soon after, Sergei stopped to ask him a question: "Father Serafim—"

The elder man held up his hand to silence Sergei. "Do not call me 'Father' again, except in the presence of other monks. 'Serafim' is enough."

Before Sergei could ask why, Serafim explained, "Training you to vanquish other men has nothing to do with my calling as a monk. I've taken vows of nonviolence, and I will die before killing another human being. I have seen and done enough killing." He would say no more about it. Instead, he set his gaze upon Sergei, who suddenly felt naked, then transparent. And Serafim said, "I see that you also have another name. So when we are alone I will call you . . . Socrates."

When Sergei finally managed to speak, he stammered, "H-how did you know . . . ?"

"I . . . looked into it," said Serafim.

"If you . . . look into such things—and if you knew I was here—then why did you make me wait before revealing yourself?"

Serafim paused. "I needed to observe, to assess your heart and your character. So I waited until the time was right."

Sergei now saw the old monk in an entirely new light. It was like gazing down at the rippled waves of Lake Ladoga: Sergei could not see beneath the surface, but he sensed great depths.

D ESPITE S ERAFIM'S UNUSUAL PRESENCE and intuitive abilities, it was difficult for Sergei to imagine him as a great fighter. In the past, perhaps—when he was young and strong. But now, thought Sergei, despite the force of his words, Serafim looked more like someone's elderly grandfather than a master of combat.

Serafim must have sensed Sergei's doubts. At the next training session he said, "Attack me any way you wish. But make your attack sincere. Do your best to strike me." Serafim's tone carried the clear message that he would not tolerate a halfhearted effort. So Sergei gave it his best.

Sergei couldn't even get near the old monk. Not only that, he didn't know what the man was doing; he only knew that he couldn't seem to connect with, or even *find*, the elderly father.

Whenever Sergei tried to kick or punch or sweep or trap or grab or throw, he found himself on the ground, again and again, without any clue as to how he got there. And Serafim held him down with one hand, one knuckle, one finger. Sergei was physically unable to rise. Once, he found himself falling, only to realize that Serafim had not even touched him.

Razin had been right. Sergei had found the master. And it was one of the most frustrating encounters of his life. When the old monk challenged Sergei to push him off balance, he tried many times without success. He recalled the time he'd tried to push over Alexei the Cossack—it was like trying to push over a mountain. But with Serafim, it was like trying to push over a feather and not being able to do it.

The old man would evade Sergei, trip him, twist him, turn him, and throw him to the ground with his hands, with his feet, and only with his mind, it seemed. Serafim never actually struck him until near the end of their session, when the old monk administered a light blow that left Sergei stunned and unable to move for several minutes. Had Serafim intended to injure him, Sergei wondered what damage he might have done.

The next day Serafim asked Sergei to join him for a walk through the snow to a small orchard above the farm. As they walked, Serafim began. "I've looked into your situation . . . your quest . . ." He paused, then: "You know the scripture, 'Vengeance is mine, sayeth the Lord.'"

Sergei nodded.

"What gives you the right to play the avenging angel?"

"I have no right at all," Sergei answered. "Nor can I know if my wife's soul will rest easier for it. I only know that mine will . . ."

"So you believe . . ."

"So I believe."

"You can't undo what these men have done—"

"But I might stop them from destroying more lives." What Sergei left unsaid was that in fulfilling his vow, and perhaps dying in the process, he might find salvation for his soul and join his wife and child in a better place, if such a place existed.

"Is there no way I can dissuade you from this course of action?" Serafim asked.

Sergei shook his head slowly.

The old monk sighed. "All right, then, I'll take you into the shadows. I'll give you what you want . . . so that one day you may want . . . what I want to give you."

"What *do* you want to give me?" Sergei asked.

"Peace."

"There's only one way I'm going to find peace."

"Through death."

"Theirs or mine. Maybe both," Sergei replied. "And I can't wait much longer. I need to find them soon—three months, six months, a year at the most."

Serafim's eyes again fixed on Sergei. "The timing of events is not for us to say."

"You believe it may take longer?"

He nodded.

"How much longer?"

Serafim paused. Then he said, "In an instant a life may turn around; a heart may open in a moment of grace. But preparing for that moment can take a lifetime . . ." Serafim began to pace as he continued, "Learning can happen quickly. Unlearning takes longer. If you're willing to start fresh . . . well, it may be less than ten years—"

"I don't have years!"

Serafim's eyes blazed. "You must be an important man to make such demands on God, and supremely wise to know how long things should take . . ."

As they left the orchard and turned back toward the skete, a chastened Sergei changed the subject: "How many other students have you taught?"

Serafim sighed. "None have learned from me what you seek."

"Why are you willing to teach me? Isn't there some sort of initiation?"

"You've already been initiated—by Razin and . . . by your life."

"What do you really know of my life?"

"I've seen enough."

Sergei shook his head in wonder, still mystified by the old monk. "So you're going to teach me, just like that, for nothing in return?"

"It would be a mistake to view my instruction as a personal favor, Socrates. I'm not doing it for you; I only serve God's will. And I do this because . . . helping you may yet serve a higher good that neither of us has foreseen."

. 29 .

MOST OF ZAKOLYEV'S MEN, and all of the women they had collected along the way, desired a more permanent camp—like the villages from which some of them had come. But their leader's response remained the same: "It's harder to hit a moving target."

So it was a surprise to all when the Ataman called his men around the fire in their temporary campsite near the Romanian border and announced, "Prepare yourselves! Tomorrow we ride north to build a permanent camp. Long ago I found a site deep in the forest north of Kiev. No huts this time—real cabins. And, listen well! I make this prophecy: We will soon have more women and children to form the beginnings of a new Cossack dynasty. Our time has come! From this hidden place we'll ride forth and strike at the Jews, then vanish. We will leave behind no living witness, except for one child each year, too young to remember, whom we will make one of our own. Over time, our legend will grow. We ride for Church and Tsar!"

This last exclamation, which drew cheers and raised swords, was said for the benefit of any remaining believers. His men needed to feel that they served a higher cause. Zakolyev served his own will, and his will alone.

And so it was that he led his growing community of would-be Cossacks to their camp in the north, hidden deep within a forest. With tools acquired in various ways, the men set about cutting trees and erecting real cabins. The work was good for morale, the women seemed glad enough, the children played, and for a time they did not murder or pillage. It was a time of settling. Even the restless Korolev contented himself with simple labor.

Soon after the men finished building the cabins, the Ataman announced that Paulina's mother, the woman Elena, should move her belongings to his cabin and live with him in order to watch after the child. Elena did as she was instructed.

Zakolyev's sudden domestic decision seemed out of character. But for the first time in his life, he felt something like love. Not toward Elena, but toward the child. Elena's place in his household was utilitarian at best; she did not share his bed but slept on straw matting in Paulina's room. It would always be called Paulina's room, and the child would remain, along with the boy Konstantin, the primary object of Zakolyev's affection.

It is good that fathers tell stories to their children. So one night Father Dmitri told young Paulina a tale of her past. "One day, not so very long ago, there lived a man and his wife, and they were happy and good, so a beautiful little girl was born to them. And I was that man, and you were that little girl."

"And my mother was Elena," she said.

He shook his head sadly. "Elena is not your true mother, but you must never reveal this secret."

This revelation was not really a surprise to Paulina; Elena had never felt like a mother to her. "Is Shura my true mother?"

"You are lucky to have old Shura, but no, she is not your mother."

"Then who—"

Father Dmitri cut her off. "Do not interrupt your father!" Then, in a softer voice, "You must be silent until I finish, Paulina. Your true mother—my beloved wife—was murdered by a monster . . ."

Paulina's eyes opened wide with horror. On the Ataman's strictest orders, she had remained insulated from any mention of violence or death or even the purpose of the raiding parties. She knew only that her father and his men went out on patrol to serve someone called the Tsar.

"What . . . what did the monster look like?" she asked, afraid and fascinated by this dark revelation.

"He looks like any other man—about my age, yet with white hair, wizard's hair. And this wizard has the power to enchant with his voice, telling sweet lies that confuse before he kills. The only way to destroy this monster is quickly, before he can speak and weave his spell."

Father Dmitri was utterly convincing in his tale, which he told in a trembling voice, as if he actually believed it himself.

Every child has nightmares. From that day on, Paulina's took the shape of a white-haired monster who looked like a man.

The men were puzzled by the Ataman's new paternal role, and the women were quietly bemused to find an endearing quality in a man they feared. Some of the women asked Elena whether the Ataman had become a husband as well.

She would not speak of it.

THE NIGHT that Ataman Zakolyev adopted his new domestic role, a period of relative normalcy entered the camp as the men concentrated on building rather than hunting Jews. Oddly enough, it was the dogs that completed this settled atmosphere.

Prior to finding a permanent settlement, Zakolyev had killed the growling canines along with their owners. But now he allowed those dogs whose loyalty could be bought with a few scraps of food. On occasion, Zakolyev was seen scratching an animal behind the ears. They were perfect followers, always ready to lick the Ataman's hand and show absolute obedience. The smarter children did the same.

Zakolyev let the youngest do as they pleased—running wild like the dogs and amusing themselves. But as soon as they were old enough, the children were given menial duties such as cleaning the outhouses, washing clothes in the river—whatever the adults found distasteful or dull.

Like the children, the dogs earned their keep: No stranger could approach without warning. The dogs also cornered stray horses and herded sheep acquired from recently deceased Jews. So the animals became a part of the camp, hunting with the men and watching with rapt attention as the women prepared the food, hoping an errant hand might drop a slice into their waiting jaws.

So the dogs barked and chased sticks thrown by youngsters, men built hearths in sturdy cabins, and women prepared food and cared for the children, as in any other Cossack camp. But fires were allowed only at night, when the smoke would dissipate in the darkness, or during rain or snow, which would suppress any sign.

Few could ignore the Ataman's growing preoccupation with security—but no one as yet detected the seeds of a growing obsession, as Zakolyev started seeing Sergei Ivanov lurking in the shadow of a tree, peering out from behind the barn, or staring at Zakolyev from the foot of his bed late at night.

Soon enough, the effects of Zakolyev's nightmares carried over to the light of day: a twitch of his eye, the jerking turn of his head, a muttered phrase directed at no one. At times he appeared distracted—he would stop whatever he was saying or doing and stare into a world only he could see. Circles appeared under his eyes, and he grew more remote from his men. At the same time, the Ataman came to view himself as a mythic figure, strengthened by his suffering, rising above other men. Fraternizing with a shrinking inner circle, he now gave orders through Korolev, who made sure they were carried out with brutal efficiency.

Meanwhile, life went on in the camp. When the men returned from hunting—animals or Jews—they would sit by the campfires and tell stories of their youth and drink toasts. But they chose their words carefully when their leader was nearby, or even when he wasn't. Zakolyev declared a death penalty for anyone who undermined his authority or compromised their location.

There was little danger of detection. Their cabins lay hidden deep within an expanse of forest in a small clearing a hundred meters from a flowing stream. And a short distance through the trees, the stream turned to a waterfall, pouring over the cliff and thundering straight down, twenty meters to the rocks and shallows far below. Below the base of the falls, the stream became a torrent of white water, with steep drops and rapids. Because it was not a navigable stream, no small boats would pass, and the camp lay far off any beaten path. They would remain undisturbed.

THE NINE CAMP CHILDREN—four girls and five boys—glad for this permanent home near a real waterfall, played happily in the shallows until one of the boys waded into the stream too close to the edge, slipped, and was washed over to die on the rocks below.

After that, the Ataman forbade Paulina or Konstantin to play near the top of the falls. The boy who died, he declared, had neither intelligence nor luck. He would not be missed, except perhaps by Shura.

Like the other boys his age, Konstantin enjoyed exploring the woods, carrying on make-believe adventures, and riding a horse whenever he was allowed. Spending time with a young girl was not high on his list, even if little Paulina looked up to him. But from the time he had first seen the infant girl years before, he had developed a fondness for her that brought him both delight and mortification.

He still remembered how, when Shura had first asked him to hold the infant while she tended to another, Paulina's tiny hand reached out as quick as a trained fighter's to clutch the sleeve of his woolen shirt. Then she cooed so sweetly and looked up at his face. As he gazed into her large eyes, Konstantin saw the world as she saw it—a place of mystery where all people were good and all things were possible.

That luminous moment ended abruptly when one of the older boys walked past and called him "wet nurse." As soon as he could, Konstantin disengaged himself and rushed away to help the men.

Later, when Paulina had learned to walk and talk a little, she would follow Konstantin, running on her little legs, trying to keep up with him, crying out, "Kontin! Kontin!" because she couldn't say his full name. From that day on he would become her Kontin. As time passed, he would watch over her protectively.

The Ataman had given Elena strict orders that Paulina was not to play with any of the other girls—only the boys. His daughter was to dress as a boy and would be trained in hand-to-hand combat by Great

Yergovich and all his best fighters. In the meantime, if anything happened to her, the responsibility would rest heavily on the shoulders of Elena and Konstantin. Which meant that if she came to harm, nothing would be resting upon their shoulders at all.

Although Father Dmitri clearly favored Paulina, he seemed to care about Konstantin too—but there were times that the Ataman looked at Konstantin so strangely that the boy felt afraid and didn't know what to think.

Konstantin was glad that Paulina lived in a cabin with people who cared about her, or at least took care of her. Sometimes he wondered who his own parents were, but such thoughts led nowhere, so he let them be. Still, he made it his business to listen closely to the men in case a stray conversation might provide a clue to his past.

At night he would often sit and draw pictures or whittle in the corner of the barn where some of the men drank and talked. A boy with sensitive ears could overhear many things, and Konstantin was as invisible as the dogs who curled up beside him.

When he was younger, he had wanted to go out on patrol with the grown men. But when he heard them speak in hushed tones about all the killing, he wasn't so sure. The time would come when he'd have to choose whether to become one of them or . . . or . . .

His young mind could find no other option. This life was all he knew; the rest was only dreams.

. 30 .

Some weeks later, as Sergei prepared to begin the next session, Serafim threw a punch toward his face. The movement took Sergei completely by surprise, but he evaded, as he had learned in the past. Serafim swung again; Sergei parried.

"Move naturally," said the monk, taking his shoulders and shaking them, pushing this way and that. "Less like a soldier, more like a child. You're far too tense. Even as you move, relax . . . always relax."

"I am relaxed."

"There's relaxed," Serafim said, "and then there's *relaxed*."

"Even in mortal combat?"

"Especially then," he said, continuing his attacks. "More men die from fatigue than from lack of skills. Only when you learn to relax under pressure, to relax in motion, can you fight longer and live longer. So practice relaxing in all that you do—in the kitchen, in the laundry. *Let* movement happen instead of making it happen." After a pause, Serafim smiled and said, "Be patient, Sergei. Old habits die hard, and tense warriors die young."

For the next week Sergei repeated the word *relax* under his breath a hundred times a day, taking a deep breath and releasing any unnecessary tension—especially while doing physical labor or training. "Your training is not just about punching or kicking," Serafim reminded him. "It's about everything you do. Remember: Here and now . . . breathe and relax . . . in battle and in life."

Exasperated—feeling more tense than ever—Sergei pleaded,

"Please, Serafim, I don't need you to constantly remind me to relax and breathe. I understand your point!"

"*Doing* is understanding," Serafim said.

As they walked the island paths, Serafim had Sergei inhale and exhale in time to his footfalls until he could inhale for twenty counts and exhale in the same manner. Serafim could do ten counts more—he had lungs like huge bellows.

As another frozen winter passed into the new year, practice only became more frustrating. Serafim chided him at every turn: "You still cling to the familiar, Socrates, to rote techniques you've repeated a thousand times. But you can't preplan for every situation. Reality will surprise you every time."

During this phase of training, Serafim began to attack him at random, as Razin had done. The elder monk would strike Sergei day and night, at odd times: when Sergei was running errands on rough or slippery ground, by a lake or in the forest, and sometimes even in the hallways of the hermitage. No place was safe—once the old monk even attacked Sergei while he was relieving himself.

Finally, Serafim made his point: "Each situation is unique, Socrates. Your opponent will be unpredictable; so must be your defense. Confrontations get messy, sloppy, slippery, off balance, unorthodox, and unpredictable. Anything can and does happen: Your opponent may have a concealed weapon or companions waiting nearby. He may seem drunk, then suddenly alert. He may turn out to be stronger or faster than you. Don't assume; don't predict; don't guess what your opponent will or will not do next. Just stay aware and respond naturally to whatever arises in the moment."

"Are you saying I should move without thinking at all?"

"In combat, there's no time to think. Beforehand, you may plan and strategize, but all plans are tentative and must change on the spur of the moment. Whatever happens, there's only one certainty: It will not go exactly as you expect. So expect nothing, but be prepared for anything. Relax and trust your body's wisdom. It will respond on its own."

"I think I experienced that . . . with Razin."

Serafim nodded. "You've experienced it, but now you need to master it—even when injured, overwhelmed, or on your worst day. That means throwing away any preconceived notions about your adversary's personality or emotions. None of that matters. Whether it's a fist or a stone or saber or charging horse, a force comes in—you move, you breathe—and in any given moment, your body will find its own solutions."

"Easier said than done," said Sergei.

Serafim smiled. "I think you're starting to understand."

I<small>T</small> BEGAN when Serafim picked up a fist-sized stone and, standing three meters away, said, "Hold up your hand and catch this rock!" He threw it with such force that it nearly broke Sergei's hand. "Remember the pain," he said. "It's called *resistance*. In life, stress happens when you resist. The same is true in combat. No matter what comes your way, if you take a rigid position, you experience pain. Never oppose force with force. Instead, absorb it and use it. Now you can learn how yielding can overcome even a superior force."

Serafim started by gently tossing fist-sized stones, underhand, toward Sergei's chest. "Step out of the way and catch them smoothly," he said, "matching the speed of the stone with your hand so there is no sound at all . . ."

Later, the monk brought out a heavy oak staff and swung at Sergei from the side. First he instructed Sergei to take a rigid stance, like a solid vertical wall, and experience the pain of impact. After that, Serafim instructed Sergei to swing the staff at him, and he demonstrated how, by moving and leaning away from the staff at the last moment—the way Sergei absorbed the stones with his hand—Serafim could absorb the blow, reducing its force by more than half.

"That's fine if someone swings a staff," said Sergei. "But suppose it's a saber? I can't just absorb the cut of a blade."

Serafim scratched his beard, as if pondering the question. "In that case, I suggest you get out of the way."

The next week, and the week after that, Serafim threw more stones, faster and faster. Sergei was to move off the line of force and silently catch the stone, absorbing its force. As time passed, he graduated from stones to knives—thrown slowly at first, then faster. Later he learned to evade and absorb pushes, punches, and kicks in addition to blows of the staff by moving with a wavelike motion.

"These games are well and good," said Sergei in a sudden fit of impatience. "But when will I be ready to learn advanced skills—and work with weapons and learn to fight like animals, like the Chinese monks do?"

"First of all," said Serafim, "there are no advanced skills; there is only skillful movement. Imitating tigers or monkeys or dragons has a certain aesthetic appeal, but I suggest you become the most dangerous animal of all—the human animal, who uses both instinct and reason. Your most formidable weapon is between your ears. Those who focus only on strength are defeated by cleverness, unpredictability, flexibility, and deception."

IN EARLY AUTUMN, as the cold winds again buffeted the island, Serafim led Sergei to the edge of a sheer granite cliff that plummeted down to waves breaking twenty meters below. "Stand with your back to the water and your heels just at the edge," he instructed. "There are times you may find yourself having to fight at the edge of a precipice— on a bridge or a cliff such as this. The moment fear arises and you begin to tense up—that's precisely when you need to soften, breathe, absorb, and evade. If you tighten, you fall."

Sergei glanced behind and almost lost his balance. "If I fall—"

"You will not likely die," said Serafim, "but it will be . . . unpleasant."

As Serafim gently pushed, Sergei swiveled, giving way. Serafim continued, pushing the right shoulder, then the left; the hips, the torso. Sergei evaded, gave way, maintaining his balance as the pushes grew more forceful.

He did the same as Serafim poked at him with the tip of a knife.

Finally Serafim said, "Turn around," and Sergei faced the crashing waves far below. He could no longer see the pushes; he would have to sense them coming, and instantly give way. A moment of tension, and he would fall over the edge—

Serafim began slowly, gently, all the while softly reminding Sergei, "Fear is a wonderful servant . . . but a terrible master . . . Fear generates tension, so breathe and relax . . . You don't have to rid yourself of fear . . . just train yourself to respond differently."

Staring down at the drop below, Sergei had to remind himself why he had dedicated his life to this training as Serafim's pushes came in with more force, then turned to slow punches. Next came the knife—the sting of the blade, poking, pushing, piercing his skin as he moved like water—

Suddenly, Serafim punched Sergei's shoulder blade—it took him by surprise and he fell.

For a sickening moment, everything seemed to spin . . . then his instincts took over, and he managed to stay upright by flailing his arms and legs, which closed just before he hit the water with a *ka-fump*.

The impact punched up through his legs, hips, spine, and neck. Then silence and icy water. His stomach cramped—he felt like someone had kicked him in the groin.

Struggling back up toward air and light, he broke the surface with a gasp and heard the crash of waves and the caw of gulls. Looking up, Sergei saw the small figure of Serafim high above, pointing to Sergei's right. He swam that way and found a small beach—none too soon, for he could no longer feel his arms or legs. As he hiked and climbed back up to Serafim, Sergei considered how much more he still had to learn.

A WEEK LATER Sergei was just limbering up when Serafim suddenly lunged at him with a knife. It came out of nowhere: One moment Serafim was smiling, relaxed, standing with empty hands. The next moment a blade flew toward Sergei's throat. Instantly, his hands came up and he leaned away. Not a very sophisticated defense, but at least he had moved without thinking, as Razin had taught him.

"Everyone responds differently to an attack," said Serafim. "Some fighters flinch and turn; others lean forward or back. We begin with your own instinctive response. Here, I'll show you what I mean." He handed Sergei the knife. "Thrust the blade toward my throat." Sergei did so halfheartedly. Serafim slapped the knife away with such speed that it stuck into a wooden beam three meters away. Then he slapped Sergei's face. "A sincere attack!"

The next time Sergei attacked—sincerely—Serafim leaned back and to the side, bringing his hands up to his throat. "This was my own instinctive reaction the first time I was tested," he said. "Now, notice how I build upon it."

When Sergei attacked again, Serafim moved the same way but followed up with a slight turn of one elbow, and Sergei found his knife hand trapped. Then Serafim swiveled smoothly back, and the knife was torn from his grasp and pointed back in his direction as Serafim held his wrist in a painful lock. "You see? We begin with a natural response, then let each body take the path of least resistance to solve the problem. There are no wrong movements. The only mistake is not moving at all."

Nearly every afternoon, unless he was called away, Serafim joined Sergei to observe and instruct—correcting, demonstrating, giving new exercises, and sparring with Sergei, testing his slow and steady progress.

Serafim revealed clever and deceptive ways to move in at angles to disarm and defeat an assailant armed with a pistol or a saber, and corrected Sergei's mistakes—not with words, but with pushes, touches, and taps. Working silently in this way, Serafim taught Sergei's body directly, without abstract concepts.

When Serafim finally did speak, he reminded Sergei, "In lethal combat, it won't matter what brilliant ideas your mind understands."

Over time Sergei passed through many stages of practice. He trained even when he was fasting or feeling ill or tired. By training through fatigue, he discovered that he could handle himself even in the worst of times. When physical strength and speed were lacking, he could develop relaxation, balance, timing, and leverage.

Nearly a year had passed since his training had begun. Whenever Sergei was about to quit from exhaustion or frustration, Serafim would say something like, "When running up a hill, it's all right to give up . . . as long as your feet keep moving." Sometimes the only thing that kept his feet moving was his memory of Anya, and his vow to avenge her death.

Sergei thought often about Zakolyev and his men. Each month's delay might mean innocent lives lost—but if he attacked before he was ready, he would lose any chance of success.

As precious time passed, this dilemma continued to plague him.

. 31 .

WHEN PAULINA was eight or nine years old—no one kept track of birthdays in Zakolyev's camp—she remained, as much as ever, Konstantin's friend and admirer. Still, much had changed since she began her training with Old Yergovich. Now that she had her own pursuits, Paulina could no longer spend as much time with Konstantin except when she could slip away during a rest period. Since they had less time together, they valued it all the more.

Konstantin's life had changed too—his bright mind was now hungry for challenges, and his curiosity grew. He could understand things the other boys did not. And what he didn't understand, he could figure out. He sought to learn whatever he could from his elders, and one of the few men who could read, flattered by the boy's admiration, showed him the Cyrillic alphabet. After that, Konstantin taught himself to read; he found several books thrown in a pile of discarded belongings, taken from people the men called Jews.

One of these books, written by a man named Abram Chudominsky, told of a voyage across an ocean to a land called America. Word by word, Konstantin made his own journey through the book; then he read it again, and then again. He thought that someday he would like to voyage in a great ship across the sea to such a place. Konstantin wished he could have met the man who wrote this wondrous story.

To read and to dream undisturbed, Konstantin built a special hiding place—a little cave he had hollowed out of the thick foliage, just across the stream near the top of the waterfall. Later, he revealed his secret place to Paulina, and they met there whenever their duties allowed. Tucked away from the world, they would whisper and laugh, and he would read to her from his favorite book, and show her the alphabet, and teach her how to sound out the words and write the letters.

THEN, on the eve of 1900, a restlessness and malaise gripped Zakolyev's camp. Some of the men, whose childhood religious devotion had degraded to childish superstition, were worried about Judgment Day and feared for their souls. While they believed their continuing raids were righteous, the blood and screams spoke otherwise. Only Korolev slept well.

The Ataman continued to rule with quiet courtesy and random terror. If you pleased him, he could be generous. If you betrayed him, it would not go well for you. For all his moodiness, Zakolyev was not lazy. He held the respect of his men by training harder than most. Yet he maintained his real power not by speed or strength, but by keeping the others off balance. Korolev could be more ruthless, but no one was less predictable than Ataman Dmitri Zakolyev. None of the men, women, or children ever knew what he would do next.

On one occasion some months back, a drunken Brukovsky had muttered complaints about the Ataman's strange behavior these past few years and suggested that he himself could lead as well as the Ataman— maybe better—perhaps hoping someone would affirm this. But no one said a word. Konstantin overheard this, along with the few silent men who looked down at their hands, pretending they had heard nothing so it would not taint them. But the Ataman, who had a way of learning every secret, got word of the incident. Some believed that Zakolyev could read men's thoughts, which left most of his men in a state of constant anxiety.

Soon after that, Konstantin was allowed to join the men on patrol as serving boy—another privilege given to him by Father Dmitri. So he was present when the Ataman and twelve of his men sat around a large table, eating and drinking their fill, when Zakolyev, in a good humor, observed, "We sit like Christ and his disciples at the Last Supper, only I'm not going to be crucified anytime soon." Then he looked around, searching each man's eyes.

As they raised their glasses and toasted the Ataman's long life, Zakolyev walked around the table, laying an approving hand on some men's shoulders. But when he reached Brukovsky, who had just taken a long drink of vodka, Zakolyev reached around and cut the man's throat so deeply that vodka spilled out with his life's blood.

The Ataman surveyed the blanched faces of his men, as he casually threw the body to the floor, sat at his place, and finished Brukovsky's meal. "We must not waste food," he advised, always the thoughtful leader.

Despite a growing concern in camp over the Ataman's behavior and state of mind, there was no more talk of rebellion. For a long while after that incident, any talk at all was brief, careful, and rarely above a whisper.

Not even Korolev was safe from the Ataman's ire. One cold evening in February, Zakolyev found Korolev in the barn, having just returned from hunting. The Ataman looked around the loft and in the stalls to make sure they were alone, then Zakolyev asked his lieutenant, "Do you remember the man Sergei Ivanov, whom we left facedown in the dirt some years ago? You snapped his woman's neck, if that helps refresh your memory."

There had been so many incidents, so many faces that meant nothing to the one-armed giant. Yet he did recall the man Ivanov, and how the Ataman had foolishly ordered Korolev to let him live . . .

Korolev was wrenched back from his recollection by the sharp edge in Zakolyev's voice. "I ask you again, Korolev, do you believe that he was still alive when we left him?"

"You asked me to leave him," Korolev answered. "I did so. Yes, I believe he was still alive, but his head was bloody—"

"I didn't ask for speculations; I asked what you remember!"

Zakolyev had grown more anxious. His visions of Sergei Ivanov, both dreaming and awake, had increased of late. Now he deeply regretted his impulsive decision to let Ivanov live. It was eating at him; his head ached and stomach churned just thinking about it. Korolev had been right: Ivanov's sorrow would turn to anger, and sooner or later he would come for vengeance. Even now the monster searched for Zakolyev in his dreams.

AT THE TURN of the new century, a sense of peace and celebration reigned at St. Avraam Rostov skete, and the brothers prayed for humanity at this auspicious time. Then the new year dawned like any other day, with a cold sunrise and prayer and service—and for Sergei, more training.

Spring arrived with migratory birds, the trickle and rush of streams, and a colorful array of blossoms, and the island was born anew. The work that Sergei did in the fields, the laundry, and the kitchen gave him a sense of connection to the community at large and a healthful balance to his combat practice.

In this manner, and with these routines, four years had passed on the timeless island of Valaam, where change was measured in centuries. Word reached the monastery of a Boxer Rebellion in China; warriors had banished Japanese and Westerners from their land, and Mother Russia had sent soldiers to occupy Manchuria. When this news trickled down to skete Avraam Rostov, it was met with brief nods before attention returned to higher matters.

Meanwhile, Sergei's training progressed: Serafim taught him to move his arms, legs, hips, and shoulders independently. "Allow your mind to be concentrated on a single point, yet everywhere at once," said Serafim. "Relax the body and release the mind. By remaining fluid and open, you can strike one opponent in front of you while your leg is kicking another behind you, even as your body is moving or turning. Your opponents will think they are battling an octopus."

Serafim also reminded Sergei that no matter how many men surrounded him, he would never have to fight more than one man in a given moment. "Even if ten or twenty men attack, most of them get in each other's way. Of the three or four who threaten, you move toward the closer man—don't wait for him to reach you."

That very day Serafim taught him to juggle two stones, then three. "Fighting multiple opponents is very much like the juggler's art," he said. "You toss objects into the air one at a time, but in rapid succession. If your attention fails in juggling, you drop a stone; if your concentration fails in battle, you lose a life. So stay relaxed, focused, and always moving as you face one man . . . and the next . . . and the next . . . with an expansive mind and flowing body . . . with a peaceful heart and warrior spirit."

ALTHOUGH SERGEI had first come to Valaam for combat training, he and Serafim also had other obligations that were a necessary part of the skete's existence. Serafim was constantly busy, engaged in his spiritual guidance to the monks and his healing work with the sick and injured. But afternoons, for the most part, were dedicated to training.

As frustrating as these sessions could be, Sergei looked forward to each one because he never knew what was coming next. One day, and for weeks after, Serafim showed him how to throw knives with his right or left hand—overhand, underhand, from standing, lying down—and while running or rolling.

Then Sergei learned to apply the right force to devastating pressure points that could paralyze an arm or leg—and how to strike two or even three men at once in a spinning, whipping motion, and redirect an opponent's kick or punch to hit one of his fellow assailants.

During this phase of training, Serafim caught Sergei staring intently at an intimidating ax he had raised. "Relax your gaze," he instructed. "Rather than fixating on your opponent's arms or legs or eyes, stay aware of everything around you. An open gaze expands your awareness and conveys a powerful message to your adversary's mind that he is only a temporary problem you will soon put out of the way. So look through, beyond the opponent, as if you are hardly concerned with the attack, yet remain completely aware."

"Is that possible?" Sergei asked.

"You'll find out soon enough," Serafim assured him.

As the months passed, Sergei came to realize that his hermitage duties—his hours of service and contemplation—were not merely a distraction, but an integral part of his training. Movement practice and the rest of life interpenetrated one another, blending into a unified existence. Almost without his noticing, the practice of combat shifted to the practice of living.

"How could it be any other way?" Serafim said. "I would not have wasted my time merely teaching you how to vanquish your enemies. Our time together has far more to do with living than with fighting. And I still pray that you will find a way to let go of your vendetta."

Sergei said nothing. There was nothing he could say.

By THE MIDDLE of Sergei's fifth year on Valaam, his training increased in both breadth and depth. Because Serafim always pushed him to the edge of his abilities, he noticed this gradual transformation not only in his combat, but how he moved more gracefully when sweeping the floor, opening a door, or washing the bowls and utensils. His body felt . . . different, somehow. Without doubt, Sergei's fighting skills improved, but he had also become as much a part of the skete as young trees were part of the island. The outside world, engaged in its own pressing affairs, neiher knew nor cared that a young man named Sergei Ivanov had finally learned to move like a child.

Some weeks before, Serafim had reminded him, "A young child responds freshly to each moment, without plans or expectations. This is a good way to fight . . . a good way to live." Now Sergei had made another kind of journey, back to innocence. He could no longer recall what his mind or body were like when he had first arrived on Valaam seeking a mysterious master. He could not yet match his teacher's prowess, but Sergei had gained the ability to *see* what old Serafim was doing—and it intrigued him as never before.

He recalled a story Serafim had told about a man who was always tired and who prayed each day for more energy. His prayers were never answered, until one day, in a fit of despair, he cried, "Please, oh, Lord, fill me with energy!" And God answered, "I'm always filling you, but you keep leaking!"

Sergei was no longer leaking—not as much, anyway—and his energy seemed to build with each passing day as he prepared for the task ahead.

I N T H E C O M I N G W E E K S Serafim pressed, prodded, poked, twisted, and struck sensitive pressure points to cause increasing discomfort. "Notice," he said, "when I push here, you feel fear; when I press here, you feel sorrow. No two people are exactly alike in this. But whatever emotions arise, let them pass through you as you focus on your goal."

The old monk also began to slap Sergei in the face to momentarily stun him, until the time came that he could concentrate and move right through the pain. Afterward, one of the monks noted the "healthy glow" in Sergei's cheeks as they worked in the kitchen. "Your practice must be invigorating," the brother said.

Sergei smiled, thinking: If you only knew . . .

One evening soon after, Father Serafim called in four of the brothers to assist with an exercise. As ethical pacifists, the island monks did not approve of such fighting practice, but the brothers deferred to Serafim's wisdom in this unusual form of service. So they agreed to hold tightly to Sergei's legs, arms, and head as he lay on his back on the floor. As instructed by Father Serafim, each pulled and twisted rigorously in a different direction, inflicting some pain. Sergei's task was to stay relaxed. He found this exercise surprisingly difficult—perhaps because it brought back sensations of having been pinned down on that day of horror years before. But by relaxing and using creative movements, he was able to escape each time.

"As long as you stay relaxed and mobile," Serafim remarked, "you'll never again become weighed down by many hands."

Sergei recalled the day he had finally told Serafim about the events that first drove him on this quest. As the elderly monk nodded, Sergei had the eerie sense that his words only confirmed what his old teacher had already seen . . .

As Sergei's reverie ended, he heard Serafim continue: ". . . Rather than immediately trying to break free, maintain physical contact; it enables you to know the location of an opponent. If he grasps you, you actually have him; you can then move your body in such a way as to throw him."

The instructions and practice went on and on and on. That winter, Sergei grew agonizingly aware of his every weakness, imbalance, and point of tension. When he told Serafim that he seemed to be getting worse, the monk smiled. "Not worse—you're making the usual mistakes but to a lesser degree. Life is about refinement, not perfection. And you still have refining to do."

The training was not without its humorous moments. The next afternoon, as Serafim was administering more pain training with a leather whip, one of the brothers walked past, shook his head, and muttered, "They would have lined up for this in the Middle Ages."

As the brother departed, they both laughed. Then, more seriously, Serafim said, "No healthy person seeks pain, Socrates—nor do I enjoy administering it. But such training, judiciously delivered, conditions you so that pain in battle has less power to shock or discourage or slow you down."

After that, each time Sergei felt the sting of the whip's sharp blow, he thought of Zakolyev.

In the spring of 1903 Serafim blindfolded Sergei for a part of each session to enhance his sensitivity and awareness. He led Sergei through the forest, saying, "In case you're temporarily blinded, you need to continue fighting with whatever senses you have remaining."

After some falls and bruises, Sergei began to feel his way around obstacles, developing greater acuity in hearing. Beyond that, he sometimes sensed the energy of objects around him. All the while, Serafim provided pushes from the back, front, or side, and Sergei had to soften instantly and move or roll. If at any time he lost track of his teacher's whereabouts, Serafim would hit him over the head with a stick. On their return to the skete, Serafim led Sergei into a room where he had to guess how many other monks, if any, were present.

And at random, Serafim would instruct Sergei to close his eyes and describe his surroundings in as much detail as he could. This encouraged him to pay acute attention to his environment rather than getting lost in thought. "You are learning," Serafim said, "how to think with your body—how to leave your mind and come to your senses."

Serafim tied thin ropes to Sergei's ankle and elbow and pulled him off balance as he fought imaginary opponents. He also tied one then both of Sergei's arms behind his back, forcing him to fight with his shoulders, chin, hips, head, feet, knees, or torso. "If you can't use anything else," Serafim urged, "use your wits. You may surprise yourself with your abilities, even against great odds."

Sergei also learned new ways to escape from holds and twists— headlocks, armlocks, and different chokes—by striking in clever ways to a variety of targets. He then studied ways to defeat one or more opponents while standing or lying on his back or side or stomach and while rising to his feet, so he could fight when disabled, or on difficult terrain, or from awkward postures.

As SERGEI'S MIND turned to his mission, and to those he would fight, he told Serafim, "Some of my adversaries are larger and stronger than I. One of them is a giant—"

"It doesn't matter," the monk answered. "Big men can fight well at a distance, but softness, fluidity, and speed can overcome size and strength. A shorter man can work on the inside, at close range. Every body type has its strengths and weaknesses, so work to minimize your

weaknesses and focus on your strengths. You can even overcome superior speed by responding instantly to an attack rather than waiting until
it is launched."

That summer, when Serafim decided that Sergei was "finally ready
to learn," they met in the forest clearing, and Serafim showed him several extremely clever movements for evading and disarming a swordsman. Holding a razor-sharp saber, gliding across the earth, and cutting
through the air, Serafim said, "Learning to use a blade helps you defend
against it."

After Sergei had practiced for weeks with various attacks and strikes
in the manner of the samurai of Japan, Serafim asked him to draw a
saber from a scabbard as quickly as he could and strike him.

As Serafim stood relaxed and alert, three meters away, Sergei was
about to draw the sword and advance quickly and strike as Serafim had
instructed. But as soon as he started to move, Serafim was standing next
to him, locking Sergei's sword arm so he could no longer draw—then
he demonstrated how he could then disable Sergei in several ways.

"Never fear the weapon, only the man wielding it. Focus on your
opponent while he focuses on his knife or saber or pistol. He invests his
power in the weapon but forgets the rest of his body. And the very
moment you might want to back away from a weapon, go in without
hesitation! Close the distance and disable him before he can use it. Stop
the attack before it begins."

It took many more weeks of patient practice until Sergei could close
the distance between himself and an adversary in a fraction of a second.

THEN ALL AT ONCE, it seemed, Sergei's training took a different
turn. As they walked back to the skete in the brisk air of late September,
Serafim spoke about patience, and the ethics of combat. "You have done
well these past years, Socrates, but skill training is only the beginning.
The movements of the highest warriors are relaxed and expansive
because they fight for a cause larger than themselves. Only by surren-
dering to God's will does one find victory in battle and serenity in life."

Serafim started pacing again, as he did whenever he was about to emphasize a point. "The true warrior, Socrates, retains his humanity even in battle. In winning a brutal victory, you may still lose your soul. Those who fight the dragon may become the dragon."

These words, and the spirit behind them, penetrated not only Sergei's mind but his heart. He gazed at this peaceful old warrior-monk who for the past seven years had assumed the role of mentor. It seemed ironic that Sergei was never to call him "Father," because that is what Serafim had become, filling a role that Sergei had missed since childhood.

That night, after Sergei had said a prayer of love and remembrance for Anya and his son, he gave thanks for Serafim's generosity of spirit and his simple humanity.

Sergei had known from the beginning that Serafim had no wish for him to follow this course, yet each day without fail—unless church duties took him elsewhere—this island father gave Sergei a part of his life and experience. He received nothing in return except Sergei's gratitude. For Serafim, it seemed reward enough to serve the mysterious will of God.

This truth made Sergei love him all the more.

. 33 .

AFTER HER MORNING SESSION with Yergovich, Paulina raced through the woods toward the river, laughing with delight, barely escaping Konstantin's grasp. Konstantin might have caught her, but he chose to let her get the better of him. The way her training was progressing, soon he would not be able to catch her even if he tried.

No longer a boy but a tall youth, Konstantin remained her protector and friend. Not that Paulina needed protection anymore; she could handle herself amazingly well for an eleven-year-old. Besides, none of the older boys would be so foolish as to bully Zakolyev's favorite. But when she was younger, he had to protect her from herself. Paulina had tried every kind of risky stunt with wild abandon: climbing trees to the high branches, walking a slippery log over a deep culvert. Now she was growing up as wiry and swift as any of the boys, and far more skilled at combat.

Paulina could already outrun and outfight many of the older boys. Yergovich was training her in the traditional Cossack style of fighting, which depended more on flowing movement, balance, and agility than on brute strength or size. All in the camp agreed that she had a talent for it, although no one dared ask why Ataman Zakolyev insisted that every man teach her everything he knew. Only Korolev declined to involve himself in "children's games."

The Ataman doted on Paulina more than ever these days, but his maudlin sentiment turned to fatherly severity when it came to her combat training. He demanded nothing less than her best effort each and every day—at morning, afternoon, and evening practice sessions. For her part, Paulina never complained. She had both the willingness and energy for it, and took pride in her newfound expertise. In fact, she applied herself with a focus that impressed all who watched her progress.

KONSTANTIN KEPT TO HIMSELF much of the time, dreaming and reading and drawing images in the dirt or sketching on parchment with charcoal from the fire. He also thought about Paulina. He missed her gentleness and innocence, qualities that he had lost somewhere along the way. Having her with him felt like stepping out of a dirty hut into a fragrant forest. Sometimes he watched from the shadows as Great Yergovich led her through her training.

Yergovich was a massive figure, taller than any man in camp except for the giant, Korolev. With his girth, he reminded Konstantin of a bear, especially with his thick brown beard and hairy neck and chest. He had a bear's power—and while he could not move as quickly as some of the younger men, he could anticipate their attacks.

Years before, he had worked as a bricklayer. Then one day, in a saloon, he had gotten into a tussle with Tomorov. A minute later, Tomorov and the others who had come to his aid were lying on the ground, not seriously hurt except for their pride. When Zakolyev appeared, Yergovich told him, "I can teach these young pups to fight properly." So he had joined them and proved himself worthy. Now none could defeat him except Korolev, who once nearly broke the old bear's head. But Korolev got a few bruises in the scuffle, along with a grudging respect for the big man.

After that, they called him Great Yergovich. He was obedient and trustworthy and didn't ask questions, which made him a good teacher for Paulina. He valued his position as instructor and enjoyed seeing the girl's progress. Great Yergovich had no family of his own, only a friendship with Shura, the only woman his age in camp. In a sense, it was Yergovich and Shura who had parented the growing girl.

Yergovich got on well enough with all the men but Korolev. He didn't like the way the giant looked at Paulina. Korolev knew enough to leave her alone, but Yergovich didn't trust this tiger who played tame when it suited him but waited, his tail twitching.

So the bear and tiger kept an uneasy truce.

Each day Yergovich led Paulina through a rigorous course of warrior games and exercises—running, swimming, climbing—and fighting skills some of the men had never seen. He had saved his secrets for her. He resolved to train Paulina so well that if the time ever came, and he wasn't there to protect her, she would at least have a chance against the one-armed man.

K ONSTANTIN, meanwhile, was hungry all the time. He grew out of his shirt and shoes. He had to go barefoot for a while until he found an old pair of boots in a pile of discarded clothing. He felt clumsy, and once in a while his voice cracked. He thought a lot about the older women and about what they did with the men—and might do with him someday. Then he would think of Paulina and feel bad; after all, she was still a girl.

With all the changes, she remained his one constant—someone who cared about him no matter what. Konstantin now felt a jealous animosity toward Father Dmitri, whom Paulina so admired. She had seen only one side of the Ataman; to her he was a protective, involved father, interested in her progress. The Ataman had never given Paulina a reason to fear him. She did not know the real Dmitri Zakolyev, and Konstantin could not bring himself to tell her.

At the same time, Konstantin hid his growing attachment to Paulina. He was once a brother to her, but now his feelings had deepened and changed. He knew he should be thankful that the Ataman did not object to their friendship—as long as Konstantin didn't distract her from training.

His role in the band, as a servant but never a warrior, had been defined years before, when the Ataman first assigned him to help care for Paulina. So it was no surprise that none of the men encouraged him to learn fighting skills.

He was, in fact, relieved to stay out of the raids and the killing; he had other interests and talents. From the growing pile of discarded belongings taken from murdered Jews, he found a precious set of brushes and pigments. So while Paulina pursued her training, Konstantin practiced his own craft with charcoal and brush on paper or on any surface he could find. The hours would pass unnoticed as he drew and painted—trees and huts and horses and birds, and sometimes even images from his dreams.

Only when Konstantin thought about his future did a sorrow settle upon him. He couldn't imagine living this way for years—waiting in camp with the women and Yergovich for the "real men" to return from patrol. The other youths his age, some of whom now rode with the men, thought Konstantin strange.

Only Paulina understood him.

But now he wasn't so sure about anything. When they found time alone, he felt awkward, no longer able to say what had come so easily before. So he only asked her about her training, and she told him with such enthusiasm that he knew they were still friends.

Konstantin loved the way Paulina's bobbed hair, the color of rich earth, bounced as she ran. She was pretty, even in boys' clothing. He had tried to draw her face once; they both laughed at his first attempt. He could draw her again and again but never capture her beauty. She would have been in danger from some of the men were it not for Father Dmitri's protection.

Father Dmitri. The thought of him brought a rush of righteous anger at the great deception, the hypocrisy, the secrets and lies. Paulina still saw only what she wanted to see—and what they let her know: the Ataman's disciplined life, and the patrols helped in service of a faraway tsar. She never heard about the charred bodies left behind.

Konstantin knew that he should tell her, but each day of silence made it more difficult to speak the truth. She wouldn't believe it; he would lose her trust. She might even hate him. And if she confronted Father Dmitri, it could mean catastrophe for them both.

He would just have to wait until she woke up to the truth on her own.

Possessed of a good mind and heart, Paulina assumed the same qualities in those around her. She had witnessed Father Dmitri's moods and fits of anger, of course, but a child easily overlooks her father's foibles. Insulated from the world by his orders and preoccupied with the life he had arranged for her, Paulina had little time to consider life's larger questions. She had accepted that as the Ataman's child she received special training and responsibilities. She did not envy the other women's timid, submissive manners as they cleaned, cooked, carried water, and served the men.

But sometimes, in the quiet moments before sleep, she wondered what it might feel like to live an ordinary life in the company of other women.

At least I have the old bear, she sighed. And I'll always have Kontin.

. 34 .

It was spring of 1905. Nine years had passed since Sergei had arrived on Valaam. Nine years of service, contemplation, and training in combat and in life. Sergei was now thirty-two years old. His youthful temperament gave way to a more reflective state of mind, a sobering sense of maturity, humility, and perspective—the first stirrings of the transformation that Serafim had once predicted.

Since his wife's death, Sergei had spent more than a decade preparing for a single act of retribution. Sometimes it seemed a form of madness; other times it seemed a just and honorable cause. A man kills your family; you show him the gates of hell. It was as simple as that.

He was now a formidable warrior, having surpassed without realizing it Alexei the Cossack and even Razin. A growing energy and power flowed through him—intimations of mastery, of invincibility, tempered only by Serafim's regular thrashings.

With Sergei's metamorphosis came a growing sense of restless impatience as he confronted the question he had asked many times before: How long will I let Dmitri Zakolyev walk the earth? His mind stretched south, to the Pale of Settlement, where those men were likely shedding innocent blood.

Sergei decided that the time had come for him to leave. But it would not be easy to say goodbye. He both admired and envied Serafim for the peace he had found—a state of grace that Sergei might never know. But he had glimpsed the possibility that he might someday grasp what the island father had wished to teach him.

He announced his decision at their next meeting. "Serafim, it's time for me to be on my way."

Serafim only scratched his beard and said, "Well, that may be so . . . but I wonder, Socrates, how do you expect to destroy so many men when you can't even defeat a tired old monk?"

"Are you saying that I have to defeat you before I can leave?"

"You can leave anytime you wish. This is a hermitage, not a prison."

"I mean leave with your blessings."

"You've had my blessings from the day we met. Even before—"

"I think you understand what I'm saying, Serafim."

The old monk smiled. "By now, we understand one another. I was merely suggesting that if you can defeat me in a sparring match, that would be a good sign of your readiness."

They had sparred many times in the past, of course, but this would be different. It would no longer be a child against a giant. Sergei now had not only speed and youth, but the edge of constant training. He even practiced in his mind while he ate, worked, sat—even while he slept. Yes, he was ready.

Sergei nodded, and so did Serafim.

They circled. Sergei took a deep breath and made a direct but deceptive attack, trying a feint. Unresponsive to bluffs, Serafim just stood relaxed while Sergei danced around; then the old monk stepped forward and waved his arm. He almost threw Sergei off balance with this misdirection, but his student wasn't having any of it—he maintained his focus and balance. Then Sergei managed to grab Serafim's robe and step in to throw—

The teacher seemed to disappear like a puff of air.

While Sergei kicked and punched and swept and elbowed, Serafim deflected so subtly that Sergei felt no resistance anywhere. Nothing connected. The monk was never where Sergei expected him to be, so he gave up expecting. In that moment he could see and feel everything: Serafim, the sky, the earth. Sergei managed to throw him, but as Serafim fell, he threw Sergei, and they rolled to their feet in perfect unison. Their battle continued, but the conflict had disappeared. There was no Sergei and no Serafim. Just energy moving.

Then, as Sergei stepped forward, before his foot touched the ground, Serafim seemed to vanish from one spot and reappear in another, and his foot hooked the underside of Sergei's calf. The next thing he knew he was spread-eagled on his back and Serafim knelt above him, ready to deliver the final blow. The match was over.

It was the closest they'd ever come to a real contest. Serafim wasn't just toying with Sergei; he could no longer afford to. Sergei could finally discern the qualities his teacher possessed and where they were still lacking in himself. Despite the outcome, this represented a major breakthrough: Sergei had absorbed months' worth of training in those few minutes. They both knew it. But he was not going anywhere, anytime soon. His training would continue.

And it was about to change in a way he never could have anticipated.

As THEIR NEXT SESSION BEGAN, Serafim announced, simply, "All your past training was only a preparation for what I'm about to show you. This is your rebirth, the one practice that is primarily responsible for whatever modest skills I have attained. You could have begun this practice from the first day we met, but it would have taken twenty years. In preparing you these past years, I've given you the shortcut you so devoutly wished. With your present skills, this final practice should take no more than a year to master. We shall see . . ."

It would be the most radical method of combat training Sergei had ever encountered. And it began with six words: "Prepare yourself," said Serafim. "I'm about to strike."

Sergei relaxed into an expansive state of awareness as he had been trained to do. He waited, ready. Then he waited some more. Serafim seemed to be just standing there like a statue . . .

Sergei took a slow deep breath, and another. Finally, he said, "Well? When are you going to attack?"

"I am attacking," responded Serafim.

"I don't understand . . ."

"Shhhh. Silence please. Words only pull your attention into your lower mind, and you miss what's going on around you."

In the silence that followed, Sergei finally saw it: Serafim's arm and whole body were indeed moving toward him, but so slowly that the old monk appeared to be standing still.

Another minute passed. "Are you joking?" Sergei said. "What's the point of this?"

"Notice each passing moment," Serafim said slowly, in a soft voice. "Feel your entire body, from your toes to your head to the tips of your fingers. And match the pace of your response with the pace of my movement."

Sergei sighed and made the best of it, moving more slowly and deliberately than ever before. It felt both pointless and frustrating. Still, he followed the old master's movements during the minutes it took for Serafim to complete the hooking punch he had launched several minutes before.

Moving this slowly, Sergei noticed points of subtle tension and willed himself to relax his thighs, his stomach, his shoulders . . .

When the first movement was complete, Serafim began another, although it was difficult to tell. At this point Sergei broke the silence. "Serafim, I can appreciate the value of practicing in slow motion. But hardly moving at all? I can easily block anything—I could clean the kitchen and return before you hit me."

"Relax . . . breathe . . . observe," Serafim repeated. "Move as I do . . ."

So they continued, as slow and silent as the sun's path across the sky, into the dusk.

TIME STOOD STILL as the practice continued. Many weeks passed before the pace of Serafim's movement noticeably changed. They still moved as if through thick molasses, but at least the motion was clearly perceptible.

Sergei began to correct imbalances previously unnoticed and to relax profoundly as he moved. Whatever came, his body responded naturally, without effort. Awareness now infused every part of his body.

Sergei began to sense the relationship of every body part, even his internal organs, and the bones and joints and the lines of energy flowing from the earth up through both their arms and legs, which became whiplike extensions of their centers.

Once in a while Serafim would whisper something like, "Move like seaweed . . . floating . . . rising . . . falling . . . turning." But mostly they continued in silence, because no words were necessary. Movement became deep meditation, and at times, as energy welled up into Sergei's heart, it became a form of prayer.

In the months that followed, Serafim continued to attack in a slow, flowing manner with a punch . . . a kick . . . a knee . . . an elbow . . . left hand . . . right . . . jab . . . hook . . . cross . . . kick . . . grab. From every possible angle. The sun moved. The shadows changed. And the seasons passed.

By midsummer, after thousands of attacks, each strike took only a minute, and a new sense of flow and rhythm grew. Sergei's thoughts had long before abandoned him; now it was all a play of energy. Every response happened by itself—mindless movement, effortless response. Sergei could have continued in his sleep, yet this was the opposite of sleep; it was pure awareness, no self, no other as Serafim and Socrates moved as one body, like wind through the seasons.

By autumn, each movement took only fifteen seconds . . . then ten . . . then five . . . yet Sergei hardly noticed. The pace had become immaterial. Whatever force entered was absorbed, redirected; the principles penetrated the marrow of his bones. He had embodied masterful skill, yet "he" was doing none of it.

Winter came; the attacks now whipped in rapidly. Every strike was neutralized effortlessly. Sergei did nothing but remain aware.

In a moment of illumination, Sergei grasped how Serafim moved — with an efficiency and grace that amazed him. More incredibly, he could do the same.

Having ceased all resistance in mind and in body, Sergei had become empty—a hollow conduit of life force. He had long ago learned to trust Serafim; then to trust his body; only now had he come to trust All That Is.

Spring arrived—another cycle of the seasons. Now Serafim attacked like lightning—faster than the eye could see—but it made no difference at all. The movements were a blur of motion, so fast that a year ago Sergei would once not even have perceived them, much less had time to respond. But speed and time no longer mattered.

Then, without warning, Serafim stopped moving.

Sergei nearly fell over. His body was vibrating. He felt a sparkling mist of energy whirling around them.

"We created quite a stir," said Serafim.

Sergei nodded, smiling, as the spring sun disappeared over the hills to the west.

"What now?" he asked.

"Nothing more," said Serafim. "Our practice together is complete."

For a few moments Sergei heard only the wind in the treetops. Not certain he had understood, he asked for a confirmation: "Are you saying that my training is over?"

"Training never ends," Serafim responded. "It only evolves, depending upon your purpose. You now grasp the essence of movement, of relationship, of life. You've also learned something about combat. You accomplished what you came for.

"Tomorrow we can go for a walk and set aside this talk of killing. You may yet consider a higher calling.

"Serafim . . . you know—"

"Tomorrow," the old monk interrupted. "Let's speak of it tomorrow."

As soon as they met on the following day, Sergei began: "You know that I made a vow, on the grave of my family—"

"A vow you made to yourself, not to God. In truth, Socrates, you have no opponents but yourself. Make peace within, and there will be no one who can overcome you. And no one you will wish to overcome."

They walked on in silence before Sergei responded. "I once had a teacher who told me that commitment means doing what you set out to do or dying in the attempt." Sergei turned to face Serafim and addressed him in his spiritual role. "I'm committed, Father Serafim—I have to face them."

The old monk looked weary. "Will you not stay here among us, as one of us, if only for a few more years?"

"While those men run wild?"

"Men run wild all over the earth, Socrates. Nature runs wild—with hurricanes and earthquakes and plagues and locusts. Even now, innocents die by violence and by starvation, in the tens of thousands all over the Earth. Who put you in charge? Who gave you the wisdom to know who is supposed to live and who should die, and by what means? Who are you to know God's mind?"

Sergei had no answer, so he asked a question: "To what God do you refer, *Father* Serafim? The God of mercy and justice who saw fit in his infinite wisdom to take my family? Is this the God you pray to?"

Serafim raised his bushy white brows in a quizzical, appraising look. "So, Socrates, you finally confront what has been weighing on you for so long. I wish I had an answer—some sweet words to heal your heart. But God remains a mystery even to me. There was once a wise man named Hillel, one of the Hebrew fathers, who said, 'There are three mysteries in this world: air to the birds, water to the fish, and humanity to itself.'

"I have found God to be the greatest mystery of all, yet as intimate as our heartbeat, as close as our next breath . . . surrounding us, like air, like water . . . always present. But the mind cannot fathom God, only the heart . . . That is where you will find the faith—"

"I stopped believing in God years ago."

"Even nonbelievers are embraced by God. How could it be otherwise?" Serafim looked deeply into his eyes. "Abide in the mystery, Socrates. Trust it. Let go of knowing what should and shouldn't be, and you will find your faith once again."

Sergei shook his head. "Your words have always tasted of truth, Father . . . but somehow I can't quite grasp their meaning."

"Once you couldn't even grasp my robe. And look what has occurred with a little patience—"

"And a lot of practice."

"Yes. And perhaps it's time to practice . . . another way." He paused then, waiting for the right words. "Your training has already taught you the limits of the mind. The intellect is a great ladder into the sky, but it stops short of the heavens. Only the heart's wisdom can light the way. Your ancient namesake, Socrates, reminded the youth of Athens that 'Wisdom begins in wonder . . .'"

"But beyond these lofty words, Serafim—what am I to do?"

"What is anyone to do? Put one foot in front of the other! You are only a player in a drama greater than anyone but God can conceive . . . sometimes I'm not so sure that even God can make sense of it!" he said, laughing. "We can only play the role we are given. Do you understand? Those who appear in your life—whether to help or to harm—are all given by God. Meet all of them with a peaceful heart, but with a warrior's spirit. You will fail many times, but in failing you will learn, and in learning you'll find your way. In the meantime, surrender to God's will, to the life you were given, moment by moment."

"How can I know God's will, Serafim?"

"Faith does not rely on knowing anything with certainty," he said. "It requires only the courage to accept that whatever happens, whether it brings pleasure or pain, is for the highest good."

With those words, they reached the hermitage.

. 35 .

THE YEARS had not been kind to Dmitri Zakolyev, nor had the nights. Once lean and taut, now gaunt and drawn, his hollow cheeks gave the impression of a walking corpse. His eyes shone, not quite from madness, but from his zeal over a single obsession. It was as if his vision, once grand and expansive, had shrunk to a single point, and that point was Paulina and her training.

Paulina, in the summer of 1906, was still lean and wiry, with growing energy, awareness, and maturity. Her progress had quickened as well, to the continuing awe of those who witnessed her astonishing skill.

Yergovich had trained her well. But Zakolyev no longer trusted the big man; he no longer trusted anyone except his daughter. Even Korolev was suspect; he had seen the way the giant sneered and turned away when his Ataman approached. Not only Korolev, but the others as well. The Ataman heard them whispering behind his back.

His only hope lay with his daughter. She would win back his honor, authority, and respect; she would give him peace. Nearly every day he watched her practice, but as he sat, his mind turned in upon itself; the daily world faded into fragmented sounds and images—words, grunts, screams, and blood.

His mind would return with a jerk as he remembered where he was—weary to his very sinews, unable to fend off the living nightmare as the monster cut his mother's life to bloody ribbons of flesh. And her cries were joined by ghosts of the Jews, coming for him, relentless.

He still led every frenzied raid, demanding one onslaught after another. Yet his mind wandered even then, preoccupied with Paulina, in whose hands he had placed his hopes, his very life—this girl becoming a woman, this woman becoming a warrior. Paulina was his dagger, his savior, his sword. Only her victory could stop the screams.

. 36 .

OVER THE NEXT FEW DAYS, Sergei spent hours in contemplation; he had much to ponder. He and Serafim went for many walks together across the island. Sometimes they shared the silence; other times they spoke. But they no longer discussed anything more to do with combat.

Sergei's questions were larger ones now. The answers would come not from Serafim but only from within: Should he hold fast to his vow? Was he showing commitment or rigidity? Would he choose war or peace? Could there be a higher way? And finally it came to this: Would Anya be gladdened by the death of those men—or by his own death in the attempt?

Sergei wasn't certain anymore, and he chastised himself for his lack of resolve. Maybe Zakolyev was right in calling him a weakling and a coward. If Sergei did not confront his enemy, what was the point of all his training these past years? He was like a loaded gun ready to be fired.

Yet a gun could be unloaded and a sword slipped back into its sheath. That was what Serafim would say.

A story came to him—one that Serafim had told some months before, perhaps intended for this moment. He had spoken of a proud and hot-tempered young samurai who routinely cut down any peasant who gave the least offense. In those days, samurai were a law unto themselves, and such behavior was accepted according to custom.

But one day, after another killing, as he cleaned the blood from his blade and returned it to his scabbard, the young samurai began to worry that the gods might disapprove of his actions and send him to a hellish realm. Desirous to know about eternity, he visited the humble abode of a Zen master named Kanzaki. With expected courtesy, the samurai removed his razor-sharp *katana* and set it alongside him, bowed deeply, and said, "Please tell me of heaven and hell!"

Master Kanzaki gazed at the young samurai and smiled. Then his smile turned to raucous laughter. He pointed to the young warrior as if he had said something hilarious. Wagging his finger, still laughing loudly, Kanzaki said, "You ignorant bumpkin! You presume to ask me, a wise master, about heaven and hell? Do not waste my time, idiot! You are too stupid to possibly comprehend such things!"

The samurai's temper flared to the boiling point. He would have killed anyone else for even pointing at him in such a way. Now he fought to restrain himself despite these insults.

Master Kanzaki was not finished. He remarked casually, "It's quite clear to me that not one of your lineage of louts and fools could understand a word—"

A murderous rage came over the young warrior. He grabbed his katana, leaped to his feet, and raised the sword to take the Zen master's head—

In that very moment, Master Kanzaki pointed to the samurai and said calmly, "There open the gates of hell."

The warrior froze. In that instant, a light illuminated his mind, and he understood the nature of hell. It was not a realm beyond this life but within him now. He dropped to his knees, laid his blade behind him, and bowed deeply to his teacher. "Master, my gratitude knows no bounds for this brave lesson you have taught. Thank you. Thank you!"

Zen master Kanzaki smiled, pointed to him once again, and said, "There open the gates of heaven."

Maybe I'm that samurai, Sergei thought as he turned over the soil in the garden of skete St. Avraam Rostov.

THE NEXT DAY, as they walked, Sergei told Serafim the story of his life, from his earliest memory to the time he came to Valaam. When he had finished, Serafim said, "Your story, Socrates, has only begun. And remember this: Your past does not have to determine your future—yet you carry your history like a bag of stones slung over your shoulders." Serafim stopped and pointed to an old pilgrim working in a nearby garden. Many of the elderly stoop over not only from age, but from the weight of memories."

"Are you suggesting that I forget my past?"

"Memories themselves are faded paintings. Some we cherish; others are painful. There is no reason to throw them away. Just tuck those you want to keep in a safe place, to review as you wish. The past is not meant to intrude on the present. I care less about where you've been than where you're going."

"And where am I going?" Sergei asked. "Have you seen?"

Serafim looked at him intently. "I have seen something . . . but we will speak of that soon. In any case, I remind you again that there is nowhere to go. *Now* is all you have. Wherever you walk, you will always be 'here.'"

"But even now, the past is a part of me."

"Only pictures," he repeated. "The time has come for you to make peace with the past, just as you must accept the present. What happened, happened. All a perfect part of the process of your life—"

"Perfect?" Sergei said, suddenly angry. "The death of my wife and son?"

Serafim held up his hand. "Calm yourself. You hear and interpret in my words at a different level than they were spoken. I refer to a higher meaning: It was perfect because it sent you to me, as God will send you onward, to whatever you need to experience next."

"How can you know this?"

"Know this?" responded Serafim. "I don't even know if the sun will rise or whether I'll wake up in the morning. I don't know if God will grant me my next breath. So I choose to live on faith rather than knowledge—and accept whatever comes, welcome or not, bitter or sweet—all of it, a gift from God."

"More words, Serafim. What am I supposed to do with them?"

"Do nothing with them. Go beyond the words to the place within you that already knows—"

"Knows what?"

"That each day is a new life; that each moment you are born anew. This is one meaning of grace, Socrates. Sometimes all you can manage is to pay attention, and do the best you can."

"You make life sound so simple."

"It *is* simple, but I did not say it was easy. And I promse you this: One day you'll grasp its fullness, and it will be so clear and simple that you will laugh with delight. Meanwhile, all I can do is plant seeds. The rest is up to God."

Sergei PONDERED Serafim's words, willing them to penetrate him. Instead, another question arose: "Serafim, from the first time we met . . . how could you know so much about me?"

The old monk considered the question and finally answered, "Years ago, Socrates, before I became a monk, I was a soldier. I fought in terrible battles and saw carnage that no man should have to see. Then there was another . . . sorrow . . .

"So I traveled to the East, searching for meaning, for peace. I had little hope for either one. I visited many lands and learned of various paths to God. I learned that all paths are good if they lead to a higher life. I chose the Christian faith, but I haven't abandoned the gifts received when I studied other ways, different paths up the one mountain.

"I discovered certain gifts that were always in me, but certain practices helped me to cultivate them. One is the gift of healing. Even as a boy, I had energy that pulsed through my hands. I believe this energy comes from a spiritual source. My other gift is insight . . . and foresight. It works like a blossom that opens when light enters. And I see things—in dreams and reveries. That is how I know certain things, but never with certainty."

"I've often wondered about this ability of yours . . ."

"To understand it, you have to experience it. When you open to God, you can *know* all because you *are* all. You discover that the past, present, and future are all occurring now. This is how I can sometimes see and know."

"Have you seen what my future holds?"

"I see what may be, not what must be. The actions you take will shape your future for better or worse. Such is the power of choice."

"But can you tell me anything at all about what lies ahead?"

Serafim paused to consider his words. "With every spiritual gift comes a responsibility. My visions are meant to help me advise, not predict. If I told you what I've seen, it might help or harm you—and I'm not wise enough to know which.

"In any case, it might interfere with your free will. You are not here on Earth to trust me; you are here to trust yourself, to follow your own path. What if I had seen you vanquishing your enemies when you first arrived? Would you have bothered to train all these years? Would my vision have assured this course of action? What if I saw you lying dead? Would that have made you abandon your plans?"

Serafim again fixed Sergei with his gaze. "I don't always understand what I see, Socrates. I can't tell you with any certainty whether you will kill these men or forgive them."

"Forgive them? I'll send them to hell first!"

"They are already in hell."

"That's no excuse!"

"No, of course not," he answered. "There are no excuses for anything. Most of the time, I can't even find explanations. But one day you may come to see these men as part of your larger self. In that moment all else falls into place. You may be called upon to fight, but you'll know that you are only fighting yourself."

Serafim paced again as he continued. "What I'm going to tell you now, I've never revealed it to anyone—but now it may help you to understand.

"I was once married. I was young and in love, and we had three children. When I was off to war, they were killed by brigands."

In the silence that followed, a bird sang. Then Serafim continued. "Like you, Socrates, I vowed to find those who committed this crime. And, like you, I prepared myself—"

"Did you find them?" Sergei asked, waiting for a sign.

"Yes. And I killed them, every one."

Sergei took a deep breath, struck by this tragic bond they shared. "Serafim . . . when you found out what happened to your family, was it also your darkest hour?"

Serafim shook his head. "It was at first, but my darkest hour came after my 'victory'—after I had slaughtered those men. For in doing so, I became one of them—"

"But you weren't one of them! You aren't—"

"You fight the dragon, you become the dragon," Serafim repeated. "It still weighs heavily on my soul. I can't change what I've done. Ever. But do you now understand one of the reasons I decided to instruct you? Because I hope you won't make the same mistake."

In truth, Sergei was finally ready to seek another way of life, but a vow that deep—a vow he had worked nearly a third of his life to fulfill—left traces to which he still clung. "Even if I no longer seek revenge," he said, "someone has to stop them, Serafim. Why not me?"

Serafim looked into his eyes once more, searching, then he said, "Maybe you're right. Maybe you should go hunt them. Kill them all. Make them suffer the way you suffered. Do you think it will end there? You had better kill their children as well because they will come after you. So kill them too, and experience a hell deeper than any you have yet seen. Or perhaps you'll feel no response at all. You may even find satisfaction in their suffering. And the devil will smile on that day because you will have become the evil you sought to destroy."

After a time, Serafim added a final plea: "Your loved ones will find peace when you do, Socrates. So ask yourself: What is the way to peace? Must you make war to find it? Or can you create it, here and now? Those at war with themselves are defeated at every turn. So make peace with yourself . . ."

After a pause, Serafim added, "I understand the depth of your beliefs and your feelings—the painful memories and resolutions. But not every emotion needs to become an action. Whether you remain here, or whether you ride on, I ask you to give your life over to a higher will. Master your emotions the way you weather a storm—by building a shelter of faith and patience until the storm passes. Liberate your life from the tyranny of impulse, desire, and compulsion. Become God's warrior, God's servant.

"But . . . how can I know God's will?" Sergei asked.

Serafim smiled. "Many men and women wiser than I have asked that question, Socrates. I only know that God speaks through your heart, and that your heart will show the way . . . to becoming a true man . . . and a peaceful warrior."

Serafim's words struck like arrows. Yet one question remained—a question Sergei could not dismiss: "What of those men?"

"Enough of those men!" Serafim said. "They seem to have possessed you! Have you not let them live in your mind long enough? Have you the courage to show them the mercy and compassion they denied to you and your family? These questions lie at the heart of Christ's teachings. But few listen. Are you listening?"

Serafim paced again, as if words came more easily when he was in motion. "We both know that you are a formidable warrior. But can you wage peace? You know how to die, but have you learned how to live? Will you destroy or build? Will you behave with hatred or love? This is the choice you have before you."

"And all my training?"

"Nothing is ever wasted," said Serafim. "You've learned the warrior's way—so fight! Make war on hatred, battle against ignorance, fight for justice! But I tell you this: You cannot kill darkness with more darkness. Only light can banish the shadows from this world."

Sergei could hear Serafim's deep breathing as the old monk gazed inside himself. Then Serafim said, "In any event . . . those men will die without your help."

"Have you seen this . . . in a vision?" Sergei asked.

"Not a vision, no—only an understanding of how such men end up destroying themselves. They will all die, in any case, as all men must die . . . and the question remains: What will you choose? Consider it carefully. What kind of a life would your Anya wish you to live?"

Then they parted, and Sergei walked the paths of Valaam, letting Serafim's words blend with his own thoughts. In all his years of training, lusting for the blood of evil men, he had come to know his own darkness. Sergei finally understood why men and nations can rise up against each other—how each act of retribution, desperation, and ignorance fuels the tragic acts that follow.

As Sergei passed through the forest, his hatred, like any fire, finally extinguished itself. And when he finally surrendered his grip on this long-held mission, Sergei found in its place a troubled peace. In letting go of the past, he he had lost a part of his future. Before, he knew where he was headed, and why. Now his mission to kill his enemies, his vow of vengeance, had ended. No goals or purpose remained.

Sergei floated between heaven and earth, connected to neither.

37

Having trained every afternoon for all those years, Sergei now found a space opening in his days, in his mind, and in his life. A tremendous amount of energy was now liberated and pulsing within him. He experienced a quickening of thought, insight, and understanding. With his attention free from a long preoccupation, and this chapter of his life now complete, new possibilities rose into his mind.

Sergei had come to a turning point, a crossroads: He finally forgave himself for his human failings and accepted that he'd done the best he could on that day in the meadow—that despite his efforts, he was not able to save his family. This truth helped him make peace with the shadows of his past. For the first time since his family's death, he felt that he might have a new life to live.

The time had come to write a letter to Valeria. He sat down immediately, in the common room where he had spent countless hours in training, and wrote the words that flowed from his heart to his mind:

Dear Valeria,

I know that I have lost the right to call you Mother, but I continue to think of you that way, just as Anya will always be my beloved wife. In the time that has passed, I hope your heart has healed enough that this letter will not reopen old wounds but instead may bring gentler memories of love and of the family we were. I cherished what I found in your home. Overwhelmed by the loss of Anya, I later grieved losing you and Andreas as well.

I will not ask your forgiveness. I only send my love and gratitude for the kindness you showed to me during the happy times.

With abiding love, and prayers for your health,

Sergei

It was a long-overdue message. He did not expect a reply. Sending it was enough. He only hoped that Valeria might one day bring herself to read it.

38

THE NEXT TIME Sergei saw Serafim, the old monk took him completely by surprise. It was not a punch or kick this time, but it might as well have been. The first words Serafim spoke were, "You must leave the island, Sergei—and soon."

Sergei stood stunned, his mind regrouping. "Leave?" he asked. "Leave to go where?"

"I'll explain as we walk. When I'm done, I hope you will gather your belongings and say your good-byes."

Mystified, Sergei decided to keep his mouth closed and listen. The father began: "Do you recall when, several days ago, you asked me where I thought you might be going, and I said that we would speak of it later?"

"Yes, I do."

"Well, I now know. The time has come. I only just received the letter. They are gathering at the roof of the world."

BY EARLY AFTERNOON Sergei had packed his few things and said his farewells to the brothers at St. Avraam Rostov skete. They nodded, smiled, then turned back to their duties.

Before meeting Serafim at the island farm, Sergei sat for a few minutes in a silence made more sacred by their imminent parting. In that silence, Sergei contemplated all that Serafim had told him . . .

"Our purpose together is finished," the old monk had said. "But there are others who may be useful . . . a gathering of masters, all good and trusted friends. Each comes from a different religious tradition . . . They cherish their paths as I do mine. But they've transcended their reliance on conventional teachings and turned to the esoteric, hidden truths and internal practices. They explore the intertwining roots within every religion, the one river beneath the many wells.

"I can't be sure who will appear, but you may meet a master of the Sufi tradition . . . a Zen Buddhist roshi . . . a Taoist sage . . . a yogi of the Hindu path . . . a rabbi of the Jewish faith . . . a woman Kahuna from Hawaii . . . a nun and Christian mystic from Italy . . . a Sikh master . . ." Then Serafim smiled, adding, "And you will likely meet a man named George, who fits into none of the traditions, yet all of them. It is he who has called them together.

"There is a proverb favored by those in this fellowship: 'One Light, many lamps; one journey, many paths.' Each of these masters serves as such a lamp, bringing his or her own principles, perspectives, and practices to open doors to the world of spirit—the internal path of awakening—"

"Awakening to what?"

"To the transcendent," Serafim answered. "And in service of this great purpose, they meet in friendly debate to compare and contrast, to test, and to share with one another in free and open inquiry. Their goal, I believe, is to find the most central, core practices for body, for mind, for spirit—to begin a new, universal way free of cultural dogmas or trappings.

"I won't burden you with all their names, which you'll learn in good time. Just know that they will gather soon—in the next three months— which is why you cannot delay.

"The journey will be arduous," he added, "but you've made arduous journeys before."

"You haven't told me where I'm going," said Sergei.

"Yes—of course. Look here." Serafim reached into his robe and took out a map. "I've marked the route: You'll be riding to a point north of the Hindu Kush, in the region of the Pamirs, which some call the rooftop of the world. That high place, at the crossroads of India and Tibet, China and Persia, is where I send you in my stead—to the Fergana Valley, and a city called Margelan."

Serafim handed him a letter. "It is a brief introduction. Go to serve them . . . and to listen and learn. Consider this my parting gift.

"The timing seems too perfect for me to doubt the rightness of this opportunity," he continued. "This possibility fell into place only when you decided, of your own free will, to let go of your quest for retribution.

"Your decision to take a higher path justifies all that I've taught you over the years. In making that choice, Socrates—by not repeating my sad history—you've given me a gift whose value I cannot fully express."

SERAFIM HAD ANOTHER GIFT AS WELL—a sturdy mare, one of the few stabled on Valaam. With the approval of the island fathers, Serafim had also provided supplies and a hundred rubles, in case of need. "The mare is yours to keep," he said, "as long as she will carry you."

Sergei named her Paestka, which means "journey."

Father Serafim stood watching as Sergei cinched up a saddle that one of the brothers found. The old monk's eyes shone, and his skin was translucent, as if he were made not of flesh but of light.

Before Sergei mounted, he turned to say good-bye, but Father Serafim raised his hand to silence him. "For us, Socrates, there are no good-byes."

With a final look between them, Sergei Ivanov rode to the dock, boarded a ship, and vanished from the world of men.

Part Six

———

A

RISING

STORM

Talents are better nurtured in solitude,
but character is best formed
in the stormy billows of the world.

JOHANN WOLFGANG VON GOETHE

. 39 .

TWO YEARS PASSED. And on a perfect spring day in 1908 Sergei Ivanov reappeard, riding west to St. Petersburg. Although his name remained the same, the man himself had changed in ways both subtle and deep. This peaceful warrior breathed deeper, sat taller, and laughed easier. His eyes shone with an inner light. Beyond these outward signs, casual observers might think that little had happened to him in the town of Margelan. They would be vastly mistaken.

He knew their names now, and their hearts: Kanzaki . . . Chen . . . Chia . . . Yeshovitz . . . ben Musawir . . . Pria Singh . . . Naraj . . . Maria . . . and George, who had called them together.

After a difficult journey east, Sergei had served as their assistant and, later, a sort of apprentice. He listened and watched as they discussed different forms of meditation on images and inner sounds: chanting . . . breathing and concentration methods to amplify internal energy . . . inner work to open intuitive sight . . . hypnosis and working with the lower and higher mind . . . the three selves . . . from kirtan to kaballah, and the deeper truth within both the conventional and transcendental realms.

Those in the fellowship also practiced movements from various martial traditions, such as the slow-motion *T'aiji*, but such practice was aimed at efficient movement for vitality and health—for rebuilding, not destroying.

One day Yeshovitz and Naraj were debating a point, and Sergei found himself stepping into the fray. "I believe Yeshovitz has the more realistic view," Sergei said. Immediately, they asked him to leave for the day—for his audacity, he thought—but when he returned, they had decided to use him as an experimental subject: Sergei would practice each of the disciplines they agreed upon and report what he had experienced. So he came to understand and experience the results of these practices.

After some months had passed, he no longer recognized himself. His face had changed—lines of worry were replaced by a smooth, youthful glow. The old scar on his arm had nearly disappeared. His body felt like that of a child. Only his white hair remained to remind him of the past. But the past, and time itself, had become little more than a useful convention, an illusory idea—his attention now rested in the present moment, with his head in the clouds and feet on the ground.

There, in the city of Margelan at the roof of the world, Sergei had faced an initiation—a gauntlet of nine tests that gained him entrance into the fellowship as one of their own.

Then the time came to part. Each member of this fellowship carried new understandings and hope for humanity. They left with a certainty that for anyone truly interested, the so-called mystical states could become a normal part of human experience.

Sergei carried this realization lightly as he and Paestka entered St. Petersburg and considered his most immediate intentions: He would pay a visit to Father Serafim to share the gifts and blessings he'd received and to convey his gratitude. After that, he would find work, save money, and make his long-overdue journey across the sea.

But first he would visit Anya's grave.

Standing there, in the stillness of the meadow he had left so long ago, he gazed upon flowers now growing upon the mound of earth. A breeze caressed his face as he stood in silent communion with the love of his life.

Then a new impulse arose: He would visit with Valeria and Andreas. Sixteen years had passed since he had last seen them. If he had made peace with the past, they might have done the same.

In the early evening Sergei found a stable for Paestka and a much-needed grooming and feeding and rest. As he had years before, he visited a barber, had a long bath, and, completely open to whatever might follow, again appeared at Valeria's door.

He had certainly not expected a crying Valeria to throw her arms around him, speaking so quickly he could barely understand.

"Sergei! Sergei! My prayers have been answered. We never thought we would see you again! After your letter came—it must have been two or three years ago—I sent Andreas to Valaam, to find you, but you had gone. Oh, Sergei, I grieved so for Anya, but then I grieved for you too, and for how we parted. You've no idea how much I wanted to take back the words I had spoken. Oh, but you've come back to us! Can you forgive me, Sergei? How you must have suffered!"

Valeria began to cry again. Sergei reached around her aging shoulders and comforted her, and old wounds were healed.

Then, abruptly, Valeria's eyes opened wide. "Oh! Andreas doesn't know you're here. He will be so surprised! And Katya too—I didn't tell you—he is married, Sergei, and I have a grandchild, little Avrom, with another on the way."

Valeria was out of breath, but it didn't slow her down. "They will be home soon. I must make dinner, something special. Oh, Sergei, forgive me—I haven't let you say a word. You must tell me everything. Soon, when we are all together. And I have much to tell you too!" she called back as she rushed into the kitchen.

When Andreas arrived with his family, and he spied Sergei, he gave a joyous roar and a brotherly embrace. He too had changed over the years. Sergei guessed that Katya, a serene-looking, black-haired woman, now rounded with their second child, had much to do with this transformation. They made introductions, then Katya took Avrom away to change his diapers while Grandma made dinner and the men talked of many things.

Andreas began by telling Sergei of his own travels to Persia and his successful rug importing business. "And it wouldn't have been possible without your . . . well, we can discuss that later."

D URING DINNER, Andreas told Sergei, "Since you have been away, you may not know—the pogroms have continued under Tsar Nikolai—and on my travels I've seen terrible poverty and misery. It's been a golden age for those who have gold, Sergei, but the poor grow bitter, and there is growing talk of revolution. I fear for those who live comfortably here in St. Petersburg."

"All the more reason for you to consider emigrating with me to America."

Valeria took Sergei's hand and said, "In this I have not changed. I'm too set in my ways to leave the soil where I was born, and where my husband and daughter are buried."

A silence filled the room after that. It seemed the right time to ask, "May I take you to your daughter's grave?"

"Yes, I would like that," Valeria said with a sigh. "After all these years."

As soon as the dishes were cleared, Valeria sat down and said, "Now, Sergei, you must tell us about your life—all that has happened since our sad parting."

How does one convey the years, the life and depth and passion, into a few words told after a dinner meal? Sergei was doing his best to summarize his vow of retribution, and all the years of searching and preparation, ending on the island of Valaam, when Valeria interrupted—

"Oh! Sergei, with all this excitement . . . seeing you again—there is a letter for you from Valaam. We received it six months ago, and I saved it. Just a moment!"

Valeria rushed into her room then returned, handing him an envelope. He opened it and read:

Sergei Sergeievich:
　　I pray this letter finds you at the address you left with Father
Serafim. He would have wanted you to know that he passed from this

world last December. He was at peace with God. If I may say, I believe
that he remembered you with a certain fond regard.

Brother Yvgeny, skete St. Avraam Rostov

Sergei would not be going to Valaam after all.

In the space of a deep breath, he said a silent good-bye to his spiritual father, friend, and mentor. Blessings be upon you, Serafim, he thought. I am one of the many souls you saved.

Sergei would take more time later to reflect on his time with his old master, now residing with the other angels. When he looked up he said only, "A good friend has passed away."

AND WHAT ARE YOUR PLANS?" asked Andreas.

"Stay with us," Valeria interjected. "We can make room—"

Sergei smiled. "Perhaps for a little while, Mother—until I leave for America. I'll need to find employment, to earn my passage—"

"That won't be necessary," said Andreas with a broad smile. "Excuse me for just a moment . . ."

When he returned, Andreas placed three jewels on the table in front of Sergei, saying, "These will cover your passage and more—not that we're in a hurry to see you leave . . ."

Sergei looked down at the sparkling gems. "Andreas—these must be worth a great deal—I can't take your jewels."

Andreas laughed, Katya looked delighted, and Valeria was completely beside herself. Leaning forward, she said, "Sergei, these gems don't belong to Andreas; they belong to you."

"What? I don't understand."

"It was the clock," she said, as if those words revealed everything. Sergei's puzzled expression only made her smile more; then it faded as she explained, "Years ago, on that terrible day . . . after I sent you away . . . the clock fell from the mantel and shattered. I was so distraught that I saw nothing. "

Andreas took over: "When I returned home and saw the smashed clock, I thought there might have been a robbery. I rushed through the apartment, found Mother in her room, learned what had happened . . .

"Only later did I return to the sitting room to clean up. That's when I found them: Mixed with the clock fragments, an assortment of gemstones were scattered on the floor. I placed them in a cup and set them in the cupboard. In the back of my mind I knew that they were valuable, but neither of us could think about much of anything just then."

Sergei was starting to grasp it. "So my grandfather had hidden gems . . . inside the clock?"

Andreas nodded. "Twenty-four of them."

No one spoke as Sergei absorbed this revelation. His thoughts traveled back to the time he first found the clock and read his grandfather's note. It had said, *Always remember that the real treasure is within.* Sergei smiled as he imagined how Grandpa Heschel must have enjoyed writing those words, pleased by their double meaning.

He heard Andreas say, "The gems are your inheritance, Sergei. And you can't imagine our pleasure passing them on to you."

Andreas looked at his mother, and at Katya, then said awkwardly, "I must tell you, Sergei, we kept them safe for five years, but when we heard nothing—we didn't even know if you were alive—we sold two of the smaller gems . . . to help me get started in my business, and to help with expenses. Now we have money enough, and I can repay—"

Sergei raised his hand to silence Andreas. "Please, say no more of it."

Andreas started to shake his head when Valeria interrupted. "Sergei, my son is too proud to ask. But if you could consider a gift of two more, for the growing family—"

"Of course," Sergei said.

Valeria brought out a small velvet bag she had made, and she poured the gems onto the table between them. The afternoon sun glinted off their facets, causing some to sparkle a translucent green, others a deep rich red, and the clear gems diffracted rainbows.

Knowing that Andreas would take only the two smaller gemstones,

Sergei selected two stones of generous size and slid them across the table to Andreas—then two more. "For your family."

And it was done.

Valeria put the remaining eighteen jewels back into the velvet pouch and set them before Sergei, who asked, "Do you have any idea of their value?"

"We sold the two stones to Yablanovich, a jeweler and trusted friend of your grandfather," Andreas answered. "He gave us sixteen hundred rubles for one gem and two thousand for the other—and those were the smallest in your collection. The rest he appraised. I can still recall it clearly.

"When I asked him the value of the stones, Yablanovich took an eyepiece out of his shirt pocket, examined the stones one by one—he turned them, weighed each—and then he said, 'I cannot tell you their value—that is for each person to decide—but I can tell you something of their worth in the marketplace. So let me put it this way. Today, you can purchase an excellent meal in a fine eating establishment for twenty-five kopeks. This stone,' he said, pointing to the smallest ruby, 'would buy you three such meals a day for many years. And this one,' he told me, touching an emerald, 'will purchase far more. As for the gems of alexandrite—they are more valuable than diamonds, and if you live modestly, they will meet your needs here or in America for the rest of your life.'

"You are a wealthy man, Sergei," Andreas concluded.

WHEN VALERIA AND KATYA had taken the dishes to the kitchen, Andreas drew Sergei aside and said in a more serious tone, "This may not be a good time, Sergei, but . . . could you tell me exactly what happened . . . that day in the meadow? I've wanted to ask you all these years . . . if it's not too painful . . ."

"It will always be painful," Sergei replied. "But you should hear it all." So he told Andreas how his sister had died and what Zakolyev had done afterward. Seeing Andreas's face turn ashen, Sergei regretted saying so much.

"Thank you for telling me," Andreas said, staring down at the floor. "I would have always wondered . . ." He looked up and added, "Mother will also want to know, and now I can tell her the truth but . . . I'll spare the details."

Sergei nodded.

Then Katya returned and the couple retired, leaving the rest of the evening to Valeria. She and Sergei spoke long into the night, bridging the years that had separated them.

. 40 .

THE NEXT AFTERNOON Sergei took Valeria and Andreas to visit the meadow and grave site. They sat quietly together with their own thoughts and prayers. Clouds passed slowly on the spring wind and their emotions changed like the sky.

To Sergei, Anya felt so close that he could see her behind his closed eyelids. He saw her as she was then and would always be, forever young. He heard her voice and the sound of her laughter. He sensed her touch and knew that while he lived, she would always be with him, until they met at last in a place beyond this life.

On their return to the city the three of them spoke little, but Valeria reached out and took Sergei's hand—then murmured something so softly he nearly missed hearing it. "Those poor babies . . ."

"*What?*" he said. "What did you say, Mother?"

She answered in a sad, wistful voice, "Oh, I was just thinking about the babies who died with their mother before they ever had a chance to be born . . . how they now rest in the meadow—"

"Babies?" Sergei interrupted. "I don't understand."

"I—I thought you knew, Sergei. Oh—I'm so sorry, you didn't—"

"Valeria, tell me."

"Anya had confided in me, but . . . she didn't want to disappoint you if the midwife was wrong. The woman seemed certain that Anya was carrying twins. I know that she was planning to tell you . . . I thought she already had."

Sergei stared blankly. *Babies.* Two lives inside Anya. Sergei's mind raced back in time, stitching together words and images: Valeria remarking about the size of Anya's swollen abdomen. Anya joking, "With so many kicks, I must have a dance troupe inside." Then the horrific image, the gaping wound, the bloody tangle of intestines and . . .

Sergei had seen the death of one child; then he had been knocked unconscious. He had found only one . . . If there had been a second child, he would have seen it—

And so would have Dmitri Zakolyev.

In an instant Sergei knew the wonderful, terrible truth: Another child, a twin boy, might still be alive. After all these years . . . in Zakolyev's sight, within his reach. He could not be certain, but there was a chance—a good chance—that they had a second child, a son who still lived.

These revelations unfolded in a few heartbeats. Valeria would have assumed that both infants died with their mother. It was all he would ever let her know, unless he found his child and brought him home.

"Sergei? . . . *Sergei?*" Valeria's voice snapped him back.

"I'm sorry," he said. "I was just thinking . . . of Anya. And I was surprised to hear about the two babies. It's hard news, even now . . . to know what might have been."

"Yes," she said with a sigh. "What might have been . . ."

SOMETIMES we make choices, and sometimes they are made for us. Once or twice in a lifetime, we grasp how all that happened before has led us to this moment. Sergei now felt an urgent new sense of purpose: If his son lived, he would find him. To do so, he had to find Zakolyev.

But what would he tell Valeria?

In truth, Sergei was no longer driven by hatred or a personal mission to use violence to stop the evils in the world. As Serafim had reminded him, Sergei had neither the responsibility nor the authority to play God's assassin. But he would need a credible reason for his abrupt departure—one that did not generate in Valeria any hopes that might later be crushed. So he would tell her the truth—that he was leaving to search for Zakolyev and his men. His official motive—stopping evil men from doing more harm—was one that Valeria would support despite her concerns for his safety.

When Sergei told Valeria about his change of plans, she started to protest, but then only nodded sadly, and said, "Please be careful, Sergei, my son." She realized that he might not return for months or even years—and while neither of them spoke of it, they both understood that they might never meet again.

As Paestka carried Sergei south across the rolling hills and plains, he took stock of the situation, drawing upon his past searches. It was not likely that one man on horseback could find a band of marauders that struck quickly, left no witnesses, then returned to hiding somewhere in the vast expanse of Ukraine. He could only trust that his senses, refined by life in the wild, years of contemplation, and his intuitive powers might now show him the way. He would ride south to pick up a trail of rumors, smoke, and tears.

When he found them, he would use stealth and strategy, observing from a distance to discern their numbers and routines. He would seek out his son, if he was to be found, and wait for the right moment to speak with him alone. Such a plan wouldn't be easy, but it was far better than riding boldly into camp and starting a bloodbath that might endanger his child.

Beyond that, Sergei would just have to see what unfolded. Only a fool underestimated his adversaries. And as Serafim would have said, "All plans are tentative."

THAT SPRING OF 1908, fifteen-year-old Paulina disobeyed her father's wishes for the first time: She told her trusted Konstantin the long-held secret. She hoped that sharing her burden with him might somehow lift the darkness that had recently descended upon her.

As she passed Konstantin on the way to morning practice, Paulina slipped him a note she had printed in letters he had taught her: "Meet me in our special place. Before afternoon training."

Konstantin looked up from the note, enlivened by the prospect of a few minutes alone with her. He tried to imagine a future with Paulina, but it had never quite taken shape in his mind. How could it? He had nothing to offer her—no possessions except for the clothes on his back, remnants discarded by others in the camp, plunder once worn by murdered men.

During the break between training sessions, as soon as Father Dmitri had left to talk with some men, Paulina ran into the forest and across the footbridge over the stream that tumbled down the falls. There in their small cave hollowed out of the thicket, where they once hid as children, Konstantin was waiting for her.

In the few minutes before they would be missed, Paulina told Konstantin to lean close. His heart quickened as she placed her hand upon his shoulder and whispered in his ear: "Years ago, my father told me a secret I was never to reveal: Elena is not my mother . . ."

She waited while he absorbed this revelation, unaware that he already knew this. Then she added, "My real mother was killed by a monster with white hair, and . . . and ever since that day, I've had nightmares about a white-haired wizard who can paralyze with his voice, coming to kill me. I struggle to kill it before it can speak, but it always utters one word. I can never remember the word, but in the dream I die."

Her voice trembled as she whispered these words. It was not likely that anyone would overhear them, but Paulina leaned close because she enjoyed the nearness; she needed it.

"Surely it is only a story the Ataman told you," he responded.

Paulina shook her head. "Father Dmitri has told me that the monster is real. He is a man named Sergei Ivanov."

She moved back and watched Konstantin closely, searching for a reaction—a sign to justify the secret shared, the risk taken: surprise, curiosity, even disbelief—anything.

He only furrowed his brow.

"What is it, Kontin?"

Distracted by the memory taking shape, he said, "It's just that . . . I'm troubled to learn about your mother's death . . . and how it happened . . ."

He wasn't telling her something. Of this, Paulina was certain. She started to speak, to question him, when suddenly she jumped to her feet in alarm. "Oh! The time—I have to go!" Paulina scrambled quickly out of the thicket. Yergovich would be waiting, and angry. He would not report her tardiness, but if her father had returned . . .

With that panicked thought, Paulina raced back across the footbridge over the stream and back to the camp.

KONSTANTIN WAS STILL THINKING about the name, Sergei Ivanov. He had overheard it before, in a conversation long ago. He recalled the name for good reason: That man might be his father.

Konstantin had always assumed he was one of the orphans whose parents had been killed—until he'd heard Shura muttering to one of the men about Sergei Ivanov. Konstantin had listened carefully and caught a few words: "one infant killed . . . a boy . . . the other taken." Konstantin had the sense that they were talking about him, since he'd left Shura and Tomorov only moments before and then sneaked back to eavesdrop through a crack in the log wall.

This new revelation left him with no choice. He had to stop Paulina from hurting this Sergei Ivanov. But how could he tell her? If she spoke of it to Father Dmitri, the consequences were unpredictable and dangerous. Besides, he was not certain that Ivanov was his father. Everything could fall apart over a few words he might have misunderstood.

Speaking out, even to Paulina, could mean his own death. Yet how could he remain silent?

T HAT NIGHT, as Paulina was just drifting to sleep, Father Dmitri entered her room, sat on her bed, and gazed at her for a long time before he woke her. "Paulina, you've been a good and obedient daughter . . . you have made me proud. You don't live like the ordinary girls, because you are not ordinary. You have special gifts and a rare destiny. Like your father."

He paused to let these words, as kind as any he had spoken, make their impression, then he reached behind his neck and removed something Paulina had never noticed before. He handed her a silver locket on a chain. She took it, not knowing what to do. "It is a gift," he said, "to celebrate the day you were born to me."

A single tear slipped down Paulina's cheek. She turned away and wiped her eyes as Father Dmitri spoke again. "Open it," he said, pointing to a small clasp.

Inside the locket Paulina found a tiny, faded photograph of two faces—a man with a dark beard and a pale woman. As she gazed at the photograph, her father spoke again. "They are my mother and father—your grandparents." Then he added, "Do you remember what I told you about the wizard who murdered your mother? The man Sergei Ivanov?"

She nodded.

"He also killed your grandparents—these faces you see in the locket. It all happened on the same day." He drew a long breath, and Paulina saw that even now he was grieving their loss. She reached out to touch her father's hand. "Oh, Father . . ."

He pulled his hand away and spoke rapidly. "We all lived happily in a small Cossack settlement. I had to go away on various duties, so I left you with your mother and grandparents in the safety of the camp. You were only an infant.

"I returned early from my business and found you with Shura, who told me that your mother and grandparents had left you and gone for a ride to a meadow by a lake. I decided to join them. Just as I rode into the meadow, I was surrounded by armed men who bound me . . ."

Trembling with rage, he continued, "As I struggled to free myself, Sergei Ivanov raped and killed your mother, then turned on your grandparents and he cut them down. I've waited until now to tell you the whole story, but you had to know, because of . . . a duty I'm going to ask of you.

"Long ago, I vowed to find and kill this monster who took your mother, who took them all . . ." Paulina had never seen Father Dmitri cry, and the effect was devastating. "I have men of my own," he managed to continue, "hard men like Korolev. But it's not for them to avenge the death of my wife and parents. That duty has fallen on me, as a matter of blood and honor."

He looked into her eyes and added, "I grow older . . . and I won't live forever . . . so I pass this torch, this honor, to you." He studied her expression before explaining: "Sergei Ivanov knows my face . . ."

Zakolyev paused to let Paulina grasp his meaning—that as a young woman and a stranger to this man, she would have a decided advantage, a tactical edge. My child, my future, he thought, will hunt down the monster who has haunted me all these years . . .

Then he added, "If I had a son, it would be his mission; instead I have a gifted daughter. Now you know why you've been training all these years; why I have such faith in you; and why I gave you this locket: so you'll never forget who killed your mother and your grandparents."

"I won't forget," said Paulina, her eyes cold and hard—like those of her father, Dmitri Zakolyev.

THE NEXT MORNING Paulina rose early for practice. On the way to meet Old Yergovich at the barn, she saw Shura leaving her cabin to fetch water. Realizing that Shura must know the truth about her mother's and grandparents' death, she called out to the older woman.

Shura set down her buckets and approached, always glad to see Paulina. But when Shura's smile abruptly faded, Paulina turned to glance behind her and saw Father Dmitri standing by the cabin, watching both of them. He gestured to Paulina that she should get to training. When Paulina turned back to Shura, the woman had already picked up the buckets and hurried away without glancing back.

That day Paulina had one of her best practices, defeating multiple attackers. In years past the men had held back, treating her like a novelty; now they sparred as roughly with her as they did with each other. She got some bruises and sprains, but they healed quickly enough.

The men outmatched her in reach and strength, but even Great Yergovich—who could squat under a small horse and lift the kicking animal off the ground—could not get his hands on her. Paulina was more supple and far quicker than any of them. She seemed to be able to see into their bodies, sense their point of weakness, then throw them off balance again and again. What surprised them the most was her power. Paulina could kick like a horse. The force that came from her didn't seem possible in a woman her size. It was as if she were drawing her power from the Earth itself.

Her hands, feet, and elbows found the pressure points that, when struck, would render the strongest man unable to move. If a fighter tried to grab her or throw a punch, she would punch a nerve in his arm.

If a man kicked at her with his right leg, he would find the left one swept out from under him.

Paulina had no real desire to kill anyone—not even the white-haired monster who had haunted her dreams. She wasn't at all certain she could bring herself to break his neck, crush his windpipe, or stab a knife through his heart. Yet this mission meant everything to her father, so she did her best to prepare herself.

When she had asked why Father Dmitri didn't just use a rifle or pistol, he'd said, "A rifle can miss or misfire; so can a pistol. The hands or a knife are the surest of weapons at close range . . . and the most satisfying."

Satisfying. A strange word, she thought. And sometimes a strange man, she realized. But he was, after all, the leader of a Cossack band, and an expert in such things. Still, elements of doubt began to seep into her mind. Paulina's life had become a complex puzzle . . . and she was just beginning to notice the missing pieces.

Finally Zakolyev knew that none of the men could defeat her—except perhaps for Korolev, who still refused to "spar with a child." It was just as well: Korolev, if provoked, might go for the kill. Zakolyev had enough of a challenge keeping the blue-eyed giant away from his daughter for purposes other than combat. So, despite this affront to his authority, Ataman Zakolyev ignored Korolev's avoidance of sparring duty. He did this for Paulina. He did everything for Paulina.

ATAMAN DMITRI ZAKOLYEV AWOKE in another sweat-drenched night terror. The cries faded only when his eyes snapped open. A wisp of memory appeared, then was gone. He rubbed his forehead, trying in vain to erase the ghostly afterimage, dreams of the dead . . . the voice of an old schoolmate . . . the face of a girl he deflowered . . . everyone whispering, walking away . . . a child receding . . . a day in the meadow . . . confusing flashes . . . all because of Sergei Ivanov, the monster who killed his wife.

He moaned aloud, then looked around to be sure no one had heard. "Dreams, only dreams," he muttered, rising, pacing.

Soon Sergei Ivanov would die at Paulina's hands. It had to be soon.

STANDING ALONE in the darkness, remembering her father's words, Paulina touched her locket. She sighed as she looked up into the night sky, wishing her father had never told her of her mother's death or her mission. Her innocence had faded; along with it, her belief in a world of love and kindness. Now Konstantin seemed to be growing distant, and this mission . . . this mission that clouded her future . . .

After that, her rare smiles masked a growing melancholy and a terrible resolve—because she had accepted the torch he had passed, and made her father's mission her own. Aware of his suffering in the night as he muttered and moaned in his sleep, Paulina now suffered confusing dreams of her own—a mysterious, changing landscape of forest and meadow . . . the sad face of a woman who might have been herself, only older . . . The dream-woman's mouth moved, but Paulina didn't understand her words. Sometimes she saw the white-haired man, but his back was always toward her, so she never saw his face.

She awoke to a world no less confusing. Now that her body had started to fill out, the men looked at her differently—particularly Korolev, who made her skin crawl. She tolerated his presence by pretending he was only a ghost. As long as her father maintained his authority, she would be safe—and her fighting skills gave her less to fear from any man.

A few days later, as Paulina was about to enter the cabin, she heard Oxana speaking in hushed tones to Elena. Paulina stopped to hear her say, "Yes, the Ataman has grown 'concerned' and 'anxious' . . . and another of our men, Leontev, was killed in the last raid . . . Will these purgings never end?" Oxana quickly added, "I tell you this only out of love and concern for Ataman Zakolyev."

"Of course," said Elena.

When Paulina entered, the women changed the subject abruptly and Oxana hurriedly left. The camp had changed, Paulina noticed—people skulking about, speaking in whispers, wearing false faces. Elena was especially careful. Then Paulina wondered: Have they changed, or am I only just waking up?

Once, when Paulina was younger, she had asked what the men did out on patrol. She was told only: "Patrols for the tsar."

She wanted to ask Shura more about this, but she never seemed to get the chance. Shura would nod respectfully when they passed each other, but rarely spoke more than a few words. So Paulina was surprised when, on the day after the men had returned to camp, the old woman stopped and looked like she wanted to say something.

"What is it?" Paulina asked.

Shura just stood there, looking at her.

"Shura?"

The older woman looked slowly right and left. Then she said, "I was there . . . soon after your birth. I nursed you."

A little embarrassed to think of such things, Paulina retorted, "Yes, you've told me—"

Shura glanced around then said, "Paulina . . . you do care about me, don't you?"

"Yes, of course, but I don't understand—"

Again Shura interrupted her. "You wouldn't want to get me into trouble, would you? If I told you something, could you keep it secret?"

"Even from Father Dmitri?"

"Especially from . . . him," Shura answered, shuffling anxiously. Then she seemed to make a decision. "Things are not as they seem. The mark on your neck—"

Paulina touched her neck to feel the raised birthmark. "My birthmark? Like my father—?"

"Yes—no!" said Shura. "Not like his. It was a stick from the fire—I can still hear the screams . . ."

"What are you saying?" Paulina cried, louder than she had intended. But when she saw the frightened look on Shura's face, now pale, Paulina's voice softened. "Shura, I don't understand . . ."

Shura only babbled on: "So tiny . . . when they brought you. Such a precious child . . . you are not like him. He has killed so many . . ."

Then Shura saw one of the men approaching and scurried off, leaving a shaken Paulina to sort out what the old woman had told her.

. 42 .

By summer 1909, Sergei had searched for more than a year without finding any solid clues to Zakolyev's whereabouts. He had found the charred remains of isolated cabins and several farmhouses that might have been Zakolyev's handiwork, and he had marked each location on a map, but they revealed no pattern he could discern.

One night Sergei dreamed that Paestka and he were a tiny speck, no bigger than a gnat eternally wandering across a huge map of Ukraine, looking for another dot that always moved away from them. He awoke in frustration. He was beginning to think that Zakolyev might have moved his camp to Siberia or to the north.

No, he reasoned, they had to be in Ukraine, where atrocities against the Jewish people continued. But Ukraine, stretching more than a thousand kilometers from the north to the south and from west to east, tested his strong heart and will. He might as well have been searching for a coin buried in a forest.

Sergei zigzagged west then east and ever southward, toward Kiev, the center of Ukraine. He followed rumors like a scent but found only trails of smoke that dissipated in the wind.

Avoiding the larger city centers, Sergei sought out isolated cabins, farms, and small settlements, where Zakolyev's band was more likely to strike. Near one such settlement he spoke with an elderly Jewish man who, lacking a horse or mule, was pulling his own cart. The old man offered to share a little bread from his meager stores.

"Thank you, but I need information more than food. Have you heard of any recent pogroms?"

"Who hasn't?" the elder replied. "In settlements outside Kiev, Minsk, Poltava, and elsewhere, horsemen appear from nowhere. Wolves dressed like men. No, worse than wolves, because they kill their own kind—men, women, children, it's all the same to them. For what reason? What reason?"

When Sergei asked him where such marauders were last sighted, his eyes turned down and he would not or could not speak. He only shook his head slowly, back and forth.

As WINTER CAME, Sergei's patience grew thin. He rode across frozen soil, wrapped in his long burka, leaning into the wind. Grim and haggard, he pushed Paestka onward. But doubts plagued him.

For all his skill and discernment, Sergei could not track men by sniffing the air, nor could he see the faces of men in a bent twig. He needed tangible signs, omens, clues—a sense of direction. Until he found something tangible he could only follow rumors to gossip, and gossip to settlements, where he might find witnesses. In the meantime, his questions were answered by puzzled looks and fingers pointing in different directions.

He fasted and prayed for a clear path to his son, but no sign appeared. Then he thought, Maybe I'm asking the wrong question. His breathing changed, and he descended into a deep trance and lost all sense of his body. In that state he asked, *Where is Dmitri Zakolyev?*

The answer came in a form quite different from the one he expected. Out of the void, the face of Dmitri Zakolyev flickered before him—the same sallow skin, blond hair, and dead eyes. He had not imagined that face; he had actually *seen* it—and he felt the full force of Zakolyev's torment and madness. He felt it as his own.

At that exact moment, as Dmitri Zakolyev lay sleeping, the face of Sergei Ivanov suddenly loomed before him. He awoke in a panic, seeing Sergei the Monster standing over him. He gasped for breath, his eyes wide, peering into the darkness. The face of his enemy showed no anger but something closer to . . . pity. Then the face vanished.

Zakolyev rose quickly and paced frantically, pounding his head with his fist. A momentary impulse arose, to tell his daughter the truth. But what was the truth? If only he could remember . . .

When they were children, Konstantin and Paulina were almost inseparable. Now Konstantin cherished each brief opportunity to meet—like the time he found Paulina between training sessions, sitting with her feet in the cold stream above the falls, not far from their hiding place. He sat down next to her, removed his shoes, and let his bare feet join hers in the brisk waters. In that moment, he nearly asked her to run away with him. But words failed him—he had no idea where to begin. So he said nothing, out of cowardice, out of love.

Paulina now looked at her Konstantin in a way that made her blush at times. She had seen one of the men with Oxana, out behind the barn. It had seemed coarse and crude, with the noises they made.

But now she wasn't so certain. It was as if her mind and body could not agree on this, the end of innocence. Paulina had no one with whom she could share her inner turmoil, not even Konstantin. Especially not Konstantin.

ONE MORNING after Elena had left the cabin, Paulina opened her locket and was gazing at the faces of her grandparents when Father Dmitri passed by her room and said, "Get to practice. Yergovich will be waiting."

Paulina sighed. Yergovich was always there, waiting. One day she would rise earlier and get to the barn before him. But not today. She was too tired—she felt off balance, cranky, and . . . something else she couldn't name.

As Father Dmitri was about to leave. Paulina pointed to the photograph and said, "Father, I've been curious . . . you don't look at all like your father—your hair is light and his is dark, and—"

"Do not trouble me with such nonsense!" he said. "Just remember who killed them, and increase your efforts in training!" He slammed the cabin door.

Hurt and angry at this unjust rebuff, Paulina trained so furiously that morning that she pulled a muscle in her arm while throwing Great Yergovich. She flinched with a stab of pain.

"What's wrong, little one?" he asked.

"It's nothing, Bear—just a strain. I'll be all right; don't tell my father." She tried to lift her arm, then bit her lip.

"No, it is not all right," he said. "Go put your arm in the stream until you cannot feel it. Then rest."

"No rest!" she cried. "I need to train harder!"

"First you soak your arm, then we'll see."

"First you soak your head!" she cried, running off too fast for the Bear to catch her.

Paulina sat alone in her room, as depressed as she could remember.

Rubbing her arm, she decided that maybe she should put it into the cold stream. It would take her mind off her father's anger. She had no idea why she had displeased him with a simple question. He was the one who had given her the locket in the first place—and it was a natural question. But apparently not one he wanted to hear . . .

She turned to find Father Dmitri standing in the doorway of their simple cabin, looking disheveled and distraught. Paulina silently chastised herself for losing control. She wanted to apologize, but something held her back. Why should she apologize? For what?

She just stood there, staring at the floor until he spoke. "Paulina, I'm sorry I spoke with you harshly. I didn't want to talk about your grandparents because it brings back too many terrible memories."

He came and sat on her bed. His voice was hoarse with emotion as he said, "I know I bear little resemblance to my father, but not every child looks like his parents. It's lucky that you do not look like me. You are fortunate to resemble your mother. Still, you and I share a birthmark . . ."

He pulled back his straw-colored hair to reveal a red mark on his neck, like the one she bore.

"We are the same blood, you and I," he said, touching her hair. "That is why I've trusted you to . . . why you need to train even harder. I remind you that Sergei Ivanov is not only a well-trained fighter; his voice also has the power to deceive and enchant . . . make you believe that earth is sky and black is white. So when you meet him, you cannot give him a chance to speak his lies or he will confuse and then kill you." Father Dmitri had told her this so many times she had memorized his words.

When he turned and left her, Paulina touched the raised mark on her neck. She hated the monster Sergei Ivanov for making her father suffer. One day she would find him. One day he would pay.

SEVERAL DAYS LATER, during an afternoon practice, Paulina was frightened to find blood on her pants and on her leg. Yergovich excused her without another word; he must have thought it was serious too. She ran from the barn back to her cabin and tried to find the wound. She wasn't hurting—just a little cramp deep in her belly. She wondered if it was some kind of illness.

Shura entered the cabin a few minutes later. "Yergovich told me," she said—and she was smiling, which only confused Paulina more. "It's normal, means you are a woman, now—no longer a girl. About time; you're later than most. The bleeding will happen every month. Now go change your pants. For a day you will probably need to train lighter." Shura gave her a few pieces of cloth and said, "When you bleed, put some of these up in between your legs." Then she turned and left before Paulina could ask her about anything else.

What other mysteries don't I know? she wondered. What else have they not told me? She touched her neck, recalling what Shura had said about a burning stick.

THE NEXT DAY Paulina fell ill with chills and fever. She couldn't keep her food down. Her head spun, and she couldn't even stand. She had never been so sick. Elena avoided her, but Old Shura came and put cool cloths on Paulina's forehead, touched her cheek, and made warm drinks that tasted awful.

Hazy images passed through her mind in that netherworld between waking and sleeping. There was something she wanted to ask Shura, but she couldn't think of it . . . Then other questions arose that she had never thought to ask . . . about herself and the world around her. What does my future hold? How many years will I spend hunting a man who might not even be alive?

She needed to see Kontin—to talk with him, to take his hand, to look into his dark eyes . . . He was her eyes and ears, her connection to the world—a world outside the barn, her purpose, her prison . . .

Her reveries were interrupted by a harsh voice. "Get out of bed!" said Father Dmitri, standing stiffly in the doorway, staring at her. "You have to train, if only a little!"

Paulina tried hard to rise but fell back and slept.

When she next opened her eyes, a wet cloth lay across her feverish brow. She looked up to see Konstantin sitting on her bed, stroking her hair. "Kontin!" she whispered. "What if my father finds you here?"

"Shhhh," he said. "He's away on . . . patrol." He sat with her, and his smile lifted her spirits, even though it was a sad smile. She closed her eyes to save his image as he spoke softly to her with a tenderness she had not heard before.

"Paulina," he began in a whispered breath, leaning close to her, his breath in her ear, his hand stroking her hair. "You once told me a secret. Now I'll tell you one so you will know that I trust you . . . and that I care." He took a deep breath and looked into the distance. "If you share what I'm about to tell you with anyone, it will mean my death . . ."

Paulina, half in and half out of delirium, murmured, "You'll never die . . . always here with me . . ."

"No, Paulina, listen—please! I need to tell you now, and you have to believe me! You've been kept in the dark about so many things—I don't know all of it. But you can't kill Sergei Ivanov—"

Konstantin turned back to Paulina. She was fast asleep.

As KONSTANTIN LEFT Paulina to confused dreams, Zakolyev and his men were thundering down on a small, isolated farm. The farmer Yitschok had been urged by friends in a nearby town to move closer, where there might be help should trouble come, but Yitschok had disregarded their advice. "What is one to do?" he'd said with a shrug. "The Pale is large. They have not come anywhere near. And would I be safer near a settlement?" His friends only shook their heads; Yitschok was right—if these murderers came, there would be no safety anywhere.

Zakolyev's band murdered Yitschok, and his wife and children. And Korolev did more than his share before the woman died. Zakolyev's men set the farmhouse aflame. Sullen, they moved mechanically, no longer under any illusions that they were serving the Mother Church or the Tsar—only the Ataman's will.

An argument broke out when some of the men wanted to take the children and others didn't. Zakolyev cut them off. "Kill them. Now. Do it quickly!" His version of mercy, and they obeyed.

Before they torched the cabin, Zakolyev's band confiscated anything of value. Later, the Ataman would search through every trunk saved from the fire, rifling through photographs and other personal items. But today he found a special prize—one of the finest horses he had ever seen, deep chestnut, wild eyes—a warhorse if he had ever seen one.

As flames danced from the farmhouse behind them, lighting the evening sky, Ataman Zakolyev laughed. In a manic mood, he slipped a halter over the frightened stallion and announced, "I name him Vozhd—Chieftain!"

All was well for another moment, until the fool Gumlinov blurted out, "He is indeed a great horse, Ataman Zakolyev—but of course you recall that my horse has also been called Vozhd these past three years. Surely we cannot both have a horse with the same—"

Gumlinov's words stuck in his throat when he saw Zakolyev's expression—abruptly calm, almost serene as he approached Gumlinov's horse, joking to his trusted man, "Well, thank goodness you are named Gumlinov instead of Zakolyev, or people would have trouble telling us apart." This broke the tension, and the men, including Gumlinov, bellowed with nervous laughter.

The laughter died as Zakolyev drew his saber and with one stroke sliced through the knee of Gumlinov's horse, completely severing the leg. With a shriek, the shocked animal tried to rear up but instead toppled over, its severed leg spurting blood. As the animal whinnied in agony, a horrified Gumlinov stumbled backward, his eyes darting from his suffering horse to Zakolyev.

The rest of the men stared in silence, their mouths open. They had seen the Ataman do many strange things, but this—cruelty to a horse— was sacrilege, and their Cossack blood boiled.

So it was that the last of the mortar holding together Zakolyev's mind began to crumble. He picked up the severed leg as if it were a piece of wood, and said in a calm, lighthearted tone, "At least now we will be able to tell our two horses apart." Tossing the leg over his shoulder, the Ataman walked to his old horse and mounted, gripping the halter rope that held his new steed. He called down to Gumlinov, "Better find a new name for your horse—or better yet, find a new horse to name."

Zakolyev wheeled around, and the others followed, leaving Gumlinov to put the poor beast out of its misery. Soon the dead and bloodied horse lay at Gumlinov's feet. Twenty meters beyond lay the burning pyre of another family of Jews. Then Gumlinov lifted his saddle over his shoulder and started walking toward an old mare they had let out of the corral.

A loyal member of the band for fifteen years, Gumlinov did not dare to kill Dmitri Zakolyev; but he would love the man who did.

He had decided not to follow the others to their next raid farther north—not on a broken-down, swaybacked horse. Let them butcher the next village without his help. "I'm tired of killing horses," he said, "tired of killing Jews."

D**URING HER FATHER'S ABSENCE**, Paulina grew strong enough to get out of bed and limber up. She had always liked stretching; it made her feel like a cat.

She missed Konstantin. She wanted to feel his hand stroke her hair again—or had she just imagined it? Maybe it was only a dream, she thought. But he had said something to her; she could still remember his breath in her ear. Was it something about her father? She felt angry then, without knowing why.

The next day she asked Elena, "Have you ever seen Konstantin with any of the other girls?"

"I really don't know," Elena said curtly, "but I don't think so."

Paulina was relieved but wary. She placed little trust in Elena's words. The woman was no more than her father's servant—always formal and distant, ever so careful with the Ataman's daughter—as if Paulina were a duty like cleaning and cooking. Elena didn't care about her; that was clear. Then why did she pretend? Why did everyone pretend?

Paulina felt like she lived in a cabin of secrets, in a camp of lies.

. 44 .

In April of 1910, as his search continued from village to village, Sergei rounded a hill and saw in the distance the still-smoldering ruins of a small farm. The stench called forth memories of the Abramovich cabin those many years ago. For a moment he felt physically sick with grief for those buried beneath the rubble.

Riding closer, he spied a man standing near the ruins, stooped over by grief, his head bowed in prayer. Dismounting, Sergei walked the last thirty meters to avoid startling the older man, who might not welcome a mounted rider at the moment—especially one who looked like a Cossack. As Sergei approached, he continued scanning the ground for tracks.

When Sergei drew near, he stopped and stood respectfully, waiting until the grieving man looked up, at last aware of Sergei's presence.

"I'm sorry," Sergei said. "Were they relations?"

"Are we not all related?"

"Yes, I believe we are." This old man reminded Sergei of his grandfather Heschel.

"They were my friends. Now they are ashes."

"Did you see what happened . . . the men who did this?"

"I was riding to see Yitschok and his good wife . . . and his three children . . ." He sighed and after a long pause added, "and as my cart approached, I saw smoke in the distance. I hurried to help, thinking that the barn might be burning. But then—before the farm came into sight—I heard the shouts of men, then . . . a woman's scream . . . and the children . . . oh, the children!" He held his head in his hands.

"You heard men? How many?" Sergei asked, drawing him back to the present.

"How many? I don't know . . . maybe ten. I only saw them from a distance. I was hiding . . . like a coward—"

"Like a wise man," Sergei said. "You saw them ride away?"

"Yes." The man shivered then shook his head sadly.

"Which way were they riding? Please. It's important."

The man hesitated, then pointed to the southwest.

Sergei led Paestka twenty meters in that direction. His pulse quickened when he came upon the hoofprints of at least ten horses—the freshest trail he had found since his search began. If Zakolyev's band had done this, they might have only an hour's lead—two at the most.

Before riding off, he returned to the old man. "Can you describe any of them?"

"No, I was hiding. But there was one who seemed taller than the rest—a giant. That's all I know."

"Thank you. I'm so sorry about your friends. Do you need anything before I go?"

"Nothing you can give, I'm afraid. I will go and tell the others. They will come. We live in a settlement twenty kilometers to the south. If you ever come there, ask for Heitzik."

Old Heitzik nodded in farewell, and was about to leave, when he faltered, clutched at his chest, and fell.

Sergei ran to him.

"It . . . it's all right," he said, trying to rise, but clearly in great discomfort. "It's happened before. Just the shock of seeing this."

"What can I do?" Sergei asked.

"If you could help me to my cart." He rose slowly, painfully, then tried to walk but couldn't, so Sergei carried him. "Thank you. I'll be all right. My horse is as old as I—she knows the way."

Clouds were building; it might rain soon. Now Sergei had a trail he could follow. He might even overtake them before they reached the forest. His son had never felt so close.

Heitzik grimaced in another wave of pain. "I'll be all right," he insisted. "You go . . ." He could barely hold the reins.

Sergei sighed, having made his decision. "Give me just a moment—I'll ride with you to your settlement." Heitzik nodded, and Sergei saw the relief on his face.

He mounted Paestka and did another quick ride around the ruins. He found the body of a horse, its throat cut and one leg severed at the knee. A swarm of flies buzzed around the carcass. He tried to make sense of this, but couldn't.

The tracks led south. He ached to follow these men while the trail was warm. He looked back at old Heitzik, hunched over on the cart seat. He tied Paestka to the back of the cart, climbed up, and took the reins. "All right, horse," he said. "Take us home!"

"The horse's name is Tsaddik," murmured the old man. He added, "I only reveal his name to friends." Then he was quiet.

By the time they reached Heitzik's settlement, it was nearly dusk. Rain clouds had settled heavily over them and a few droplets fell. A woman ran out to meet them and pointed to Heitzik's home. By the time Sergei got him to the door, it was dark and the rain had begun to fall in a downpour.

Few tracks, if any, would remain.

While Heitzik's wife, Devorah, was helping her husband to bed, she spoke to Sergei as if he were family: "It's dark. It's raining. Please—put your horse in the barn across the street and stay the night. In the morning, you'll have a good breakfast with us. With food in your stomach, you can be on your way. Or stay with us as long as you wish." Then she hurried to attend to her husband.

Sergei had also heard her unspoken words: *Thank you. May God bless you. You are not a stranger to this house.*

Serafim had once said, "A man's character reveals itself most clearly when he makes a choice under pressure." Sergei had made his choice; he hoped it was the right one. But in making that choice, he might have lost the way to his child. He wasn't going to be able to find tracks at night in the rain, so he accepted the hospitality of these Jewish people—Grandfather Heschel's people, his mother's people. His people.

. 45 .

On an otherwise pleasant day in early spring, the dogs began barking wildly. A stranger had entered the camp. Nearly naked, his clothing torn and shredded, he cursed loudly and waved a saber in the air. His hair and beard were long and tangled, as if he had lived in the wild—not a man but a forest creature. One of the dogs growled ferociously, just out of reach. Another attacked him and was cut down.

Zakolyev and his men were away on a raid, and nearly all the young men including Konstantin were in the forest gathering wood, leaving only Great Yergovich on guard. On seeing the savage, a child cried out in alarm and ran screaming. Paulina emerged from her cabin just as Great Yergovich rushed to investigate.

Yergovich and Paulina saw the stranger at the same time, but they were both too late to save Shura, who was just rounding the corner carrying water from the stream. Startled, the nameless man spun and slashed Shura with the sword, nearly severing her head. An enraged Yergovich dashed in to take the life of this intruder, but he made the fatal mistake of underestimating his adversary, thinking him a *bezoomnii*—mindless, crazy. Yergovich approached boldly to frighten off the poor witless fool.

As Yergovich drew near to him, the man threw his sword in a spinning arc. It pierced the heart of Paulina's Old Bear, who stumbled backward and fell with a look of surprise on his face as the light faded from his eyes.

Paulina stood stunned, at first thinking that the wild-eyed stranger might be the monster Sergei Ivanov. But she quickly realized that this crazed and babbling bearded stranger was not a monster but a man possessed by demons and bent on destruction. He would surely attack the other women and children—

She had no memory of what happened next, but Oxana, peering out the door of her hut, saw it all.

A FEW MINUTES LATER, the young men returned, their arms filled with firewood. When they saw the bodies of Shura and old Yergovich, and a stranger lying facedown, they dropped the wood and ran to investigate. Konstantin was the first to reach Paulina, now slumped against a wall nearby and weeping. He sat down next to her, put his arm around her, and held her close.

Just before dusk, Dmitri Zakolyev, Korolev, and most of the others returned. As soon as the Ataman saw the bodies of Yergovich and Shura—and the corpse of a stranger lying farther away—he cried, "What happened? Where is Paulina?"

"I saw it, Ataman," said Oxana. "A crazy man came into the camp!"

Zakolyev leaped off his horse and shook her. "Where is Paulina?" he repeated, but Oxana babbled even faster, as if to save her life.

"After he killed Shura he threw a saber and killed old Yergovich— but Paulina saved us! She walked up to the wild man and held up her hand as if to say 'Stop!' He pulled the saber out of old Yergovich, and he let out a horrible shriek and attacked Paulina. She moved so quickly! One moment she was in front of him; then she was beside him, so his saber missed her. She struck him many times, and he fell and died."

Zakolyev was breathing hard, trying to control himself. He said softly, "Oxana, I'm going to ask you only one more time. *Where is Paulina?*"

She pointed toward the Ataman's cabin. "I . . . I think Konstantin— he walked her back to your cabin—"

Zakolyev released Oxana and ran toward the cabin.

Paulina had begged Konstantin to leave the instant they heard the men riding in. When Father Dmitri found her she was sitting alone, still in a daze, staring into space. She had avenged the death of Shura, who had mothered her, and the death of the man who had taught her better than he knew. She was shocked by how easy it had been to take a man's life—sickened because she had *wanted* to kill him—but also because of something he had said . . .

At first he had only raved in words she didn't understand, but then he'd muttered a few words in Russian. That's when Paulina realized that he had not just stumbled onto them, he had searched for and found the camp. He had cried out, "Murderers! . . . killed my wife . . . my children . . . for what reason? Because we are Jews!" There were tears in his eyes. She didn't understand the rest of his mutterings, but his voice had the sincerity of one who spoke the truth.

The wild man's words made Paulina face what she had long ignored. She now knew where the men had found the horses, sheep, trunks, tools, books, and many other things as well. And she knew what kind of men they were . . .

Just then her father burst into the room in a panic. "Are you all right?"

Her answer came slowly, her voice a monotone. "I'm not injured, if that's what you mean." She looked up and saw what she had never seen with the eyes of childhood: Her father had aged; he was drawn, weary, haunted. His eyes were like those of the wild man. No, they were far colder.

Zakolyev let out a sigh of relief. "All right then. You did well—Oxana told me—and soon you'll be ready." He started to reach out to touch her hair, but she moved away.

He pretended not to notice. "You rest," he said. "Tomorrow I will find you another instructor."

Staring at the floor, Paulina responded, "I don't think I'll be needing another instructor, do you?" When she looked up, the doorway was empty.

Dmitri Zakolyev had left to wash himself in the river, to scrub his body raw, to cleanse his mind. Then he would try to sleep. He did not like losing Great Yergovich and the woman Shura. They were both use-ful—and he was furious about this breach of security. Yet this strange twist of fate had tested his daughter in mortal combat. So it had turned out well in the end.

She was ready.

S OON, SHE THOUGHT. He had said it would be soon. She hoped so; she wanted to get it done, get it over with, find out if she had any life on the other side of this mission. As the reality and inevitability of it dawned on her, Paulina shivered. She knew she could fight, and now she knew she could kill. But was she truly ready to kill Sergei Ivanov? Paulina touched the locket, held it gently in her fist, as if it contained the souls of her grandparents. She tried to imagine what her mother must have thought before the white-haired demon killed her.

Yes, she could kill him, and she would. Everything depended on it. Not only her life—for if she failed she would surely die—but even if she survived, she could not live with the shame. She wished her father had never given her this weight to carry. But he had. So she would not fail him. Now seventeen years old, Paulina wondered how much time, how much life, she might live beyond that.

What has happened to me? she thought. I once had dreams; now I have only this dark purpose. Paulina sighed. No, I have more. I have Kontin . . .

T HE NEXT DAY the Ataman began muttering about moving the camp once again. Pacing like a caged tiger, he spoke without direction, as if he were talking to the air or to himself. "We have grown soft and comfortable, like a quaint village of Jews!" he ranted. "Remember what I told you long ago: We must be moving targets—so we must move!"

He slipped in and out of a dark inner world that no one could reach. Then, without apparent cause, he would wake from his trance and issue orders with complete clarity. Some hoped he would forget about leaving the camp. Others whispered about leaving themselves.

Zakolyev could no longer clearly distinguish between the waking world and the nightmares that raged in his sleep, shifting and changing like patterns of smoke rising into the night sky.

But he took consolation in the knowledge that someday soon, Paulina would be the last sight that Sergei Ivanov ever saw. If he saw her coming at all. And justice would be done.

Meanwhile, Korolev watched Zakolyev's descent into madness with growing disdain. And whenever the ripe little Paulina passed by, Korolev's cold blue eyes would follow.

. 46 .

SERGEI LEFT Heitzik's village with little hope, but with new provisions and the blessings of a family. The cold rain had ended, leaving the air crisp and fresh—a good day for tracking if any tracks remained.

He returned to the ruins, now cold, and to the spot where he had seen the tracks. He found not a single trace of hoofprints in the muddy ground. Still, he had a direction. Or did he? Think! he told himself. Would these men, led by Zakolyev, whose existence depended on secrecy, leave the scene of a massacre in the exact direction of their camp? Not likely. Their initial trail led southwest, toward the Podolia region, and Bessarabia beyond—not the best region to hide.

But suppose they changed course and circled—where? To the north, his instincts said. Toward the forested region near Kiev where he had once found tracks before they disappeared in a streambed. He knew the region well by now, and if he were Zakolyev, that's where he would go.

His knees told Paestka to go forward at a walk, along the line of old tracks. Up ahead the ground might show some sign. He found nothing for fifty meters . . . a hundred . . . two hundred. But at about three hundred meters, he saw the faint marks of many riders. He followed the tracks until they disappeared.

Then he backtracked until he found the hoof markings again, and rode in a circling course ninety degrees to the right until he was heading northwest. He found nothing, so he backtracked again, then covered ever-widening circles all afternoon. As the sun dropped low in the short days of early spring, he was about to give up for the day when something caught his eye. A single hoofprint. He walked in a circle and found more, leading north and east. He had found their trail.

There were times he lost the tracks again, but he could see other signs where they had ridden through tall grasses or underbrush. He looked for broken branches at the height of a rider's head or shoulder or slung rifle—places where horses pulled up plants to eat while walking, or shrubs pushed out and down due to the circular motion of their hooves. He silently thanked Alexei for those few lessons in tracking.

He had hoped that they would head directly back to their camp, but the trail led to the outskirts of the town of Nizhyn, where the tracks were finally lost in a morass of hoofprints and the ruts left by of many travelers on horseback and buggy. There was no trail left to follow.

It was not likely that they had remained long in the town. But on the faint hope that he might learn something, Sergei entered and decided to spend the night in a room and eat a prepared meal.

He found a barn for Paestka and a small boardinghouse for himself, run by a heavy, middle-aged woman with a bun of gray hair pinned to her head. She showed him to his room and announced that the dinner meal would be ready in twenty minutes.

Sergei decided to go down to the saloon across the street and question a few locals about riders who might have passed through. He ordered a glass of vodka to warm his bones and blend in with the other customers. He sat quietly for a while, listening to random conversations. He was just raising the glass when he heard a man at the table behind him muttering to himself: ". . . sick of it . . . slaughtering for Zakolyev . . . no honor . . . last time, no more . . ."

Suddenly alert, Sergei quietly put the glass down. He sat still and listened, but he heard nothing more than the man's breathing, pouring, swallowing. He picked up the bottle and casually walked to another table, where he could observe the lone man dressed in the clothing of a Cossack. It had been many years, but he still had a familiar look about him. One does not forget such men.

Soon the man rose unsteadily and, still muttering, staggered up the street. Sergei followed at a distance, until the drunken man entered another boardinghouse. Then he waited and watched through the long night, his dinner and bed forgotten.

In the morning, he thought, this man may return to his camp.

Eᴠᴇɴ ʙᴇғᴏʀᴇ the incident with Gumlinov's horse, the men had unspoken doubts. Now everything was falling apart—the Ataman was acting like a crazed jackal.

In another raid, two more men had died. One was killed by a Jew who charged with a pitchfork as his wife hugged their children in the doorway. He managed to stab Chertosky before one of the men cut him down. Another of their men was stabbed in the back by a brave boy who had leaped out of hiding. It was his last act.

As Zakolyev's men rode back to camp, those out of the Ataman's earshot muttered about riding off, sickened by what their lives had become. One of the men said softly to a nearby rider, "Perhaps I'll become a monk."

The other answered, "Too late for that—our souls are already lost . . ."

Jᴜsᴛ ʙᴇғᴏʀᴇ her afternoon practice session, which she did in solitude, and mostly out of habit—and before her father's expected return from patrol—Paulina searched the camp for Konstantin. She found him sitting on a rock outcropping overlooking the falls, staring down at the water pounding on the rocks far below. Sitting next to him, Paulina told him that she would soon be leaving to complete the task her father had given her. "Few young women have ever undertaken such a mission," she said, as if trying to convince herself. "For this purpose he freed me from the duties of other women . . . gave me special privileges and protection . . ."

Paulina looked intently at Konstantin, desperate for his approval, but his expression revealed nothing. "He told me I was born to do this," she continued, her eyes pleading, her hand grasping his arm. "Oh, Kontin, I hope I'm ready! My father needs this victory so badly for his . . . peace of mind."

Then she reached down the front of her blouse—a gesture that made Konstantin gasp—and pulled out her locket. She showed him the faded picture of her connection to a past of which she had no memories. "I do this for them as well," she said. "Father insists on sending Tomorov with me. I wish you were coming instead . . ."

He nearly spoke then—almost told her everything he knew—but what did he know for certain? And if he told her, would she believe him? Or would it mean catastrophe for both of them?

Paulina had hoped that Konstantin might share her sense of destiny—that he might be glad for her—but the look of dismay on his face, despite his efforts to hide it, turned the moment to sorrow.

THAT VERY AFTERNOON, after Paulina left for her training, Konstantin finally made his decision: he would leave this camp—he would tell her everything and convince Paulina to leave with him. He had gone over it again and again, but any path his mind traveled, it reached the same destination: They had to go together; it was their only chance for happiness. They would run for their lives and for their future. They had to take flight this very night.

Konstantin was no fool—he knew that choosing between familiar lies or bitter truth would not be easy for Paulina—and he held only the barest hope that she loved him enough to abandon all she had known.

If she could not bring herself to join him, then he would go alone, a desolate flight carried only by the hope that he might one day make his fortune and return for her. And at least he would be able to say good-bye to the one person who reminded him that love was still possible in this dark world.

KONSTANTIN RAN to the barn, where Paulina practiced, looked around to make sure no one else was inside, and said quickly, "Paulina, this afternoon, meet me at the falls. Tell no one you're coming!" Then, before she could speak, he ran off, thinking that if they left in the night, no one would miss them until morning.

All might have gone well if Elena had not just returned from the latrine and overheard Konstantin's words to the girl. She stopped, just out of sight as the young man ran off. Then she continued back to the cabin.

LATE THAT AFTERNOON, as Konstantin waited in the thicket of brambles near the top of the falls, he had time to think of many things. He wondered why Father Dmitri had never discovered this spot, then worried that perhaps he had.

Konstantin also thought about prayer. Some of the men had spoken of God and heaven and hell, but that was the extent of his religious education. He had never prayed before, although he had seen others do it. He prayed now, not quite sure whom he was addressing—but if there was some all-powerful being who might be listening, he asked for Paulina's safety. He could not pray for her love, for that was only hers to give.

Dark clouds had blown in, turning a bright afternoon to dusk. Paulina would arrive within the hour—if she were coming at all. He whispered another fervent prayer. "Please let her go with me!"

A steady rain had begun to fall, which might help cover their tracks. He would be a rabbit that would evade Zakolyev the fox.

Two rabbits, he reminded himself. Two.

. 48 .

Bʏ ᴇᴀʀʟʏ ᴀꜰᴛᴇʀɴᴏᴏɴ ᴏꜰ ᴛʜᴀᴛ ᴅᴀʏ, Sergei had dropped far behind to avoid being seen by the rider ahead. This meant that he could no longer see his quarry, but the trail was fresh and easy to follow, despite the rain showers. Eventually, the tracks led to the edge of a forest. Sergei quickened his pace; he could now draw closer without being seen.

An hour passed. Sometimes the hoofprints were mixed with others, until Sergei came to a rushing stream, where the tracks disappeared altogether. Tracks don't just disappear, and horses don't fly, thought Sergei; the man's horse had walked upstream. So Sergei followed, checking the banks on either side as the water rushed past Paestka's knees and then her strong thighs. It would be deeper ahead, and faster. Soon he heard white water surging over rocks. It was not a river for travel by boat—a good place for an isolated camp.

Sergei listened for any telltale sounds but heard only the steady pounding of a waterfall just ahead.

Part Seven

———

THE

SEARCH

FOR

PEACE

Everything that begins also ends.
Make peace with that
and all will be well.

THE BUDDHA

W HEN THE MEN RETURNED in the late afternoon, a few women and children ran to greet them, only to find grim expressions on dirty, tired, and sullen faces. Covered with blood and soot, they had brought back two more riderless horses. No bodies were draped across the horses because the dead were thrown into the flames.

"The Jews killed Chertosky and Larentev," muttered one of the men to Oxana before he headed for his cabin. Oxana had lived with Oleg Chertosky, and she cried over his loss—but she could feel no hatred for people who were only trying to defend themselves against armed men.

The Ataman was in a bad state. He had killed a woman before Korolev was finished with her, and they'd had angry words. As soon as they arrived, Zakolyev turned his back on Korolev as if the man didn't exist. Then he led his new horse into the corral, removed the saddle, and carried it to the barn, where he planned to check on Paulina's practice.

She was finishing her routine when she saw her father standing in the doorway, staring at her but not really seeing her. He nodded absent-mindedly before departing.

When he arrived at his cabin, tired and distracted, he hardly took notice of Elena, sitting by the fire, until she looked up at him and forced her usual smile.

T HE ATAMAN had lost his mind and his men. Korolev was con-vinced of this after they had almost come to blows during the raid.

Korolev decided he would never again take orders from any man. It was time to leave.

But before he rode away, he would have the girl, Paulina—as a parting gesture for the lunatic leader. He had waited far too long to pluck the ripe young woman. He would only have to wait a few moments more, just out of sight, until Zakolyev left the barn and headed to his cabin.

Paulina had just finished her final stretches, and her body still wet with perspiration. She was about to rush off and tidy up before meeting Kontin, eagerly anticipating what he might say or do, when Korolev entered the barn, his knife drawn.

"Get on your knees!" he commanded, shutting the door.

Paulina knew that the time had finally come—Korolev was going to force himself on her . . . and her father was not going to be able to protect her this time.

As he drew near, Korolev threw a surprise kick to her belly. The kick missed, as he had known it would. He followed up with a backhand strike to where he anticipated she would move. It stunned her, but Paulina rolled and recovered.

They both knew it would be over in a matter of seconds, one way or the other. Korolev had tremendous power, devoid of mercy or conscience. Paulina had speed, determination, and a few surprises of her own.

When he came at her again, she leaped past him and drove her heel up behind her, kicking him in the groin. The air escaped his lungs, and he went down. As she came in to finish him, Korolev swept her support leg and kicked the side of her knee.

Paulina gave way to absorb most of the force, but the kick had done its damage—her leg collapsed and she fell. Then he was on her, straddling her hips, pinning one of her arms with his knee, sweating, excited, victorious—

Out of the corner of her eye, she saw the blade flashing down. In that fraction of a second, she realized he was going to kill her and *then* rape her—it made no difference to him—and a fury coursed through her body. Since his one arm held the knife, he was momentarily open. As the blade descended to pierce her chest, Paulina's arm shot out.

Filled with a primal hatred, she deflected the blade and in the same motion drove her knuckles deep into Korolev's windpipe. She heard a *crunch* . . .

Korolev released the blade and instinctively clutched at his throat, trying to get air. Paulina kicked again into his groin, lifting the giant off the ground with a terrible sound. He lay there making sucking, gasping, choking noises. Then with a shudder, Korolev died as violently as he had lived.

A RAIN BEGAN TO FALL as Paulina hobbled in pain back to the cabin. Finding no one there, she collapsed upon the cold hearth and cried in convulsing sobs. She dreaded what her father might say or do when he learned that she had killed his second in command. Then she realized that she didn't care. If any man ever deserved death . . .

Still, Paulina was badly shaken; she needed to talk to Konstantin—

All at once she remembered: He was waiting for her—she hoped he was still there! Paulina leaped to her feet and started to run but cried out in pain and fell. She pounded the stone hearth. Furious at her father, at her leg, at the world, she rose again and forced herself into a limping run toward the stream, to the falls, to her Kontin.

. 50 .

THE POUNDING RAIN, and a forest full of chirping insects, made Konstantin want to scream for silence. Another hour had passed as he sat here, hoping, praying, listening for her footsteps. If she came, all would be well; they would be together. If she did not come . . . He tried to imagine what he would do.

I can read and write and draw, he thought, and I know my numbers. I will find work in a city far away, perhaps even in America. I will learn a new language, and I will make my fortune. Then I will return one day and ride into the camp on a great horse with a sword and rifle and with a band of fighting men I've hired. And I will tell Dmitri Zakolyev, "I come from America; I have come for Paulina." I will say the words in English, and if he does not understand, that will be too bad!

Just then, Konstantin thought he heard over the sound of rain and crickets, and water pounding on the rocks below, approaching footsteps. Ecstatic that she had come, Konstantin emerged from the foliage, smiling in anticipation . . .

Instead of Paulina, he found Ataman Dmitri Zakolyev standing before him, not three meters away.

A MOMENT of cold panic washed through him, followed by an impulse to run. Such a gesture would have been futile. So he froze in place and waited as the raindrops fell.

Zakolyev made no attempt to approach. Instead, he stood relaxed. Konstantin glanced around as the Ataman spoke soft words that Konstantin never imagined he would hear. "I have known for some time that you care deeply for Paulina. I've also noticed that she cares for you. And why not? You have a bright mind and good character.

"It may seem strange, my coming to you now, here, but there are pressures building for everyone, and I have given it considerable thought. You know I have always liked you, Konstantin . . ." Father Dimitri sat on a large stone and gestured for Konstantin to join him. "I expect that Paulina will want to marry before long. And I will not have her marry any of the other men, nor will I have her passed around from man to man. So marrying you may be the best solution. But you and I must have an understanding . . ."

Konstantin could not believe his ears. He was suspicious, of course; yet what the Ataman said made sense and sounded sincere. In any case, Konstantin knew two things for certain: Either the Ataman was telling the truth, in which case he was safe for the moment and his life might work out far better than he had ever imagined, or the Ataman was lying, and he was in grave danger. But if he rejected this offer, sincere or not—if he turned and ran—he would not live out the next hour.

He approached warily, as Father Dmitri patted the wet stone next to him. This was Konstantin's moment of truth. As he sat down, Father Dmitri smiled and placed a hand lightly on Konstantin's shoulder and said with what seemed genuine affection, "You have grown, Konstantin. Yet you still look Paulina's age."

The rain had ceased and rays of late-afternoon light broke though the clouds. At that good omen, Konstantin risked a smile in return. He wanted so much to believe Father Dmitri that his wary mind did not consider three critical questions: First, if Father Dmitri truly wanted his daughter's happiness, why had he trained her as an assassin—to kill or be killed? Second, and more pressing, how had the Ataman known he was waiting here? And third, where was Paulina?

SERGEI HAD LOST THE RIDER'S TRACKS, but he continued upward, following the turbulent river on faith, until he reached a small pond surrounded by boulders at the base of a high waterfall. There he found a winding path upward—a path made by men. He tethered Paestka to munch on the wet grass. Wiping his rain-soaked hair back from his eyes, Sergei climbed the steep and slippery trail . . .

When he reached the top of the falls, the rain stopped, and he heard, over the sound of the roiling water far below, someone speaking.

PAULINA LIMPED along as fast as she could, but her painful leg had given way and caused her to fall again. Konstantin, with his dark eyes and sad smile, would be waiting for her. Once she reached him all would be well. She struggled on through the slick mud, blinking in the rain, peering ahead into the cloud-shrouded light. Now twenty meters from the stream, as the rain gave way, she saw two figures sitting together on the far shore of the rushing stream, near the top of the falls.

She stopped and stared. It was Konstantin . . . and her father. They stood and turned as a third man stepped out of the forest.

WHEN SERGEI EMERGED from the trees, he thought for a moment that he had stepped into a dream. Zakolyev didn't quite believe it either; he stared as if he were seeing a ghost. Then his face quickly returned to the familiar mask as he wiped back his wet hair.

Seeing this man for the first time since Anya's death, Sergei felt his body tense—then he took a breath and let himself relax, his senses on full alert, scanning the immediate area above the falls.

They were alone, just the three of them: Sergei, Zakolyev, and a young man about the age . . .

Sergei turned his attention back to Zakolyev and wasted no words: "I've come for my son."

Zakolyev sighed, as if resigned to some unpleasantness. He knew that the moment of reckoning had arrived. "Sergei Ivanov," he said, forcing a mirthless smile, "we meet again. And now you say you've come by to pick up your son? Without even a word of greeting? Well, I'm willing to overlook your lack of courtesy. And as it happens, you're in luck. As you see, he stands here before you. His name is Konstantin, and I give him to you."

Elated by this wondrous turn of fortune, Konstantin started to speak as Dmitri Zakolyev reached around his shoulder.

Sergei saw the knife flash just as Zakolyev grabbed the young man's head, put the knife to Konstantin's throat, and cut—

In the next instant, as if by magic, Sergei had transported himself three meters forward—he slapped the knife hand down to the young man's chest, pinning it, then broke Zakolyev's arm and disarmed him. With his other hand, Sergei grabbed Zakolyev's hair and jerked his head back so far it nearly broke the man's neck; then, pushing Konstantin out of harm's way, he stunned Zakolyev with an elbow strike, knocking him to the ground, where he lay stunned.

Paulina arrived in a state of total confusion. She had just seen—or thought she had seen—Father Dmitri try to cut the throat of her Kontin. And the white-haired man had saved him.

Zakolyev came to and saw Paulina. "Kill him! Kill the monster!" he screamed at Paulina, commanding her with all his authority.

"No!" yelled Konstantin. "Paulina, no! You can't! He's my father!"

The words made no sense. Nothing made any sense. But Paulina's body responded to years of training and followed the will of the man who had raised her. Her painful leg forgotten, Paulina closed the distance and flew at the white-haired monster who had killed her mother and haunted her dreams, leaping in with a devastating kick—

She landed with a splash in the stream above the falls and whipped her head around—the white-haired man was no longer there. She rolled, twisted, spun, saw him behind her, and attempted a leg sweep, but somehow it missed. Without hesitation, she leaped up with a barrage of lightning blows, but Sergei Ivanov evaded her every strike.

Something felt wrong. Nothing in her years of combat training had prepared her for this. It made no sense; the monster had not struck a single offensive blow. Was he truly a wizard and merely playing with her?

Again she lashed out at him—and again the man deflected but did not return a single blow. Panting as they stood in the shallows above the falls, Paulina stopped for a moment to gather her wits.

JUST THEN THE CLOUDS PARTED, opening to the last rays of the setting sun. And as a beam of light illuminated her face, Sergei got his first clear look at this amazing assailant: It was the face of a girl—not any girl, but the face of Anya. In that moment of recognition, sunlight glinted off the locket around her neck. And he knew beyond any doubt.

His search was finally over.

Again Zakolyev screamed, "Kill him! Now is your chance!" But the authority was fading from his voice.

Konstantin cried out again, "Stop, Paulina, please! He's my father!"

"No," Sergei said to the boy without taking his eyes off the girl called Paulina. "I wish I were your father—but I don't have a son. I have a daughter, and she is standing before me now."

Paulina stood frozen, not knowing what to do.

Zakolyev lay still, his arm broken, his eyes waiting, watching. Then he commanded her one last time: "Kill him, Paulina!" he yelled, his voice shrill and desperate. "Complete your mission! He killed your mother!"

She crouched, circling the white-haired man. He just stood relaxed; his face was serene. And he was crying.

Confused, not knowing what to think, how to feel, she pointed to Zakolyev and said to the white-haired man, "But . . . he's my father—"

"No!"

Paulina turned to see Konstantin walking toward her, his shirt wet and bloody from a cut on his chest. "No, Paulina. I'm so sorry I never told you . . . I was only a little boy, but I remember when they brought you—"

Then Zakolyev was on his feet with another knife in his left hand, his mind gone, madness driving his legs forward through the river in a frenzy, leaping—

Sergei looked over Paulina's shoulder to see Zakolyev flying toward them both—and he couldn't tell who Zakolyev was aiming to kill. Moving faster than Paulina could see, Sergei pushed her out of the way—

She fell and rolled, thinking it was an attack. But when she came up she saw Father Dmitri Zakolyev, his knife raised in his left hand, flying at Sergei Ivanov.

Sergei watched Zakolyev careening toward him in slow motion. The world was silent. Not a sound intruded, as he waited, relaxed, breathing, his hands resting at his sides. This was the moment he had trained for.

As Zakolyev rushed in and the knife stabbed downward, Sergei moved at the last instant like a ghost—as the point of the blade was about to pierce coat and flesh, Sergei was no longer there. He had somehow moved off the line of attack, turned his body slightly, and with a subtle wave of his arms had thrown Zakolyev headlong through the air, into the river toward the edge of the falls.

But as the mystified assailant had flown past his enemy, he had reflexively reached out and clutched Sergei's coat—

Zakolyev's momentum, combined with the treacherous footing and powerful current, jerked Sergei off his feet.

Horrified, Paulina and Konstantin watched Dmitri Zakolyev and Sergei Ivanov as both men slid over the precipice and disappeared.

. 51 .

T WILIGHT. A clearing sky at dusk. An anguished Paulina, supported by Konstantin, limped along the shore to the top of the falls and peered down to the rocks far below, where they saw the twisted, broken, lifeless body of Dmitri Zakolyev.

Sergei Ivanov had vanished.

She couldn't yet grasp the truth or take in all that had happened. But despite her confusion and grief over the cataclysmic events that had transpired, a spell had lifted. The life she had known and lies she had believed lay shattered at the base of the falls. She could not fathom what might lie ahead, but for the first time she sensed the possibility of a different world now, with Konstantin by her side.

She clung to him as they slowly made their way down the winding path toward the foot of the falls. Ataman Dmitri Zakolyev, the man she had called Father, was dead. The body of Sergei Ivanov, the man who had saved Kontin, had washed downstream. But if he still lived, he might help her make sense of the world once again.

S URPRISED BY HIS SURVIVAL, in a state of grace, Sergei crawled up the bank of the river about twenty meters below the falls to find Paestka peacefully grazing nearby, unconcerned about the dramas of the human world.

Sergei was bruised and cold but bore no serious injury. He made his way back to the foot of the falls, found Zakolyev, and pulled him out of the pounding water and into the underbrush. For a moment he saw images of their boyhood together, as fellow cadets, and their survival training, and their struggles. Then the images faded as Sergei took the small shovel from the saddlebag and dug a final resting place for Dmitri Zakolyev, covering him with the wet earth.

"I had not intended to kill you," Sergei said, "but I'm glad you are gone . . ."

He had no stone to mark the grave nor any more words to say, but as he gazed down at the mound, Sergei faced the fact that his worst enemy had midwifed his daughter into the world, had protected her and trained her, and in his troubled way had fathered her. He bowed his head and gave thanks that his daughter was alive. He thought of Anya then, and how glad she would be . . .

Paulina and Konstantin joined him there, gazing down at the grave, saying their own farewells in silence.

While the people of Zakolyev's camp went about their business, ignorant of what had changed, the three of them hiked back up the winding path—Sergei leading Paestka, and Paulina and Konstantin holding tightly to one another's hands.

While they ascended, Sergei told Paulina the story of the locket—where it came from and how it came into her hands. Not the details, but enough so she might begin to understand.

By the time they returned to the top of the falls, Sergei had finished his story. A purple light still infused the sky when they heard shouts of alarm from the camp, carried through the still evening air.

"Korolev is dead!" someone shouted.

"The Ataman is missing!" yelled another. "We are under attack!"

A few moments later Tomorov and five other men carrying saber, knife, and pistol caught sight of the three of them standing there and raced toward them to kill the white-haired intruder.

Sergei stood relaxed. Expecting nothing, ready for whatever came—

But as the men drew near, Paulina stepped in front of Sergei and faced them. "Stop! All of you!" she said, her small voice ringing with authority. As she raised her arm, the men stopped and waited. "It's over!" she said. "Ataman Dmitri Zakolyev is dead—gone over the falls. And believe me when I say this: You do not want to fight this man. If you do, you will face me as well!"

The leaderless men grumbled and stared and shuffled their feet. They didn't take orders from a woman—not even Paulina. But there was something familiar about that man . . .

Tomorov the scout had a long memory. He recognized the white-haired man—the one who had followed after they had beaten him and killed the woman and child. Tomorov remembered enough. "Come on!" he said to the men. "We have no more business here."

They backed off and away, and like blind men, they stumbled through the camp to gather their belongings and saddle their horses. The place stank of death, and they wanted no more of it.

Sergei looked at the wound on Konstantin's chest. "It isn't deep and will heal well enough," he said.

"Better my chest than . . . thank you for saving my life," Konstantin said. "I . . . I'm sorry that you aren't my father too. I wish you were . . ."

Sergei looked at his daughter, and, seeing how closely Paulina held this young man, he smiled and said, "We may yet find a way to grant that wish."

The events of that day—the death of Korolev, Kontin nearly taken from her, and the death of the man she knew as her father—rushed in upon Paulina. She started to pant, and her chest heaved. Konstantin held her as she found release.

Some time later, when she was able to speak again, Paulina looked up at Sergei Ivanov. "I had learned to hate you . . . all my life . . . How can you be my father? How can I know that it's true?"

Sergei had no proof to offer. So he said, "You've had a difficult day, Paulina. We all have. Let's ride away from here, make a camp in the woods. And in the morning we may all see more clearly."

His words made sense. A good beginning.

Sᴇʀɢᴇɪ, Pᴀᴜʟɪɴᴀ, ᴀɴᴅ Kᴏɴsᴛᴀɴᴛɪɴ rode out of the camp together. No one interfered or seemed to care. Someone had set the barn ablaze. Looking back, Paulina turned to Konstantin and said in a weary voice, "Today—before I came to the falls, Korolev tried to . . . attack me. We fought . . . and I killed him."

Sergei turned to her. "Did you say you killed the one-armed giant, the man Korolev?"

She nodded, biting her lip. "Do you know him?"

He hesitated, but then decided that she should know the whole truth: "Korolev was the man who killed your mother."

Paulina turned her head away so he would not see her tears. So she had completed her mission after all—killing the monster who had murdered her mother. Her years of training had not been wasted.

That night Sergei lay awake for a time, wondering how he might earn her trust.

The next morning he was already up and tending the fire when Konstantin woke, then Paulina. They didn't speak at first, but Sergei knew what was on her mind—the proof she sought. When he had first awakened, an idea had come to him. He would have to take a risk . . .

As Sergei handed the two of them some berries he had found nearby, he said to Paulina, "Do you notice the resemblance between me and your grandfather . . . in the locket?"

She didn't need to look; she had memorized their faces. "Yes," she said. "But many people bear a resemblance."

"There's something else," he said, "if it's still there. You see, when your mother and I were married, I took five strands of her hair and wound them into a tiny circle, a lock of hair the same color as yours, and I placed that lock behind the photograph of my parents—your grandparents."

Paulina's eyes opened wide. She had never thought to look behind the photograph. She quickly opened the locket and carefully pried up the round piece of photographic paper and looked as Sergei held his breath—

There was no lock of hair. Nothing. When Paulina looked up, her eyes were again guarded.

"Wait!" said Konstantin. "There's something stuck to the back of the photograph." Paulina turned the photograph around. And there, pressed into the faded paper, was a tight little circle—five strands of her mother's hair.

Sergei smiled. "Her name was Anya, and she was as lovely as you are."

Soon after, they broke camp and mounted their horses.

Paulina had brought only the locket and a few personal items. Konstantin had left everything behind save for a few of his drawings, folded and placed into the cover of a book.

"Your book," Sergei asked as they rode north. "What is it about?"

"About a journey to America, by a writer named Abram Chudominsky," he replied.

Sergei nodded, committing the book and author to memory. "America is where I intend to go," he said. "And I hope you will both join me . . ."

Paulina said only, "Where do we ride now?"

"To meet your grandmother and uncle, who would like very much to make your acquaintance."

T HEY RODE IN SILENCE for some time after that—not because they had little to say, but because they had so much—it was difficult to know where to begin. Sergei thought it best to wait until Paulina was ready.

About midday she began, with one question following another. Sergei answered them all, telling the story of his life and her lineage, until she seemed satisfied.

It wasn't until the second day of their ride north that Paulina began to speak—slowly at first, then faster, as if to reassure herself of her memory and hear it aloud in the safety of Konstantin's company. She told Sergei Ivanov all that she remembered. Konstantin embellished where he could and told his perspectives as well.

Sergei took it in and silently grieved her strange childhood and all the years they had lost.

As the days passed and their tales were told, lulls in the conversation grew longer, until Sergei and Paulina spoke little. But now there was a tenuous comfort in the silence between them, and when Paulina cast speculative glances at Sergei, they were not without a certain regard. Or perhaps it was only gratitude for his long journey to her side.

Upon their arrival and joyous welcome in St. Petersburg, after all introductions and greetings were made, Paulina and Konstantin shared their first Shabbat meal with Sergei, Valeria, Andreas, Katya, and their children, Avrom and Leya. Grandmother Valeria Panova gave special thanks and cried with happiness on that special night.

Sergei's life once again took on a dreamlike quality as he gazed around the table drinking in these faces he would remember all the days of his life. Realizing that this moment would not last, he cherished it all the more.

Sergei stole yet another glance at his daughter and marveled at her resemblance to Anya—the eyes, the hair, the shape of her cheeks, the line of her mouth—so alike yet so different.

Paulina was only now learning about the larger world. In the past few days, Valeria and Andreas had taken her and Konstantin on a tour of the city. Konstantin was curious about everything, and had a hundred questions about customs and social manners, banks and commerce and travel. Paulina spoke less but looked and listened.

Then, on their second Shabbat night, during a lull in the conversation, Sergei quietly announced that he had a gift for Paulina. He placed three gemstones on the table in front of her. "These jewels," he said, "come from your great-grandfather Heschel Rabinowitz, and from his father before him. I now pass them to you. They are quite valuable and will provide funds for you to begin your new life together."

Paulina looked down at the jewels that sparkled like her eyes in the candlelight. She turned to look at Konstantin, then back to Sergei. "I . . . I thank you . . . Sergei." She still had trouble calling him Father—it sounded strange to her.

Paulina was quiet the rest of that evening—preoccupied. Her mind had accepted that somehow all the people around the table were relations: father, grandmother, uncle, aunt, and young cousins. Yet they were strangers to her—even the brave and generous Sergei Ivanov, whom she had known for only a few short weeks.

After the meal, Sergei spoke enthusiastically of America, where he and Paulina and Konstantin would soon go. He made a last plea for Valeria, Andreas, and Katya to join them, but without success.

Even as Sergei spoke of their future, Paulina had reached a resolution about her past: She would put it behind her and never speak of it again. Even this night was part of her past. Her future had not yet begun.

And on the previous night, Paulina and Konstantin had made another difficult decision as well . . .

THE FOLLOWING WEEK Sergei returned with all necessary certificates and papers for Paulina and Konstantin. "A little money in the right hands can work wonders," Sergei explained with a smile. He had also booked their second-class passage out of Germany on the great steamship S.S. *König Friedrich*.

Five days later—after a bittersweet farewell and promises to write—Sergei, Paulina, and Konstantin set out toward Finland, to find passage on the Baltic Sea to the port city of Hamburg.

IN THE FIRST DAYS OF TRAVEL, conversations seemed strained and awkward, sometimes dying out almost as soon as they had begun. Sergei realized that while Paulina's mind had accepted him as her father, and a woman named Anya as her mother, only Konstantin had found a place in her heart.

During their voyage, Paulina and Konstantin kept mostly to them-selves. But then, almost two weeks into the journey, as the great ship neared the coast of America, Paulina made a special effort to include Sergei in the conversation over dinner. Once, it seemed, she was about to say more, but she fell silent, as if unsure how to proceed. She glanced over at Konstantin, who gave her a look and a nod, then said, "There will be no better time than now."

Paulina turned to Sergei. "Sergei . . . Father, could we go up on the deck?"

On the aft deck, out of the wind, Paulina drew Sergei aside, took a deep breath, and said, "I . . . first I want to thank you for everything . . . saving Konstantin's life . . . and what you went through to find me . . . all your kindness and generosity . . ."

Sergei started to speak—to tell her that he understood, but her words tumbled out: "I am glad that you, a good man, are my father . . . maybe there is also some goodness in me . . ."

She hesitated, then looked into his eyes before adding, "And now you have completed what you set out to do, and . . . and Konstantin and I must go our own way. Just the two of us . . ."

Then her voice grew more resolute: "We must go to find our life and you must find yours. I wish you a good life, Sergei Ivanov, wherev-er you may go . . . I will remember you fondly, but . . . I also have much to forget."

Konstantin appeared, slipping one arm around Paulina. With the other he reached out to clasp Sergei's hand and said, "When we find our place and have news to tell, we will write to the address given us by Paulina's grandmother." With that, he excused himself. Paulina started to follow, but turned back to Sergei and added, "I believe that my moth-er . . . would be proud of you for what you have done."

Then, for the first and last time, Paulina drew close, reached up, and kissed Sergei on the cheek—a daughter's kiss so tenuous and tender that Sergei's heart nearly broke open. He could not even protest when she took the locket from her neck, placed it in his palm, and closed his fin-gers around it.

Sergei stood alone and stared out to sea, thinking how Serafim had taught him, many years before, to expect nothing but be prepared for anything. He had foreseen this parting—he had known it would occur. Just not so soon . . .

So many emotions washed through him that it was impossible to distinguish one from another. He released his feelings and his future into God's hands. When they reached America's shores, Paulina and Konstantin would vanish from his life as abruptly as they had appeared.

Yet all in all, it had turned out well. Sergei had found his daughter, alive and healthy, and had helped her start a new life. She had just done the same for him. She had spoken her truth and it set him free.

As the shores of America came into sight, and the bow of the great ship cut the ocean waves, Sergei gazed upon his new land. His eyes took in every detail—the sparkle of sun, the textures of sea and sky, the life abounding. Someday, he thought, even if men voyage to the stars in flying ships, that adventure will be no greater than this one, here on Earth.

In the next moment, the sea breeze vanished and the world was still and silent, as three faces appeared to Sergei, one after the next, so vivid they seemed to float in the air before him: First he saw his father—not stern as in his photograph, but with soft eyes and a smile that opened Sergei's heart; then the face of Serafim brought tears of gratitude—and a moment later, Sergei was gazing at the rough-hewn face and deep eyes of Socrates the Greek, as he had appeared in Sergei's boyhood vision those many years past . . . and as these three images became one in Sergei's mind and memory, the following words came to him like an ancient song: *As we die from one life into the next . . . we may also die and be reborn in a single lifetime . . . and the story, the journey, goes on and on . . .*

Sergei remained still for some minutes, until he again felt the wind ruffling his snow-white hair. Stepping into a sheltered place, out of the wind, he reached inside his shirt pocket and took out the locket Paulina had returned to his safekeeping. Carefully opening the clasp, Sergei gazed at the photograph of his mother and father then peered behind it, expecting to find the lock of Anya's hair.

For a few moments, Sergei forgot the world around him, and the taste of his tears mingled with the scent of the sea. For he had found not one, but two separate locks of hair that he would treasure for the rest of his days.

Sergei said a silent prayer for his daughter as a wind gusted in from the north, and it seemed that he could hear Anya's voice, as it had once spoken to him in his darkest hours. She had said, "Have faith, my darling. Our child is safe in God's hands."

So she is, he thought. So are we all.

When I was young, I believed that life
might unfold in an orderly way, according to my hopes and expectations.
But now I understand that the Way winds like a river,
always changing, ever onward, following God's gravity
toward the Great Sea of Being.
My journeys revealed that
the Way itself creates the warrior;
that every path leads to peace,
every choice to wisdom.
And that life has always been,
and will always be,
arising in Mystery.

FROM SOCRATES' JOURNAL

REVELATIONS FROM THE YEARS THAT FOLLOWED

ALL FOUR OF MY GRANDPARENTS came from Ukraine, but I was especially close to my maternal grandparents. When I was a boy, Grandpa Abe used to tell me stories while we cracked open walnuts from the tree in their backyard. Like many people from the old country, he didn't say much about Ukraine or Russia but spoke of smaller, more personal incidents that could have taken place anywhere—a horse he had longed to ride, a favorite river where he learned to swim by jumping from a rowboat into the cold, clear waters. He awakened my imagination with folktales, like the one about a rainbow bird that no one could catch except a clever and patient little boy like me . . .

Grandpa Abe died when I was four years old.

My grandma, whom we called Babu, didn't tell stories. But she made the best peanut butter and jelly sandwiches and was an expert at cleaning behind my five-year-old ears. I remember Babu fondly, as an old white-haired woman who wore flowered dresses.

When I grew up and went away to college, I didn't see Babu much until the early 1970s, when I moved back to southern California for a time. She was about eighty years old then, mostly bedridden, and her eyesight was failing, so I read to her from one of my various works in progress.

One Sunday I decided to read her an early draft of this book compiled in part from a journal that Socrates had given to me with some details about his life. Since the story took place in Russia, in the old country, I thought that Babu might enjoy it. As I began, I wasn't at all

sure that she was paying much attention—that is, until I first said the
name Sergei Ivanov. Hearing that name, Babu leaned forward, and her
clouded eyes opened wide.

"Are you okay, Babu?" I asked.

"Yes, yes—go on," she said, staring into space.

The name Sergei Ivanov is not uncommon in Russia, so I thought
she might have known someone by that name.

It wasn't until I spoke of the boy, Konstantin, that Babu held up her
hand and interrupted me. "Stop right there!" she said.

I had never heard her speak so emphatically before. But it wasn't just
her voice that got my attention. It was the tears filling her old eyes.
Wiping them gently with a tissue, Babu began telling me about her
early years, and the story of her life . . .

What she told me revealed more than I could ever have hoped for
or imagined about family secrets, and my heritage.

W HILE ON BOARD their steamship to America, Konstantin met
a well-dressed French-Canadian émigré. The man, a Monsieur Goguet,
owned a fashion design company. After studying several of Konstantin's
sketches, Goguet offered him a job on the spot, making illustrations in
the company catalog.

So directly after they arrived in New York, Konstantin and Paulina
emigrated to Toronto, where they rented a small flat.

Paulina eventually gave birth to two daughters. In 1916 their family journeyed across Canada to Vancouver, British Columbia, and from
there they finally moved to the west coast of the United States.

As for Sergei, he traveled on foot, by horse, and by train for several
years, and his occasional letters to Valeria and Andreas bore postmarks
from places across America. Later he made contact with one of the masters he had met in the Pamir and was called back across the sea on an
urgent mission. All correspondence ceased for an extended time.

In 1918, after Valeria passed away, Andreas managed to get his family out of Communist Russia just before the iron curtain closed. Then, as happened to so many immigrant families, everyone lost touch.

Sergei eventually returned to America and settled in Oakland, California, a mere five hundred miles from his daughter, although neither of them knew the other's whereabouts.

Sometimes he thought he saw Paulina in a crowded marketplace and almost called out her name. He often wondered where she was and how she and Konstantin were faring. He would have been glad to know that Paulina and her husband were doing well, devoted to their family and future. But their daughters never learned more than the most sketchy details of the past. Paulina would not speak of it, and Konstantin honored his wife's wishes.

However, the story doesn't end there.

Years earlier, when Paulina and Konstantin had first emigrated, Konstantin was asked to state his name. Since he didn't have a last name, he decided to take a new name for a new country. The only one that came to mind was Abram Chudominsky, the author of his first and favorite book. When they entered the new country, the clerk at immigration wrote it down as Abraham Chudom. So it was done, and Paulina took his new last name and changed her first name to Pauline.

Pauline and Abraham had named their two daughters Vivian and Edith. Both girls grew to adulthood in southern California. One of those daughters, Vivian, married a good man named Herman Millman, with whom she had two children—a daughter named Diane and a son named Daniel . . .

Not until my grandmother Babu, whose legal name was Pauline Chudom, told me her story—from the time she grew up in the camp of Dmitri Zakolyev to her motherhood in a new land—did I grasp the hardships, heartbreak, and eventual triumph that shaped my grandmother's life.

So it was that my great-grandfather, Sergei Ivanov, whom my mother had never known, became my mentor, when we eventually met in 1967 in Berkeley, California.

Now I understand why he smiled that night that I impulsively chose to call him Socrates, after the Greek sage so admired by my great-great-grandfather Heschel Rabinowitz and his beautiful daughter, Natalia.

MY GREAT-GRANDFATHER Sergei Ivanov, known to me as Socrates, was a resourceful man—more than I ever could have realized. Those of you who have read *Way of the Peaceful Warrior* may recall that in 1968 Socrates told me, "I've been watching you for years." A few years after that, when I first opened his journal, I noticed that his first entry was dated February 22, 1946—the exact date of my birth, twenty-two years before we ever met.

During our time together, Socrates never revealed our family relationship—maybe for the same reason he chose not to intrude in (my grandmother) Paulina's life or that of her family. Nor did his journal notes make that final connection. I had to learn the truth from Babu herself, who told me that she had written once to Valeria many years before, to inform her about their new names, their whereabouts, and their children.

Babu had briefly met and exchanged a few words with Sergei only one other time—at my grandfather Abraham's (Konstantin's) funeral. Later, when I searched my earliest memories, an image came to me: I was only four years old then, standing next to my mother and fidgeting in my dark suit. As they lowered the casket bearing Grandpa Abe's body, my mother started to cry.

I looked up and around at the faces of the people gathered there and noticed a white-haired man looking right at me. He seemed somehow different from the other people there. He looked right at me and nodded before he faded back into the other faces and was gone.

I now realize that Socrates knew of my birth and chose to begin writing his journal on that day so that he might someday share it with me. That same journal, along with the story of Babu's life, enabled me to share his story, their story, with you.

I believe that my great-grandfather Sergei Ivanov had watched over me all those years like a guardian angel, waiting for the right time. Socrates was good at waiting. He had learned patience many years before, on his many odysseys, on his long journeys to the light.

Late one night, in the predawn hours,
an ageless white-haired man sits quietly outside an old Texaco station
leaning his chair back against the wall.
He owns the station and works the night shift.
His name is Sergei Ivanov.
Dan Millman, a young college athlete,
is walking home when he stops
and, on impulse, approaches the station office.
He's not sure why he does this—
maybe to get a soft drink or late-night snack . . .
Socrates smiles to himself through half-closed eyelids.
He is here. It begins. The final chapter.

The torch is passed in:
Way of the Peaceful Warrior

Acknowledgments

N o o n e is smarter than all of us. Many people past and present helped bring this book to life. Many writers, philosophers, and mentors served as way stations on my odyssey.

Candice Fuhrman, my literary agent, first told me to write "the book about Socrates" and guided the project from the beginning.

In the early stages of development, Sierra Prasada Millman, Joy Millman, and Nancy Grimley Carleton all provided invaluable editorial feedback from first to final draft. My daughter's editorial analysis of the first draft enabled me to see the story with fresh eyes, to reshape the narrative, and to make that literary leap to the next level.

Publisher Stephen Hanselman acquired the book in an act of faith, generosity, daring, and uncanny good taste. Gideon Weil, my capable editor, provided skill and support at every level of the publishing process. With the rest of the outstanding HarperSanFrancisco team of Jeff Hobbs, Sam Barry, Linda Wollenberger, Claudia Boutote, Margery Buchanan, Terri Leonard, Priscilla Stuckey, Mickey Maudlin, Mark Tauber, Jim Warner, Anne Connolly, and JulieRae Mitchell, Gideon took the book from manuscript to finished form and out into the world.

Special thanks to Terry Lamb for his beautiful cover artistry.

John Giduck, founder of the Russian Martial Arts Training Center in Golden, Colorado, gave generously of his time and expertise, providing detailed research notes and invaluable suggestions about both Russian culture and martial arts.

The Russian System Guidebook, written by Vladimir Vasiliev, one of the world's foremost teachers of the Russian Martial Art, served as a rich resource. And special thanks to Valerie Vasiliev, who, while caring for her family and performing innumerable other tasks, answered many questions that helped establish authenticity related to Russian traditions.

Other experts in their respective fields who helped me keep my facts straight include Rowan Beach, Elissa Bemporad, PhD; David E. Fishman, professor of Jewish history at the Jewish Theological Seminary of America; Lawrence H. Officer, professor of economics at the University of Illinois at Chicago; Professor Harlan Stelmach and Mary K. Lespier, Humanities Department, Dominican University of California; Four Arrows (Don Trent Jacobs), professor at Northern Arizona University and Fielding Graduate Institute; William Harris, MD; David Galland, MD; Father Vladimir of the Holy Trinity Russian Orthodox Church, Toronto, Canada; and Joe Cochrane of the North Bay Cooperative Library System. Any errors of fact are mine, not theirs.

Thanks also to early manuscript readers Douglas Childers, Linda and Hal Kramer, and Sharon and Charles Root for their insight, candor, and encouragement.

Each of my daughters (in birth order)—Holly, Sierra, and China—has contributed, in ways both practical and mysterious, to my creative endeavors and reminded me about the important things.

My wife and guardian angel, Joy, for three decades has renewed and enriched my life through her loving support and practical wisdom. Always my first and final reader, she offers sage advice that helps me improve both my writing and my life.

Finally, I want to acknowledge the loving sacrifices and generosity of spirit provided by my late parents, Herman and Vivian Millman, which made possible all that has followed, and my grandparents, Pauline and Abraham Chudom, and Rose and Harry Millman, all émigrés from Ukraine, on whose courage their families relied, on whose labors we depended, and on whose shoulders we now stand.

For information about Dan Millman's work:

www.danmillman.com

S P E C I A L   O F F E R

Order these selected Thorsons and Element titles direct from the publisher and receive £1 off each title! Visit www.thorsonselement.com for additional special offers.

Free post and packaging for UK delivery (overseas and Ireland, £2.00 per book).

The Alchemist Paulo Coelho (0 7225 3293 8)	£7.99 – £1.00 = £6.99
The Monk Who Sold His Ferrari Robin Sharma (0 00 717973 1)	£7.99 – £1.00 = £6.99
Twisted Fables for Twisted Minds Barefoot Doctor (0 00 716485 8)	£12.00 – £1.00 =£11.00
Living Your Best Life Laura Berman Fortgang (0 00 711183 5)	£9.99 – £1.00 = £8.99

Place your order by post, phone, fax, or email, listed below. Be certain to quote reference code **715E** to take advantage of this special offer.

Mail Order Dept. (REF: **715E**)   Email: customerservices@harpercollins.co.uk
HarperCollins*Publishers*   Phone: 0870 787 1724
Westerhill Road   Fax: 0870 787 1725
Bishopbriggs G64 2QT

Credit cards and cheques are accepted. Do not send cash. Prices shown above were correct at time of press. Prices and availability are subject to change without notice.

BLOCK CAPITALS PLEASE

Name of cardholder   _____
Address of cardholder   _____
                                        _____
                                        _____
Postcode   _____

Delivery address (if different)

                                        _____
                                        _____
                                        _____
Postcode   _____

I've enclosed a cheque for £_____, made payable to HarperCollins*Publishers*, or please charge my Visa/MasterCard/Switch (circle as appropriate)

Card Number: _____
Expires: __/__   Issue No: __/__   Start Date: __/__
Switch cards need an issue number or start date validation.

Signature:_____

thorsons
element

Make
www.thorsonselement.com
your online sanctuary

www.thorsonselement.com

Get online information, inspiration and guidance to help you on the path to physical and spiritual well-being. Drawing on the integrity and vision of our authors and titles, and with health advice, articles, astrology, tarot, a meditation zone, author interviews and events listings, www.thorsonselement.com is a great alternative to help create space and peace in our lives.

So if you've always wondered about practising yoga, following an allergy-free diet, using the tarot or getting a life coach, we can point you in the right direction.

thorsons
element